ELODIE HARPER

The Death Knock

KT-377-292

MULHOLLAND
BOOKS

HODDER

First published in Great Britain in 2018 by Mulholland Books
An imprint of Hodder & Stoughton
An Hachette UK company

This paperback edition first published in 2019

1

A CIP catalogue record for this title is available from the British Library

Paperback ISBN 978 1 473 64221 8
eBook ISBN 978 1 473 64218 8

Typeset in Plantin Light by Hewer Text UK Ltd, Edinburgh
Printed and bound in Great Britain by Clays Ltd, Elcograf S.p.A.

Hodder & Stoughton policy is to use papers that are natural, renewable
and recyclable products and made from wood grown in sustainable
forests. The logging and manufacturing processes are expected to
conform to the environmental regulations of the country of origin.

Hodder & Stoughton Ltd
Carmelite House
50 Victoria Embankment
London EC4Y 0DZ

www.hodder.co.uk

To my husband Jason Farrington, harbour and tempest

The Devil, that proud spirit, cannot abide to be mocked
Thomas More

Ava

My sight is the first to adjust. Bars of light, so faint they blend into the dark, are falling across my face. Drowsiness washes over me, a terrible heaviness, and I want to close my eyes, to fall asleep again, but somehow I know this is wrong.

I don't know where I am.

I try to sit up, but seem to have been paralysed. The top of my forehead scrapes against something hard. I can see wooden slats in front of me. I breathe out, afraid, and dust puffs back, mouthfuls of it. Instinctively, I push my hands upwards, but there's nowhere for them to go. I'm pushing against a solid barrier. My elbows scrape wood, rough and splintered. I'm hemmed in on all sides, trapped inside a wooden box.

Panic seizes every joint in my body. I'm on fire with fear, twisting and hammering. It's impossible to move to the side, to sit up, I'm pressed downwards, flat on my back. There's no room to extend my legs, no room to kick, even though, frantically, I try. I'm not screaming but gasping, breathing in lungfuls of dirt, scraping the skin from my knuckles as I fight against the wooden ceiling too close to my face.

Then, suddenly I stop. My heart is in agony, trapped against my ribs, like I'm trapped against the slats of this box. I feel it thumping. *Panic will kill you*, a voice says in my head. *Breathe.*

So I breathe. I think of nothing but the breath, shallow and ragged at first, but getting slower. *Someone put you in here*, says the voice. I feel panic rising again, but the voice returns. *Think. Who put you in here?*

And so I try to remember. But nothing comes. Terror rises again. I count the slats above my face to calm myself. Two, four, six, eight. I remember the bar. I remember Jon laughing, Laura leaning over, her blue boots tucked neatly underneath her. An ordinary Sunday night, surrounded by friends, people I know. Did we speak to anyone new? But the memory stops at Laura's boots. I can see them so clearly in my mind's eye, their heels resting on the metal bar of the stool, ankle cut, vintage, fake suede, powder blue. Almost luminous in the dark. I even remember the day we bought them, a bargain at a second-hand store, Laura's glee as she found them in the basket, yanking them out from amongst the battered Dr. Scholls. *This isn't helping,* I tell myself. *Try to remember that night.*

Other fragments come back to me. Jon buying more drinks, though I stopped after two, switched to Coke, wanted to finish my coursework the next day. Not drunk then. I try to remember leaving the bar, try to picture Laura's blue boots swinging off the stool, making their way out of the door, clacking onto Bedford Street. Then it hits me. I wouldn't remember that, I went home early. Alone. I will myself into recalling the journey, but I can't. There's a vague sensation of smothering, something over my face. Or is that a false memory, a fantasy my mind has created to make sense of what's happened?

Perhaps it was a blow to the head. That might account for my confusion. I feel a stab of terror. What if there's permanent damage? I reach up to feel my skull. It's cramped in the box, and hard to manoeuvre, but I'm just about able to pat against the back of my head, tentatively feel my forehead. There's nothing matted like dried blood, no lump I can feel.

Nothing else comes back to me about the journey home, and I don't try to force it. I know how it would have been. The walk to the bus stop. The journey to campus, the walk to halls. A trip in the dark, accomplished fearlessly a million times.

I try to work out which was the riskiest stage in that mundane journey, soothing myself by playing detective in my own kidnap, when I hear the sound of footsteps. I brace myself, about to cry for help, but then another thought seizes me. What if this is *the kidnapper*? My heart speeds up and I stay silent. The footsteps seem to be going up or down stairs. I hear a bolt scrape back, the creak of a door.

It's hard to breathe I'm so afraid, and then the footsteps come closer. It's a slow, heavy tread, deliberate. Somehow I know, I just know, that I mustn't cry out, I mustn't scream. Then a thud. Whoever it is has sat down on my box. They are sitting over my heart, blocking out the bars of light, strips of faded denim crushed between the slats by their weight. It makes me feel even more claustrophobic.

Be still, I tell myself. But it's no good, my breathing is fast and shallow, whistling through my teeth. Then I hear a sound that makes me want to cry. His voice.

'I know you're awake.'

Frankie

The phone rings just as she takes a mouthful of tuna sandwich.

'Bollocks!'

No prizes for guessing who it is. Frankie looks balefully at the screen, lit up with the familiar number. Briefly she imagines letting him wait, finishing her supermarket meal deal, snug in the front seat of the car. Instead she takes the call with a sigh.

'What now? You know I've been filming *all* morning? I've literally just stopped for lunch.'

'My heart bleeds,' says Charlie, her news editor. 'Well, eat up, I've got another job for you. I need you to go to Great Yarmouth. We've had a tip-off about police presence near Vauxhall rail bridge.'

'Seriously? But that could be anything, maybe somebody's dumped a bike in the Bure.' It's the second time this week Charlie has dispatched her to hang around the police on a punt. The first, a body on the beach at Wells, turned out to be a suicide. 'I mean, come off it,' she says. 'The bridge is two streets away from the police station, what self-respecting killer is going to leave someone there?'

'Our caller said there was quite a lot of activity. Doesn't sound like a bike.'

There's the familiar edge of steel in her news editor's voice. Charlie is convinced that the recent discoveries of two murdered women could be the work of one killer – even though the police won't confirm that – and he's been sending reporters to check out every crime scene since. Frankie sighs again. She's not going to win this. She never does. 'OK, I'm on my way to Great Yarmouth. Who's my cameraman?'

'Well, that's the thing. Given it *is* a punt, we thought you could film it yourself. Might just be a bike in the river.'

'Bastard.'

Charlie laughs. 'Have fun.'

Charlie's postcode takes Frankie to North Quay just before the Bure meets the Yare. It's Great Yarmouth's old industrial heartland but many years have passed since any fortunes were made in fishing here; now it feels more like the outskirts of town than the centre. She drives slowly alongside a row of houses before they give way to a car rental company and a half-derelict industrial estate. Numerous wind-battered signs announce there are units to let. Frankie's satnav orders her onto a track leading to the river. The car jounces as tarmac turns to cobbles and the buildings thin out, taken over by dirty scrubland that's barely contained by mesh fencing.

The track stops as she approaches the brown water of the Bure and she's about to curse Charlie for a wasted journey when she spies a snapper, leaning his considerable bulk against the mesh to take a photo. Whatever he can see is obscured by a warehouse at the edge of the river. Frankie parks up and walks to the boot of her car, hauling out her camera. The brittle autumn sunshine doesn't take the edge off the wind, which stings her cheeks as she hurries to join the photographer, tripod bumping against her thigh. As she gets closer she recognises him. It's a man in his fifties, an acquaintance of her cameraman Gavin, who's worked for years on the local paper. He's not much of a talker.

'Hi Dave,' she calls. 'Anything interesting?'

'You could say that.'

Standing beside him, Frankie sees there are several police cars parked on the forecourt of the empty warehouse. Blue and white tape flutters in the breeze. She waits for Dave to elaborate but he continues snapping as if she isn't there.

'Not a shopping trolley in the river, then?'

'Nope.'

Dave doesn't even turn in her direction. He clearly takes competition between news outlets very seriously, or else he's a grumpy git. Frankie sets up her own camera. There are figures on the scrubland beyond the cars, uniformed officers and a couple of forensic suits, but they're too far away for her to see much. She might get a better view if she zooms in. She presses her eye to the rubber ring of the viewfinder and turns the dial on the lens. The blur of sludgy brown and green coalesces into sharp lines. Frankie draws back as if the camera's burned her.

'Shit, is that a body?'

The continued snapping tells her she's correct. Frankie hesitates, then looks down the viewfinder again. White trouser legs and blue feet block most of the view, but she can see a hand, its pale fingers curved upwards, and the shape of a slender arm resting on the mud. She doesn't press record. The person lying on the wasteland by the river will mean the world to somebody, and even if they don't, even if they are utterly friendless, no self-respecting editor would show a dead body on the teatime news. Feeling queasy, she goes through the motions of her job. If it's a murder, they'll need pictures of the scene. She zooms out, taking a few shots at a wider angle, then some close-ups of the police tape and cars. Beside her, Dave is screwing his lens cap on, getting ready to leave.

'Have you spoken to the police?' Frankie asks. 'Have they confirmed if the death is suspicious?'

'Not my job,' he says, walking off. 'I just take the pictures.'

Frankie leaves her camera – she can't imagine anyone will steal it with half the East Anglian Constabulary a few yards away – and heads towards the water, looking for a way through the fence. As she approaches the Bure, it's hard to believe this is the same river that tourists sail on through the Broads. It laps gently against the rusting corrugated metal shoring up the bank, sluggish and dark, the colour of stewed tea. The red ironwork of the pedestrianised Vauxhall rail bridge curves over the water to Frankie's right and on the opposite bank there's a supermarket car park. Nobody will be sending postcards of this spot home.

She squeezes past the fence where it meets the water, ignoring the warning signs, resting one trainer on the concrete verge to shove her way through. Safe on the other side, she walks towards the panda cars, but doesn't reach them. One of the officers, a brunette about her own age, has spotted her and heads her off.

'This is a police investigation. Can you get back please.'

'I'm really sorry to disturb you,' she replies. 'My name is Frances Latch, I'm with the Eastern Film Company.' She reaches into her pocket for her press pass. 'We were just wondering if the death is being treated as suspicious.'

'I'm sorry, you'll have to call the press office. I can't talk to you.'

In spite of herself, Frankie's eyes have flicked over to the body lying in the mud, still some distance away but close enough now for her to see clearly. It's a young girl, blonde highlighted hair blown over her face. She's wearing a filthy short-sleeved pink top and jeans. For a moment, Frankie has an absurd worry she must be cold, she hasn't even got shoes on, then the reality hits her. 'Oh my God,' she says, stepping backwards. 'The poor girl. Her poor family. Who would do that?'

The officer takes hold of Frankie's arm, steadying her. 'You shouldn't be here, OK? Just let the police do their job. We'll have updates for the media later.'

'I'm sorry, I'm so sorry,' Frankie says, stricken. 'Somebody killed her, didn't they? Somebody killed her.'

Perhaps the officer senses her horror, understands she isn't only speaking as a journalist, because Frankie sees the closed look on her face waver, and reads the answer in her eyes. She releases Frankie's arm. 'Off you go now,' she says, her voice hoarse.

Stumbling slightly on the uneven ground, Frankie turns and heads back towards the fence. The police officer's voice rings out as she reaches it. 'And don't fall in the bloody river!'

Frankie is conscious of the memory stick as she walks into the newsroom. A small orange oblong with a metal edge, giving nothing away about what's inside. It's not as if she actually filmed the woman's body, she reminds herself; those pictures aren't in her hands, though they are certainly in her head. The pale arm, the pink top and, worse, the vulnerable, crumpled shape of her on the ground. How long had she been dead? Who is she? It feels wrong somehow that Frankie didn't see her face, it's one more aspect of her humanity erased, and yet she's also relieved not to have that image playing over in her mind too.

The newsroom is almost empty at this time of day; other reporters are still out filming, just one or two hunched over their edit machines, cutting packages for the evening show. She heads to the newsdesk, picking her way over the mess of bags and discarded newspapers, and taps Charlie on the shoulder.

'You're back,' he says, spinning round on his chair to face her. As always, he's wearing a headset with an earpiece and mic, to save him from picking up the constantly ringing phone. It makes him look like he works in telesales, though she can't imagine anyone less suitable to flog double-glazing. 'I've been on to the police,' he continues. 'They're not identifying her yet, though they have confirmed they've found a woman's body and the death's being treated as suspicious. Are your rushes online?'

'No, I thought I'd ask traffic to do it,' she says, holding up the memory stick and nodding towards the central bank of desks where production sits.

Charlie looks embarrassed. 'Of course. Sorry it ended up being so grim.'

'All part of the job, I guess.'

He nods, no doubt relieved she isn't going to start weeping over him. 'I think for today we'll do a live from the scene, just give whatever information we have at that point, but I'd like you to start digging for more. See if anyone knows who she is.' He reaches out and takes the memory stick from her. 'Don't worry about giving that to traffic,' he says, putting it on the desk. 'I'll do it.'

There's still a half-drunk cup of tea on her desk from this morning. She shoves it aside to make room for the fresh one, and sits down, logging on to the East Anglian Police website She clicks through their news alerts, looking for any press releases about missing people. If Charlie is right, and there's a link with the last two murder victims, Sandra Blakely and Lily Sidcup – who were both working as prostitutes – it's possible nobody has declared this latest woman missing yet, but it's still worth a try. All she finds is a pensioner with dementia who wandered off from his home on Sunday. No young woman has been recorded as missing in the last month.

Frankie takes a sip of tea, and opens up Twitter. She types in 'body Great Yarmouth' and reads through the results. At the top there's a short update from the *Norfolk Times*; the bare facts, which she already knows, plus one of Dave's photos of the scene. She scrolls through the other tweets, most of them trite RIP messages in response to the newspaper article, before she notices an image that's been retweeted multiple times. She opens it fully, then immediately wishes she hadn't. It's a photo of the young woman, lying on the mud, taken from horribly close up. The photographer must have been standing right over her. She can see the dead woman's pink top has sequins sewn on it, and there's livid bruising on her neck. Her face is still almost entirely obscured by hair. Frankie reads the text above it.

There's only a fucking dead body by the Bure!!! WTF??

The poster is someone called @M_VanMan but his photo is just a silhouette with no biog. Frankie reads the replies, which are mainly abuse directed at him for tweeting it: **Disgusting** says one **Have some f***ing respect.** VanMan's attempts to defend himself **I did call the fucking police FYI, knobhead** gain him little sympathy. As always, there are some messages whose nastiness, even though she half expects it, takes her by surprise. **Probably just a junkie. Killed for crimes against fashion, lolol, is that top from Tesco??**

She is about to log off, when one tweet makes her pause. **OMG I think that's my flatmate!!!!** It was posted twenty minutes ago by @Pixie95. She's not an egg; her profile shows a heavily made-up young woman, pouting for a selfie, who gives her location as Great Yarmouth. Frankie looks at Pixie's other recent tweets, all replies to concerned messages. **Yeah, Han went missing last week. OMG can't believe it. So so sad if its her!!!!** She seems to be relishing the drama of it all, a bit too much for Frankie's taste, but it's possible she really does know the victim. She follows Pixie and sends her a message.

Hi I'm Frankie a TV journalist, can you follow me so we can chat? Very sorry about what's been happening.

A few minutes later she has an interview with Pixie set up in Great Yarmouth and a possible name for the victim: Hanna Chivers.

'Not sure about this, Franks,' Gavin says, as they drive slowly along the terraced street. It's behind Marine Parade and several of the houses seem to be B&Bs, with flower baskets and striped awnings. 'Could be anyone online, couldn't it? How do we know this Pixie person is who she says she is?'

Frankie's cameraman has a deep distrust of the Internet. Gavin is on Facebook, but only, she suspects, because his adult children harangued him into it. He posts something about once a year, if that. 'She's not really called Pixie, she's called Leah Wilcox,' she says.

'Exactly. That's my point.'

'Just here.' She touches his arm. 'I think it's this one.' The house is painted cream, its windows tacked on like boxes in a style the Victorians seem to have favoured for every English seaside resort. Gavin parks up and gets his camera kit out of the boot, refusing Frankie's offer of help. His short grey hair sticks up in the wind, a frown of concern on his thin face as she knocks on the door.

'You the news people?'

Leah stands in the doorway, one elbow propped on her hip and what looks like an enormous joint hanging from her fingers.

'That's right,' says Frankie. 'Thanks for having us.'

'Come in, then,' she says, wafting them over the threshold and padding barefoot through the dark hallway. Frankie follows her without turning round. She doesn't need to see the furious expression on Gavin's face to know it's there. Leah takes them into the front room. A young man sits on a black faux-leather sofa holding a Fosters can. He raises it slightly as they walk in, but says nothing. Leah plops herself down on the sofa without introducing him. She takes a drag from her roll-up. There's a strong smell of weed.

The only other place to sit is a small beanbag, so Frankie stays standing. Gavin puts his camera on the floor and leans on the tripod without setting it up. 'Thanks for seeing us,' Frankie says again, getting her notepad out of her bag. 'Before we do any filming, what makes you think the murdered woman is your flatmate?'

'Han went missing about a week ago. I told her work she was sick, just in case she needed some time out, you know?'

'Did she often do that? Go missing, I mean?'

'Dunno. She's only been here a month, hasn't she?' Leah turns to the man beside her. 'Didn't know much about her to be fair, did we? Just that she worked at the hairdresser's across town. What's it called again? Curly Sue.'

Frankie jots down the salon name. 'Why did you tell her work she was sick?'

'So they wouldn't fire her.'

'You didn't think to call the police or her family at all?' says Gavin, not even attempting to make his question sound less like an accusation. Frankie shoots him a look.

'Don't know her family. And I didn't want her to get in trouble or anything at work, thought she'd just taken off for a few days.' Leah looks upset. 'Fuck. Do you think I should have called them?'

'Well, maybe it's not her,' Frankie replies, unsure what to say. No point making Leah feel worse.

'She has a top like the one in that photo. And it did look like her hair.' Leah's voice quavers. 'What if it really *is* her?'

'Hopefully it's not. What's she like?'

'Bit stuck up, I thought,' says the man with the Fosters can. 'Kept herself to herself. Except that time she went mental over some stupid fucking parcel.'

'A parcel?'

'Yeah, somebody sent her broken glass in the post. She freaked out.'

'That sounds pretty weird,' Frankie says. 'And they sent it here, even though she's only just moved in?'

'It *was* a bit creepy,' Leah says. 'I don't think there was a note or anything, just bits of glass. I chucked it out for her,' she adds, tossing her head. 'So she didn't have to deal with it.'

Gavin nods towards the window. 'I think we may have company.'

Through the netting Frankie can see two uniformed officers are getting out of a police car. The doors slam and they walk out of sight. A moment later, there's a knock at the door.

'Shit,' says Leah, grabbing her companion's can and dropping the joint in it. 'Open the bloody window, Jez!' The young man leaps to his feet.

There's another knock and a scrape that sounds like the letterbox being pushed open. 'Anybody home?'

'Just a minute,' Leah calls, hurrying out of the room.

Frankie and Gavin look at each other but say nothing, keen to overhear whatever the police have to say. Jez is flapping the netting out of the open window, trying to disperse the smell.

'Leah Wilcox? I'm DS Ian Darlow from the East Anglian Constabulary, this is PC June Wright. Can we come in please?'

'It's Han, isn't it? Oh my God, oh my God!'

'Careful, love. Let's just go inside where you can sit down.'

A moment later, Frankie is facing the police officer she met that morning. PC June Wright looks far from delighted to see her. 'You again!'

'We were just here to do an interview,' Frankie says, gesturing unnecessarily at Gavin's tripod. 'Leah said she thought the victim you found this morning might be her flatmate.'

'I'd strongly advise you *not* to have the press here right now.' DS Darlow turns to Leah, who looks terrified. 'Your choice, of course, but I wouldn't advise it. Not at this stage.'

'It is Hanna, isn't it?' Leah says. 'Oh God, Jez, I didn't think it would be her, not *really*. Jesus.' She slumps down on the sofa.

The two police officers are staring pointedly at Frankie and Gavin, clearly waiting for them to leave. Frankie knows there are plenty of journalists with enough brass neck to try to tough this out but she isn't one of them. 'We'll just be going,' she says. 'Very sorry, Leah,' she adds as she passes her. Leah doesn't seem to hear. PC June Wright moves to sit down beside her, putting an arm round her shoulders.

'I'll see you out,' says DS Darlow.

There's a scuffle as Gavin's camera clips the police officer and they nearly get stuck in the narrow hallway. 'We had no idea you were coming,' Frankie says as he opens the front door. 'We weren't trying to intrude. I didn't even know for sure if it was her flatmate.'

'I realise that,' he replies. 'And I'm not going to take you for fools, you've clearly worked out who the victim is. But I'd ask you to wait until it's official before making that public.'

'Of course,' Gavin says.

'Is her death being linked to the other two murders?' Frankie adds. 'I'm asking off the record.'

Ian Darlow gives her a long, hard look. 'No comment,' he says, pulling the door shut and leaving them standing on the doorstep.

'Blimey!' says Gavin. 'That was bloody awkward!'

But Frankie doesn't reply; she's already calling Charlie on the newsdesk.

Ava

'*I know you're awake.*'

I can't answer, I can't even scream. I think I'm going to black out from the terror. My mind can't accept this is happening; maybe if I say nothing it will stop, I will wake up. The denim shifts out of sight as he gets off the box. There's a scuffling noise and I think he's getting down onto the floor. Then a shadow looms over me. I see it's a face, encased in a padded ski mask, dissected by the slats. An eye presses against one of the gaps, and it stares, unwinking, into my own. Fear squeezes my chest.

'Hello, in there. Cat got your tongue?'

I open my mouth but no sound comes out. *Don't antagonise him!* screams the voice in my head. Half-remembered stories about kidnap victims who survive flash through my mind. It's the ones who don't annoy their captors, who don't panic, that make it through. The ones who play nice. I know I have to answer him. The effort of speaking makes it feel as if I am dragging the word out of my throat with sandpaper.

'Hello.'

He laughs. 'Feeling comfortable in there?'

'Not really. Can I get out please?'

The brown eye stares at me, until I feel naked beneath its gaze. 'Hmmm, not today. Today, I think you can stay where you are.'

I'm desperate to ask why I'm here, plead with him to let me go, but I know deep in my bones that this would be useless. It would only make him feel more powerful, feed his cruelty. I try to keep the conversation unthreatening.

'My name's Ava. Ava Lindsey. I'm studying at the University of East Anglia.'

'I know who you are. Cool customer, aren't you, Ava? I thought you might be. I've been watching you for a while. My prim little psychology student.' The hideous eye winks at me. 'Got an even better view now.'

'Are you interested in psychology, then?' It's a ridiculous question, but I want to change the subject, I can't bear that black dot of a pupil boring into me.

'Come on, Ava. That's not really what you want to ask me, is it? You want to ask why I've brought you here, what I'm going to do with you. Why haven't you?'

'Well, I figure that if you want to tell me those things, you will.'

The eye shifts suddenly out of sight, the voice echoing as he moves away. It must be a near empty room I think, maybe a basement. 'Clever girl,' he says. 'You're right, I don't like questions. For that you get some water.' For one wonderful moment, I think he's going to open the box, then I feel cold liquid splash down hard on my face. I gasp, spluttering, then realise that if I want to survive, I will have to try to drink. Knowing I may only have a few seconds, I close my eyes and open my mouth, swallowing as the water falls. It's mixed with dust from the wood, I can taste the tang of creosote, and lying on my back, keeping my mouth open with the water tipping down my throat, I nearly choke. I manage a few swallows before he stops. I blink the water from my eyes, trying not to cry.

'Better?'

Anger, more bitter than the chemical taste on my tongue, fills my mouth. I hate this man. 'Yes, thank you.'

'I'm glad. As a reward for being a good girl about the water, I'm going to tell you a little bit about why you're here.' There's an alarming creaking noise in the joints of the box as he lies face down on its lid, his body directly above mine. My small space grows darker. I can see both eyes through the slats now, and traces of his wet pink lips as he speaks close to the wood. It's suffocating, the sense of him lying on top of me. 'Do you watch the news, Ava, or is it just Freud for you?'

'I don't really watch the news, no.'

'So you haven't seen anything about dead women being found in Norfolk?'

Oh God, please no. 'I . . . I'm not sure,' I stammer.

'Well, it's a shame you've not been watching me as closely as I've watched you. That's a bit disappointing. The police aren't helping frankly, it's not entirely your fault, they could have made more of it. I think you'll help me there. I'm doing a little experiment, you see, Ava. An experiment in fear. None of the others passed, I'm afraid. I'm hoping you might be different.' He laughs again, and I can feel his hot breath on my face, blowing dust and drops of water into my eyes. 'That would be nice, wouldn't it? If you were the one who lived. Shall we try that?'

I feel as though the scream trapped inside my lungs is going to tear me apart. I open my lips to speak but no sound comes. *This can't be happening.* My breath catches in my throat. 'Yes,' I hear myself say.

Frankie

Walking through the door of her flat, Frankie nearly stumbles over Jack's shoes and flings her keys on the bench. Bags that neither of them has bothered to unpack yet form a mini obstacle course on the path to the open-plan kitchen. They've only just moved in together. She can't help thinking of Leah and Jez's dark front room, where Hanna lived for the last month of her life. It's very different to the flat she and Jack are renting. Light and modern, right on the riverside off King Street, it's in one of her favourite spots in Norwich.

She crosses to the kitchen, moves to dump her bag on the laminated worktop that doubles as a breakfast counter, then thinks better of it and lowers it to the floor. All the surfaces in this flat are alarmingly white and Scandi-looking. Frankie imagines herself leaving a trail of mess wherever she puts down her belongings. At least Jack is too much of a geek to notice he's moved in with a dust devil.

He often works late, and she knows he'll be staring at plants at the John Innes Centre for a good hour yet. Of all the professions she imagined for her life partner, food technologist was never one of them. She smiles. At least if climate change ruins all the regular crops, Jack will be safely on hand making a genetically modified variety.

She goes to the fridge and pours herself a large glass of white wine. It's wonderfully cold. She stands for a moment, letting out a deep breath, trying to let the stress of the day drop from her shoulders. Soon after she had spoken to DS Ian Darlow, the police had confirmed Hanna Chivers' name to the press. Thanks to Leah, they had a head start on the rest of the local media. Charlie sent her straight to Hanna's hair salon, Curly Sue, for that most hated errand in journalism: the death knock. Even the hardest of hacks feels their heart sink when dispatched, like the Angel of Death, to disturb a grief-stricken family.

Frankie had called first, but nobody answered the phone. It took her a while to psych herself up into walking to the door, phrases like 'paying tribute' and 'dreadfully sorry to disturb you' waiting on her lips. The manager of the salon had spied her and Gavin through the glass, walked swiftly to the door and pulled it open before Frankie had a chance to knock. Frankie had stared at the woman's face, seen her red-rimmed eyes, and the image of Hanna Chivers lying barefoot on the wasteland flashed into her mind. She saw Hanna's hair, tangled over her face, and wondered if this woman had cut it, if she had run her fingers through the highlights that had been left to blow uncared for in the wind. Her pre-prepared speech deserted her.

'I'm so sorry,' she stammered. 'I'm so sorry.'

The other woman burst into tears.

They got their interview, so Charlie was pleased, but by the time Frankie left the salon she felt drained, and a little tainted from playing voyeur to another's pain. Maureen Grey, Hanna's old boss, alternated between shock and tearful grief. Hanna was eighteen years old, she told them, and had just finished her apprenticeship at Curly Sue, where she was one of Maureen's best stylists. 'She was so alive, just so *alive*,' Maureen kept repeating. 'When the police told me she was dead I couldn't believe it. You must have the wrong girl, I said, it can't be Hanna, it can't be. She had real spirit, you know? A proper bright spark. She was always here early, always laughing. A bit cheeky maybe, if I'm honest. Not afraid to answer back. She wanted to run her own salon one day. I'm sure she could have done.' At the thought of all Hanna would now never accomplish, Maureen had been unable to continue, and Gavin turned off the camera while she cried. Frankie had thought that was quite enough to put Maureen through, but she insisted on continuing. Frankie asked if all seemed well in Hanna's private life. 'She didn't gossip much,' Maureen told her. 'No chat about any boyfriends, which I guess is unusual. Though I know she'd had a bit of trouble in the last month. Didn't like her new flatmates much. She mouthed off about them a few times.'

In Frankie's experience, calling on the bereaved either results in being turned away immediately, or finding yourself with someone desperate to be heard. Maureen was the latter. It felt heartless abandoning her, she clearly could have spent the rest of the day talking about Hanna and drinking sugary tea, but Frankie had to do her live. She left it as late as she could, almost missing her slot. She was so flustered she forgot to mention the exclusive line from Leah about Hanna being sent glass in the post.

Standing now in the flat, she can hear the sound of footsteps passing in the hallway. Her neighbours must be back. Sure enough, she hears the sound of keys jangling, the gentle thunk of a closing door and then, after a pause, the muted strains of the *Goldberg Variations*. Just as well they're not living next to heavy metal fans, the walls are a bit thin for the price she and Jack are paying. She pulls up a stool and sits down at the breakfast counter, massaging her temples. The glass of wine is in front of her, condensation forming on its surface. She shouldn't get too comfortable. Dinner isn't going to make itself. A day of horror washed down by nothing but alcohol is no way to spend the evening. Still, she doesn't move yet, instead staring at a small drop of water as it runs down the side of the cold glass.

The next morning Jack gets up early and makes them both porridge, a peace offering for being home so late the night before. Frankie had given up and gone to bed by the time he got in. It was hard not to feel a little aggrieved, even though it wasn't his fault. After such an awful day she had wanted to talk to him.

'At least you should be able to report on something new now,' Jack says, setting the honey down between them. His hair is still wet from the shower, the dark brown curls leaving a damp stain on his collar.

'You're joking, aren't you? Charlie is *obsessed* with the idea it's a serial killer. There's absolutely no way he won't squeeze a day two out of the story. After all, we haven't even had a police interview yet.' With an unerring sense of timing, Charlie's number flashes up on her mobile. Frankie rolls her eyes and takes the call. 'Don't tell me,' she says to her news editor. 'You've lined up a nice day filming at a garden centre.'

'Ha bloody ha,' he replies. 'Can you go straight to Yarmouth rather than come in to the office? Police say the family absolutely don't want to talk, which is a shame. I suggest you and Gavin go to the scene, see if anyone leaving flowers knew her and will say anything. I think we'll send somebody else to police headquarters. They're not taking any questions, so it's just going to be some copper reading out a statement.'

'Great. So that's a day hanging out by the Bure talking to bereaved teenagers? Gavin will be delighted.'

'Always happy to oblige,' says Charlie, ringing off.

Frankie puts the phone down. Jack is staring at her. 'Are you going to be OK? Couldn't he have sent someone else? You had to deal with it all yesterday.'

Not for the first time, she wishes she didn't have to explain her job to him. 'The fact I did it yesterday is the point. It means I've made the contacts and know the story.' She spoons some honey onto the porridge, stirring it in. 'It's fine, don't worry. I've got Gavin with me.' She doesn't add that in spite of the horror, and although some part of her never wants to think about what happened to Hanna Chivers ever again, another part wouldn't want to be doing anything else.

The track she drove down yesterday is no longer deserted. A shrine sits at the bottom of it. Tealights in jam jars, bunches of flowers and cards, rest against the mesh in a growing pile. If there's anything worse than a death knock, perhaps it's loitering at places of grief, waiting to pounce on unwary mourners. She and Gavin stand as far back as they can to avoid making anyone uncomfortable. They film a short clip with one of Hanna's teachers, retired now, but a number of the well-wishers have never even met Hanna, they've just come to 'pay their respects'. A few are not averse to being filmed placing their tributes by the fence, staring thoughtfully at the candles.

Police cars are still parked in the deserted warehouse yard and a white tent has been erected where Hanna's body lay. Gavin gets some shots of forensic officers busy at the scene. The wind from the Bure is icy, and they are about to pack up and leave when a teenage girl arrives, bearing a service station bouquet. She has streaks of purple and platinum in her black hair and mascara smudged under her eyes. It's obvious she's not here to sightsee. She walks to the spot by the fence with her shoulders hunched over as if she's in physical pain. Frankie waits until the girl has laid her flowers, then approaches.

'I'm really sorry to bother you,' she says. 'My name's Frankie, I'm from the Eastern Film Company. Did you know Hanna?'

'She was my best friend.'

'I'm really sorry. This must be terrible.'

'She'd been through so much. Like seriously, so much shit. And then for something like this to happen. It makes me so angry.' The girl wipes one hand across her eyes as the tears spill over, smearing more mascara.

'What had Hanna been through?'

'Well, you know she was in care? She came to Norfolk when she was thirteen. That's when we met. We were at school together. She was Hanna Raynott then. Her foster family were all right, I suppose, but it's not the same. And then they took in some lad, and he was a right twat. Han couldn't stand him. She moved out after school, lived with me and my mum for a bit.' She pauses, biting her bottom lip. 'I just feel so bad, you know? We were best mates and I didn't even notice she was missing. When she didn't text me back last week, I just thought she was being a bit crap.'

'You shouldn't feel bad, it sounds like you were a real friend to her.' Frankie pauses. 'Sorry, I didn't catch your name.'

'Hollie.'

'Hollie, I hate to ask this, and feel free to say no, but would you like to say a little bit about Hanna for the news? My colleague Gavin is just here with the camera. We're running a piece about her on the programme tonight.'

'I guess so,' Hollie replies. 'Not sure what I can say though.' Gavin, who has been waiting nearby as discreetly as possible, hands Frankie the microphone and hoists the camera onto his shoulder, before the young girl can change her mind. Hollie looks up at him, a little uncertain, pushing the lock of purple from her eyes. 'Are you going to be filming me?'

'Yes, but it's not live. We can stop and start all you like. Just look at me, not the camera. Try to pretend Gavin isn't there.'

With a nudge from Frankie, Hollie starts talking about Hanna, about her kindness, her bravery, about the loneliness she felt in care, the friendship the two girls had, the plans they'd made. She talks quickly, gabbles even, as if determined to make it through the ordeal without crying. And all the while Frankie can see the white tent behind Hollie's head and feels a growing sense of rage. Somebody out there is responsible for all this pain; they've stolen a young woman's life and left her like trash on the wasteland, and now they're walking about, free while everyone who loved her is left in agony. She feels so angry she can hardly breathe.

'Did she say anything to you before she went missing? Like, was anyone following or bothering her? Her flatmates said she got sent some glass in the post.'

'Really? Not sure I'd trust them to be honest, she didn't like them much.' Hanna shakes her head. 'There was just the blog. That really upset her.'

'A blog? What about?'

'It was the trial, wasn't it? Some wanker wrote this whole nasty blog about it, saying that Han made up being assaulted. It was really shitty.'

'I didn't know Hanna had been assaulted.'

'Yeah, it was some perv when we were fifteen. Grabbed her outside the club toilet. Tried to stick his hand down her pants, but she punched him in the nuts.' Hollie smiles slightly, and Frankie can hear the pride in her voice. 'He perved over the wrong girl. She recognised him when he raped somebody else and it was in the papers. Han gave evidence at the trial, got him banged up and everything.'

'She sounds very brave.' Frankie feels another wash of sadness. All that bravery, and strength, for what? Hollie is squinting up at her, chewing her bottom lip, looking spiky and vulnerable. As Hanna must have been. 'What did this blog say, then?'

'It was like a riff on what Han said at court. Whoever it was must have got hold of her statement, and then they just put nasty comments all over it, making out how she was a liar.'

'Sounds horrible. Is it still online?'

'Yeah, yeah, it is!' Hollie says, bouncing slightly on the balls of her feet. 'Police are so fff—' She pauses like a schoolgirl who realises she's talking to a teacher, and glances over her shoulder in case any of the officers standing by the panda cars might have heard her – 'so flipping useless, we complained about it, but they never took it down. Said the website wasn't registered. Or something. So it's still there. Hanna even changed her name to Chivers, after her nan, just so the stupid blog didn't come up all the time. How crap is that?'

'That's awful,' says Frankie. 'Do you remember what the website was called?'

'It had the weirdest name, like really weird. *Killing Cuttlefish*.' Hollie hugs her arms round herself and shudders. 'Like, what's that about? Some really gross stuff on there. Makes you wonder about people, doesn't it?'

Frankie gets in the passenger seat of Gavin's car, slamming the door shut, waiting for him to pack the camera in the boot. Her fingers are bright pink from the cold and she has to sniff to stop her nose from streaming. She gets her phone out of her bag, to turn it off silent. Four missed calls from Charlie.

'Can you believe it!' he says, when she rings him back.

'Sorry, I didn't listen to your messages.'

'The BBC filmed her!'

'Who?'

'Hanna. They filmed a short interview with her at her further education college last year, some report on more government cash for apprenticeships. Somebody over there must have stuck her name in the archive, just in case, and it came up. The lucky sods.'

'I suppose they're not sharing the footage?' Frankie asks. Charlie just snorts in reply. She turns as Gavin lets himself in and sits down beside her. 'Well, we're on our way back now. We spoke to a teacher, as well as her best friend, and found out a load of stuff about her past. Seems she pissed off some fairly nasty people.'

'Great!' says Charlie. 'Well, you know what I mean,' he adds, obviously realising how he sounds. 'Fill me in when you get back.'

It takes Frankie a while to get round to looking up Hollie's blog. She doesn't have enough signal to check it in the car, and then back in the newsroom, she gets caught up watching the footage of Hanna on the BBC website, like everyone else. It's only about thirty-five seconds long. A few shots of her brushing a client's hair at the college salon, a close-up of her hands, another close-up of her face, with its frown of concentration, and then a brief clip. *I think apprenticeships are great, you know? You can earn as you learn and all that. When I've got my own salon, I'll definitely have apprentices there.*

It feels odd listening to her voice; she sounds incredibly young. Frankie plays it several times, trying to wipe out the memory of Hanna's dead body, without much success.

She closes the tab with the video and types 'Killing Cuttlefish' into the search engine. Some very odd suggestions for videos on YouTube come up, but only one website with the same title. She opens it. At first it's blank and she thinks maybe it's been taken down by the police after all, then a blob of ink splatters across the white screen, turning it black. A circle appears, exactly like the opening titles of a James Bond movie, but instead of 007, a female silhouette walks into the spotlight. She stands still. A small red dot appears over her chest, growing larger and larger, until the whole page is red. White text appears.

Enter Forum

Frankie clicks on it. A welcome message appears, the letters fading up through the red. Brother, make yourself at home. You are with friends. Here you can rage against the Feminist Gynocracy. Here you can dream. Here you are free. A box in the bottom right hand corner reads: Join the Conversation.

Frankie enters the forum, a long list of posts, all by different writers with peculiar pseudonyms. She reads a few and finds herself entering a strange parallel world of grievance in which women run everything and men are oppressed; doubly put upon by the constraints of chivalry and feminism. She guesses it must be an extreme version of Men's Rights Activism, a movement she has heard of before, but knows little about.

There's no search bar to pick out Hanna's name, so she's forced to plough through the forum and nearly gets lost down the rabbit hole. A series of posts advocate a brave new world that is no longer run by 'Feminazis' or 'The False Principle of Female Consent'. Instead, one blogger called @BetaBloke suggests women should be held in common, thus losing their sexual power over men. Posts below the line are full of rage about the bitches who have made the writers' lives a misery and the entire site seethes with discontent.

Even after reading a few posts Frankie is none the wiser about the significance of the site's peculiar title, and she's forced to google some of the other jargon; there's a lot of chat about red and blue pills, which she doesn't understand. The website is clearly aimed at long-standing believers and no explanations are given. After some research she learns the terms are fairly common in the MRA world, a metaphor based loosely on a film she hasn't seen, called *The Matrix*. The blue pill is a drug everyone takes to stay in a state of false consciousness, the world where men are supposedly in charge. The red pill is The Truth, whose takers understand that feminism rules, and that in reality, it's women who use and abuse men. The premise is so absurd it ought to be funny, but Frankie is starting to find the bile anything but laughable.

The website seems to be UK based, given the references are almost all British. In amongst articles aimed at specific women – including the octogenarian TV chef Mary Berry – she eventually finds the piece on Hanna Raynott. The writers at *Killing Cuttlefish* evidently don't have any qualms about the illegality of naming victims of sexual assault.

Written by someone who goes by the name @Feminazi_Slayer2, the post's main target is the woman at the centre of the rape case, Amy Spencer. Her attacker, Jamie Cole, was simultaneously convicted of raping Amy as well as three counts of indecent assault against teenage girls, including Hanna. According to @Feminazi_Slayer2, the trial was a charade. The headline runs **Jamie Cole: Another Victim of 'Rape Culture'**.

So the Feminists claimed another scalp this month: hapless 22-year-old Jamie Cole. Poor old Jamie was set up by a quartet of shrill little sluts, you know the kind I mean. Happy to get pissed out of their tiny minds, running round in little more than their panties, but all too keen to scream 'Fire!' as soon as some poor sap takes them up on their offer . . .

And on it goes. After his opening rant, the blogger proceeds to pick apart all four women's impact statements, looking for proof that they were lying. Frankie can't bear to read more than is necessary (she skips the section on Amy Spencer after reading that her cracked ribs were because she 'liked it rough') and scrolls straight down to Hanna's statement. Like all the other women's stories, the teenager's simple account – which Frankie imagines being read in the childlike voice she's just heard on the video – is constantly interrupted by the blogger's comments.

So now we get to Hanna Raynott, the youngest of the quartet, but by all accounts something of a wild child. Not that we hear anything about her tearaway, binge-drinking antics in her 'victim' impact statement. Au contraire, butter wouldn't melt, but reading between the lines we can see her little lies and slip-ups.

I was fifteen when Jamie Cole assaulted me. I was with some friends at a club, having a night out before the start of our final GCSE year. It had been a stressful few months, but I was finally feeling good about myself, and we were all having a good time.

So first off, what's a fifteen-year-old doing in a club? Last time I checked, night clubs were for over-eighteens. So we've hardly got a little innocent here. Then there's the entirely irrelevant whinging about her stressful few months. Ah, Diddums. What relevance does that have to Jamie? Zilch, that's what.

Jamie came over to the bar and insisted on buying us some drinks but then wouldn't leave us alone.

The poor sap 'insisted' did he? So by her own admission, they were quite happy to quaff his booze but not to tolerate his company. Charming.

He got quite abusive and kept wanting to snog my friend Hollie. After we told him to go away, we thought he had got the message, but an hour or so later when I went to the toilet, he was waiting outside the door when I came out.

Here I think we get to the nub of the whole thing. He wanted to 'snog my friend Hollie.' A little jealousy, methinks? Hell Hath no Fury etc. And she admits Jamie **was not interested in her** while there were witnesses, but suddenly he's sneaking after her to the loos? More likely she gave him the wink to follow her there.

When I tried to get past him he grabbed me, and tried to get hold of my breasts. I shoved him away but he jammed me against the wall and stuck his hand in my knickers. He managed to get his hand inside me, and scratched at me with his fingernails. I was very frightened and in a lot of pain but I managed to punch him and get away.

All very traumatic, I'm sure. IF IT EVER HAPPENED. I think the last line is the crucial one here – if she's strong enough to punch him away, how did he get his hand in her panties? By invitation, that's how.

What happened really affected me. I was scared to go anywhere on my own afterwards and felt really dirty and disgusted. I worried about getting an infection from his scratches. He made me feel anyone might pick on me at any time, that I wasn't safe. I already found it hard to trust people and this made it so much worse.

Blah, blah, blah. The usual spiel. You'd think these 'victims' just copied each other wouldn't you? Same little lines fed to them by the Feminazis to repeat over and over. Dirty, Disgusted, Not safe BLAH, BLAH, BLAH.

I tried to forget all about it, but I couldn't. My school work was affected and eventually I told my form teacher what had happened. I feel guilty sometimes thinking if I had reported it straight away, maybe he wouldn't have hurt anyone else.

Again this is so transparent it's laughable. She reports 'the assault' AFTER her grades drop? Blatantly just looking for an excuse. Honestly, sometimes I wonder how so many twats sitting on juries have been conditioned to believe this crap. It's the power of the Blue Pill, people.

That night meant nothing to Jamie Cole, I was just a thing to him, but I have had to relive what happened over and over again in my head.

Again the language of the woman scorned: 'That night meant nothing to him' etc. Upset he never called you after your little fumble were you, sweetie? Looking for a boyfriend? Maybe try not being such a slag.

I hope one day he understands how much hurt he's caused.

Yeah well, the poor bastard's in jail now honey pie, so I guess he's having a worse time of it than you, hey? You better hope nobody **really** gives you what's coming to you. BITCH.

By the time she reaches the end of the post, Frankie's stomach is churning. Just as Jamie Cole had abused Hanna, the poster's comments, pawing and picking at the teenager's words, are another violation.

'You fucking bastard!' she says, staring wide-eyed at the screen.

'Badmouthing me *again*? The Yarmouth job wasn't that bad, surely?'

She turns round to see Charlie standing behind her chair. 'No, it's not you for once. It's that blog I told you about. It's fucking awful.'

'Budge over, then,' he says. She gets up so he can sit down, then leans over to watch him read. Perhaps because she had been infected by the blog's bile, it comes as a strange relief to see the disgust on his face. But what was she expecting? The MRA are a weird minority; most men aren't like that. 'Jesus,' he says at last. 'I feel like I need a shower. That really is revolting stuff.' He shakes his head as if to rid it of the blogger's words. They both pause for a moment, staring at the screen. 'This looks like a credible threat to me. Do the police know about it?'

'According to Hollie, Hanna complained but the police couldn't take it down. So it's been sitting online for nearly a year. She even had to change her name over it.'

'We certainly need to ask the police if this website is forming part of their investigation. If we can confirm that, I'll feel happier sticking our necks out to lead on it.' Charlie moves the cursor, slowly scrolling through the text. 'Do you want to see if there's any mention of Sandra Blakely or Lily Sidcup on here?'

'You're still convinced it's the same killer?'

Charlie sighs. 'I know you're all saying I've got carried away on this one, relying on my famous intuition.' He stops scrolling and swivels his chair to face her. 'But seriously, the answer's yes. Three women strangled and dumped in a matter of months. Let's face it, Norfolk isn't normally that eventful. And after reading this, there's obviously some local guy wandering about with a massive grudge against women, and against one of our victims in particular. Not like the nationals would have reported on a sexual assault case in Yarmouth, this guy must have sat in on the trial, or read about it in the local papers.'

'But maybe he's only connected to Hanna?'

'Well, I guess *someone* will have to go through the blog to see if any of the other women's names come up.' He looks at her pointedly.

'What? No, you're joking, that'll take hours! There isn't even a search bar.'

Charlie presses Command + F and a search box pops up on the screen. He shakes his head at her. 'Call yourself a reporter? There you go, get cracking.'

Ava

When he's gone the first thing I feel is relief. His weight was unbearable. I couldn't feel it, not physically, but it left me doubly hemmed in, by the nearness of his body and his stare. Yet when I'm alone, it's even worse.

What if he never comes back? What if he leaves me to starve in here? I start hyperventilating. I don't mean to, but I can't help myself. The sense of physical containment in the box is agony; I feel like I'm buried alive. I try to stay calm, but there's a loud buzzing in my head and bright spots before my eyes. I wonder what happened to the other women, the ones before me, and the fear is so intense I'm suffocated by it. I start screaming and find I can't stop. I don't want to be here, I don't want to die, I can't bear it, I have to get out.

I don't know how long I scream and punch against the box, but I stop when my throat is burning and the pain in my hands starts to cut through the terror. My nose is almost blocked from all the crying and I have to blow it against my shoulder. With a flush of embarrassment, even though there's nobody here to know it but me, I realise I've wet myself. But the itch of the denim, damp and stuck to my thighs, is nothing compared to the pain that seems to be raging in every joint of my body.

This is how people go mad says the voice in my head. *Distance yourself.* I try to imagine myself in one of my psychology lectures at uni, hearing Professor Marks talk about the rational observer, the technique you encourage patients with anxiety to develop so they can step outside their own situation. I feel a tiny flash of calm, all too brief, like the beam from a lighthouse at sea. I close my eyes and breathe out, trying to calm down. The desperation to escape is so fierce it threatens to drown out every other thought with its incessant, beating drum, but I can't let that thumping noise in my head dominate. At this moment, escaping is out of my control. All I can control is how I react to my situation. Even though it doesn't feel like it, I still have some choices.

An image flashes into my mind. My brother Matt lying in bed, looking away from me as I hold his hand. I hear my own voice, talking to him. I'm trying to sound sympathetic, but the bitterness cuts through, its ice beneath the water's surface.

'Only you can control how you feel, Matt. When you decide to feel better, you will.'

No wonder he told me to fuck off.

I almost smile. Then the thought of what he must be feeling at this minute, and what his anxiety might be doing to him, hits me like a punch to the chest. I can't think of Matt, I have to think of myself. I have to plan how I'm going to stay alive.

'I'm going to survive,' I say aloud. 'I'm going to get out of this box.' My voice sounds croaky from the screaming. I carry on, speaking more loudly. 'I'm not going to let that fucking bastard win. I'm going to get out of here and I'm going to survive. The police are going to find me. It will happen.'

That makes me feel a little better. I decide to go through what I know, checking it off, trying to look for clues. I'm in a box. It seems pretty solid, no chance of punching my way out. I heard a bolt, so even if I managed to get out, I'm still locked in. No point wasting any more energy thumping away; I will need every bit of strength to get through this. The man who's put me here claims he is a serial killer. My breath starts to accelerate at that and it takes a huge effort not to give in to panic. But I'm not dead. He doesn't mean to kill me, not yet. He said something about a fear experiment, a trial that the other women failed. I'm not sure that makes me feel better.

Deliberately, like a person with vertigo standing at the edge of a cliff, I look over into the abyss. All my worst fears are there.

Rape, torture, physical pain. Death. I step back. If I spend too long staring all that darkness in the face, it will swallow me. I can't allow myself to go mad with terror. My only goal is to survive, and I will endure anything to get out alive. There's no point thinking about *what* I might have to suffer until it happens. The box is bad enough.

Finally, steeling myself, I think of him. The eye against the slats, the voice. I have to turn him from a monster into a man. It's going to be hard. The only way I might manage it is if I pretend I'm studying him. I'll have to pretend he's a patient and I'm treating his psychopathy. I almost smile. Perhaps I'll write a paper on all this one day. I try to imagine Professor Marks asking me about him. *What did his behaviour tell you about who he is?* He likes power and control, that's a given. He likes fear. I remember the way he poured the water, as if it were some sort of reward for my behaviour. He likes to manipulate. And then a thought comes that gives me another tiny prick of hope. He likes talking.

Engaging him, keeping him entertained, that's my biggest chance. Whatever he says to me, I mustn't let it throw me. I have to use it as a weapon to discover who he is.

The effort of staying calm has exhausted me. I've never been so tired. Somehow, in spite of the fear and the pain, I drift off to sleep.

It's completely black when I wake. My thighs are icy cold and sting from half-dried pee, and my body aches from twisting and hammering at the box. But all of that discomfort fades when I realise what has woken me. The sound of a bolt scraping back. Adrenalin hits me and I gasp. A click, then light brings the slats back to view. I'd forgotten how close they are to my face.

'Wakey, wakey.'

The light dims as he covers the box. He's lying on top again, his mouth wet and pink against the gap. And his eyes.

'Hi,' I say. Even I'm shocked by how normal my voice sounds. 'What's up?'

The mouth purses in surprise. I almost laugh. 'It's like that, is it?' He sounds annoyed and my momentary buzz at having wrong-footed him is snuffed out by anxiety. He likes control. He won't like to be laughed at. I'm furious with myself.

'Can't you sleep either?' I say, hoping my tone sounds sympathetic.

'I ask the questions,' he snaps. I say nothing, but in spite of my fear I feel contempt for him. For his pettiness. The eyes continue to stare at me. 'I came to give you something.' My heart quickens, wondering what game he is playing now. I say nothing. 'Don't you want to know what it is?'

I pause, wondering what sort of trap this might be. 'If you'd like to tell me,' I say at last, knowing I can't refuse. In answer I hear a patter on the box. At first I think it's more water, then I realise he's dropping shards of glass. Some fall through the gaps, landing on my clothes and my skin. I scream in shock. 'Stop it! What are you doing?' A sliver lands on my mouth and instinctively I brush it off, cutting my finger. I whimper, raising my hands to protect myself.

'That's you, Ava, that's you,' he says. 'I've been trying to tell you for a while. Didn't you notice?' The glass is still falling. I have no idea what he's talking about. This seems to make him furious. 'Jesus, you women. How fucking stupid *are* you? The tokens I left you, bitch. The *tokens*.'

I force myself to think and suddenly understand. 'What? The jam jars and things? That was *you*?' I remember the first box arriving. I thought the glass had broken by accident on the journey. It was a jam jar full of wild flowers, posted to me at uni in a cardboard crate, soaked through with water. No message, just a small blank card of a Greek vase. My friend Jon had laughed about a secret admirer. In the second box the glass was intact, but the flowers had died. A bit creepy, but nothing too frightening. I had meant to mention it to Professor Marks when I next saw him. I certainly didn't call the police. The sender had probably misjudged how much water the flowers needed, I thought.

Except he hadn't.

'For saying you're a fucking university student, you're a lot denser than Hanna. She understood right away. *She* knew what my gifts meant.' Then he laughs. A creak and he has swung himself off the box. He is light on his feet, and I can hear him skipping about on the hard floor. 'Whose grave am I dancing on? Is it Hanna's? Or yours? Who shall I lay flowers for?'

I feel too sick to reply. I cry silently while he capers around me. Then there's a splintering crunch and I realise he's taken a crowbar to the lid. I scream and cover my eyes, terrified he's going to smash the metal into my head. Instead I feel his hands on my wrists, yanking me upwards. He's pulling me out. Glass falls from my clothes and my hair. My limbs are numb and cramped and I stagger, falling into his arms in a parody of a rescue. Too weak to stand, I let him lead me over to the corner of a small, concrete room, where there is a pile of blankets. I collapse onto them. Beside me is a dirty glass of water. My heart leaps, my throat is so dry and sore. I snatch the glass and drink before he has a chance to take it away.

'Feeling better?' he asks. Looking up, I see he's standing over me. His ski mask is thickly padded, distorting the shape of his face into a monstrous ball. It hides everything except the wet lips and his eyes. Behind him I can see a door. There's a bulging plastic bag dumped in front of it. I wonder what might be inside.

He pushes his shoe towards me. At first I flinch, thinking he's going to kick me, then I realise he's nudging a Tesco sandwich in my direction. It's egg mayonnaise. I rip the wrapping off and eat it. The bread is cold and soggy, but I have never been more grateful for the taste of food.

He watches me eat. 'Nice?' he says.

'Yes, thanks.' My voice is small but the words come out automatically, politeness an instinctual reflex, like breathing.

He turns and walks back towards the shattered box. I see it's a roughly made, coffin-shaped crate, the sort you might find in a shipping container. Briefly, I imagine charging him from behind as he bends to pick it up, wresting the crowbar from him, smashing his face in and escaping. I even try to flex my legs to stand, but realise almost immediately that I don't have the strength. I can't move. There's a deadness in my limbs and every part of my body hurts. Instead I just watch.

'So here's the thing,' he says. 'Why don't we have a little trial without the box. See how you behave.' I wait for him to say more but now he's standing with his back to the wall, unlocking the door behind him without looking at it. He manages the manoeuvre in a deft and practised motion. With a sense of dread, I realise he's done this many many times before. Still looking at me, he drags the box with him into the darkness and slams the door shut.

Frankie

'I can't believe the lawyers wouldn't let you say anything on the show last night,' says Gavin.

Frankie glances at him, his hair ruffled by wind blowing through the small opening in the car window as he drives. 'Well, we could say we understood the police were looking at threats made to Hanna online, just not as much detail as Charlie wanted.'

She leans back, shifting her weight. The drive to Wells-next-the-Sea is Norfolk at its most rural. They are cruising across a bright green horizon, flat fields rolling out so far into the distance it's impossible to imagine their end. The round flint tower of the church at Little Snoring is the only punctuation mark in view. It gets steadily taller as they approach, the narrow windows a reminder of its ancient function of defence rather than prayer.

It *had* been a bit disappointing that the lawyers were so nervous of the blog. There was much hand-wringing about Ofcom and the possibility of prejudicing any trial, which seemed far-fetched given the blog was anonymous. Still, it means even Charlie hasn't felt able to coax a day three out of Hanna Chivers' murder, particularly as they couldn't find any mention of Sandra Blakely or Lily Sidcup on the *Killing Cuttlefish* forum. This came as something of a relief to Frankie, who has found the blog hard to evict from her thoughts.

At least today she doesn't have to drive to the job herself. It's even worth putting up with Gavin's Édith Piaf CD blaring out as they hurtle over the country lanes, just to put her feet up. Frankie's least favourite part of reporting is all the miles she has to cover. 'Lunch in the fast lane', as Gavin calls it.

'Nice day for the seaside,' he says.

'Yeah, we should have time to grab a sandwich on the seafront before heading back,' Frankie says, watching the gravestones as they pass. Édith's jaunty harmonica is starting to jangle her nerves. 'What do you reckon is the deal behind this couple we're interviewing?'

'Bit creepy if you ask me,' says Gavin. 'Not sure blokes like that deserve a second chance.'

They have been assigned a domestic violence story. The boyfriend has reformed thanks to therapy, and now the couple want to tell the world that abusers can and should seek help. 'I know what you mean,' she says. 'But then again, at least it shows he knows it was wrong. And better that than just repeating violent behaviour. After all, what are you going to do with people who've abused their partners? You can't just chuck them on the scrap heap of life forever, people do learn from their mistakes.'

'Would you be with Jack if he was a reformed wife-beater?' asks Gavin, glancing over to look at her. She doesn't answer. He nods. 'Exactly.'

The flat is in an alley off Straithe Street. They navigate their way down the narrow road towards the harbour, Gavin nearly knocking over a mass of bright plastic buckets and spades for sale on the tiny pavement. He hefts the tripod higher over his shoulder.

'Just here,' says Frankie, guiding him into a small cul-de-sac. There's barely room for them both and the camera kit. Weeds sprout up through the tarmac. The wall on their left seems to be the back of a shop, boxes of stock blocking its windows. She heads to the door on their right and knocks. A hand-written sign declaring 'NO JUNK MAIL!!!!!' is stuck in its dusty windowpane. They wait. The place is quiet save for the cries of seagulls wheeling and calling overhead.

'Maybe you should—' Gavin starts, but before he can make his suggestion a shadow appears behind the grimy glass. There's a sound of multiple locks and the door opens.

'Are you from the Eastern Film Company?' A woman blinks at them from the doorway. She has sandy hair and eyes so pale it's hard to tell the colour.

'Yes that's right. I'm Frances, this is my colleague Gavin.'

The woman opens the door. 'I'm Debbie. Come in.'

They follow her through a tiny dark hallway into the front room. Frankie nearly chokes on the overpowering smell of air-freshener. It's a cheap chemical one, sickly sweet, and makes the room feel stale. Gavin looks round for somewhere to put his tripod down, but the room is stuffed full of knick-knacks and cuddly toys. Shelves of shiny porcelain cherubs and fawns simper at Frankie from the mantelpiece, and she nearly trips over a large stuffed bear with 'Hug Me!' stitched across its stomach. Unlike the dusty front door, this room is meticulously clean.

'I'll go get Martin,' says Debbie. 'Make yourselves at home.'

'Blimey,' whispers Gavin when she's gone. 'Got enough stuff, haven't they? Not sure how we're going to film in here. If I move, I'll break something.'

'We'll have to stick them both on the sofa,' she says. 'There's nowhere else. Perhaps if we move this bear ...' She picks up the massive soft toy and is in the process of trying to ram it into an armchair when a voice makes her jump.

'Moved in for a hug already?'

She turns round, the bear in her arms. A thin man is smiling at her from the doorway, holding hands with Debbie. 'What? Er, no, just trying to make space for Gavin's camera,' she says, embarrassed to be caught in the act of rearranging her host's living room. 'Hope you don't mind.'

'No, that's fine,' says Debbie, looking flustered. 'There's far too much junk in here anyway.'

'Poor Huggles,' says the man. 'Not sure he'll appreciate being called junk. He was a present from our first date.' He's obviously trying to be funny, break the ice, but nobody laughs and there's a mortifying silence. 'Here, I'll put him out of the way.' He steps forward and takes the bear off Frankie. 'Would you both like tea or coffee?'

'A tea would be lovely,' says Gavin. 'White, no sugar.'

'Same for me, thanks,' says Frankie.

'We really should have a clear-out,' says Debbie, when Martin's gone. 'My son hates all this stuff.'

Frankie isn't sure what to say to that so she just smiles.

'You all right to sit on the sofa, sweetheart?' Gavin says to Debbie. 'We'll get the shelves in the background, give the shot a bit of depth.'

By the time Martin comes back in with the tea, Gavin has managed to rearrange the furniture so that Frankie is perched on a tiny stool by his tripod with the correct eyeline for Debbie and Martin on the sofa.

'Thanks,' says Frankie, taking the teas. 'Are we all right to get the interview out of the way?'

'Sure,' says Martin, sitting down close to Debbie and taking her hand. 'Bit nervous about this.'

'Everyone always is, but it's not live,' says Frankie. 'Anything the pair of you are unhappy with, you can stop and start again.' She looks down at her notepad. She hasn't written down any questions; she almost never does, preferring to let the interview unfold like a conversation. 'So the first question's easy, can we have your names for the tape.'

'I'm Martin Hungate and this is Debbie Richards.'

'And Debbie, what was Martin like before he got help?'

'Well, it was awful, wasn't it?' Debbie looks at Martin for confirmation and he gives her hand a squeeze. 'It was great when we started going out, but then he just seemed to get angry and resentful. Not letting me do stuff, calling me names. Just constant belittling basically.'

'And Debbie's too kind to say,' says Martin. 'But I could be violent too. Only once or twice, but it's never acceptable. I know that now.'

'When you say violent . . .?' Frankie leaves the question hanging, unfinished.

41

'Kicking and biting,' says Debbie, going red, as if she's the one who is ashamed.

'That must have been awful,' Frankie replies, trying not to look too surprised. She hadn't expected biting. A row of fairies is staring at her behind the couple's heads; her eye is drawn to the bright red smiles and tiny white teeth on their china faces.

'I'm so ashamed,' says Martin, who, unlike Debbie, isn't blushing. 'It was the last incident that made me realise there was something really wrong with me and I needed help. We were at a restaurant, having a row, and I slapped Debbie and kicked the table over.'

'I suppose with other people seeing what was going on, you knew you had to tackle it. It couldn't be kept secret any more. Is that why you went for help?' Martin looks at Frankie as if he's seeing her for the first time. She meets his gaze. An unpleasant current passes between them.

'No,' he says. 'That's *not* why. Debbie told me she was leaving me, and I knew I had to change. I knew how much I loved her, and that she deserved better.'

'He's a completely different person now,' says Debbie, placing a hand protectively on her boyfriend's knee. 'That was two years ago, and I don't think we've rowed since.'

'And what sort of form did the therapy take?'

'Some of it was together, as a couple, and some of it was just me addressing anger issues. But the main thing,' says Martin, 'is getting you, as an abuser, to accept full responsibility. So you can't make any excuses. None of it was Debbie's fault, it was entirely down to me.'

'It's great that it's worked for you as a couple,' says Frankie. 'But some people are saying this sort of therapy shouldn't be made part of public services. That it's wrong to focus taxpayers' money on abusers rather than on women's refuges or things like that. What would you say to that?'

She has addressed the question to Martin but it's Debbie who answers. 'Well, I think this is still about protecting the victims of domestic violence,' she says, her tone sharp. 'I was the victim here, and now my life is much better. So if people say targeting the abuser isn't helping the victim, they should think again.'

Martin smiles, putting his arm around Debbie, giving her shoulders a squeeze. 'I don't think I can add to that,' he says.

Frankie breathes in the sea air, feeling the salt scour the last of the air-freshener from her lungs. She and Gavin sit on a bench, eating chips in the sunshine. They had persuaded Martin and Debbie to come out to the quayside for the rest of the filming, and Gavin got a few shots of them walking hand in hand beside the water.

'So what's the verdict, Gav?'

'She seemed a nice lady. Not so sure about him.' He makes a face. '*Biting?*'

'I know, that was an awkward moment, wasn't it? Poor Debbie.' Frankie takes another mouthful of hot, vinegary chips. She keeps meaning to eat more healthily – her jacket's getting rather tight – but life always feels too short to pack herself a salad in the morning. 'Thought she made a good point though, that his therapy helped the victim in this case.'

Gavin sniffs. 'Maybe. But I still wouldn't fancy a pint with him.'

Frankie stares up at the sky, its vast expanse of blue softened by a few trails of white cloud. In the breeze, she can hear the tinkle and creak of the boats' masts. She'd like to spend all day here, walk up towards Holkham beach. She looks over at Gavin, sees he's finished his chips and takes a final mouthful of her own.

'Guess we'd better get back,' she says, scrunching up the greasy paper. 'But can we give Édith a rest this time? Please?'

The weather is still fine when Frankie finishes work, and Charlie lets her head home early before the end of the programme. The first few autumn leaves lie on the path and she scuffs at them as she walks, wondering if the new boss will be as accommodating about working hours when she arrives; Kiera Williams is due to take over tomorrow. It's been an uncertain time in the office. The company's last boss David Hall had been hugely popular, and his retirement, though expected, was greeted with dismay. Frankie had half thought Charlie might apply for the top job, but he told her he was too much of a hack to become a manager. He's already met Kiera, but was unusually tight-lipped when asked what she was like. 'Very corporate,' is all he said.

Frankie reaches her building and feels a surge of happiness to be living here in this spot, right on the river. She takes the stairs at a run, but it seems that she's less fit than she thought because by the time she reaches the third floor, she's out of puff. She leans against the door, searching for her keys. To her surprise she can hear Jack's Pavarotti CD playing. She hadn't expected him back this early. She lets herself in and finds him sitting at the breakfast bar, bent over his computer. When he isn't staring at plants, Jack is forever playing online chess with strangers in Russia or Brazil, or doing maths 'for fun'. She's not too sure about all of his activities; he's very keen on Internet security, and once accessed their neighbours' data accidentally because the firewall he had put round his own data was apparently a bit too strong. It all sounded rather like hacking to Frankie, but she doesn't know enough about it, and as a naturally nosy person she's probably less shocked by the idea of Jack snooping than she should be.

'I didn't notice the time,' he says, getting down from the stool and going over to give her a kiss. 'I meant to watch the show tonight, I almost never catch you on TV. How was it?'

'Oh, you didn't miss much. It was a piece on domestic violence.'

Jack pulls a face. 'Charlie sends you to all the fun stuff, doesn't he?'

'That's just news, I'm afraid,' she says, though in regional telly that isn't strictly true. Her friend Rachel, another reporter, seems to get wall-to-wall punting trips and stranded seals.

She wanders over to the counter and picks up the small pile of post, leafing through the papers. There's their energy bill, which Jack has already opened, a flier about pizza deliveries and a postcard. It's black with a photo of an exquisite alabaster vase, almost translucent, just a hairline crack along its lip. It looks like something from a museum, Ancient Egyptian or Roman; she's not sure of her history. She turns it over but there's nothing, just a sticker with her name and address. It must be a flier from an antiques store she thinks, turning it over again, though it seems odd not to give any details.

'What's that?' Jack asks, standing at her shoulder.

'Just a couple of circulars,' she replies, gathering the card up along with the pizza flier and dropping them both in the bin. 'Do you fancy walking down Riverside and eating out tonight? It's a lovely evening.'

'That sounds brilliant,' Jack says, putting his arms round her. Frankie smiles at him, the strange card already forgotten.

Ava

Nineteen and a half steps long, seventeen steps wide. That's how big my cell is. I don't know what that is in metres; I was never very good at maths.

I have walked it over and over, counting and counting and counting. After being cramped up I was worried about getting my strength back and desperate to move about. The weakness in my legs is improving now the circulation's come back, but I'm still really sore, and the cuts on my knuckles throb. It was such a relief at first to be out of the box, to be able to move, but now I feel like I'm just in a bigger box.

Even when walking makes me dizzy I don't stop. I have to keep moving to stay warm. This place is so cold. I'm grateful I wore a jumper to the bar that night. I shuffle round and round, wrapped up in the dirty blankets like a tramp, muttering to myself. The blankets are scratchy and have an animal smell – I think it's horse – which makes me feel oddly comforted. It takes me back to the stables my grandparents rented out, the last working part of their run-down farm. They weren't sentimental people, but my grandfather loved horses. Children, not so much. He horrified Matt and me when we were small, the way he'd stalk across the fields with his gun, aiming at rabbits. Sometimes I hear his voice, harsh and long dead. *Pull yourself together, girl!*

I've found talking to myself helps, though it's an effort to think up new words. Instead I recite the entire Anglican Communion Service. I haven't been to church in about five years, yet the prayers have somehow stayed with me. We used to sing it every Sunday, Matt and I, in the High Church that reminded Mum of

46

her Catholic roots. *And He shall come again in Glory, to judge both the quick and the dead: Whose Kingdom shall have no end. And I believe in the Holy Ghost, the Lord, the Giver of Life, who proceedeth from the Father and the Son* ...

I don't believe in any of them, as it happens, but chanting it in the singsong melody is soothing. It stops my mind from juddering to a halt altogether.

As I walk, my eye is constantly drawn to the door. I know the feel of every inch of its horrible surface. Rough, unforgiving, solid. I've thrown my full weight at it, kicked it again and again, rattled the handle until I thought it would fall off. But I always come off worse, the door isn't budging. It doesn't even have a deadlock, just a simple Yale, with the latch to open it on the outside, like a sick joke. When I finally accepted defeat, I cried, resting my cheek on the wood, sobbing my heart out. The door absorbs kicks and tears with the same indifference.

So I avoid it on my endless journeys round and round. Every now and then I stick out a hand to touch the wall with my fingertips. It's concrete, the surface uneven, as if the cement was slapped on without much care. It's cold.

There's one part of the wall I don't touch. I always move my hand when I reach The Stain. It's a brown mark, almost human-shaped, and has acquired capitals in my mind. The sight of it turns my insides to water. It looks so like a person, bent with pain. Sometimes when I look at it, I imagine I can hear someone else. I know it's only my own breath, laboured from fear, but I can't shake the feeling it's one of the others. That she's still here, somehow. Still trapped here after death. I try to practise professional detachment, find it interesting that even when there are *real* horrors to be faced, my mind creates fanciful ones. But I still take care not to touch the dark mark as I pass.

At the top of the wall opposite the door is a small grille. It filled me with hope at first. I spent God knows how long jumping up trying to see through, shouting for help. But the only thing it brings me is an icy draught. The silence is profound. No sound of

the street, no cars or voices, the heavy nothingness of the countryside. When day comes, I see there are wisps of grass at its edge,
which makes me think I must be in a field somewhere.
Underground. A tiny shaft of light comes through at what must be
late afternoon and I move across the room with it, so the light falls
on my face.

I think of my family.

It makes me cry whenever I imagine their worry, the desperation they must be feeling about what's happened to me. Then the
frustration at being trapped in here, at being unable to go to them,
tears at my chest like a dog in a cage.

Instead I make an effort to remember the fierceness of my
mother's hug, the way she never gives in. I know she won't give up
on me. Every minute I'm here, she'll be thinking of me, willing me
home. I try to send her messages in my mind: *I'm here, Mum, I'm
here, I'm alive!* Some part of me believes she can hear. I think of
my dad trying to keep it all together, saying trite optimistic things
that drive everyone mad. And Matt. I don't like to think of his
reaction. So I relive funny moments; the impressions he did of the
teachers when we were children, the practical jokes he played,
pushing each other on the swing. I stop the action in our late teens,
before the depression took hold, and then replay it.

*And I believe in one Holy Catholic and Apostolic Church, I acknow-
ledge one baptism for the remission of sins . . .*

Hunger makes my stomach growl. My body craves a proper
hot meal, but I'm not as starving as I might be. The bag by the
door had food in it. Four more egg sandwiches and seven apples;
not very filling but better than nothing. And there's water. I try to
ration myself, leave at least some of the apples, as I don't know
how long he will be gone. I think of the hideous puffball mask and
don't know what's more frightening: him coming back, or being
abandoned until the food runs out. *Don't think of that.* I quicken
my pace, shuffling round in another lap of the cell.

My favourite part of the room, after the grille proved a dead
end, is the light. The electrics are crude, the wiring snaking up the

wall over the cement, but there's a switch by the door and when I press it, a single bulb lights up in the centre of the ceiling. It means I never have to be in the dark. That counts for something.

I've had to use the bucket, adding to the stink in the room. It's a relief to have one, I suppose, but when I pick it up to use it, I realise it already smells bad. That's when it hits me. Somebody else has used it before. One of the other women.

And I look for the resurrection of the Dead, And the Life of the world to come. Amen.

On my hands and knees, I find traces of them on the filthy floor. Hairs. Some long blonde ones, and some dark brown. I lay them across my palm. I stare at them and the terror is so absolute I feel numb. It cuts me off from my own body as if it's somebody else's hand they're resting on and it's somebody else in this room, living this nightmare. I can hear breathing, whistling with panic, and I don't know if it's mine.

Frankie

Frankie is already near Cambridge, on her way to film a story at the city's Science park, when her hands-free set rings.

'Hello?'

'I need you to turn round.' Charlie's voice crackles over the speaker. 'The police have called a press conference. Major new development in the Hanna Chivers enquiry. This is it. They're going to announce it's the same killer. Network news are on their way.'

'Blimey. Great first day for the new boss.'

'Yes, well, make sure you don't fuck it up.'

'Thanks.'

'Always happy to oblige.' Charlie rings off. He's joking about the new boss, she knows that. But it's not the most encouraging remark.

Frankie parks badly, taking up a space near the door marked POLICE ONLY, one wheel over the white line. She's running late, every minute of the long drive across three counties adding to her stress levels. She hopes the presser hasn't already started.

At the reception desk, she rummages for her ID, out of breath, hair plastered over her face.

'Frances Latch, Eastern Film Company. I'm here for the press conference on Hanna Chivers. I think it's being held by DSI Nigel Gubberts?'

'Fill this out please,' says the woman at the desk, handing over a security pass form. Frankie writes her details in a barely legible scrawl, slinging the pass over her neck. The woman points down the corridor. 'Second door on the left.'

'Thanks.'

She hurtles into the presser just as Nigel Gubberts walks in. It's a typical police meeting room; pale blue walls, boxy corporate chairs, no distinguishing features. But unlike the usual half-empty seats in a regional HQ, the place is packed, unfamiliar journalists from network news crowding out the local hacks. Frankie slinks into a space at the back, squeezing past Malcolm, the man from the Press Association.

'Late again, Frankie?'

She pulls a face and dumps her bag. At the front she can already see Gavin set up with his tripod, filming. His grey hair is askew at a mad angle and he's stuck himself in prime position, a couple of national cameramen standing well back, out of the way of his sharp elbows. Frankie smiles to herself, knowing there's one part of the news gathering she doesn't have to worry about. Then Detective Superintendent Gubberts starts speaking.

'Thank you for being here. As you are aware we have a major development in the enquiries into the deaths of Hanna Chivers, Sandra Blakely and Lily Sidcup.' He blinks owlishly, blinded by flashes from the newspaper photographers. 'We have reason to believe all three women were the victims of the same perpetrator or group of perpetrators. Their deaths are therefore now being treated as a single investigation.' A murmur goes round the room. More clicks and flashes. Gubberts bends over his notes, his bald patch shining with sweat. 'We are asking the public to help us catch whoever is responsible. If you have any information about the women's last known movements, or about the days leading up to their disappearances, then we are urging you to please get in touch with us.'

He pauses as another officer projects an image onto the screen behind him. It's a blurred photo of a gaunt woman with dyed blonde hair. 'This is Sandra Blakely. A thirty-eight-year-old mother of two originally from Swaffham. At the time of her death she was working as a streetwalker in Norwich.' The slide changes to a CCTV image of a figure walking down a dark residential street. 'She was last seen by a colleague, wearing a red puffa jacket and black trousers, walking down Edgedon Avenue in the Carrow Road area of the city around 2 a.m. on the 22nd of April this year. We would like to know if anyone saw Sandra get into a car that night, or if they saw her talking to anyone.'

The photo changes. 'This is Lily Sidcup. She was twenty-six years old, originally from Lowestoft, and also working in Norwich as a streetwalker.' Frankie stares at the laughing brunette. The photo was taken in a sunny garden, one she herself has seen. She remembers looking at it through the window when she inter-viewed Lily's grieving parents. 'Lily was last seen on the 30th of August, wearing a denim jacket and a distinctive short green dress like this one from Primark.' A double slide appears as he speaks, showing a picture of the dress and a grainy image of a figure in a Londis store. 'We have CCTV of her at the grocer's that day near her home at 4.23 p.m. Colleagues say she had been planning to work that night, but so far nobody can remember if they saw her. Again we are appealing for witnesses.

'And now we have Hanna Chivers.' The detective superintend-ent pauses and the eighteen-year-old apprentice appears behind him. It's a very familiar photo to Frankie, who has used it in her news reports. It looks like a selfie taken in a bathroom mirror, perhaps in a bar. Another girl standing beside Hanna has been cropped out. She wonders if it was Hollie. 'Hanna was last seen by her colleagues at Curly Sue, a hairdressing salon in Great Yarmouth, on the 10th of September at just after 6 p.m. It was the end of the working day and she had told them she was going to the supermarket. Her flatmates say she never returned home. We are currently examining CCTV to see how far we can trace her jour-ney that evening.'

Gubberts looks down at his notes and coughs, then raises his head to stare at the journalists, his expression grim. 'Today we are also concerned about the safety of another young woman, twenty-year-old Ava Lindsey, a student at the University of East Anglia, who has gone missing.' There's a collective intake of breath and the detective is almost whited out by a barrage of flashes. A fourth smiling young woman now looks out at the assembled hacks. She has a pixie cut, the hair dyed pink. Her grey eyes are direct and challenging. An image flashes into Frankie's mind: those eyes covered by pink hair as Ava lies on the mud. She feels her chest constrict. 'Ava is from West Sussex and was last seen by friends on Sunday evening. They had been enjoying a night out at The Blue Bicycle in Norwich. Ava left her friends at about 10.20 p.m. and made her way home. We understand she had not been drinking heavily and would have been very capable of finding her way. Her disappearance is entirely out of character and she has never gone missing before. We are asking Ava, or anyone who knows where she is, to get in touch with us as a matter of urgency.' Nigel Gubberts stops to take a long glug of water from the glass in front of him, then folds his hands, ready for the onslaught he must know is coming. 'Now, are there any questions?'

Malcolm's hand shoots up in the air. He waits for the microphone to be passed back. 'Malcolm Collins, Press Association. Can you tell us what's caused you to think there is a single killer?'

'We made the decision to combine the three investigations following Hanna Chivers' post mortem report. That's all I can tell you at the moment. I'm sure you understand I can't release details about the evidence.' He nods at a reporter from the *Norfolk Times*. 'Yes, George.'

'What makes you believe Ava Lindsey's disappearance is linked to the deaths of the other women? And why has it taken you so long to link all the cases, haven't you lost valuable time?'

'If I can answer the second part of your question first. There's no question of us losing time. Detectives from the first two murder enquiries have been sharing information for some weeks, but in order to run this as a single investigation we needed to reach a certain threshold in the evidence. We feel we've now reached that point.' Gubberts pauses, takes another sip of water. 'As far as Ava Lindsey is concerned, we very much hope there *isn't* a link. But her disappearance is totally out of character, and given the current situation, we think it best to take it very seriously. We would appreciate publicity from the media to help locate her as soon as possible.' Gubberts points to a big-haired young man in the front row. 'Yes?'

'Luke Heffner, Commercial Television News.' Frankie notices Luke's cameraman has turned round, zooming in to film his face. The reporter pauses, giving his colleague time to frame up, then carries on in his cut-glass accent. 'You *claim* you've not lost any time and you *hope* there is no connection between the murder and missing person investigations.' Luke pauses to show how little credence he gives either idea. 'Nonetheless, Ava Lindsey is the fourth young woman to disappear in the county in just a few months. The last woman's body was found dumped by the side of the road, not far from Great Yarmouth police station. The killer is obviously winning, do you think he's also deliberately showing up the incompetence of your investigation?'

It's more a statement than a question, designed to demonstrate the brilliance of Luke's probing at the expense of the poor plodding police. If Nigel Gubberts's increasingly pink face is anything to go by, the strategy is working. It's a fair point for Luke to make, Frankie supposes, but she finds the young man's self-importance, so obviously engineered for the camera, excessive. Even worse, as the representative of CTV News, he's affiliated with her own employer, which means she's bound to end up working with him.

'Well, Mr Heffner, this isn't a game, innocent people have died so I don't think "*winning*" is an appropriate way of putting it . . .'

'Quite, and those innocent people died on your watch,' Luke shoots back.

'People can be assured we are working around the clock to ensure the perpetrator is brought to justice. That's why our public appeal for witnesses today is crucial. Yes, next question please?'

'Leonard Smythe, *London Daily Times*. Any evidence this missing girl Ava Lindsey was on the game like the others? Aren't we talking about a prostitute killer here?' Frankie rolls her eyes. The other hack ploughs on. 'I mean, was she really going home from that bar, or could she have been meeting a client?'

Nigel Gubberts looks even more irritated than he was with Luke Heffner. Lights from the cameras pick up beads of sweat on his hairline. 'The first two victims, Sandra Blakely and Lily Sidcup, were both sex workers, but the third victim, Hanna Chivers, was an apprentice hairdresser in Great Yarmouth, and there's absolutely no evidence that either she or Ava Lindsey were involved in the sex trade.' The detective pauses, shuffling the papers in front of him. 'So in answer to your question, *no*, that's not a line of enquiry we're pursuing. We don't believe the victims' professions are the key to the investigation.' Frankie looks at Ava's smiling face and wonders where the young student is being held while they sit here talking. Perhaps she's already dead. She sticks her hand in the air.

'Frances Latch, Eastern Film Company. Obviously Ava Lindsey is a *missing* not a *murdered* person. How confident are you that you can find her alive?'

'Yes, well, clearly that's our number one priority.' Nigel Gubberts turns to look directly at the cameras. 'And I would appeal to anybody who might know where Ava is right now to get in contact. She has a family who miss her and are desperate to have her home. This is a young woman with her whole life ahead of her, please think of that, and get in touch.'

The press conference drags on for almost an hour as every journalist in the room goes after their pound of flesh. Then, with the look of a fox whose hole is finally in sight after being pursued by baying hounds, the detective superintendent escapes from the room. Frankie is making her way towards Gavin through the crush when somebody taps her shoulder.

'Frances Latch? I'm Luke Heffner. Our newsdesk said you'd be able to get me archive footage of the previous murders. I'll need them for tonight's evening news.'

Frankie squints up at Luke, who is taller than she expected. She hadn't been able to make out much of him from behind, except for his perfectly coiffed hair and expensive suit. Now she sees he's probably even younger than her, mid-twenties maybe, with preppy good looks and a subtle coat of bronze foundation dusted over his face. He makes her feel like a scruff-bag with her too-tight jacket and emergency trainers. She left her 'on-camera' shoes in the car.

'OK, no worries, I'll speak to my news editor, he'll get them sent to you.'

'Thanks. I'll be editing in the satellite truck outside the university halls of residence if you need me.' Luke pats her arm as if he's the one granting the favour and heads off.

'Bit of a prick, isn't he?' says Gavin behind her, voicing her own thoughts.

Frankie smiles. 'You said it. So what next? I guess we head to the university and try and talk to Ava's friends?'

'Us and the rest of the world,' Gavin grumbles, lifting the camera onto his shoulder.

Frankie has speaker phone on as she drives back to Norwich. Her friend Priya Malik, who is producing tonight's show, explains she wants the story told in two reports. The first on the announcement that the three murders are linked (the killer is already being called 'the Norfolk Strangler' by the press) and the second report devoted to Ava Lindsey.

'I'd like you to do the second piece,' Priya says, as Frankie hurtles along the road back into town. 'We've set you up an interview with Professor Peter Marks, Ava's tutor, the press office say he can speak for the university. Then it's just a question of grabbing whichever students will talk.'

'OK, I'll do my best. What's the new boss like?' There's such a long silence, Frankie thinks the call has cut out. 'Priya? Are you there?'

'Don't worry about that now, just get to the UEA.'

'Blimey! She's that bad?'

'Everything's fine, just concentrate on your report. Speak later.'

'Well, that's fabulous,' Frankie mumbles to herself, after Priya has gone. She turns the radio on, and carries on driving.

Gavin arrives at the university before her. He's in a furious mood, convinced he got snapped by a traffic camera after belting up the A11. 'It's all Charlie's fault,' he says. 'What's he doing making us cover this side of the story? It would have been quicker to send someone from Norwich if they're doing two reports. And I hate bloody vox pops!'

Frankie struggles along beside him as they trek across the concrete jungle of a campus. She offered to carry his tripod earlier and is now regretting it. The thing weighs a ton. Normally Gavin is far too chivalrous to let her carry anything. He must be feeling really aggrieved. 'We don't have to vox pop any students just yet,' she says soothingly. 'It's an interview with her tutor first.'

'What's he going to say?'

'I don't know, I only spoke to Priya.'

'Well, I'm not trudging up to some rubbishy room with nothing to film but a white wall in the background and some stupid set-up shots of him tippety-tappeting on a computer. He can come down here. Looks nice outside, it's a sunny afternoon. We'll shoot him against those trees.' Gavin stops abruptly, and Frankie can see he's not going to move any further. Gratefully, she drops the tripod.

'I'll just run along to reception and get him, then.'

Professor Peter Marks is already at the front desk when she arrives, saying goodbye to another reporter from a rival broadcaster. The two journalists nod at each other. Ava's tutor must be doing the rounds today, Frankie thinks. She goes over to introduce herself.

'Is it all right if we do the interview outside, Professor Marks? My cameraman has set up by some trees, to get a bit of autumn colour on campus.'

'Of course.' He smiles, shaking her hand. He's a tall, slim man, rather young-looking for a professor. 'Whatever you think best.'

He holds the door open for her and they walk out into the sunshine towards Gavin.

'It's terrible what's happened, you must all be very worried,' she says. 'Had you been teaching Ava long? What's she like?'

'I've been teaching her since last year. Ava is a very able student, she's going to make a good psychologist one day,' he says, his hands pushed deep in his grey trouser pockets. 'She always struck me as an exceptionally calm person, with real insight into human behaviour.'

'Not somebody likely to take off without explanation?'

Peter Marks stares straight ahead as they walk side by side along the grass. 'No. Absolutely not.'

'Did she have any enemies at all?'

'*Enemies?*' He half frowns, half smiles at the word. 'Of course not, no. I think she did get a few people's backs up in the science department, she was a passionate supporter for environmental issues when she arrived, but really you expect that with idealistic young people. And I got the feeling she'd moved away from any actual activism this year.'

They reach Gavin, standing by his tripod. Frankie introduces them and Professor Marks immediately manages to take the edge off Gavin's grumpiness by complimenting him on the location he's chosen. 'One of the prettiest spots on campus,' he says. 'You must have a good eye.'

Professor Marks clearly cares about Ava, so it's a disappointment that he comes across as rather cold in the interview. Frankie keeps prodding him to be a bit more personal, but the tutor only says, 'I couldn't tell you that,' or 'I didn't know Ava socially, only as a student.' His only truly interesting reply is one she cannot use. It's after she asks what message he would have for whoever might be holding Ava captive.

'I wouldn't have any message for them,' he says, then looks over towards Gavin and holds his hand up. 'Can you stop filming for a moment please?'

'Of course,' says Frankie. 'What's wrong?'

'I don't mean to be patronising, but you do realise that whoever is holding Ava will almost certainly be watching all the news coverage, feeding off it to give themselves a sense of control, and quite possibly using it to manipulate her?'

Frankie is stunned. 'Er, well, I guess so.'

'The police will have their own profiler, and any message they have for this man – and I strongly suspect it is a man – will be filtered through their own knowledge of the case. I have nothing to say to him.' For the first time, Frankie sees a flicker of anger underneath the smooth exterior. 'I have only contempt.' Peter Marks stares at her, perhaps waiting for another question, but his sudden change in tone has taken Frankie by surprise. 'If that's all,' he says at last. 'I'd better be getting back.'

'Of course, yes, thank you for your time,' she says, shaking his hand. She and Gavin watch him stride back across the grass.

'Funny fish,' Gavin remarks.

An hour later she's heading back to the newsroom. The vox pops hadn't been too bad, although she didn't find any of Ava's close friends, perhaps because there seemed to be almost as many reporters as students hanging out in the university's concrete amphitheatre. At one point Frankie asked a boy whether he knew Ava, only to find he was an especially young BBC radio producer. But although she did manage to get some students to talk, the whole exercise makes her uncomfortable. It's too similar to her job earlier that week accosting mourners at Hanna's shrine. She hopes the report on Ava doesn't feel like an obituary. Of course it's only human to feel sympathy, but she's surprised by the intensity with which she wants the student to come back unharmed.

The most promising lead she picks up is not an interview but a mobile phone number, given to her by a psychology undergraduate in Ava's year. The number belongs to Laura Jenkins, Ava's friend who was with her on the night she went missing. She hasn't responded to Frankie's messages in time for an interview today, but it's the type of contact she hopes might prove useful later.

When she walks into the newsroom, she has a quick look around for the new boss, but can't see anyone who might be her. Charlie spots her and beckons her over to his desk.

'Right, it's going to be tight to get this on air, but you can work with Caz in the edit suite.' He puts a hand out to stop her from rushing off. 'Also I've said Luke Heffner from national can have your interview with the professor. He didn't get time to do it himself and Kiera is keen for us to share material. I'll send the rushes to his truck once they're online.'

'Fine by me,' she says, already heading for the stairs.

The report ends up being more than a little tight; they almost miss their deadline. They are still laying the last shots as the presenters read the headlines and Caz the video editor has to live roll from the edit suite. Not something Frankie wanted to happen on Kiera's first day. She also has an unpleasant shock when Caz plays through the rushes. Gavin had, accidentally, kept recording during Professor Marks's off-the-record remarks about the killer. She sends Luke a brief email, explaining they had agreed not to use the last answer and asking him to respect that, but she gets no reply. She hopes it's because he's too busy.

She and Caz watch the programme from the comfort of the edit suite, then when the national news starts they both walk back into the newsroom for the debrief. Caz holds the door open and Frankie sees Kiera Williams, the new manager of the Eastern Film Company, is already standing by the newsdesk, a sheaf of notes in one hand. She's a tall, thin woman, with glossy auburn hair, wearing a houndstooth print suit, its tight skirt cut on the bias. She looks over at Frankie and Caz as they file in. 'Well you two certainly kept us on our toes!' She's smiling, but there's no warmth in her face.

'Frankie had to drive over from the press conference. There was very little spare time,' says Charlie. Kiera glances down at him. He's sitting a couple of feet away from her, his chair pulled back to let her take the floor. Since their old boss David Hall retired, it's been Charlie's job to debrief the programme. Frankie wonders if he's going to have cause to regret not going for the top job himself.

'So, not a *bad* show,' says Kiera, ignoring Charlie's remark. 'Perfectly respectable lead, though I think we could all have done with the report being finished a *little* sooner.' She nods at Frankie. 'That's something I intend to introduce. All packages should be ready fifteen minutes before we go on air.'

'But that would only have given us forty-five minutes to cut it,' Frankie says, then immediately wishes she hadn't.

'I'm not interested in excuses,' Kiera replies. She's still smiling, but only just. 'Nobody said newsgathering was *easy*, but good habits are *so* important. From now on we'll be operating a three strikes policy on reporters who file late. I'll exclude today's programme, obviously.'

Nobody asks what happens after the three strikes. Frankie looks over at Charlie, who appears to be studying his shoes with interest.

'On to the rest of the show,' says Kiera. She proceeds to fillet their efforts, ignoring the unwritten rule that new bosses wait at least a week before criticising the programmes they've inherited. Frankie comes off comparatively lightly. Neil is told his scripting is pedestrian, Zara's presenting is 'stiff' and even Gavin's filming doesn't escape censure – 'Was it necessary to have *so* many shots of students' shoes walking by? Such a cliché.' Worst of all are her ill-concealed digs at Charlie's newsgathering skills. No wonder Priya had nothing good to say about the new boss. It's clear that Kiera Williams doesn't intend to brook any competitors in her new Norwich fiefdom.

The debrief over, Frankie stuffs scattered belongings on her desk into her bag, getting ready to go home. She bends to pick her mascara up off the floor. A pair of sensible shoes clump into her line of vision.

'Got time for a drink, old girl?'

Frankie looks up. It's Zara Hyde, Kiera's 'stiff' presenter. She's only recently been promoted from reporter, forcing Paul Carter to share his throne. The Eastern Film Company's long-standing anchor is not at all pleased by the new arrangement, and in fairness to him, Zara is an unconventional choice for the studio sofa, more at home in mac and wellies than a glamorous dress. This evening she had worn a pinstripe trouser suit, a choice almost certainly prompted by Paul's complaint that she doesn't wear enough skirts. Now that she's in jeans and an old T-shirt, obviously having rushed to get changed as soon as the show ended. Frankie is sure Zara only accepted the promotion for the extra money, her heart still on the road.

'Why not?' she says, getting to her feet. 'I'll just text Jack and let him know.'

Frankie swings the bag onto her shoulder, typing out her message to Jack as they head into reception. Before they can make it to the revolving glass door, Ernie the security guard calls them over.

'Your admirer has been hanging round the car park again,' he says to Zara, leaning his large frame over the front desk. 'I saw him on the CCTV. I've been out and warned him off, but I suspect he's still loitering nearby. Are you sure you don't want me to get the police to have a word with him?'

'Brian's been hanging around *again*?' Frankie asks.

'Oh, come on, he's harmless,' says Zara. 'Just after autographs. He's got to be one of our most loyal viewers.'

Frankie and Ernie exchange glances. They both know who Brian is most devoted to: Zara. He certainly isn't waiting around for selfies with Paul Carter, the programme's much more famous presenter.

'It's up to you, Zara, I can let it pass today, but if I see him again this week we really will have to tell the police.'

'If you have to,' says Zara, wrinkling her nose. 'But poor old Brian's totally harmless.'

Ernie's far too polite to contradict her directly, but Frankie can tell he's not convinced. She supposes his former life as a prison officer has made him more suspicious than most. 'You can never be too careful,' he says.

'Honestly,' mutters Zara, as they push their way round and out. 'Talk about overkill.'

'He's only doing his job,' Frankie replies. 'And Brian is a bit weird.'

Zara laughs. 'When Colin Firth wore a knitted jumper like that on *Bridget Jones* he was a heart-throb. It's not Brian's fault he looks more like Uncle Fester.'

Outside there's no sign of Zara's diehard fan or his trademark knitwear anywhere near the premises. Ernie must have succeeded in scaring him off. They cut into the network of Norwich's narrow alleyways and end up at Frank's bar. It's a quietly eccentric place, all wooden floorboards and mismatched chairs with half a fairground horse on one wall. Old books and candles fill its darker corners. Zara shuffles some students along the bench at the back so they can sit down. The pale light from the windows behind them almost makes it feel like a summer evening.

They order tapas and a couple of glasses of white wine. Zara looks much more at home in her scruffy clothes than she did in the pinstripe suit.

'So how's it going with Paul, any better?' Frankie asks.

Zara grimaces. 'As if. He keeps asking me when I'm going to get pregnant. Think he's hoping I'll go off on maternity and never come back.'

'God, how rude! How does he even know you and Mark are trying?'

'He doesn't. He just heard I'll be hitting the big Four-O soon and seems to think I ought to get a move on. Seriously, every time there's a report with a cute baby in it, which let's face it, on regional news is practically every week, he gives me this smarmy look. Last night he even said "tick-tock" and winked.' Zara starts laughing. 'It's funny really. I can never work out if he's trying to be chummy or just a bastard.'

'A bastard, I'd say,' says Frankie, sipping her wine. Zara and

Mark are having IVF and she feels like punching Paul. 'Still, I suppose you have to laugh about it.'

'Not sure there will be much laughing with Kiera in the hot seat,' Zara says. 'I caught Paul oozing his charm all over her earlier. Getting in early.'

Frankie grimaces. 'Bit of a change from David, isn't she?' She pictures their old boss, with his curly grey hair and tweed jacket, always the first in and the last to leave. One of the gentlest souls in the business, he had spent a lifetime building a friendly oasis in a cut-throat industry.

'Not a promising start,' says Zara. 'Let's just hope Norfolk knocks the edges off her.' They sit in glum silence, pondering the alternative. 'Still,' she adds. 'There are worse things. Like your report tonight. That story puts it all in perspective. Those poor women. Held captive, then killed. Fuck.' Their tapas arrives and Zara takes a forkful of spicy potatoes. 'She's dead, isn't she? The missing student. She must be.'

'It doesn't look good,' says Frankie. 'But I'm not sure he's killed her. If you think about it, there was a gap between Hanna Chivers going missing and her body turning up. And he dumped her quite blatantly, like he was taunting the police.' She thinks of Peter Marks and his analysis of the killer. 'I think if she were already dead, we'd have found her.'

'Not sure that isn't even worse.' Zara shudders. 'What's he doing with them? The police haven't mentioned anything about sexual assault.' She catches sight of Frankie's face. 'Sorry, didn't mean to upset you.'

'No, it's fine. Just something about this case really gets to me.' She runs her finger round the rim of the glass. The bar is filling up, getting louder. The waiter has started lighting candles at tables across the room. 'Don't you sometimes worry that we're part of it? That some of this is for the media?'

'Like what?'

'Well, the bravado. Dumping Hanna where he did. Snatching Ava a couple of days later. Not just taunting the police, is he? The killer's making sure it's in the news. That we're all over it.' She dunks a piece of bread in olive oil, and the black vinegar soaks through, giving it a bitter taste. 'Makes me feel complicit somehow.'

'I wouldn't stress about it. I know what you mean, but you can't help that. We're just doing our jobs.' Zara punches her on the arm. 'Don't eat all the tapas while I go to the loo.'

Frankie takes out her phone when Zara has gone, starts idly flicking through tabs on the Internet. She hesitates, then logs onto the forum on *Killing Cuttlefish*. Ever since she found the site, she keeps going back to it; she's not entirely sure why. She's already checked it once today to make sure there's nothing about Ava, and so she isn't really expecting the post that appears at the top of the page.

MSM cream their pants over Norfolk Strangler.

Frankie stares at the title. It's written by @Feminazi_Slayer2. After a moment she clicks on the link.

The Brainless Wonders of our beloved Mainstream Media have been outdoing themselves today. It seems we have a serial killer in our midst – oh joy for the hacks – but he's going after hookers – oh horror for the PC brigade!

Seeing fuckwit reporters tying themselves in knots about how to say PROSTITUTE KILLER was a particular pleasure. Where do they learn these phrases? 'Women who were employed as sex workers' – that's PROSTITUTE to you and me – or even better describing that raddled old tart Sandra Blakely as 'a mother of two'. Some mother. Her children must be delighted to see the back of the revolting old junkie.

But it's worth suffering through all the useless reports to see that HANNA THE SLAG got her just deserts in the end. For all you put Jamie Cole through, for all the lies you told in court, for all the pricks you teased, I hope you rot in Hell, BITCH.

'Frankie! Are you OK? What's the matter?'

She hadn't realised her friend had already got back. Zara is leaning over the table towards her in concern.

'Oh, it's nothing.' She closes the tab and places the phone face down on the wood. 'Just that awful website I told you about. There's been a post saying vile things about the victims in the Strangler case.'

'What are you doing *reading* that crap? Seriously, woman, put it away.' Zara pushes the wine bottle towards her. 'Have a drink, please. That website's for sad, nasty men typing away in their mums' spare bedrooms, winding each other up and pining for the girlfriend they'll never have. Promise me you won't keep reading it, OK?'

'OK,' says Frankie, without much conviction. 'I'll try.'

Frankie

'*We go live now to Norwich, where retired electrician Donald Emneth says he knew all the women reported missing in the investigation police are calling Operation Magna. Our reporter Katie Greenaway is with him . . .*'

The television blares out as Frankie makes breakfast. Her eyes are burning. She woke too early this morning, fury stopping her from sleeping. She butters her toast aggressively at the white countertop. An especially violent scrape sends half of it flying across the room.

'Bollocks!'

Jack looks up from his coffee. The toast lies, butter down, on the living room's new slate grey carpet. With a sigh he ambles over to pick it up and drops it in the bin. 'It wasn't your fault,' he says.

She knows he's not talking about the toast. Ever since she saw Luke Heffner's report on the late news last night, Frankie has talked about little else but what a bastard he is. In spite of her email, Luke had run the precise section of Peter Marks's interview that the professor had asked her not to record. She had watched it air on television in outraged disbelief. 'I just can't believe he'd *do* something like that,' she says. 'It's such a crappy trick. Really unprofessional.'

Across the living room, breakfast telly is still yammering away. Frankie has had it on all morning, nervous that the overnight team might also have used Professor Marks's interview clip for their morning reports. But the only story in town seems to be a local eccentric called Donald Emneth claiming to have an 'affinity' with the case. She's already heard what he has to say and so points the remote at the TV to turn the sound down.

'I'm sure if you explain what happened Professor Marks will understand it was an accident,' says Jack.

'That's not the point! He specifically said he didn't want to talk about it because it would be bad for Ava.' She bangs the butter back into the fridge. 'That's the worst bit. Even if Marks is wrong, Luke's made it look like the press don't give a stuff about her.' She heaves herself up onto a stool by the worktop and starts eating the remains of her toast. 'Why would he *do* that? Just for a slightly snappier line in a report.' She takes a swig of coffee, aware that she needs to give it a rest. Even Jack's sympathy will run out eventually. And at the back of her anger lurks a nugget of anxiety, not just for Ava but for herself. Luke hadn't only run the clip in his report, he had really milked it, using it to discuss the psychology of serial killers at length in his live. If Kiera was watching she will be wondering why on earth Frankie didn't use it too. Charlie's always been supportive of her scruples, but she has no idea if the new boss is going to be so accommodating. The last thing she needs is a ruthless hack like Luke tramping all over her patch and scooping her on her own material, making her look bad.

'Honestly, try not to worry,' says Jack, pouring them both some more coffee. 'Maybe the professor wasn't even watching.'

The newsroom always feels different in the morning, even a grey one like today. There's a semblance of order. The long-suffering cleaner has repaired some of the daily damage and newspapers are stacked in a pile on Charlie's desk rather than spread across the room in a hurricane of pages. He's working steadily through them when Frankie arrives, his head buried in one of the tabloids, trying to glean a story that might fit in their programme.

'Morning,' she says.

'Hello you.' He looks up, pulling his glasses down from the top of his head. 'We need to chat. There's been a complaint.'

Frankie thinks of Professor Marks and her stomach lurches. 'Really? Oh shit.'

He waves a hand. 'Nothing serious. Get yourself a cup of tea and come join me in a minute.'

They sit huddled in front of Charlie's computer screen, reading through the email together. It has a dismaying amount of caps lock in it.

'He thinks *I* made him look bad?' she says. 'The guy went on television and told the world he used to bite his girlfriend!'

'Marvellous, isn't it?' says Charlie, who seems to be enjoying the email much more than Frankie. 'Self-delusion is always such a treat. I think I'll have fun sending the reply.'

'And what's this bit? "Your reporter Francesca Larch clearly has HER OWN DUBIOUS AGENDA." He even got my name wrong. What a dick.'

'All very entertaining. What's this business about you and Gavin trashing his front room?'

'It was stuffed full of hideous trinkets and cuddly toys. We could barely move.'

'You didn't break anything though? The company's not going to get an invoice for the replacement of some priceless porcelain cherub he inherited from Great Aunt Jenny?'

'No, I just moved a giant teddy bear out of the way of Gav's tripod so we could film. That was literally it.'

'That's fine then. Just don't touch his bears in future.' Charlie is laughing and she can't help joining him, even though the email has made her feel uncomfortable. She can normally tell when people are going to be difficult, but Martin Hungate had gone out of his way to be charming. Then she thinks of the flicker of animosity when she asked him a question he didn't like. The warning was always there, she just hadn't paid attention.

'Seriously though,' she says. 'I'm a bit worried now that we broadcast a report saying he was a reformed character. Far from making him look bad, perhaps we've gone and given an unhinged wife-beater some credibility.'

'Yes, that had occurred to me too. But I think you asked sufficiently challenging questions. And as far as I remember from your report, you barely used any clips with him, it was mainly an interview with his girlfriend.'

'Maybe that's what got up his nose,' Frankie says, thinking of the pale-eyed woman, trapped in a house full of kitsch, passive-aggressive love tokens. 'Poor Debbie.'

'Well,' says Charlie, spinning in his chair to face her. 'You'll be delighted to know that's not the only madman I've got lined up for you today.'

Frankie groans. 'Not that guy on telly this morning?' she says, thinking of the scrawny, wild-eyed man with a shaggy beard claiming he had 'helped' all the missing women. 'He's just some crank, desperate for attention. Shouldn't we leave well alone?'

Charlie tuts. 'Hardly. He's all over the nationals. You can't go soft on me now, I'll have to report you to the new boss.'

She knows it's a joke but Frankie looks round. 'Where is she?'

'London. Some meetings with head office.'

'That's a *shame*. Who's going to implement the fifteen minute rule?'

Charlie raises an eyebrow at her. 'I didn't hear that.' He turns back to his computer screen. 'So, I've got you a name and address. Donald Emneth, he's over in Costessey, not far from where girl number two was dumped.'

Frankie heaves herself to her feet. 'Please tell me it's not a self-shoot.'

'Would I do that to you?' He sees her face. 'All right, don't answer that. Ray's already on his way there.'

Even if Charlie hadn't given her his address, she would have been hard pressed to miss Donald Emneth's street. Three satellite trucks dwarf the row of bungalows and the quiet road is full of people clutching notepads, cameras and takeaway coffees. She spots Ray loitering near a privet hedge, dark glasses on, having a smoke. She parks up and walks over to him.

'You'll have to wait your turn with Captain Birdseye,' he says, nodding in the direction of their bearded prey standing in his front garden gesticulating at another reporter and camera crew. 'There's quite a queue.'

'Did you see the news this morning?' she says. 'I don't think he's right in the head.'

Ray shrugs. 'Still might be the killer, I suppose. So it's as well to get a few shots of him, they'll be handy at the trial.'

'You don't think he did it surely? Why would he invite the press into his garden?'

'She's right, it's never the mad ones.' Malcolm from the Press Association joins them. He looks haggard with dark circles under his eyes and there's a large white blotch on the shoulder of his navy jumper. He follows the line of Frankie's gaze and peers at the stain. 'Toby was sick this morning. Bang on cue for Daddy's good-bye cuddle. Babies.' He shakes his head. 'Don't have one, you'll never sleep again.'

'No need to tell me, mate,' says Ray, taking a drag. 'Our youngest has just started toddling. You just wait till they get to that stage. Bloody nightmare.'

The two men laugh. Frankie isn't keen to get sucked into this fatherly chat; she knows the next stage will be an exchange of phone screensavers, the bragging disguised as complaints, followed by questions about when she and Jack are going to 'get started'. She's feeling unusually chippy about it, with her thirtieth birthday just a few months away. 'Our Ancient Mariner,' she says. 'Do you think the police are likely to arrest him?'

'Be surprised if they don't,' says Malcolm. 'They'll have to take him in for questioning at least. Looks a bit iffy if he did know all the girls. Assuming that's not a lie.'

Frankie can see the other TV crew are heading out of Donald Emneth's garden gate. He's still talking to the reporter, jabbing at the elbow of her bright blue coat. 'We'd best head over,' she says.

'No point hanging about, we'll have to interview him at the same time as one of the others.'

'See you, Malcolm,' says Ray, lifting the camera up from where it was resting by his feet. They head down the road. A couple of newspaper reporters are already in the garden. With a sinking feeling, she sees Luke Heffner dart out of a satellite truck just ahead. By the time they get to the bungalow, his cameraman is rolling. Donald Emneth shouts into it while Luke nods sagely.

Ray and Frankie join the gaggle. She doesn't introduce herself; there doesn't seem much point. Donald Emneth is clearly up for talking to every journalist in the land. Ray is already in record, catching his speech, which now seems to be directed at nobody in particular. Mr Emneth is glassy-eyed, his beard even more unkempt at close quarters. He looks every bit as wired as you might expect of a man who has been live on various news channels since 7 a.m.

'. . . So I says to Lily, be careful, love, watch whose car you get into. Lovely girl, she was, she came round for tea, regular. I used to lend her money. Tried to persuade her off the game, didn't I? No sort of life for a girl like that . . .'

'And how did you know Hanna?' Luke interrupts.

'She did my hair once. Nice lass.'

Frankie exchanges glances with one of the other hacks. Mr Emneth doesn't look like he's been to a hairdresser since the 1990s.

'Why would you go for a haircut in Great Yarmouth,' she asks. 'Isn't that a bit of a trek?'

'Free, wasn't it?' Donald Emneth doesn't ask who she is or seem perturbed to find another stranger in his garden. 'Got the flier somewhere.' He rummages in his pocket, taking out a fistful of lint. 'Not there,' he says, looking down at the washed-up fragments. 'Anyway, the college advertised. Free haircuts by the young girls. Because they was training, see? Not qualified yet.'

Frankie is certain the college won't have phrased the offer quite like that. She begins to feel queasy at the idea of Donald Emneth hotfooting it to Yarmouth, eager to have his hair washed and blow-dried by teenagers.

'And did you strike up a friendship with Hanna afterwards?' asks Luke.

'Nah. I just recognised her face on the news. Little poppet. I was watching and thought, that's the little girl who did my hair. I helped her get her training done.'

'And what about Ava?' says one of the newspaper journalists. It's a young man in a pink shirt who Frankie hasn't seen before.

'Oh, Ava,' says Donald Emneth with a sigh. 'Now she was something special. I met her at a demo last year. A protest against those monster crops they're making at the John Innes.' He looks at Frankie, and for a horrible moment she thinks he might be about to accuse her of having a boyfriend who works there. 'You know what I mean, the genetically modified whatsits. The plants that are going to give us all cancer and kill the field mice and butterflies and whatnot. I helped her too,' he says with an air of triumph. 'Brought her a cup of tea. But she had already got one.'

Mr Emneth is ignoring Luke and the other two journalists now. Frankie has caught his attention and he's staring at her tight jumper.

'So just to recap,' she says. 'You're saying you helped Lily and Sandra, gave them cups of tea and friendly advice. Hanna cut your hair and you met Ava at a demo. Isn't that all a bit of a coincidence? And how can you be sure it really was Hanna and Ava, given the meetings were so fleeting?'

'Never forget a pretty face,' he says, his gaze transfixed several inches below her chin. 'Always remember a lovely girl when I see one.'

Ray and Frankie trot down the road. Another horde of journalists has turned up at Mr Emneth's front door, giving them a chance to escape. He took an unwelcome shine to Frankie, and seemed reluctant to let them get away, even asking for her number. She gave him the telephone line for the company's planning desk, and could just imagine the gratitude of her colleagues if the old man called. She would have to warn them.

'Frances!' A yell from behind makes her turn. It's Luke Heffner. She waits. Perhaps he's going to apologise for broadcasting the interview with Professor Marks.

'This demo the old guy mentioned Ava was at,' he says. 'Will you lot have filmed that?'

'Might have.'

Luke frowns. 'Well, could you check?' He looks at her as if she's a bit slow. 'Obviously if we've got moving footage of one of the girls that would be *really* helpful.'

'Women.'

He looks perplexed. 'Excuse me?'

'They're *women*,' she almost shouts. 'They're all over eighteen. That makes them women. *Not girls.*'

'Only just eighteen in Hanna's case,' Luke says, unperturbed. 'So could you check please? For the footage?' Without waiting for her reply he turns and walks back to his satellite truck. She watches him go, restraining the urge to throw her notepad at his perfectly coiffed head.

'I know he's a bit of a wanker,' Ray says, speaking quietly so there's no way Luke can hear. 'But wasn't that a slight overreaction?'

Frankie can feel anger churning in her stomach. The complaint from Martin Hungate, sleazy Donald Emneth gawping at her breasts and finally Luke, with his insufferable entitlement. But she can't really direct all that annoyance at Ray, simply because he's standing next to her. 'Maybe,' she says. 'It wasn't just that.' He looks at her, waiting for more. She feels too tired to try to explain. 'Never mind. Let's get back to the newsroom and find that archive footage. Wonderboy is right. It *would* be useful if we've got Ava on tape.'

The tape proves easy enough to find. A quick Google search for the date of the demo and she fetches it from the company's library.

Sitting at an edit machine, she plays the recording, moving through the crowd shots in slow motion. Bullseye. A flash of pink hair and there's Ava. There's something uncanny about seeing video of her. She looks so alive, her face lit with passion, waving her placard. Then the camera pans across the crowd of students and she's lost from view. In all, the clip of her lasts fifteen seconds. Not much, but enough.

Frankie watches it again, this time paying attention to the rest of the shot. She takes a sharp intake of breath. There, at the edge of the crowd, is Donald Emneth. His beard is in better trim and he doesn't have the same air of bumbling ineptitude from their filming that morning. But it's unmistakably him. Frankie freezes the frame, zooms in on his eyes.

'Charlie!' she shouts. 'Come have a look at this.'

He heads over. 'You found her? Brilliant.'

'Yes, but that's not all.' She points at the screen. Charlie bends over, peering in the direction of her finger.

'Shit,' he says. Donald Emneth is staring at Ava, a look of focused malevolence on his face.

Ava

I spend so long staring at the door handle, waiting for it to turn, that when it eventually does I can't believe my eyes. I think I must be hallucinating.

But no, he's here. I scramble to my feet. He steps into the room, locking the door behind him. We stand facing each other, just a few steps between us.

'Jesus, it stinks in here,' he says. 'You're disgusting.'

'You're right,' I reply. 'It doesn't smell great.'

'You all think you're so irresistible, don't you, covering your fucking faces with make-up? But you're bags of stinking piss and shit underneath.' He shudders, as if I might be contagious. I can't think of anything to say back, I don't know what he wants. He lowers a plastic bag to the floor. My heart leaps. *Perhaps it's more food, perhaps that means he's not going to kill me.* 'Still, you're not as bad as the first four,' he carries on. 'Fucking crack heads. Vomit and piss everywhere. Gibbering and shaking for want of a fix. God they stank.' I feel like my insides are going to shrivel up at the mention of the other women. *Four?* I don't remember there being that many missing. 'Can you believe one of the vile bitches actually came here willingly, thinking I wanted to fuck her?' He shakes his head. 'I'm done with whores now. They're too much. You and Hanna are a *treat* in comparison.'

He stares at me, as if expecting some response. I dredge my mind, but it's blank. There's nothing in the section marked 'polite small talk with psychopaths'. But I know I have to say something. 'I'm sorry you didn't like all the women who stayed here.'

'I didn't expect to like them. They were whores. You don't *like* whores. You *kill* whores.' He smacks the flat of his hand against the wall for emphasis. 'Do you know the parents of one had the gall to go on the news, bleating away about what a lovely daughter she was to some fat slag of a reporter. *Our darling Lily.* Made me laugh. *You should have seen your darling Lily after I knocked all her teeth out,* I wanted to say. Ugly bitch didn't look so pretty then. It took nothing to break her, Ava, she was pathetic. Always whining.'

My hand flutters to my own mouth, as if I can feel Lily's pain. For one dark moment I imagine I can hear her screams, still reverberating in this concrete room. I sway on my feet. He's tapping his black-gloved fingers against the side of his dark trousers, his head cocked on one side, watching. *He wants to break you too,* says the voice in my head. *Don't let him see your fear.* With a massive effort of will I force my panic back under control. 'I guess most parents love their children,' I say. 'Whatever they're like.'

He gives a slow clap. 'Very good, Ava, very good.'

I gasp. It's Peter Marks's voice, the slight Edinburgh lilt, so soft you might miss it. The same stress he always makes on my name. I stare at the masked figure in total disbelief. 'Well done. Don't *antagonise* him. Try to make him feel *comfortable.*' He stands with his hands meshed before him as he speaks, a gesture I've seen hundreds of times in his lectures. 'You always were a very *able* student.'

'Professor Marks? Is that really you?'

'Maybe it is,' says the Scottish voice, though this time it sounds more like David Tennant. 'Maybe it isn't.' With the last words he seems to shrink back into his old aggressive posture and it's the same harsh voice as before.

'*Who are you?*' I scream at him. 'What do you want?'

'You don't need to know who I am. Though I know what *you* are. You're an animal,' he spits. 'Just like the others. You might not be a whore but you're still just as dirty and revolting inside.' He starts to pace round me. '*Look* at this place. Look what you've *done* to it!' He kicks at the bucket, which wobbles but doesn't tip over. I want to retaliate, point out that anyone would smell disgusting locked in a dungeon, that all human beings crap, that men are animals too, but I don't dare. He's still pacing. I try to work out if this horrible man might really be Peter Marks, or if he was just doing an impression, playing a trick on me. I can't make up my mind. The way he changed from one to the other. It was like a hallucination. My head hurts with the confusion. The brown eyes watch me through the ski mask. 'Not that it matters,' he says. 'You all fail my experiment in the end. It's inevitable. You can't stop yourselves.'

I feel tears come to my eyes. 'You don't have to run the experiment,' I say. 'If you *are* Professor Marks, then you know me already, don't you? You know I respect you. Maybe we could work this out, maybe we could be friends.'

'*Friends?*' he says. 'Are you fucking *insane?*'

He strides towards me and I lurch backwards, try to get away, but it's useless. He grabs my arm and I cry out. 'Look at me,' he says, as I twist and struggle. 'I said *look at me.*' I turn my face towards him. His brown eyes are cold in the padded mask. He has me pushed against the wall so I can't escape. He lets go of my arm and for an awful moment, I think he's raising his hands to choke me. I start screaming, I can't stop myself. He clamps a hand over my mouth and grabs one of my breasts, twisting it so hard the pain almost makes me black out. 'Listen to me, bitch. You disgust me. Think I'm wearing these gloves for forensics? I'm wearing them because *I don't want to fucking touch you with my skin.*' He lets go and I collapse to the floor.

He heads to the door, picks up the plastic bag and rifles through it, takes out a sandwich, ripping off the packaging. Then he shakes it out of its wrapper onto the floor and stamps on it. He looks over at me. 'There you go, Ava. You can eat it off the floor. Like the dog you are.'

Frankie

Donald Emneth is crucified by the media coverage. His mad beard and staring eyes are on the front of almost every national newspaper. The coverage strays well into the danger zone of prejudicing a trial if he's charged. One tabloid even uses a screen shot of him from Frankie's report with the headline: '*If Looks Could Kill.*'

She sits with Jack on their new sofa, watching the paper review on the late news. They have already sat through all the broadcasters' coverage of Mr Emneth's interview. It's more restrained than the papers, but the cumulative effect is damning. Charlie sold the footage of Ava at the demo to all their rivals, so every viewer has the chance to judge his murderous look, repeated over and over again in slow motion. Then there's the interview: the salacious glee at Hanna's haircut, and the highly suspicious-sounding 'support' he gave to Sandra and Lily in his supposed quest to help them give up sex work.

'He was blatantly paying for their services, wasn't he?' says Jack.

'Probably,' says Frankie. She scrolls through her phone, reading some of the newspaper articles that are already online. The reports are stuffed with neighbours' damning opinions about the 'local eccentric' and one has an exclusive interview with his ex-wife, accusing him of being a pervert. 'Well, that's his life trashed,' she says, putting the phone down. 'I don't suppose he'll be inviting any more reporters into his garden now.'

'Do you think he did it though?' Jack says. 'Bit of an own goal in that case, going to the press.'

'I think he's a sleazebag,' says Frankie, scowling as she remembers his leer. 'And the fact he's incriminated himself doesn't necessarily mean he didn't do it. If you think about it, the killer has been baiting the police, almost as if he's desperate to be noticed.'

'So you're saying it's him?'

'No, but it wouldn't surprise me.'

Jack rolls his eyes. 'Talk about hedging your bets. It's as well you're a journo, not a police officer.'

'Yeah well, I'm meant to hedge my bets. Unbiased and accurate reporting is my thing. I don't want to be sued.' She waves her phone at him, one of the red top front pages still on the screen. 'Unlike some newspapers I won't name. Or national TV reporters.' Frankie is feeling the need to reassure herself about the virtue of her own reporting. Kiera gave her a roasting for the Peter Marks interview, refusing to listen when she tried to explain that the clip Luke used wasn't even meant to be recorded. '*You're a hack not a social worker!*' Kiera had snapped, stomping off. Zara had come over to give her a hug when the boss was gone, but it was all very embarrassing.

'At least if this old guy's arrested it means one less nutter protesting at work,' Jack says. 'As far as I remember that was the demo when protestors dumped a load of dirty spuds outside reception. Some sort of ridiculous gesture against the pest-resistant potatoes we're developing. Completely bonkers.' He had been working at the John Innes last year, meaning Frankie hadn't been allowed to cover the demonstration due to conflict of interest. 'A bit of luck you caught them both on film that day, isn't it?'

She knows Jack means Ava and Donald Emneth, but it makes her think of the interview with Hanna in the BBC archive. It's not the first time she's known victims of crime to appear on old, unrelated news reports, but it still feels a bit odd that *both* women have. So far, the fact they've both been on TV is the only connection she can see between them. 'Do you remember seeing either Donald or Ava at the demo that day?' she asks Jack.

He shakes his head. 'Nobody stands out at these things. It's just a mob. Your Mr Emneth's bloody typical though, claiming we're causing cancer when we're trying to *cure* it. Must say I feel a lot less sorry for Ava knowing she's part of the socks and sandals brigade.'

'Jesus, Jack. She hardly deserves to be murdered for shopping organic.'

'I was joking!' He flings his hands up in mock defence. 'Suppose I ought to be grateful to the protestors. It adds a certain frisson to splicing proteins into tomatoes, knowing you're a target for terrorists.' He smiles. 'Nearest I'll ever get to being James Bond, anyway.'

Waking the next morning before an alarm goes off is pure pleasure. Frankie rolls over sleepily to face the window. Sunlight is shining through the slatted blinds in dazzling stripes, turning the wall an even brighter white wherever it touches the paint. For a moment she just lies there, savouring the time in bed, before coffee calls. Jack is still sleeping and she slides out from under the duvet, padding across the new beige carpet.

She stands for a moment at the living-room window, looking out over the river. The morning light has turned the grey water silver and the willow trees are golden brown. A lone jogger runs along the path opposite, but otherwise it's so peaceful they could almost be in the countryside. It's a little cold to step out onto the balcony in her pyjamas, but she can't wait for summer, all the lazy afternoons she and Jack will spend there together, enjoying a glass of wine and a favourite book.

As she crosses to the open kitchen area, the black and white tiles are cold under her feet. She flips the kettle on to boil and gets out the cafetière, ladling in the coffee. It's expensive stuff Jack bought at a fancy independent shop on the Norwich lanes. Frankie can't tell the difference from the cheap supermarket brand she buys, but hasn't had the heart to tell him. The microwave pings with the hot milk and she pours out two mugs for them both, heading back to the bedroom.

Jack is still sleeping. She leans over and kisses him gently. He stirs and opens his eyes, sees her holding the coffee.

'What a lovely way to wake up,' he says, yawning. 'Thank you.'

She puts his coffee down on the bedside table and clambers back into bed with her own. 'It looks like it's going to be another gorgeous day. Such a lovely autumn this year.'

'I'm so sorry not to be spending it with you,' he says, taking a sip of coffee. 'It's just crazy at work at the moment. I think I'm in for a few Saturdays until we've got the project finished. Everyone in the lab is a bit jittery about funding.'

'It's a shame,' says Frankie, snuggling up to him. She had no idea until they moved in together that the lab was so demanding on his time. It feels like his hours are even more unpredictable than hers. 'But I understand. I'm meeting up with Priya and Zara for brunch after you go out. Anything you want in town?'

'Some more of this coffee, if you don't mind,' he says, raising his mug for another sip. 'It really is great, isn't it?'

Priya is already at the Cherryleaf Coffee House on St Giles Street when she arrives. It's a large open place with shiny wooden floors, farmhouse furniture and floral crockery; Frankie remembers eating cake off similar plates at her grandparents' house, but the retro design suddenly seems to be fashionable again. Priya's taken over a table by a window, and is sitting on a bench strewn with velvet cushions. Even on the weekend she can't switch off from being a producer; at least two of the Saturday papers are scattered amongst the china.

'Morning,' she says, standing up to give Frankie a hug. 'Hope you don't mind all this.' She gestures at the French toast and coffee she's already ordered. 'Ken has the kids this weekend. I'm discovering one of the upsides to divorce is getting some time to read and drink coffee on my own.'

Frankie knows it's been a difficult year, however much Priya always looks on the bright side. 'How were the kids this morning?'

Priya makes a face. 'Oh, don't ask. Neither of them wanted breakfast, *no that's not the coat I want to wear Mummy, why can't we*

stay with you, I don't like those shoes. I couldn't do anything right.'
She pauses. 'They've still not forgiven me for leaving their dad.'

'They'll understand when they're older,' Frankie says, thinking
of her own parents' divorce. 'Trust me. Maybe even before. I was
delighted when there weren't rows every day.'

'Hello, you pair,' says Zara, slinging her mac on the back of the
chair next to Priya. She looks at the newspapers. 'Honestly, no
time off at all?' She picks one up, folding it over to look at Donald
Emneth's photo on the front. 'They'll be sorry about all this character assassination now he's been arrested. I heard it on the radio
as I drove in.'

'Really?' says Frankie. 'I wonder if they've got anything else on
him besides the stuff he said to the press. Though I suppose put
together it sounded so incriminating the police had to take him in.'

'What will you ladies be having, then?' asks the waitress, who
has crossed over from the counter.

'I think the usual,' says Zara, looking round. 'Three egg muffins
and a big pot of coffee?' The others nod. 'And I'll have some
French toast,' she adds, eyeing Priya's half-eaten portion.

'Some bacon with the muffin for me,' says Frankie. 'And an
orange juice.'

'So what did you make of him, Frankie?' Priya asks, when the
waitress has gone.

'Jack asked me that last night,' she replies. 'He was creepy, but
that doesn't mean he's guilty. That nasty look he's giving her in
our archive footage might just have been because she turned down
his cup of tea.'

'Thanks,' says Zara, making room on the table as the waitress
brings over the coffee. 'Well, it sounds ridiculously petty to us, but
I've sat in on murder trials that were sparked by sillier supposed
slights. Lots of disgruntled men out there who think the world
owes them a woman. Usually a young, pretty one.'

'But he seems a bit, well, *dim* to be our killer though,' says Priya,
refilling her cup. 'Don't you think? I mean the last murder, that
Hanna Whatshername, she was dumped in a very public place.

Can't see Beardy having the nous to pull that off. And he's quite distinctive, surely somebody would have noticed him hanging around campus.'

'Do you ever think he's watching us?' says Frankie. Her two friends look at her in surprise. 'No, not literally sitting here watching us. I mean on telly? Following us on the news. I mean the killer must be, mustn't he? He'll want to find out how much the police know.'

'Revelling in the fame of being on the Eastern Film Company,' Zara snorts.

'Is this case getting to you?' asks Priya. 'I can speak to Charlie if it's a bit much. Get somebody else covering it for a bit.'

'No, if anything I'm enjoying the challenge of working on such a big story.' Frankie blushes. 'God, that sounds awful, doesn't it? I'm turning into Luke Heffner. Wallowing in all the misery, making it a backdrop to my ego. I bet that smug bastard would do a piece to camera in a morgue—'

'Behind me is the corpse of victim number three,' interrupts Zara, putting on a pompous tone. 'And I can exclusively reveal that she was—' The waitress cuts off Luke's imaginary script with their food. 'Ah thank you,' says Zara. 'From murder to muffins. Marvellous.'

There's a lull in the conversation as the three of them tuck in. 'So how's it going, living with Jack?' Priya asks.

'It's great. A bit weird to have somebody always *there*,' Frankie says. 'Although not today, which is a shame. He's having to do lots of extra work in the lab. Some special project.'

'Ah yes, the cancer-curing tomatoes,' says Zara. 'Just wait until you're a pair of old farts like me and Mark. He's away this weekend, but I still made coffee for two this morning.' She takes a mouthful of French toast, waving the empty fork at Frankie. 'And then you've got the joys of in-laws to look forward to. Though I guess Mark's lot aren't too bad, bless them, even if his mother does like to fuss over what I feed him. When are you meeting Jack's parents?'

'I won't be,' she says. 'I'm sure I told you his mum's dead? And he doesn't really speak with his dad, I don't like to ask him about it. Bit of a sore point.' Frankie's phone bleeps. 'Speak of the devil,' she says, fishing around in her handbag. 'He said he'd let me know how late he'll be working.' She gets the phone out and checks the screen. Her face lights up with excitement as she reads the message. 'Even better.'

'Why, what's up?'

'It's from Laura, you know, Ava's friend? She's agreed to meet me, she's free this afternoon, just for a chat, no filming. But we can work on that.'

'Working on a Saturday?' asks Zara. 'Rather you than me. Still I guess it will impress our lovely new boss, Little Miss Sunshine.'

Priya groans. 'Oh God, she's awful, isn't she? Come back David, all your crap football jokes are forgiven.'

'I reckon I need to earn a few extra brownie points with her,' says Frankie, typing a reply to Laura into her phone. 'After that bollocking she gave me yesterday.'

'At least she seems to be in London quite a bit,' says Zara. 'Any luck and Norfolk is just a brief stop on her ascent up the greasy corporate pole.'

Laura's room in halls makes Frankie nostalgic for her own time as a student. The narrow cell in the breezeblock building is a riot of colour. There's a pink tie-dye sheet pinned to the ceiling and cheap rag rugs hide almost every scrap of the threadbare orange carpet. The pin board is covered in photos of Laura and her friends. Many are of Ava.

Laura herself is a slight, nervous young woman who keeps fiddling with the end of her mousy blonde ponytail. She looks younger than twenty, or maybe Frankie is just getting old. After all, her own student days are nearly a decade ago, although it doesn't feel like it. They sit together on the bed, surrounded by mismatched glittery cushions, peering at Laura's phone.

'This is Ava and me in Vilnius last year. We went Interrailing.' Laura swipes through to another picture, showing Frankie holiday snaps. 'That's the boarding house where we stayed. Then that's us out in the countryside. We hired some bikes.'

The photo shows Ava with her familiar pink bob, smiling and squinting in the sun. She's standing next to another girl with pigtails, one arm round her shoulders. Laura is a little further off, holding two bicycles. Frankie has the same tight feeling in her chest as when she watched the footage of Ava at the demo. She hopes so much she isn't dead.

'Who's the other woman?'

'Lina. We met her and Marius out there. They're both students at Vilnius University. Marius took the photo.'

Frankie glances at the posters opposite. So much of the decoration in here is from the trip. Alphonse Mucha prints from their stop in Prague and endless Toulouse-Lautrec, perhaps from a stall alongside the Seine. She has already seen photos of the two girls by its banks in Paris.

Laura swipes through to the end of her camera shots. Her hand is trembling slightly. The screen shows Ava and a male student at a bar, leaning over the counter laughing. Ava's eyes are shut and her face is slightly blurred. She must have moved when the photo was taken. There's blue strobe lighting and the place looks vaguely familiar.

'Where's this?' Frankie asks.

'The Blue Bicycle, you know near Bedford Street? It's the night that . . .' Laura trails off.

'The night she went missing?'

Laura nods. 'It wasn't even a late one. Ava hardly had anything to drink, she was really preoccupied with her coursework.'

'Did you notice anything unusual about the evening at all?' Laura wipes her eyes and Frankie realises she's crying. She puts a hand on her arm. 'I'm sorry, you don't have to talk about it if it's upsetting.'

'No, it's just I feel really guilty,' Laura says. She stops, wiping her face again, trying to collect herself. 'I wish more than anything I could go back in time and change things. Ava hardly drank anything, but Jon and I were doing shots. We were both massively pissed by the time we went back to campus. I can't believe we let her go home on her own. The police asked if Ava might have been drugged, if she behaved oddly, and I honestly couldn't say. I knew she was quieter than usual but that's all.' She flops back, leaning against a print of a black cat on the wall. 'How shit a friend does that make me?'

'Laura, I'm sure the police already said this, but you're not responsible for what happened. Some creep chose to target your friend. That's got nothing to do with you guys doing shots.'

'I know that really. But it's hard, you know? And I just wish I could remember more.'

Frankie nods, wishing the same. Laura still won't agree to talk on camera, and if she can't get much more useful information out of her, she's going to be torn between going back empty-handed or having Kiera push her to run the drunken friends line, regardless of her reassuring little speech that Laura is not to blame. 'Did you notice anybody else there at the bar?'

'Well,' Laura says, twisting her bracelet round her wrist, a string of amber beads on ribbon. 'I don't know if he'd thank me for putting you in touch, but Brett was there that night. He might have seen something, he knows all the regulars.'

'Who's Brett?'

'Brett Hollins. He's a postgraduate student here but he works at the bar on Saturdays and some weeknights. I think he was with a friend that evening, I noticed him at a table, so he wasn't serving,' Laura says, blushing slightly. 'I'm not a stalker or anything, but he's quite fit. And I think he likes Ava.'

'Do you think she likes him too?'

'No.' She fiddles with the bracelet again, not looking at Frankie. 'Ava has been finding stuff out about herself lately. Brett's definitely *not* her type.'

'How do you know he likes her?'

'Well, Ava had some time off last term when her brother Matt wasn't well, he has depression, and Brett kept asking me where she was whenever I went to the bar.'

'Ava took time off uni to look after her brother? They must be very close then.'

'Oh God, I shouldn't have said that,' Laura says, clapping a hand to her mouth. 'Shit, I'm such an idiot. One of the local papers in Sussex put something online about Matt being depressed and Ava's mum's asked all her friends not to say anything. I wasn't thinking. *Please* don't mention it.'

'Of course I won't,' Frankie says, trying not to imagine Kiera's disapproval at her lack of ruthlessness. 'Anyway, you were telling me about this guy, Brett.'

Laura sighs, twiddling with the ponytail again. 'It's obvious he fancies her.' Her eyes fill with tears again. 'Sorry,' she says breaking off, and wiping her face with a trembling hand. 'It's just I was a bit jealous at the time, and now I don't give a crap if Brett fancies her or not, I just want her back.'

'Honestly, you've nothing to feel guilty about.'

'That's not the bit that bothers me. It's that when he kept asking me about her I told him he didn't have a chance, Ava's gay.' Laura catches her breath. 'Please, *please* don't repeat that either. She's not out yet, it's been a confusing year for her. I should never have told him, I still can't believe I did.'

Frankie shifts on the bed, feeling awkward. So far this interview feels more like a counselling session, there are so many things she's not allowed to report. Behind Laura, she can see photos of the two girls, laughing, on their adventures across Europe. Female friendship is always complicated but the young woman in front of her doesn't deserve to be torturing herself. Frankie is a journalist not a therapist and she knows it's not her role to be offering comfort, but as is so often the case when faced with intense emotion, the lines feel blurred. She squeezes Laura's arm. 'You sound like a brilliant friend,' she says. 'Don't blame yourself for anything, it's bad enough for you that she's missing.' To her consternation Laura leans over to give her a hug and starts crying into her hair. Frankie pats her carefully on the back, wondering whether it will seem crass later to ask for a copy of the photo of Ava at the bar that night.

Back at the new flat, the grown-up white lines are a shock after Laura's multi-coloured student bedroom. It makes her feel old. Frankie picks up the fliers lying on the mat – there's something about recycling and another postcard of the vase from that nameless antiques store – and dumps them straight into the bin. She heads over to the kettle and flicks it on. Jack is supposed to be back any minute and promised to pick up dinner on the way back.

The meeting with Laura was disappointing. She got the photo – that's something to offer Kiera, the last picture taken of the missing girl – but no interview. Brett might be an interesting voice, but she's no idea if he will talk yet. Of course if Donald Emneth is charged, none of it is relevant. But somehow she doesn't think he will be. She reaches over to her laptop, which she left lying on the breakfast counter, and powers it up.

The police must have something that's made them think it's the same killer, most likely forensic evidence that links the three murdered women. But is Donald Emneth really a serial killer? She can imagine him luring Lily and Sandra into his house, but Hanna is more of a stretch. He'd surely have to abduct her, which would be much harder for an old man to pull off.

Dragging over a gleaming stool, Frankie settles down in front of the screen, scrolling through her notes on the different victims. *Sandra Blakely, 38, mother of two, crack addict and sex worker, found dead on wasteland in Costessey. Strangled. Lily Sidcup, 26, heroin addict and sex worker, dumped in a layby off the A47. Also strangled.* Frankie pauses. She remembers knocking on the door of Lily Sidcup's parents' house, their tear-blotched faces as they welcomed her in. Her discomfort at eavesdropping on their grief, perched on the sofa clutching a mug of too-strong tea as Gavin filmed their desolation for posterity. Lily had been found first, even though she was killed second. She had only recently got into sex work, bullied into it by her drug pusher boyfriend, or so her mother claimed. Her family still kept in touch and had quickly noticed she was missing, unlike poor Sandra Blakely, who had long ago disappeared into a vortex of strangers' cars and quick fixes.

Then there's Hanna. Frankie closes her eyes for a moment, though it doesn't help her blot out the memory of the eighteen-year-old lying dead on the mud. Hanna obviously had a difficult background, and anyone stalking her would know she had no family waiting for her to come home at night. But she did have a steady job, and friends at work who would have noticed her absence. The killer had a stroke of luck when her dozy flatmates called Hanna in sick on her behalf.

'And now there's Ava Lindsey,' Frankie murmurs, looking at the photograph of the student with pink hair. Shuffling all the stills together on the screen, Frankie can see nothing that obviously links the women, except their sex. There's short, blonde Sandra, a little on the gaunt side, dark circles under her eyes. The photo of Lily is an old one, provided by her family, but still, she looks nothing like the other two. Hanna is absurdly young, still childlike, posing in a bathroom mirror in the poor-resolution photo.

Thinking back to the press conference, Frankie remembers the *London Daily Times* journalist with his prostitute fixation. The police said the women's professions were irrelevant, but Frankie isn't so sure. It feels like the killer has been slowly building up to more challenging, high-profile prey. First the sex workers, notoriously easy to kill, less likely to be missed. A practice run for somebody unused to murder. Then the apprentice with no family. And now the middle-class, A-star student, whose disappearance is bound to cause a fuss. She thinks back to Peter Marks, his warning that the killer would be feeding off the media coverage, enjoying the sense of power.

She sits back from the screen. 'You're not Donald Emneth, are you?' she says to the imaginary killer, as if he's standing before her. 'You've only just got started.'

The sound of the key in the lock makes her jump. Jack comes in looking frazzled, clutching three plastic bags from Morrisons. She jumps off the stool and goes to help him. 'Sorry, I didn't mean for you to do a big shop after working all day.'

'Oh don't worry, it was on the way. But it's not after work, sadly. I'm really sorry Franks, but can we do the cinema another night? I ought to start writing up my report and could do with a quiet one in. Tomorrow I *promise* I'm all yours.'

'That's fine, there was nothing I was desperate to see at the cinema anyway,' she says, unloading a block of cheese and giant container of milk into the fridge. 'Actually, if you don't mind I might text Zara. She's alone this weekend. We've not had a girls' night out in ages.'

Frankie

She has no difficulty picking out Brett. Frankie sits at the bar in The Blue Bicycle, around the same spot she remembers Ava sitting in Laura's photo. The guy serving her is tall and slim, but muscular. He clearly works out. His dark hair is flopped in a casual style she imagines it took some time to arrange, and his shirt collar is pressed into two sharp points. The lights above them ripple in different colours like sunlight on the sea, making it hard to see if the fabric is white or blue. Behind him, her reflection is in fragments, scattered amongst bottles of spirits in the mirrored shelves.

She's put a smart black dress on, and clipped in some dangly earrings to pass as making an effort for a Saturday night without overdoing it. She smiles at him, but doesn't say too much. In spite of herself, Frankie has butterflies in her stomach. It's not the thought of the attractive man in front of her, but the whiff of a possible exclusive in the air.

'Haven't I seen you somewhere before?' he says, as he mixes her Bellini.

'I work for the Eastern Film Company,' she says.

'That's right.' He shoots her a dazzling grin. The man really is gorgeous. No wonder Laura is smitten. 'I'm good with faces. You're the new presenter, aren't you?'

Frankie thinks of Zara with her unsexy pinstripe and nearly snorts. Maybe she should have worn the low-cut top. 'No, that's a friend of mine. I'm a reporter. My name's Frances Latch.'

'Brett Hollins.' He holds out a hand, damp with Prosecco. 'Sorry, I get confused between the two jobs. Obviously you're not the older woman on the sofa.' He glances at a couple waiting by her elbow, the man holding out a tenner. Brett hands over her drink. 'Excuse me a second. Don't go anywhere.'

'Don't worry. I won't.'

Frankie watches him assemble two Mojitos, crushing the mint and lime. His movements are deft and practised. She can tell he's aware of her watching.

Brett finishes serving the couple and leans on the counter to talk to her again. 'So. A journalist.' His eyes linger on the skin at the base of her throat. 'Should I be worried? Everyone says the media can't be trusted.'

'Depends if you've got anything to hide,' she says.

'You've been covering that serial killer, haven't you?' he says. 'I've watched some of your reports.' He flashes another smile. 'You're pretty good.' He's flirting but she senses something needling behind his compliment. Frankie decides it's safest to play this one as close to the truth as possible.

'Thanks. I heard the last woman came drinking here sometimes.' She takes a sip of her Bellini. 'So I thought I'd pop along and get a feel for the place, chat to a few people.'

'I saw her around.' He shrugs. 'The dead girl.'

'Dead?' says Frankie, her stomach dropping. 'She's just missing at the moment.'

'Sorry, I can't keep track,' he says. 'Is she the one that's not been found yet?'

'Yes. Ava Lindsey. Still missing.'

'Well, I hope she turns up alive. Though it doesn't seem likely, does it? A shame. She was pretty.'

'Do you know her?'

He shakes his head. 'Saw her and her friends come in here the week she went missing. They all got trollied.' He mimics throwing back a hand and downing a drink. 'Practically cleared the bar out of shots.'

'Are you sure it was Ava?'

'I wouldn't miss the pink hair,' he says. Then he leans further over the counter. 'Or the pretty face.'

His words remind Frankie of Donald Emneth. Though at least Brett has better manners and looks into her eyes. His are dark brown. He stares with an intensity that's supposed to be flattering but feels unsettling.

'Hello old girl, sorry I'm late.' Zara thumps a bag down on the stool beside her; it's a battered canvas tote, a freebie from one of the years she's covered the Chelsea flower show. Frankie hadn't lied about a girls' night out to Jack, she just hadn't thought he needed to know exactly why she picked this particular bar.

'No problem, I was just talking to Brett. Brett, this is Zara.'

He leans over the bar to shake Zara's hand. '*Two* ladies off the telly. I should be asking for autographs.'

'Oh, you do know how to flatter an old trout!' laughs Zara. 'I'll have a dry Vodka Martini, thanks.'

'Of course.' He looks below the bar. 'Though we're a bit low on olives, if you'll excuse me a minute.'

Brett heads off, and as he swings his narrow hips past the counter, Zara whispers loudly, 'Blimey! He's fit!' It's part of their cover act, two women on the prowl, but from the smirk on Zara's face, she seems to have embraced the role with gusto.

'Well, he definitely heard that,' says Frankie when Brett has disappeared from view. 'Be amazed if the whole bar didn't.'

'Good. He was meant to.' Zara rummages in her canvas bag, bringing out a men's wallet with a burst seam. She scans the room, taking in the French posters on the walls, including, of course, *La Bicyclette Bleue* with its pouting 1940s heroine gazing at bomber planes in the sky. It's early but the place is already filling up; young couples and gaggles of students sit at small chrome tables in dimly lit corners or lounge on the blue velvet banquettes. 'Christ,' she says. 'I'm at least ten years too old for this place. How've you been getting on?'

Brett's back with the olives before she has a chance to answer. 'I was just telling Zara you saw Ava Lindsey and her friends here the week she disappeared,' Frankie says as he slips behind the bar.

'Shocking case, isn't it?' says Zara, plumping herself down on the stool. 'Maybe a splash more vodka,' she adds, watching Brett dole out an over-generous helping of vermouth into her glass.

'Of course.' He smiles. 'Yes, it's very sad. That group of students came in quite regularly, not just that week. I've seen them around on campus too.' He hands over Zara's cocktail. 'I'm a post grad at the same uni.'

Zara takes a swig. 'Spot on. Thanks,' she says, salt on her upper lip.

'That's interesting,' says Frankie. 'What are you studying?'

'Philosophy. I'm majoring in Schopenhauer.'

'Schopenhauer?' says Frankie, frowning. 'Wasn't he the guy who said men fall in love with a pretty face but end up tied to a hateful stranger?'

Brett looks surprised. 'Alternating endlessly between a work-shop and a witch's kitchen. Yes, that's the one,' he says. 'Although that's a paraphrase, not a quotation. Why, are you a fan?'

'Never read him, I'm afraid. But I remember that quote from *The Female Eunuch*.'

Zara rolls her eyes, but Brett is staring at her intently. 'As I say, that's a paraphrase. Germaine Greer must have put it into her own words. She does that quite often.'

Frankie shrugs and sips her Bellini. 'Well, I've not read him.' She glances at Zara, whose eyebrows have shot up.

'Me neither,' says Zara. 'Don't think we have *too* much call for German philosophers in regional news.'

Brett taps Frankie lightly on the arm. 'Philosophy isn't just for university. It's for everyone. All the time. It's a cliché about the unexamined life not being worth living, but still true.'

She glances down. His hand is still resting on her skin.

'Hey! Am I going to have to get this drink myself?' They turn towards a spotty youth, leaning across the bar, scowling, with an embarrassed-looking girl in tow. Brett excuses himself to serve them.

They spend the next couple of hours at The Blue Bicycle, chat-ting on and off with Brett, whenever he has a free moment. Zara takes on the role of inquisitor, grilling him on his memories of the last time he saw Ava. Frankie finds herself measuring everything he says against how Kiera might react when she reports it back. She suspects that Brett might be adding details and embellishments to impress them, though she won't tell her boss that. He talks to both women, but it's clearly Frankie who's caught his attention.

After her third Bellini, she's feeling a little light-headed, and Zara has started recounting one of her previous exploits, the time she single-handedly brought down the management of a prison.

'It was drugs,' Zara says, her cheeks flushed. 'The place was awash with them. And I never really got to the bottom of whether the bosses were merrily letting prisoners get high and top themselves, or if that was just an unfortunate side effect.'

'That's why she got the promotion to presenter,' Frankie says loudly. 'It was such a great exclusive.' She looks at Brett. 'So if you're serious about wanting to see me glammed up in the studio, reading an autocue, you'll have to help out.'

'How would I do that?' He smiles at her. 'I've not been giving drugs to anybody.'

'No, but you could tell us everything you remember about the last night Ava Lindsey was here. Nobody's run an interview like that yet.'

Brett holds his hands out in a gesture of surrender. 'But there's nothing to say. They came here, they drank, they left.'

'I thought you said there was a creepy guy. You noticed some guy you hadn't seen before, watching them.'

'You *definitely* said he was creepy,' Zara chimes in.

He looks uncomfortable. 'Yes, but that doesn't mean anything. Lots of creeps hang out in bars. Both the girls were pretty. And very drunk. I suppose several men in here might have been looking at them.'

'S'fine,' says Frankie. 'Say that then. Still interesting.'

'No harm, I suppose.' Brett shrugs. 'Anything to help a lovely lady.'

'Fab!' says Frankie, getting her phone out of her bag. She fumbles and nearly drops it. 'What's your number? I'll call you.'

'*All* the girls say that.' Brett looks at her from under his floppy fringe. He makes an unconvincing ingenu.

'No, she really will call you,' says Zara.

They pay up and totter out of the bar. Brett offered to call them a taxi, but Frankie wants to walk home to clear her head and Zara decides to catch a cab in the Forum. They clatter along the cobbles and part at the back of Jarrold's department store on Bedford Street.

'The words fish, shooting and barrel spring to mind,' says Zara as she hugs Frankie goodnight. 'Poor bastard. At least lemon-faced Kiera will be pleased.'

Frankie laughs and sets off down the dark street. Saturday night is still young – it's only half past ten – and drinkers are spilling out of bars to stand with bottles and pint glasses in the dull orange light. The air is thick with loud voices and music. It would have been much quieter than this when Ava last walked home. She remembers Brett's smile and feels a pang of anxiety. It must be guilt at reeling him in that's making her uncomfortable. She tries to think of Kiera, of how pleased she will be that they've got an interview, a new line about a possible suspect. At least this should get her off Frankie's case for a bit. Over the sound of Norwich on a Saturday night she can hear the clack of her own heels along with the beating of her heart, loud in her ears from an uneasy feeling that won't go away.

Ava

After he left, it took me a while to move. It wasn't just that he hurt me; hearing Professor Marks's voice coming from that monstrous round head felt like a punch to my soul. Even now, I keep wondering if it might be him; whether the person who's doing this to me, the person who's killed other women, might be a man I trust, someone I *admire* even. I can't believe it's possible. Professor Marks has put so many of his lectures on YouTube; this bastard must have studied them. It must have been an impression, it *must* have been.

When I finally felt strong enough, I got up and prised the sandwich off the floor. Most of it was inedible, not because I couldn't stomach the dirt – I'm too hungry to waste precious food over that – but because he had squashed so much of the filling out, grinding the mayonnaise into the concrete. It made me want to scream with rage. I don't feel like a dog for eating it, whatever names he calls me. I'm not ashamed of wanting to survive. I keep telling myself that *he* is the one who is inhuman, not me. It makes me feel better to say it aloud, even though it's not to his face. *You're the dog, you bastard! Not me!*

There were other sandwiches in the bag too. Five. I laid them out against the wall in a line, made a small picnic blanket out of the Tesco bag and sat the apples on it. At least none of the food is going to go off in here, it's so cold. It made me feel slightly more in control seeing the food set out like that. I can choose when I eat it. I can still make decisions.

But it's exhausting trying to keep my own spirits up. In the end I wrapped myself in the horse blankets and tried to get comfortable on the stone-cold floor. Lying there made me cry again. The concrete is so hard and I'm so bruised. Everything is cold, nothing feels soft, or safe or warm. Yet somehow I slept. Despair saps your will to stay conscious I guess, you just want to escape from yourself. It makes me think of Matt, all those times he wouldn't get out of bed and I snapped at him or rolled my eyes. I wish I'd been more sympathetic.

Light coming through the grille woke me. For a second I wasn't sure where I was.

Then it hit me.

I couldn't breathe. I sat up but my legs were tangled in the blankets, which made me panic even more. I kicked and kicked, then flung them off and ran to the door, hammering and screaming. I ran to the grille and yelled at that, but there was only silence. I knew there would be nothing, just as I knew the door wouldn't open, yet the disappointment still felt crushing.

It was still hard to breathe. I thought I might be having a heart attack, and as my breath whistled in and out, it looked like The Stain was moving at the same time, though I guess it was just me shaking. I don't know how I came back to myself, but at some point the air seemed to fill my lungs again and I slumped down on the blankets. It's impossible to get comfortable on them, and the only way to stay warm is to walk, but I needed to rest. I'm encrusted with dirt, sweat and dried pee and every part of me feels cold or hurts. I've never longed for a hot bath so much in my life.

I've no idea of the time in here, but I decided it was breakfast and ate an apple and half an egg sandwich. It's not like there was anything else to do, and after the panic subsided, I was ravenous.

Then I waited. And waited.

I hadn't thought it was possible to feel bored and terrified at the same time, but now I know you can.

I can't get the other women out of my mind, the ones who must have died in here. I only have names for two. I say them out loud as an exorcism. *Lily, Hanna.* Did they think what I'm thinking? Feel what I feel now? Did they die in here? I've stared at The Stain so long, I feel like it's changing shape. At one point it came into my head that Lily or Hanna is standing here in the room, watching me, and all I can see is her shadow on the wall. That's what The Stain is. That's why it keeps changing. I tried to tell myself if one of them *was* still here, she'd be wishing me well, siding with me against him, not tormenting me. But there's nothing good about The Stain. I can feel the evil flow from it like an electric pulse. Sometimes I worry I'm going mad.

The only thing I can actually *do* besides walking round and round is drink, and it's tempting to keep going. I've been resisting the urge to keep knocking the water back and instead have stretched it out, so there's still enough left for however long he leaves me. But now it's getting dark again, and there's no sign of him.

Whenever my eyes keep getting drawn back to The Stain, I try to distract myself. I go through the order of service again, revisit some of my favourite memories. That's meant to help. I know, I did a module on it. Taking yourself to a safe place.

I close my eyes. In my head I'm eleven and it's the summer holidays. Matt and I take the small rowing boat out on the River Rother that runs near our grandparents' old house. I trace every turn of the banks on our route, imagining it over and over again. We pass tiny Chithurst church, its tower just visible from the water. I can hear the splash of our oars echo as we pass under the old bridge. Over the side I can see grey fishes dart by, and the trees hang over the water, leaving us in the shade. We cut through farmland, cows cropping grass at the top of the steep banks, just above our heads. At the shallow sections we get out and walk, dragging the hull across the pebbles, scraping the fibreglass. Like all my memories from that time, it's brilliant sunshine.

We stop for lunch. This is a dangerous part to imagine, with my own stomach so empty. I can't remember what our mother would have packed us, so I make it up, thinking about the things we used to eat. Ham sandwiches, Golden Wonder crisps and Babybel cheeses with their red wax wrappers. And cake. In the cold room my stomach gurgles. I ignore it and carry on upstream with my brother.

Matt does almost all the rowing. I'm far too lazy, and to be honest, not very good at it. The exception is when we approach a small wooden bridge. It looks homemade, stretching out between the trees as if it was specially designed for children.

'Here, you take the oars for a bit,' says Matt. He's fourteen, skinny and tanned in his swimming trunks. 'Keep it still when we get underneath.'

I do as he asks and he stands up, the small boat wobbling in the water at the change in the weight. Suddenly it rocks violently and I squeal in protest as he jumps upwards, grabbing the bridge so his legs hang down over my head.

'Whoo-hoo, I'm Superman!'

'Fly then!' I say, rowing off and leaving him there. I crash into a bank, clutching onto the reeds so that the boat is not too far away from where he's hanging, but still out of reach. My brother is a prankster, he meant for me to do this. It's part of the code we have, there's no need to explain what the joke is. With a shout he lets go and plunges into the water. The boat tips from side to side with the impact. I wait for him to surface and there's nothing.

'Matt?'

A splash and his head comes up beside the boat. I laugh with relief, grab one arm, help him haul himself in.

'Your turn!' he yells, pushing me overboard. It's icy cold. I splutter, treading water, weighed down by my summer dress. I grab hold of the side, looking up at him. We're both hysterical with laughter.

In my memory, my brother helps me back into the boat and we continue our journey on the Rother, both soaking wet, working out how we can dry off before we get home.

I sit back against the concrete wall, exhausted by the effort of taking my mind to another place. Again I picture my brother suspended above the water, his legs kicking where I left him hanging. I look at the door, at the handle that still isn't turning. The memory doesn't feel so comforting any more.

Frankie

On Sunday Jack suggests heading to Holkham beach, the spot where she first fell in love with Norfolk. It's another beautiful day. Frankie lets him drive, enjoying sitting back and watching the fields roll out, listening to his Brahms CDs. They don't say much but it's a comfortable silence. She looks at his profile as he concentrates on the road and finds herself comparing him to Brett. They must be about the same age, and any objective observer would tell her the barman is more attractive, but the quiet thoughtfulness she so loves about Jack's expression is entirely lacking in Brett's face. Jack glances in the side mirror and catches her watching him.

'What?' he laughs.

She smiles at him. 'Just thinking I'm going out with the best-looking geek in the lab.'

'Now *that's* a backhanded compliment!'

They arrive at the Holkham Estate car park, and wrap up before setting off; the coastal wind is biting even from this distance. They pick their way through the woods, nodding to another couple with a dog passing them on the way back. It never gets less extraordinary, she thinks, as the enormous expanse of sand and sky suddenly opens out before them. They stand for a moment, Jack putting his arms round her as they take in the view. The landscape has an unearthly quality, the way everything merges. There's no line where the sea meets the land; instead ripples of wet sand give way seamlessly to water, which in turn weaves its way through the dunes in silver ribbons, lying in wait for unwary walkers when the tide turns. And against the pale sand and sky, the black mass of trees keeps watch, like soldiers on the eve of battle. The tide and the wind are always changing the landscape, but the limitless horizon remains constant.

'Let's go,' Jack says. They set off, taking the path down onto the sand. Hand in hand, their cheeks whipped scarlet by the wind as they walk along the beach, Frankie feels completely happy.

They trek across to Wells-next-the-Sea, then cut into the town, choosing the first café they can find with a table spare. Frankie squeezes past an elderly couple by the door to claim the space, while Jack goes up to the counter to order their club sandwiches. The room is warm and noisy with the gurgle of the coffee machine and the chatter of customers. There's a slight sheen of condensation on the plastic tablecloth beneath her fingers. She leans back and looks at the wooden seagulls hanging on the wall. One of them is missing a beak. Further up, lobster baskets hang from the ceiling, another decorative shorthand for seaside.

'I said *leave it!*'

She glances towards the counter where somebody seems to be having a row. With a lurch of embarrassment she recognises Debbie Richards and Martin Hungate. They're looking over at her.

'Shit,' Frankie mutters to herself. This is the last thing she needs. Hoping to brazen it out, she raises a hand in a half-hearted greeting, a tense smile on her face. Immediately she wishes she hadn't as Martin takes it as an invitation to leave their place in the queue. She looks desperately at Jack, but her boyfriend has his back to her, oblivious.

'I hope you're proud of yourself,' Martin Hungate says, standing by the door and talking loudly at her over the heads of the startled pensioners.

'Not here, Martin,' Debbie hisses, tugging at his arm.

He shakes her off. 'Bet you had a nice laugh at our expense.'

'Not at all,' says Frankie. 'We were representing all sides of the argument. I'm very sorry if you were disappointed by the report, but I believe it was fair.'

'Fair?' Martin says. 'Making Debbie here look like some sort of Stepford Wife? You call that fair?'

Debbie has gone bright red and Frankie feels a stab of sympathy. She hopes Martin hasn't been taking out his frustrations on her at home. 'I really didn't mean to cause either of you any offence,' she says. Debbie averts her eyes.

'Do you mind?' the older man sitting by Frankie interrupts, turning round to look at her and Martin. 'Some of us are trying to eat our lunch in peace!'

Martin looks as if he'd like to say something else, but instead bangs angrily out of the café. Debbie fights with the handle, struggling to open the door, and scuttles out after him. Frankie watches them pass the window, Debbie remonstrating as Martin stomps ahead.

'Honestly!' tuts the older woman, shooting a disproving look at Frankie.

'Excuse me,' says Jack, squeezing past with his tray. It's empty apart from their table number and two sets of cutlery wrapped in paper napkins, which he sets down with a clank. He doesn't notice the other couple stiffen with irritation at the noise. 'There we go.' He scrapes back his chair and sits down, then frowns, seeing her expression. 'You OK?'

'Yes, it's nothing. Some guy who was peeved at a report I did decided to have a go.'

Jack looks around. 'Which guy?'

'Never mind, he's gone now.'

'Sorry I wasn't here to stick up for you. You should have called me over.'

'Oh don't worry,' she says. 'Getting harangued by idiots is an occupational hazard. No harm done.' She smiles at him, the knot of tension already unravelling. Jack smiles back and takes her hand over the table.

The walk back to Holkham blows away any lingering sense of unease left in the wake of Martin's outburst. In the evening, after they get home, Jack has to pop to the lab and check on his precious tomatoes, but Frankie's in such a good mood she doesn't mind being left alone. She even finds it touching, the way he frets over his plants as if they're wayward children.

She makes herself a hot chocolate, realising as she opens the cupboard that she forgot to buy more of Jack's coffee yesterday. She crosses to the window, looks at the black water of the river, lit up in patches from the windows of her block of flats. It's too dark to see much of the opposite bank. She leaves the thin linen curtains open and sits down to watch the evening bulletin on TV. It's Zara in the studio, of course. Paul always manages to wiggle out of working Sunday evenings. She sips from the warm mug, relaxed by all the sea air, as her friend looks out at her from the screen.

'*Good evening, you're watching the Eastern Film Company.*' Zara's studio smile turns grave. '*In the last hour, police have released a sixty-four-year-old man who was arrested in connection with the murder of three women and the disappearance of a fourth from Norfolk. The man, named locally as Donald Emneth from the Costessey area of Norwich, was taken in for questioning on Friday, regarding the murders of Lily Sidcup, Sandra Blakely and Hanna Chivers. A fourth woman, Ava Lindsey, remains missing. Police say Mr Emneth has been released without charge.*' Zara glances down solemnly at her papers, then looks up again, her tone brighter. '*A church in Peterborough has become the first in our region to be powered entirely by solar power . . .*'

Frankie props her feet up on the perspex coffee table, settling back into the sofa. She feels sorry the killer hasn't been caught, or Ava found, but part of her is already wondering whether Brett will agree to do the interview tomorrow. She's especially glad she made the contact now. She picks up her phone, thinking about the promise she made to Zara. Ever since their drink at the bar she has resisted going onto *Killing Cuttlefish*, but curiosity and the urge to find something else Kiera might be interested in prompts her to open the tab.

She scans through the latest blogs and spots another post from @Feminazi_Slayer2: **We Mustie find Ava the Crustie!** She clicks on it, and immediately a poor-resolution cartoon of a placard-waving hippie clutching a bomb comes up, with Ava Lindsey's face superimposed on top.

It seems Ava Lindsey, the supposedly innocent little sweetie pie who's gone missing in Norfolk, is actually a FUCKING TERRORIST. That's right folks, Ava is an animal rights activist, and the little BITCH cost the John Innes Centre thousands of pounds' worth of damage last year at a violent protest.

Of course, the MSM have nothing to say about this, do they? Oh no. Instead we get a load of hand-wringing crap about what a model student Ms Lindsey is, how her parents miss her etc. etc. etc. Imagine for a moment that Ava were a MISSING BOY who supports the MRA movement. How would the Lame Stream Media cover that, I wonder?

That's right, they wouldn't. **And that's what we call DOUBLE FUCKING STANDARDS.**

We can be as peaceful as we like, campaigning for Men's Justice, and STILL the media will cover us in shit, but a woman can be an ACTUAL TERRORIST and hey presto! she's the victim. And they say **there's no gynocracy??** Of course, Ava is no doubt safe and well right now, hanging out with her crustie mates and planning on bombing a lab somewhere, but maybe we can dream, maybe our friend the Norfolk Strangler did pay her a visit. Here's hoping you get what you deserve, BITCH.

Frankie's heart is racing. Even though the website's bile is no longer a surprise, still, every time she reads it, it manages to get deep under her skin. It's not just the hate directed at Ava, it's the wilful mangling of facts: confusing Ava's environmentalism with animal rights, lying about the scale of the protest at the John Innes. It makes her want to argue furiously with whoever wrote the blog even though she knows that would be futile.

She looks at the blog again, knowing she shouldn't, but it's like returning to a scab. Directly underneath the text she notices there's a link to a YouTube video, posted by someone calling themselves @Anabolic100. She's half expecting it to be obscene, but instead is surprised to see it's of Ava. She clicks on it.

'*Ava Lindsey is a long-time Green campaigner here on campus. Ava, what do you think the government should be doing about climate change?*' The video is amateurish, with the background in focus instead of Ava's face. It must be by a student.

'*Well, anything would be a start. The Paris Agreement doesn't go nearly far enough, we need to be taking action on all fronts, across every section of society . . .*'

Ava has an authoritative voice, her gestures firm and unapologetic. She goes on to outline a Green action plan, dwelling passionately on the damage plastic bags are doing to the oceans. In spite of herself Frankie feels a sense of disappointment she didn't have this footage when she did her report on Ava, but at least she can tell Kiera and use it in future. The thought is followed by an immediate wave of self-disgust. She closes the site, throwing the phone onto the sofa. How can she possibly be using this blog as an aid to her own reporting? Her only task should be to expose it. The phone lies beside her, a dark grey slug against the cream upholstery. 'Let's see what Kiera makes of *you*, dickhead,' she says.

Monday morning is overcast, the covering of cloud so thin it filters the light through in a flat glare, like a giant photographic reflector. Frankie parks up, squeezing in between Charlie's rusting Volvo and one of the other reporters' cars, a grey Clio. As she locks the door a voice behind makes her jump.

'Is Zara in today?'

It's Brian, standing so close she almost hits him with her bag as she turns round.

'Jesus!' she says. 'Where were you? You're lucky I didn't run you over.'

'Sorry,' he says, stepping back. 'I did wave, I thought you saw me.' He's shifting nervously from foot to foot, overweight in a faded red anorak. Even though he's given her some space, his bulk is still blocking the narrow way out between her car and Charlie's Volvo.

'Can you let me past?'

'Sorry, I'm sorry.' He shuffles backwards. 'Is Zara in today? I just want an autograph. That's all.'

Frankie steps beyond the bonnet of her car, away from Brian, unconsciously holding her bag close to her body, relieved to have open space between her and the door to reception. 'I thought she'd already given you an autograph?'

'Yeah well, I know I've asked before.' Brian looks embarrassed. 'It's just I thought maybe she could sign some old memorabilia of your show, you know, some publicity material from the 1970s.'

'You've got stuff from the Eastern Film Company from the seventies? Like what, old posters?' Frankie asks, almost interested in spite of herself. Brian nods and she laughs. 'Blimey. I had no idea it even existed.'

He beams at her. 'I love your programme. You're so lucky to work here. You're so lucky to work with Zara.' He takes a step closer. 'I don't think that Paul Carter deserves her.'

Frankie is not especially fond of Paul but she doesn't like the way Brian is trying to gossip about one of her colleagues; it doesn't feel appropriate. He's looking at her eagerly and she notices a speck of dried food on his chin. Revulsion rises in her throat, then she imagines the loneliness of his life, his probable lack of friends, and feels sorry for him. It's not his fault he's so unprepossessing. 'Look, Brian, I know you mean well,' she says. 'But you're really not meant to ask for Zara's autograph like this. If you want her to sign something, you should leave it at reception and then pick it up later, not approach staff in car parks.'

'Oh right,' says Brian, crestfallen. 'OK.'

'Take care,' says Frankie, turning and walking quickly across the tarmac. She pushes through the glass revolving doors, aware Brian is still standing where she left him.

'You OK there?'

It's not Ernie on reception today, but a new guy she's only met a couple of times. 'Yes, I'm fine. I think our number one fan is getting a bit too keen to see Zara though. Maybe you could have a word with him? I'm sure he's harmless, but . . .' She trails off, feeling guilty about adding to Brian's sense of rejection.

'Don't worry, I'll handle it,' says the security guard, moving out from behind the desk. Frankie doesn't watch him head into the car park to talk to Brian, but swipes herself into the newsroom. Charlie beckons her over to his desk, brandishing one of the weekend's prejudicial front pages. There's a look of glee on his face.

'We've had a call. About Donald Emneth.'

'Not another complaint?' she says, aghast. In her mind she leaps from a snotty email, to a reprimand from Ofcom, to a suit for libel, to losing her job. 'But I was so careful!'

'Don't worry,' he says. 'You were fine. That Luke Heffner on the other hand, skating on very thin ice, I thought. No, this is a follow-up call with a tip-off. About our beardy-weirdy.'

'I don't have to interview him *again*, do I?'

'Better than that. We've been contacted by one of Lily's colleagues. A woman called Amber Finn. She's another of Donald Emneth's "friends". Or rather he's one of her punters.'

'So he *was* paying Lily and Sandra for sex.'

'Of course.' Charlie waves a hand dismissively. 'Would you hang out with Donald Emneth unless you were paid to?'

'What about my barman? And the new blog?' Frankie asks. She had texted Charlie last night and is disappointed he's not more enthusiastic about interviewing Brett or going after @Feminazi_Slayer2.

'The YouTube footage of Ava is definitely a good find, we'll use that tonight,' he says. 'And I told Kiera you had a couple of possible leads. She wants to chat about it all when you get back.' He shrugs. 'But for now Donald Emneth is the only story in town.'

Frankie looks at a giant plasma TV above Charlie's head. There's a row of them, as big as miniature cinema screens, all playing various news channels on mute. She can see a pre-recorded clip of Mr Emneth taking his bins out that morning, surrounded by a pack of reporters, all thrusting microphones under his nose and shouting questions at him. '*They've got my jacket,*' he keeps repeating, his words coming up in real time one by one as subtitles on the screen. '*They wouldn't give it back.*' In the silver flashes of the paparazzi cameras, his eyes look wide with fear.

'I'm not so sure about this. Don't you think he's had enough of a grilling? I don't want to end up in McNae's *Essential Law for Journalists* as a case study for the chapter on defamation.'

'Would I do that to you?' Charlie asks. He has a crocodile grin. 'Trust me, you're going to be fine.'

Amber Finn's flat is in Costessey, not far from Donald Emneth's house. Frankie and Gavin sit in her immaculate front room. Two walls are painted grey, while the others are papered in a blue and silver floral print. A large pink poster of the Eiffel Tower hangs above the sofa they're sitting on and in the corner is a stack of children's plastic toys. Frankie balances a mug on her leg, trying not to spill any tea on the cream carpet.

'Lily and I weren't colleagues, not really,' says Amber, leaning over to hand Gavin his mug. She has her hair in a ponytail and wears coral-pink jeans. 'I have a very select client list. Lily was a lost soul.' She sits down in a chair opposite. 'I only met her the once. At a sex workers' support group. I think she went along because she thought they might give her methadone. She was an addict. In the industry for all the wrong reasons.'

'But you both knew Donald Emneth?'

'Donnie is well known in the community. He's a sex maniac.'

Gavin chokes on his tea. 'The old guy?' he asks. He pulls a disgusted face and looks at Frankie, expecting her to share his dismay. Not for the first time, she wishes her cameraman were more discreet. She ignores him, burying her nose in her mug.

Amber looks unperturbed. 'Donnie's a sweet old thing. He's also very lonely, the sort who wants to imagine you're friends. You know, have a cuppa, chat about life.' She leans into the side of her chair, stroking some fluff off the arm of her cardigan. 'He's got this whole fantasy that he's just helping you out. There's no harm in him. He'd never have hurt Lily. Or the other girl, what was her name?'

'Sandra.'

Amber nods. 'That's why I called your newsroom. There's a lot of crap talked about sex work, but I've been doing it a while, and I can tell you, you get a feel for the dodgy ones. The ones who might want to hurt you. And you stay well clear. I've never felt nervous with Donnie.'

'How did he come up in conversation, given you only met Lily the once?'

'We were trying to talk to her about safety, get her to set limits on who she'd take on as a client.'

'You mean not get into strange guys' cars,' says Gavin. 'Isn't that the nature of the job?'

Amber looks irritated. 'It is for a streetwalker. Not for me.'

'Is that—' Gavin starts, but Frankie cuts him off before he can ask another question. 'What did Lily say about Donnie?'

'That he was one of her regulars. She'd got in his car a few times, and then he started seeking her out. We told her to try and only go with people like him, guys she'd met before and trusted.'

Frankie thinks about previous cases where sex workers have been murdered by men they've known for years, wonders if it's ever possible to know whether a punter is safe. But she keeps her suspicions to herself. Better to ask that on camera, than risk offending Amber now. 'You must be very fond of Donald Emneth, or think highly of him at least, to be doing this interview.'

'Well, I wouldn't say I was *fond* of him. But it's not fair, all the media coverage making out he's some sort of dangerous creep. And your news editor said I could be anonymous. And paid.' She folds her arms, eyeing them both. 'Though not much. Your company's a bit tight, isn't it?'

'We don't normally pay people anything at all for talking to us. We'd be bankrupt in a week,' says Gavin. 'Think about all the hundreds of interviews we do.' He and Amber stare at each other in mutual dislike.

'As far as making it anonymous,' Frankie says. 'How anonymous does it need to be? Unrecognisable to your mum or just casual passers-by?'

'My mum's dead,' says Amber. 'And I'm not ashamed of what I do. Only reason I want to be anonymous is so my little girl doesn't get a load of shit at school about Mummy being a prostitute.' She looks at Gavin. 'Lots of people have very backward views about sex work.'

They film Amber as a blurred silhouette against one of her grey walls, the ponytail down to disguise her profile even further. It's an uncomfortable interview. Amber has plenty to say off camera but once the record light is red, many of her answers dwindle to monosyllables. Even worse, although she tries to counteract the negative coverage of Donald Emneth, whenever she does manage a more detailed answer it ends up making the old man sound more, not less, alarming.

'I wouldn't go round his house in a hurry,' Gavin says, tucking the last of his camera gear into the car boot. He slams it shut. Frankie can see Amber's face at the window of the front room, watching them, as she walks round to the passenger side of Gavin's battered Toyota.

'I know,' she says, getting in and pulling the seat belt on. 'Why did she tell us he locked her up once? How can she possibly think that makes him look like Mr Nice Guy?' They reverse out of the driveway, Amber's face still in the glass. 'I can't imagine what a dodgy punter's like, if he's a safe one.'

'Though she says he only locked her up for company, an excuse for extra tea and biscuits,' Gavin says. 'A likely tale.' He pulls into the road, and Amber's flat slowly disappears in the rear-view mirror. 'Are you going to use it? It was the best bit of the interview.'

'Guess I'll have to. Though I'd rather not. We're meant to be helping clear his name and it just makes him look even crazier. And I know he's been released without charge, but who knows in a case like this?'

Gavin glances at her, then turns his face back to the road. 'If you don't use it, Luke Heffner will.'

'What's that supposed to mean?'

'He scooped us on our own interview last time. What was all that about?'

'Bloody hell!' Frankie thumps her head back against the seat in annoyance. 'You were there, Marks asked us not to record it! I didn't use it because I'm not a complete wanker.'

'I know that, Franks, and it makes you a nice person. But not always a good journalist.' He raises his voice to drown out her protest. 'Sorry, but it's true. I know Charlie always backs you up, but this is the type of story that could make or break you. It's massive. So you can either get a bit more ruthless, or get used to Luke from national leaving us in the shade.' He looks over at her again. 'And don't forget, Charlie's not in charge any more. It's Kiera you have to think about. She's not somebody you want to disappoint. Seriously.'

'I can't believe you're telling me to suck up to Kiera. She's a total cow.'

'All the more reason to suck up to her. Listen,' Gavin says, tapping his fingers on the wheel for emphasis. 'I've been in the business a lot longer than you.' Frankie rolls her eyes. 'No, listen to me, I have. Bosses like that, they come in and they're looking to get rid of people, put their own stamp on things, make a place their own. It's not just you, we've all got to be careful. Charlie too.'

'Well, cheers for the lecture, Gav,' she says, turning away from him and watching the houses flash past the window. 'But for your information, I'm about to go to Kiera with some digging I did at the weekend, so I don't think she's going to fire me *just* yet.'

By the time they're back at the newsroom Frankie and Gavin are friends again. She knows he's not a tactful man and despite numerous tiffs over the years, they never stay annoyed with each other for long. But his warning has made her more nervous about the meeting with Kiera. She's desperate to impress the new boss.

Charlie suggests they hold their catch-up in the kitchen over a cup of tea.

'So this Brett will definitely talk?' he says, once they're all installed at a table. He's lounging on the bench while Kiera sits stiffly at the end. 'It's quite a good line, if he did see somebody suspicious at the bar.'

'Yes, he told me he'd do an interview.' Frankie glances at Kiera. 'I can text him and ask if he's free tomorrow.'

'We should *definitely* pursue this,' says Kiera, drumming her pink shellac nails on the table. 'After all, Brett might turn out to be the killer, and then we'll be the only ones to have interviewed him.'

'I don't think he's a suspect,' says Frankie, alarmed by Kiera's lurch in logic. 'The interview would just be about what he saw, you know, the strange guy watching Ava.'

Kiera purses her lips. 'The only man we know for sure was watching Ava that night is *Brett*. That's if your little student stalker Laura is to be believed.' She taps her fingers in an aggressive tattoo. 'You've *always* got to question why people agree to talk to the press about a murder case. I can think of plenty of times where the guilty party's gone to the media to point the finger elsewhere. How do we know this creep that Brett *claims* he saw even exists?' Kiera pauses to examine a nail. 'What else do you have?'

'There's also the blog on that website I found.'

'Oh yes, what *was* that? Some saddo rambling online?'

'A bit more than that,' Frankie replies, bringing *Killing Cuttlefish* up on her laptop. 'I found this sexist website that a load of weirdos like to vent on. One of the guys who posts on it targeted Hanna, saying she lied in court, and the whole thing was so nasty she had to change her name. Now this same writer, who calls himself Feminazi Slayer, is attacking Sandra, Lily and Ava on the site, saying they all deserved what they got.'

'Lemme see that.' Kiera gestures impatiently for the computer.

Charlie and Frankie watch as she reads. A pink flush appears on her cheeks and her eyes widen. Frankie knows that feeling. For the first time since she's arrived, she feels a flicker of solidarity with her boss.

Eventually Kiera looks up and turns furiously to Charlie. 'Why haven't we been all over this?'

'The lawyers didn't want us to say too much, they thought—'

'Fuck the lawyers.' She shoves the laptop over to Frankie. 'We could have an exclusive insight into a serial killer right here. This is gold dust.'

Charlie makes a face. 'Isn't that a *bit* of a leap? The blogger's an arsehole, clearly, but we don't know he's the killer.'

'He targeted Hanna, didn't he? And now he's saying all the others got what was coming. Pretty damning circumstantial evidence if you ask me. And either way, people are lapping anything up on the Strangler right now, we'd be mad not to run it.' She jabs a pink fingernail towards them both. 'Right, Frances, script your piece with Emneth's prostitute pal as quick as you can, then leave it with Caz to edit. I want you live on the programme talking about this blogger. Who is he? Is he the guy running the website, or just some random nutter who mouths off on there with all the other freaks? He must be local to know all that stuff about Hanna. Call the police, see if you can get any more from them about whether they are investigating his posts or the site.'

'What about the lawyers?' Frankie says, looking nervously at Charlie.

'You let us deal with that,' Kiera says, getting up and waving Frankie off the bench. 'Go after this blogger as hard as you can. I don't want you pulling any punches. Let's flush the bastard out into the open.'

In the studio, the light on camera one is red. They're on air. Paul Carter has leaned forward, taking charge of the interview and partially blocking Zara from the shot. All that viewers at home will see are her legs, akimbo in her navy trousers. Sit forward! Frankie wills her friend, but Zara stays put.

'So, what have the police said, Frances?' asks Paul.

The red eye lights up on camera two as the director changes shot, and Frankie talks into its lens.

'At the moment, not much. They've confirmed that the blog post *is* forming part of their enquiries, and that Hanna did complain to them about the first post, nearly a year ago.' Paul has arranged himself into the pose of expectant listener, though she suspects he's simply counting down the seconds until the shot returns to his face. Zara, she can tell, is genuinely hearing what she says. And all the while she talks, the red light is shining. In Frankie's imagination it becomes the eye of the murderer, watching her. She knows, instinctively, that she is being observed by the man who killed Hanna and Sandra and Lily, the man who is holding Ava. And that killer, whoever he is, has a cheerleader, or if Kiera's correct, possibly even an identity: @Feminazi_Slayer2. She holds the printed sheet of her prepared speech so hard it begins to crumple in her hand. It doesn't matter. She isn't going to read it anyway.

'The thing about this blog, Zara' – she says, deliberately turning her shoulders slightly to include her friend – 'is the viciousness of its tone. Nasty, snide and above all threatening. It even ends with a plea that Hanna gets *what's coming to her*. Whatever that's supposed to mean. And all this about a girl who was *fifteen* at the time of the assault described, and just eighteen when she was killed. So what was so scary about Hanna that this writer felt the need to try and crush her? We know from her friends she was a brave, strong person, a young woman who managed to stand up to the man who had attacked her and get him put behind bars. This blog post,' she says, her voice starting to shake with anger, 'is a cowardly, anonymous attack. Just like whoever killed Hanna, Lily and Sandra was a coward.' In her earpiece Frankie can hear Priya urging her to wind it up, her tone increasingly insistent, but she hasn't finished. 'The writer of this post never dared confront Hanna in person with his sordid little argument. And now he's passing his time bravely maligning the reputations of murdered and missing women. But perhaps he would care to come on our programme one evening and explain himself? Unless he's too afraid to show his face.'

'Thank you, Frances,' says Zara, cutting in. 'We appreciate you keeping us up to date on the latest in the case. We turn now to another story . . .'

The red light is off camera two and Zara and Paul are talking to camera one. Frankie is out of shot. Clive the engineer comes up to her quietly and unclips the mic from her jacket. They're live so he can't say anything, but he looks at her as he winds up the wire, and shakes his head.

After the programme Priya is beside herself. She paces up and down during the debrief, wringing her hands. Frankie's other colleagues avoid her eye, all except Zara, who says nothing but slides into the seat next to her in a sign of solidarity.

'Frankie, what were you thinking? Offering some sort of personal ultimatum to the killer, for God's sake!'

'It was an ultimatum to the blogger. And it wasn't personal. I suggested he come on the programme.'

'A blogger who you compared to the killer for being a coward. Jesus, let's just hope the bastard doesn't decide to sue for defamation.'

'I think we could say most of it was fair comment,' says Charlie. 'Well, the stuff about it being snide and nasty.'

'If she'd left it there, fine, but Frankie went sailing well over the line. Emotional, baiting, what were you doing?' Priya looks very upset, as if she's taken her friend's mistake personally. Frankie bites her lip. The adrenalin from going live is wearing off and guilt and anxiety are creeping in to take its place.

'OK, if we can get over the *histrionics* here,' says Kiera, drawing out the word with her throaty smoker's drawl. 'I thought we really *owned* the story tonight. Nice little exclusive from Frances, and a bit of drama.' She leans back, her houndstooth jacket buckling to reveal the shine of its red lining. 'Imagine our ratings will shoot up.'

'So you're happy she just compared a blogger to a serial killer?' asks Priya.

'Yeah, that was going a bit far, but I'm not going to lose sleep over it.' Kiera tosses the auburn hair from her eyes. 'I can't really see this guy suing us. According to Frankie the IP address of this website *and* this mystery blogger are so encrypted, PC Plod can't even get the article removed, let alone find out who wrote it. We didn't name the website on air. And who knows? Maybe he *is* the killer.'

It feels uncomfortable being at odds with Priya and supported by Kiera. She can tell Priya is furious, even though she's stopped speaking. Frankie turns instinctively to Charlie, willing him to back her. He meets her eye. 'I think all that about defamation is probably true,' Charlie says, talking as if there's just the two of them there. 'I'm not so bothered about us being sued. I'm more concerned about the fact Frankie just issued a challenge to a potential serial killer, or at the very least a total madman, live on air. I'm not denying it would be a great exclusive if he came on the show,' he adds sarcastically, with a sidelong look at Kiera. 'I'm just concerned he might look for a rather more personal showdown.'

Ava

The room has shrunk even smaller than the box, consumed by my hunger. All the sandwiches have gone. So much for rationing. The only thing I have left is a single apple, but I don't dare eat it. That would mean I had nothing.

I feel faint, my head ready to split open from the pain. Everything is shaky, my body and my nerves. I managed to eke the water out over the last day and night, but now there's only a tiny splash left, barely enough to wet my lips. It takes all my willpower not to drink it. The only reason I don't is because I know how much worse I will feel afterwards.

I lie on the blankets in the corner, freezing but no longer energetic enough to keep pacing, and part of me wonders if it would be easier to fall asleep and never wake up. Just disappear into the blackness. I wish I could. I want to tell Matt that I understand now, that I don't blame him any more.

It's hard to tell if minutes or hours are passing. Time is collapsed by boredom and fear and hunger. I sit and stare at the ceiling, my arms around my knees, willing myself to stay strong. I think of our mum and her favourite phrase, the one that used to drive us crazy when she used it as a spur to get us through our homework, when we sat, slumped and grumbling at the kitchen table. '*Ne quittez pas!*'

I try but fail to imagine my mum in this place. She's not a person I like to picture hemmed in. I prefer to think of her as she usually is, in charge. As children, Matt and I nicknamed her Madame Souza after the French cartoon character from *Belleville Rendez-vous*, an indomitable grandmother who crosses the

Atlantic in a pedalo to rescue her grandson. Mum pouted when she first found out. '*La grand-mère*? That's how you see me?' But we could tell she was secretly pleased.

I know she will be thinking of me right now, willing me to survive. I hope to God she doesn't think I'm dead. She must know, she must *sense* somehow that I'm alive. I touch my face. It's wet again. I can't stop crying.

I must have dozed off where I sat without realising, or else my mind drifted off into nothingness, because the sound of the bolt scraping jolts me back into myself. I don't have the energy to stand. He strides in and I can see he's carrying a large plastic bag and heavy multipack of water. I burst into tears of relief. I'm not going to die yet. In that moment I almost want to hug him.

He drops the water on the floor where he's standing and holds the bag up, swinging it slightly. 'What do you say?'

His tone sounds angry, aggrieved almost. 'Thank you,' I reply, sniffing, trying to stop myself from crying. 'Thank you very much.'

He grunts and drops it on the floor, out of my reach. I'm desperate for a long drink of water, but know better than to ask. I can eat and drink when he's gone. He's watching me, eyes narrowed through the slits of the ski mask. I'm afraid of appealing to his human side again – my breast is still sore where he twisted it – but I have to keep trying. I reach for the apple beside me, the one I've been saving. It's the only thing I have to offer. My hand shakes as I hold it out to him.

'Would *you* like something to eat?'

For a moment we stare at each other. My right hand, clutching the fruit, hangs between us. I'm afraid he will accept out of spite, leaving me with less, or worse that the gesture will make him furious.

Slowly he shakes his head. Then he lowers himself to the floor, sitting cross-legged opposite me. 'Like Eve,' he says. I think there's humour in his tone, rather than anger. Or I hope so.

I think of Professor Marks and clench my hands. Could this monster be him? Surely he wouldn't do this to me. It *can't* be him. This man is shorter, and heavier, I'm sure of it. There's a tension to his limbs; he reminds me of a coil wound up and ready to spring. He taps his fingers on the concrete. An impatient gesture. 'Most women, whatever you do,' he says, 'they don't appreciate it. It's just endless whining.'

In spite of my fear I almost want to laugh. But I don't. 'I'm sorry you've had that experience.'

He makes a darting movement, leaning forwards and backwards where he sits. 'You're not going to fool me, you know. I know you're a filthy bitch like all the rest.' I watch his gloved fingers still drumming the floor. 'But at least you're a bitch with some manners. That's what's wrong with the world, Ava.' He sighs and shakes his head. 'Nobody has any fucking manners any more.'

I stare. He doesn't seem to be joking. 'I guess that's true.'

'You guess? Are you just parroting what I say?'

'No, I was thinking about some of the stories you read in the newspapers,' I lie, racking my brains for anything I might have come across. All I can think of are columnists complaining about the younger generation. 'You know, about manners. How we don't appreciate each other any more.'

'The fucking *media*. They're the worst of it.' He slaps the palm of his hand against the floor. 'Bunch of fucking liars. Fucking *fake news*. You know it's all run by feminists, don't you? The media?'

The only media baron I can think of is Rupert Murdoch. 'I . . . I don't know,' I stammer.

'Don't pretend, Ava. I know you're a little media whore. I *saw* you, flaunting yourself on the TV, waving a banner for your fucking animal rights, prattling on and on about it on some stupid YouTube channel.' I open my mouth, about to deny that I've ever been on YouTube, that he must have mistaken me for someone else, then I remember. A film student in her final year interviewed me for a university project. She must have posted it online. I realise he's looking at me, scrutinising my reaction, just as he must have been scrutinising me for weeks. 'That's right, bitch. Ought to have been more careful, didn't you? Never know who might be watching. You're almost as bad as Hanna bragging about how she was going to be a world-famous hairdresser.' He shakes his head. 'Still, at least neither of you are fat. Nothing pisses me off more than a fat bird on the telly. Fucking *nerve* of it.' He stares, still drumming his fingers on the concrete. 'Well? Aren't you going to say anything? You had enough to say when the cameras were rolling.'

I try to remember what I said to the film student but can't. 'I guess you're right, I guess some media can be misleading,' I say.

'*I guess you're right*,' he mimics me, putting on a high-pitched voice. 'What do you mean you fucking guess?' He gets to his feet and I scramble up instinctively, not wanting him to tower over me. He grabs hold of my upper arms. 'Just playing along, aren't you? I can tell you're a fucking blue pill bitch.' I have no idea what he's talking about. He grips my arms more tightly, brings his masked face close to mine. 'I said, *aren't you*?' His touch is worse than the sensation of wasps crawling over my skin. I'm desperate to shake him off, move away from him, but I can't. 'But don't worry,' he says, his voice crooning, 'you'll soon be swallowing the red pill.' He takes his right hand off my arm, flicks the side of my head. I flinch. 'That's all part of the experiment. Getting you to see the world as it really is.'

I've never wanted to get away from somebody so badly. I want to prise his fingers off me one by one, snapping them back like twigs. 'That sounds interesting,' I say. I try to look at him while I speak, but it's too difficult. I lower my eyes in what I hope looks like a modest gesture. 'I'd like to hear about it.'

'You're in too deep,' he says, but his grip on my arms loosens. 'I can't save you. You've been poisoned by all those blue pills.'

His words, however crazy, give me a sense of hope. I can feel the adrenalin kick in. Perhaps this is how I might persuade him to keep me alive. By becoming his re-education project. Dear God I'll sign up to *anything* to get out of here. 'Please,' I say. 'Please, tell me about it. I want to learn.'

He sits down heavily on the floor, pulling me down with him. I hit my coccyx landing on the concrete but try not to wince. 'It's the fucking feminists,' he says, shaking his head. 'They've ruined it for everyone.'

He starts on a crazy, rambling theory where blue pills are poisoning everyone and red pills are setting them free. I nod vigorously as he talks, occasionally adding a *how interesting*. Though not too often, I don't want to overdo it. The pressure of agreeing with him mixed with the terror of what he might do to me is stifling, like trying to breathe with a plastic bag over my face.

At one point he fetches the water and cracks open a bottle, meaning I finally get a drink too. He takes a swig, then passes it over. I hope this means he no longer finds me quite so disgusting. We're even sitting next to each other on the blankets in a hideous parody of friendship. 'I know you're all liars,' he says. 'I suppose you can't help it. Like children.'

'What do you think women lie about?'

'Don't give me that,' he says. 'You know. Everything. That's your default. Lies and fakery. It's what you do to get what you want, the same way a man uses his strength. That's what I'm testing in my little experiment. What happens to women under pressure. How they break apart.' He looks at me. I can't see his face properly through the ski mask, just the parts sunk into the roughly cut holes for his mouth and eyes. I'm not even sure how old he is. 'Where do the cracks start, Ava? When you apply that pressure. It's like taking a glass vase and, chip, chip, chip.' He mimics holding a chisel or pickaxe in mid-air. 'You keep going until the whole thing shatters.' He leans over and I stiffen, but all he does is take the water bottle off me. 'Not that Sandra and Lily were glass vases. More like dirty, maggoty containers. Hanna on the other hand.' He sucks his teeth. 'She was surprisingly resilient. Beautiful in her own way. It took me twelve days to smash her.'

Twelve days. Is that all I have? I feel like I'm going to be sick. In front of us is The Stain. *Hanna died in this room*, says the voice in my head, *they all did*. The fear is so intense I can feel it building in my mind like water behind a dam. Black spots swim before my eyes. I move my hands under my thighs so he can't see they're shaking. 'What happened to Hanna?' I say, amazed at how calm my voice comes out.

He chuckles. 'Now that would be cheating. You're so transparent.' He reaches out a gloved hand and touches my cheek. I bite my tongue trying not to flinch. 'Like a pretty piece of porcelain. But I can still smell your fear.' He leans in, burying his face in the side of my throat, breathing in deeply. The rough fabric of the mask scratches my skin.

An image flashes into my mind, brutal in its clarity. My hands taking hold of his head and twisting. Hard.

I look down at the black shape leaning against me. I would have to grab the sides of his mask, and it would be difficult to twist forcefully enough to break his neck. Am I really strong enough? In spite of myself I hesitate. The idea of killing, even killing this man, horrifies me.

He sits up again and the moment's lost. But inside me something has changed. For the first time I wonder if I should wait to be rescued. Perhaps I'm not as helpless as I seem. I don't know if he senses a shift in the atmosphere, but he gets up. I make a move to stand too, but he holds out a hand as a warning for me to stay where I am. I look up at him from the floor as he starts pacing. He seems distracted.

'Do you miss your family?'

The change in subject disconcerts me. Is it possible he's feeling sorry for me? 'Yes, I do. Very much.'

'I pity that poor pussy-whipped brother of yours. What's his name? Michael?'

I don't want to taint Matt's name by saying it aloud to this man, but I don't dare lie either. 'Matthew.'

'That's right, Matthew.' He sucks his teeth as he paces up and down. 'Bit of a delicate flower, wasn't he?'

'No.'

'Don't lie to me!' he bellows. I shrink back against the wall. The Stain is silhouetted behind him. 'Your fucking brother was a nut job! He was in a fucking psychiatric hospital!' He punches the side of the wall, breathing heavily; I can hear it come through in ragged bursts, distorted through the mask. 'Jesus! Women can't open their fucking mouths without lying.'

'Sorry.'

'You should be sorry. Now he's dead.'

I stare at the dark shape of him, leaning against the wall. My mind can't process what he's said. 'No.'

'Topped himself.'

'You're lying!' I spring to my feet and push him in the chest with both hands. He staggers backwards. '*You're lying! You're lying!*' He catches my wrists to stop me hitting him.

'Getting hysterical won't change the facts, will it?' I kick at his shins but he holds me off. 'Not so great for your parents. Losing both children like that. Maybe I ought to let you go.' He stops, as if suddenly stricken. 'I suppose that would be kindest.'

'You have to let me out, please, *please*, let me go!' I crumple, sobbing, but he holds me by the wrists to prevent me collapsing.

'Ask me *nicely*.'

With an effort I stand up, look straight into those brown eyes. '*Please* can I go home? *Please*.'

He stares back at me. I can't read his expression at all. For one moment I actually start to hope he might say yes.

'No!' He pushes me hard so I fall backwards on the floor. 'You can't!' He's almost doubled up laughing. 'I can't believe you thought I'd let you go, Ava. What sort of an idiot are you?' I don't reply. I can barely see for crying. He stoops down to look at me, still chuckling to himself. 'At this rate I should think you might not last as long as Hanna.' I stare at his muddy green boots. They move out of sight as he heads to the door. 'But at least then you'd get to see Matthew again. If you believe in that sort of thing.'

Frankie

Jack is sitting at the white countertop when she walks in, already a third of the way through a bottle of white wine and a giant bag of crisps.

'I managed to see the show tonight,' he says, pouring her a glass and refilling his own. 'That was a bit . . . well, *different*.'

'If you're about to have a go don't bother,' she says, dumping her bag and laptop by the door. 'Pretty much everyone else has.'

He holds the wine out to her, pale and inviting. 'All right, I won't then.' She stays by the door. 'Seriously. I'm sure you must have had a good reason for saying all that. Though I'm not sure what it was . . .' He trails off.

Frankie sighs and trudges over to join him. She takes the glass from his fingers and gulps down a mouthful of Chablis. It's cold and sweet. 'Not sure I did have a good reason, really,' she says. 'I think this story is getting to me. More than it should.'

'You might not like to hear this, but is it worth asking Charlie if you can take a break from it for a bit?'

'I'm sure he'd like nothing better. I've embarrassed him and Priya enough as it is. But Kiera was delighted. Thought I "owned it" apparently.'

'You did own it. But that's part of the problem. It's not your tragedy to own.'

'Easy enough for you to say, you're not speaking to the women's grief-stricken family and friends,' she says. 'And actually it does feel personal. That website. Seriously, Jack, the guys writing on there seem to despise women, *all* women. And I've spent hours racking my brains over the past weeks trying to think about some sort of connection between the women who've been kidnapped and there isn't one – *except they're all women* – yet somehow it's not a fucking hate crime, is it? It's only a hate crime if it's about race or religion. Hating women, well, that's just too run-of-the-mill for anyone to give a toss about.' To her own surprise, Frankie is almost shaking with emotion.

'Come on, isn't that a bit extreme? You'll be quoting Germaine Greer next.'

'Yeah? Well maybe women *don't* have any idea how much men hate them,' she snaps. 'It's not a fucking joke.'

'Sorry,' he says, putting an arm round her shoulders, which stay stiff. 'I didn't mean to wind you up. But I think you're wrong, the police do give a toss about it. They don't have to call it a hate crime to care about what's happening. And plenty of men get murdered too, don't they?'

'They don't get murdered *because they're men*,' she says, trying not to lose her temper completely. 'They get murdered as individuals, or because somebody wants their money or their drugs or their car, or they've had a fight about something. It's not the same.'

Jack shrugs. 'Don't suppose it makes much difference to the dead guys though. And actually men *do* get murdered because they're men. All the shootings and stabbings out there, it's mainly guys at the receiving end. Men are far more likely to be the victim of violent crime than women, by a long shot.'

Frankie grips her wine glass. The knot of rage inside her is so tight she wants to find relief by hurling it to the floor, hear the smash and watch the silver shards dance across the tiling. She thinks about Sandra and Lily and Hanna and Ava, all destroyed by the killer's sense he owned their bodies and their lives. And he's still out there, laughing at them all; at the police, the journalists, the women's families. And now she's got a focus for her anger. Kiera's notion that @Feminazi_Slayer2 is the killer is infectious, she can't get the idea out of her head. His mocking tone, belittling Hanna, laughing at her pain. She remembers his parting shot: *You better hope nobody **really** gives you what's coming to you. BITCH.*

Frankie takes a sip of wine, trying to count to ten, to calm herself down. It isn't fair to make Jack the target of all her angst, even though she wishes he had understood, rather than trying to argue. 'Yes, I know men get killed too and that's awful,' she says, slowly. 'But that's not the point I was making.'

On the walk into the newsroom the next morning, mist rises from the river and she can feel the autumn chill in the air. It's early October, and handfuls of russet leaves swirl past her ankles as she crosses the small patch of green outside the Eastern Film Company. Traffic heads past her on the road that surrounds the office, marooning the redbrick building onto its own miniature island. She left the Fiat in the office car park last night, hoping to clear her head on the walk home, and this morning she's miscalculated the time it will take her to get in. It's very early; nobody will be there except for Charlie and perhaps today's producer.

She crosses the busy road and cuts into the narrow warren of lanes that make up Norwich's old town. She loiters past The Hive, looking in at the book display, before stopping off at a nearby coffee shop. Andy Williams is playing, making a soothing back-drop to the hiss and gurgle of the coffee machine as the waiter heats up the milk. She thanks him and pays up, sipping the hot latte on her way back. By the time she makes it into the newsroom, her cheeks are red and she feels better about the day ahead.

All the TV screens are on; various channels showing breakfast television play out silently. The room is nearly empty, although the new trainee is hunched over a computer in the corner. Charlie has his back to her. Sitting perched on the desk beside him is Priya, her furry ankle boots dangling as she leans over to look at his screen. Frankie's stomach drops. She hopes they've both forgiven her. As Priya spots Frankie, she waves her over, then nudges Charlie, who turns round to look.

'Frankie.' His voice is flat. They are both staring at her, grim-faced.

'What is it?' she asks, a fluttering in her chest.

'You'd better come here,' he says.

She walks towards them and sees the familiar masthead of *Killing Cuttlefish* on his screen, but he minimises the tab before she can see more. 'You've got to be kidding me. Has the guy complained?' she asks, incredulous.

'I don't think she needs to see this,' says Priya.

'What don't I need to see?'

Charlie reaches out and grabs the back of a chair, rolling it along on its wheels until it's resting in front of her. He pats it. 'Take a seat,' he says. 'Look, I'm afraid that creep Feminist Slayer, or whatever he calls himself, has written a blog post about you. And Priya's right, you really don't need to read it, it's pretty unpleasant. We'll be putting a call in to report it to the police.'

'The police?' Frankie thinks of the red light above the camera. So he did have his eye on her yesterday. The consequences of her challenge are so obvious, she can't believe she didn't anticipate this. *Of course* he's not going to come on the programme and explain himself; much easier to attack her online instead. She's half tempted to take their advice and avoid reading it, but knows it's only a matter of time before curiosity makes her crack. 'Let me see,' she says more steadily than she feels.

'Frankie,' Priya says, putting a hand on her arm. 'I really don't think you should. He's just a sick bastard, ranting because you caught him out. Don't give him the satisfaction of letting his twisted words into your head.'

She looks from Priya to Charlie, taking in their glum faces. It's obviously bad. 'Fuck it,' she says at last. 'I'm a hack. We see hideous stuff all the time, this is just a stupid blog post. You know I'll read it at some point. Might as well be now.'

'Well, I'll go get us all a cup of tea,' says Charlie, who can't have missed the Styrofoam cup in her hand and is clearly only exiting the scene to spare her – or perhaps his – embarrassment. As he moves, she rolls the chair up to his computer and clicks open the tab. The first thing she sees is the image. Her face, digitally bloated and superimposed onto the body of a harpy with shrivelled pendulous breasts, sits above the blog's title: **Fatty Larch gets her Knickers in a Twist.**

She looks up at Priya, raises an eyebrow in a gesture of bravado she doesn't feel. 'Well, at least it comes with a flattering photo,' she says, turning back to read.

The Eastern Film Company's fattest female reporter, Frances 'I'll-go-on-a-diet-tomorrow' Larch, has got herself all hot and bothered over this website's exposure of the Gynocracy's lies.

A paid-up Feminazi of the shrillest type, Fatty Larch made a tear-ful appeal on the local yokel news last night after Yours Truly pointed out that supposed sweetie pie Hanna Raynott-Chivers was in fact a lying little slag. Fatty has a soft spot for slags – being one herself – and seemed to feel that reporting THE TRUTH about Hanna, Lily, Sandra and the rest of them is a crime **because they're dead**. Boo Hoo, and a great loss to the world that is, etc. etc. It also seems to have escaped Fatty's notice that Slaggy Hanna was still alive and well when the first post went up OVER A YEAR AGO.

Fatty then proceeded to compare Yours Truly to our friend the Norfolk Strangler. Now I'm no particular admirer of the Strangler's modus operandi, though he does seem to be picking off **whores** rather than innocent women, so far as I can see. That aside, the last time I checked, blogging and murdering were two separate activities.

But Fatty seems to feel Yours Truly is involved in some way, so perhaps we should turn her fantasy into reality.

If you're reading this Mr Strangler, why not pick off a few more slags, then we can see if their tragic demise makes Fatty's head explode. I'd watch that on TV. Or better still, why not go for Fatty herself? She fits the slag bill perfectly. Like the rest of her shrieking sisterhood in the MSM she's a talentless little cocksucker who gets her stories from blowing men in high places. Her cunt's prob-ably seen more dicks than a hooker feeding a meth habit.

So if you're feeling murderous, Mr Strangler, you can find Fatty at the HQ of the Eastern Film Company. Failing that, she lives at the posh new development on King Street. You can enjoy lovely views of the riverside from her flat there as she chokes her last. The cow drives a red Fiat 500, RV65 reg so you should know when she's home.

Bye-Bye, Fatty. Enjoy meeting the Strangler. Hope he rapes you first, **BITCH**.

Frankie's face is blazing hot with anger, fear and embarrassment. To her annoyance she realises her hands are trembling. She clenches them to make it stop.

She's read much worse than this, but nothing has quite prepared her for the unpleasantness of being the focus of another person's hate. The tone, which swings from childish to obscene, would be bad enough, but she feels physically sick when it sinks in that this man has posted up her address for any murderous individual to see.

'I've been such an idiot,' she says, pushing the rolling chair backwards from the desk with force. She nearly bowls into Charlie, who is hovering behind her with three mugs in his grasp. He winces as hot liquid slops over one hand. 'Sorry,' she says. 'And I'm even sorrier for what I said on air last night.'

'It wasn't the smartest thing you've ever done,' he says. 'But this isn't your fault. The guy is clearly bonkers, and an absolute arsehole to boot. Even if your live about this website had been totally straight, he'd still have written it. Just calling him out was enough.' Charlie glances around the near-empty newsroom. There's no sign of Kiera but he still lowers his voice. 'And we all know you were encouraged to go after him.'

Priya nods. 'Charlie's right, the guy's unhinged. Any criticism of his precious world view and he obviously gets the poisoned pen out. I've been through his stuff online, and he's even had a pop at Sandi Toksvig and Jessica Ennis-Hill.'

'But how does he know where I live?' Frankie says. 'He must have been physically stalking me *before* the live. No way would he have had time to find all that out about my address between half six and' – she looks at the screen – '2.16 a.m. when this was posted. And how did you guys see it?'

There's an uncomfortable pause. 'He emailed it to everyone in the management team,' says Charlie.

'Great. So he knows you all by name?'

'It's not *that* hard to work out who we are,' says Priya. 'Not if you watch the programme regularly and do a bit of googling.'

'You'd have to be pretty determined though,' says Frankie. She looks around nervously. 'What does Kiera say to all this? Where is she?'

'She's not in yet,' says Charlie. 'But I called her first thing and she'll be with you when the police are here. They want to ask a few questions, get as much info as they can on this guy.'

'The police are coming to the office?' Frankie says. 'Well, that's great, everyone will have read the bloody thing by lunchtime.'

'If you think *anyone* here would read that shit and not be on your side, you don't know us very well,' says Priya, leaning over and pressing a hand to her shoulder. 'But we do have to take it seriously, this guy has encouraged a threat to your life. And he obviously knows rather a lot about the programme and who works here. We need to review our security arrangements.'

'And there are some positives,' says Charlie, forcing his voice to sound cheerful. 'If this guy is trying to make contact with Norfolk's most wanted, that means he can't be the killer himself, surely? So the chances are he's just some creep, howling into the void.'

Frankie shrugs. 'I *guess*, though all that protesting that he's not murdered anyone could just be a decoy.'

'Well, there *is* one definite upside,' he counters. 'No more self-shooting for a bit. That's got to be a bonus.'

Seeing the filthy look Priya shoots Charlie for his lame attempt at a joke, Frankie almost feels better. Then she remembers the blogger's invitation: *You can enjoy lovely views of the riverside from her flat there as she chokes her last.* Nausea rises in her stomach and she excuses herself, heading to the bathroom.

She sits in the newsroom kitchen, slumped over her laptop. Far from it being a bonus not interviewing Brett until later in the morning, Frankie has found there's little to distract her from fretting. Everyone has been understanding, as Priya predicted, but it's still embarrassing. She's moved from her desk to be out of sight, spending time clearing her email backlog and drinking her way through several instant coffees, but she keeps finding herself staring listlessly at the screen.

All she can think about is the blog. She clicks onto a rival news website, looking at their coverage of the Norfolk Strangler. There's a new update on the murder victims all being the target of an online hate campaign. Kiera will be delighted at their exclusive getting airtime. No doubt Frankie's misery will seem a small price to pay for it. Thankfully the blog about *her* hasn't been reported. She sits up a little straighter. The blogger is still the story, she isn't, and unmasking him is a legitimate use of her time.

She opens the search engine, looking at the empty search bar, not wanting to bring up *Killing Cuttlefish* onto her screen. Her fingers hover over the keyboard. The site's odd title is still a mystery. She types 'women+sexism+cuttlefish' into the waiting white box, then scrolls down the results. The first only show texts that include women and sexism, but halfway down the page, to her surprise, she sees a suggestion that highlights the third word of her search.

It's a link to a page called '*ON WOMEN*'. Beneath the title, a snippet of the relevant text appears . . . and the **cuttlefish** with its dark, inky fluid, so Nature has provided ***woman*** for her . . .

Frankie opens the page, eyes scanning the blur of words to find the highlighted passage. Random phrases briefly catch her attention as she reads. Women . . . **are big children all their lives, something intermediate between the child and the man . . . Just as the female ant after coition loses her wings . . . Hers is reason of very narrow limitations . . .**

Then, halfway through the text, she finds what she's looking for. **Nature has not destined them, as the weaker sex, to be dependent on strength but on cunning; this is why they are instinctively crafty, and have an ineradicable tendency to lie. For**

as lions are furnished with claws and teeth, elephants with tusks, boars with fangs, bulls with horns, and the cuttlefish with its dark, inky fluid, so Nature has provided woman for her protection and defence with the faculty of dissimulation . . .

'Fucking hell,' Frankie says to herself. She returns to the top of the essay, to see the author of the hideous screed, and catches her breath. It's by Arthur Schopenhauer. She sits back, remembering the touch of Brett's hand on her arm as he leaned in, telling her about the importance of philosophy. Is it possible that the man she thought she and Zara were reeling in had in fact played her for a fool? Is this the sort of website a Schopenhauer devotee might set up? Could all Brett's charm towards women, all those compliments, be a cover for contempt? Then an even darker thought grips her. Perhaps Kiera was right and there was no mystery man at the bar; Brett is covering his own tracks, not for the website, but for something much worse.

She has the urge to run over to the newsdesk, grab Charlie and tell him she's too frightened to do the interview. Then she takes a deep breath and closes her eyes. She can't give in to panic. She goes back to the search results and types in 'Schopenhauer+anti-feminism'. Immediately hundreds of results come up. She scrolls down the page, breathing out slowly. Brett's study of Schopenhauer could be pure coincidence; the philosopher is quoted on dozens of sexist websites, along with other famous thinkers of his era. She looks up Schopenhauer's Wikipedia page and ***On Women*** seems to be a very minor, if controversial, part of his work. Perhaps Brett isn't even studying it. She's still staring at the entry, trying to dispel the sick feeling from her stomach, when Nick from the sports desk comes over to the table.

'Hey Frankie. There's a caller come through for you, can you take it?'

The last thing she feels like doing is speaking to a random right now, but she can't hide from one of the most basic duties of her job. 'Did they say what it was about?'

'It was a guy wanting to talk about Donald Emneth.'

'OK. I'll go to my desk and you can put it through.'

She heads back into the newsroom. Nobody stares at her; everyone seems busy with their own story or deadline, just as they always are. She sits at her desk, nodding at Nick. The phone rings and she picks up. 'Frances Latch here.'

'Miss Latch, my name's Grant Allen, I'm calling about your report on Donald Emneth.' The speaker's voice is harsh. A smoker, she thinks.

'Which report would that be?' She tightens her grip on the receiver, steeling herself for the complaint or conspiracy theory she feels sure is coming next.

'The one when the hooker said he was all right.'

'Okaaaay,' she says slowly, hackles rising at his choice of word. 'What about the report?'

'The hooker had a point. He's been released without charge, but the man's still had his name trashed. It's outrageous. I'd like to come on your show and talk about it. That's what I do, see? My organisation, Justice for Jailbirds, it's all about giving the other side of the story ...'

'But Mr Emneth hasn't been to jail.'

'He spent a night or two in the cells, didn't he?'

The voice on the phone sounds aggrieved. Frankie rubs one hand across her eyes, wishing she hadn't picked up. She softens her voice. 'Yes, that's true. Listen, Mr Allen, what you say sounds very interesting, but there are strict rules about what we can and can't report when a case is active. This is a live murder investigation and we have to be very careful we don't prejudice any future trial ...'

'Yes, yes, I know all that,' says Grant Allen, tetchily. 'I'm not a fool. But he's been released without charge. He's no longer a suspect. So it's fine to run a story on how he's been treated badly.'

It's Frankie's turn to feel annoyed. 'There's currently one woman missing and three dead,' she snaps. 'Whatever injured feelings Mr Emneth may have don't really compare, do they?' There's silence on the other end of the phone. 'Mr Allen?'

'I heard you. Not sure that's a very responsible attitude for a journalist though. Defaming somebody doesn't matter because it's not as bad as murder, is that what you're saying?'

Frankie doesn't feel up to this today. She looks round at the newsdesk, desperate to palm her irritating caller off onto Charlie. For once the workaholic editor's seat is empty. 'The Eastern Film Company hasn't defamed anyone,' she says. 'And I didn't mean to sound abrupt. I'm not dismissing Mr Emneth's situation, I'm sure it's all been very stressful for him, but I don't think our viewers would be too sympathetic to hearing his story right now. Maybe when the real killer is caught, we might talk to you again about running something on the issue then?'

'If that's the best you can offer, I suppose it will have to do.'

Frankie makes a mental note never to speak to the man again. 'Thanks for your call, Mr Allen,' she says sweetly. 'Have a nice day.'

The police turn up half an hour before she's meant to be meeting Brett. She texts to apologise for delaying the interview and he sends back a string of kisses, which makes her cringe. She tells herself he might be like that with everyone.

The two police officers suggest speaking somewhere quiet, and Kiera shuts them all into her office. The glass is frosted for privacy but it still feels like passing buses are going to rattle the windows off their hinges. Frankie has sat in this room many times with her old boss David, for annual chats about career goals or to bounce around ideas for longer investigations, but it no longer feels familiar. All trace of his personality has been removed. The framed Norwich FC shirt he had on the wall is gone, leaving just a dark rectangle where it prevented the wallpaper from fading. Kiera has not yet moved anything personal into the room to replace it.

Frankie wishes it were Charlie here, rather than Kiera. Her boss is sitting, naturally enough, at her desk, but it has created a curious power dynamic with Frankie and the two policemen ranged round her, as if she is conducting the interview. DI Tom Osmond and DC Dan Avery have been friendly enough so far, commiserating with her over the unpleasantness of it all, though the older man, Tom Osmond, seems to be listening less attentively than his junior partner. Frankie is relieved she's never filmed either of them, or had a chance to piss them off with an awkward news report.

'So, just to go through the basics,' says Tom Osmond, licking a finger and flipping through the pages of his pad. He's a heavy man with burst blood vessels across his cheeks; he looks as though he spends more of his time at a carvery than chasing villains. 'Any contact with this blogger before?'

'None,' says Frankie. 'I mean we did try and send him a message through the website yesterday before the broadcast to give a right to reply. The site has a sort of generic contact form, not a proper email address. But nothing came back, from him or the site.'

DI Osmond nods. 'And no sense of who this Slayer person might be?'

Frankie opens her mouth to speak but Kiera jumps in. 'Obviously not,' she says.

Dan Avery is watching Frankie. 'Nobody who might have taken offence at a story recently?' His body language, leaning over towards her, partly blocking Kiera from view, deliberately shuts out her boss.

'Well,' she says. 'There was one guy we did a piece on recently, Martin Hungate. It was about him turning away from domestic violence. He wrote in and complained about me. And then my boyfriend and I bumped into him in Wells and he made it clear he still wasn't happy.'

'How did he make it clear?' Avery asks. 'Did he threaten you?'

'No, no, not at all. He just got a bit shouty. Really, it was nothing awful.' She shrugs. 'It happens.'

DI Osmond blows his cheeks out like a hamster ejecting nuts. 'Well,' he says. 'I suppose it's *something* to go on.'

'Did you report this exchange to anyone in the newsroom?' asks Avery.

'I wish you'd come to *me*, Frances,' Kiera interrupts. 'You know you can talk to me about anything.' She turns to the police. 'The safety of my staff is *paramount*.'

To look at her, you'd never think Kiera had been the one urging Frankie to flush out the blogger. The sympathetic tone is so convincing, she can't help staring at her boss, lips parted with surprise. 'Not to worry,' says Osmond, mistaking her confusion for embarrassment. 'It can be hard to admit you're upset by these things, it's tempting to ignore them or try to handle it yourself. Just make sure you report anything like that in future.'

'Anybody else who might have a grudge?' asks DC Avery.

'A few complaints in the past year,' says Frankie, thinking of an apoplectic colonel who ranted down the phone at Charlie for ten minutes over a report she had done on the fox-hunting ban. She briefly considers mentioning Brett, then dismisses the idea: studying Schopenhauer isn't a crime. 'But nothing really out of the ordinary.'

'If you could make a note of names and send us any emails you've saved, that would be useful,' says Avery, handing her a card. 'You've got all my contact details on there.'

'It was you who interviewed Donald Emneth too, wasn't it?' says Osmond, sitting back in his chair and hooking his thumbs into his belt. 'Now, *there's* an angry man. Blames all of you lot in the media for his arrest, as if it wasn't his own choice to go and shoot his mouth off. Another one that's worth watching.'

Frankie remembers the old man gazing at her breasts and pestering her for her number. It feels like every lunatic in Norfolk with a grudge has her on his radar. Her shoulders ache, wound tight by anxiety. She glances at Kiera. She wishes her boss wasn't here, listening to her fears. 'The thing I'm most concerned about,' she says, trying to talk as if she's alone with the police, 'is if this blogger is actually mixed up in the murders. Isn't it possible Feminazi Slayer might be the killer? Whoever the guy is, he seems to be local, he targeted Hanna and now he seems obsessed with the murder case.' Frankie ticks each point off with her fingers as she goes through the list, then looks at the two officers for confirmation. 'I mean, isn't that what killers do, obsess about their own crimes?' Osmond's sceptical expression makes her pause but she pushes on. 'And what if posting my address is just to create more suspects, make it harder to work out who the killer is, if I'm . . . If anything happens to me,' she finishes, unable to spell out her deepest fear more clearly. 'I'm not asking as a journalist, and I don't mean to be melodramatic,' she adds, seeing Osmond raise an eyebrow. 'I'm just scared.'

'Is there anything else that's made you think the blogger might be the killer?' Avery asks, studying her closely. 'Or any other messages you've been sent beside the blog?'

Frankie shakes her head.

'Well, look, *off the record*' – DI Osmond makes quote marks in the air – 'this blogger isn't our number one suspect. Of course we'd like to know who it is, eliminate them from our enquiries, but there's not an anonymous silhouette of this man sitting at the centre of a pin board in the Major Crime Unit. It's more likely a nasty little crank, that's our feeling.' His speech is meant to be reassuring, Frankie knows, but she finds it doesn't have the desired effect. She'd be happier if finding Feminazi Slayer *was* their number one priority, then they might actually stop him. 'Right, so on to the safety stuff.' Osmond turns to Avery, waving a large hand at him. 'You OK to go over this?'

Avery hands Kiera and Frankie a couple of print-outs. 'All our advice is written on here. The main thing, Miss Latch, is to try not to travel alone if you can help it, have a phone with you and always let other people know where you're going. Also, this Feminazi Slayer guy is online, so if I were you, I'd be particularly wary of social media – don't post anything for a while, be careful about what you do post, change all your passwords and up your security settings.'

'When do you think you might be able to get the blog down?' she says. 'My address is still up there for any violent psycho to see. Not to mention all the other crap.'

'We're working on it,' says DC Avery. 'The website isn't registered in the UK, so we're having some problems identifying who owns it as well as who posts there. Unfortunately we have to find out who runs the site before we can take it down.'

Frankie makes a face. 'Great,' she says.

'As for the rest of the newsroom,' says Tom Osmond, standing up, followed swiftly by Kiera. 'It's good you've got CCTV and a security guard at the entrance. But still worth everyone here being told they need to be extra vigilant.'

Kiera opens the door and they all file through. 'We can show ourselves out,' says DI Osmond, shaking her and Kiera's hands in turn. 'Try not to worry, ladies. It's very upsetting, but if it's any consolation, this sort of nastiness online is getting more and more common, and ninety per cent of the time it's just empty threats. Not to belittle what you're going through, of course, but it rarely amounts to anything more than a bad taste in the mouth.'

Dan Avery takes Frankie's hand. His eyes are dark grey in his sharp elfin face. 'You have my card,' he says. 'Anything that happens, or anything else that occurs to you. Call me.'

She stands next to her boss, watching Ernie the security guard let the two policemen out of the building. Kiera turns to Frankie, smiling her unfriendly smile. 'I liked the whole damsel in distress line, getting them to give us that tip-off about the investigation,' she says. 'Good work.'

Frankie tries to smile back. She doesn't want to tell her boss that being frightened wasn't a line, it was the truth.

Ava

It's daytime. I know this because of the light falling through the grille, but I no longer move to feel the sun on my face.

Sometimes I wish it was over. I wish I was dead.

When he left me I screamed until I couldn't speak, howling all my grief for Matt into this hideous cell. I want to dissolve, to be nothing, to never wake up. Is this what my brother felt like too?

Sometimes I think it can't be true. That he would never do this to Mum and Dad, not with me gone. And he wouldn't give up on me so soon, *he wouldn't*. I keep telling myself this, but I don't know what to believe. About my brother, about anything. I don't know if this man might be Peter Marks. I don't think so, but he's not spoken in that voice again, not used his gestures, so I can't scrutinise him to see if it's an impression or not. The first time was too much of a shock to judge properly. I wasn't expecting it.

The light moves across the cell and I start to feel angry. What good will my death do anybody? It's just giving this pathetic bastard what he wants. Then I think of Matt and the pain threatens to drown me. If I'm to survive I can't go down that path. I have to believe Matt is alive, and if he isn't . . . I dig the nails into my palms so hard it hurts. 'If you aren't,' I say aloud to my brother, speaking to the empty room. 'Then it's even more important I get out for Mum and Dad. I love you, but I'm not going to think about you any more.'

I try to channel my anger, hang on to it. Rage makes me feel more alive, it's a better emotion than despair. *I have to get out of here*. I think about the bastard's head resting against me and I kill him over and over again, replaying all the possible methods in my mind.

Gradually the idea moves from fantasy to planning. I'd have to take him completely by surprise. Even then, I don't think I could overpower him. He looks strong, and I'm only going to get weaker on a diet of apples and egg sandwiches. If I'm going to have any chance at all, I have to try soon. Debris from the box was the only weapon to come my way so far and I was too weak and stunned to make use of it. Though there are also the plastic bags.

I look at one folded on the floor, underneath the apples. I allow myself to imagine wrestling it over his head, holding the plastic tight while he gasps his last, the gaping mouth visible through the blue and red label, his legs kicking and thrashing on the floor, until he's not moving. My mind leaps to rifling through his pockets, finding the keys, opening the door – just a few yards in front of me – then escaping and screaming for help. I want to get out so desperately and my imagination is so vivid that thinking about it, my heartbeat accelerates as if it's really happening.

Then the images in my head take a darker turn. Rather than overpowering him, he easily manages to take the plastic bag off me, grabs me round the throat and then . . . I screw my eyes shut, shaking my head, not wanting to picture my own death. Arms round my shoulders, I rock back and forth, taking deep breaths, proving to myself that it's only my imagination; in reality I am still alive.

Suffocation. Is that how the other women died?

I stare at The Stain. That's all that will be left of me, a smudge, a lingering smell in this hideous room for the next woman to find. Or it will be if I don't try something. The risks involved are so huge I can barely comprehend them. If I make an attempt on his life, I might be bringing forward my own death. But if I don't? I want to believe the police will find me, but in my gut I know I'm on borrowed time, waiting for him to kill me.

Unless I kill him first.

Frankie

Brett is waiting for her outside The Blue Bicycle, taking a drag from a cigarette. He's a very different smoker from her cameraman Ray, who snatches his nicotine in angry shameful huffs, wolfing down cigarettes like candy in between filming jobs. Brett has his eyes half closed, and leans against the wall as if he's the leading actor in a film, savouring a moment between takes.

'Fancies himself a bit, doesn't he?' Gavin whispers, thankfully not quite loudly enough for Brett to hear. 'Bet he's a player.' She wonders if he's wistful. Gavin has been married to Monica for more than thirty years and has three adult children who, it seems to Frankie, are forever tapping him for cash.

'Imagine you broke a few hearts in your day,' she says, although she isn't sure that's true.

'Nah,' he says. 'Only ever one girl for me. Wouldn't change it.'

Gavin hasn't mentioned the blog, a rare example of tact that she's grateful for. At the moment all she wants is to feel like a professional, not an object of pity.

Brett spots them walking down the street and extinguishes the cigarette, grinding it out under the heel of his shoe. He holds a hand out to Gavin, his eyes lingering on the camera. Surely he can't have set up *Killing Cuttlefish*, Frankie thinks, still less be Feminazi Slayer.

'I'm afraid we can't film inside the bar after all,' he says. 'The manager wasn't too happy at the idea. Not ideal, the place being associated with a serial killer.'

'Never know, might be good for business,' says Gavin. Frankie snorts. 'What? No need to laugh. People are ghoulish.'

'Well, either way, he's not budging,' Brett says.

Frankie and Gavin exchange glances. That's going to complicate their filming. They had imagined lots of shots of Brett going about his business, mixing a drink, looking meaningfully over the bar. 'Any chance I could speak to him?' she asks. 'We'd be careful how we filmed it.'

Brett shakes his head. 'There's no point, he won't agree. And I'd rather not push it.'

In Frankie's experience, there's always a point in asking twice. On the other hand, she doesn't want to annoy Brett before they've shot a frame. 'OK. Well, we're on the edge of Tombland.' She turns to Gavin. 'We could do the interview on a bench near the river, and get some set-up shots now, maybe walking along the street by the bar?'

Gavin shrugs. 'It'll have to do, I suppose.' He puts down the camera and starts setting up his tripod. 'If the pair of you head back up there' – he points up the hill – 'then walk down the street towards me, I'll pan off the front of the bar and get a few shots. And make sure you chat a bit, don't just plod along saying nothing.'

Frankie and Brett set off. She hopes Gavin doesn't want to film them walking from behind; her backside must be twice the size of Brett's. Would somebody that suave come up with a childish nickname like Fatty? She looks up at him, feeling a little nervous. She wishes the blog hadn't made her so paranoid. They pause at the top of the hill, then start walking towards Gavin after he gives a wave. 'So you saw Ava and her friends around a bit,' she says. 'Did you know any of them well?'

'One of them.'

'The guy who was there that night or the girl?'

Brett shoots a sharp glance at her. 'The girl. Laura,' he says. 'Actually we had a thing. Nothing serious, but she got a bit intense. I think we only went for drinks a couple of times, that was the extent of it, but she got the wrong idea.'

They walk past Gavin and carry on. 'OK, that's good,' he yells, grabbing his tripod and crossing the street. 'Now if you can walk past me I'll shoot it from the side.' The pair of them troop part way back up the hill.

'What do you mean, the wrong idea?' Frankie asks as they set off again.

'OK, stop and turn back,' Gavin shouts. They obey, turning round as if in the world's slowest, most eccentric dance.

'She wanted a boyfriend,' says Brett. 'And I'm a mature student. It's flattering, but I'm not going to have masses in common with an undergraduate. I'm nearly thirty.'

'I think lots of thirty-year-old guys would be delighted by the idea,' Frankie says.

'Well, I'm not most men.' He smiles at her, holding her gaze for a moment, then looks away. 'I prefer a woman who's lived a little. It's sexier.'

Frankie's glad he isn't looking at her. She's not sure how to reply.

'OK. That's enough. I got the shot,' Gavin calls. 'You two can just stay there while I film the outside of the bar.'

They stop and Brett catches her arm. 'Look, I'm sorry if I embarrassed you, but you're very pretty, that's all.' He looks straight at her, making it hard to avert her eyes. 'I hope you don't mind me saying so.'

This is the moment Frankie should tell him she's flattered but she has a boyfriend. She hesitates. They haven't filmed the interview yet, and she knows Kiera doesn't want Brett talking to any other news outlets. She can't afford to piss him off. She looks down at the floor in what she hopes might be taken as shyness. 'That's very kind of you,' she mumbles. After what seems an age Brett moves his hand. She glances up at him again. A chill runs through her. Rather than the smirk she's expecting, his expression is hard and calculating. He looks like he's sizing her up. She takes a step back. 'I'd better see if Gavin needs a hand.'

She has never had a boss sit in on an entire edit before. It's not a comfortable feeling. Kiera keeps looming over the keyboard, taking control of the playback. Frankie had thought she might soften up after the police visit, but if anything she seems to be pushing her even harder.

'Let's hear that last bit again,' Kiera says, frowning. Caz duly obliges, and Brett's stunning face becomes mobile on the screen.

'I don't want to make too much of it. But I did notice a guy watching them. He was slim, dark, I didn't get the best look at his face, the lighting's pretty dim in the bar. But he had definitely clocked them.'

'And you thought this man looked a bit sinister? Why?'

'Just a bit off. Creepy if you like. But like I said before, it's not that unusual. It's a bar after all, guys get pissed, check women out and ...'

Kiera waves a hand. 'We can come out after he says the guy was creepy. Jesus, your barman could be a lawyer for all the caveats he keeps offering.' She shoots a dirty look at Frankie. 'And you don't exactly press him too hard.'

'Well, he's not a suspect. Just a witness. I didn't think it was appropriate.'

'He's not a suspect *yet*,' says Kiera. 'But if he does turn out to be the killer, that's when all this material will really be worth something. He's still our only witness for this supposed creepy guy. Could just be a ruse to throw suspicion elsewhere.' She takes a sip of tea, leaning back in her chair. The fact her team has been talking to a potential murderer doesn't seem to perturb her at all. 'But even if he *is* the killer, he's still a dull interviewee. The only other vaguely interesting remark was when he said the girls were pissed. Can you find that for me?'

Caz fast-forwards to the end of the interview. She comes back in at Frankie's question.

'How did Ava seem that night?'

'Well, she and her friends had had a few, let's put it that way. Pretty raucous. I'm not saying women bring attacks on themselves, of course not, but they would have been defenceless, you know?'

There's a pause in the recording, which Frankie doesn't fill.

The camera stays on Brett's face. His expression is sorrowful, but watching it now, she thinks his sympathy looks contrived.

'I guess what I'm trying to say is it's not surprising somebody with an agenda might pick them off.'

'That's the bit,' Kiera says, waving her mug at the screen. 'Stop it there.'

'An *agenda*,' Caz says, pulling a face. 'What an odd word to use.'

'I know it's a strong soundbite,' says Frankie. 'But aren't we sounding a bit victim blaming by running that?'

'We're making *him* sound bad, not them,' Kiera says. 'Although if they are some silly little slappers who had one too many, no point in us beating around the bush.' She looks at Frankie, her mouth twisted in displeasure. 'Journalism isn't about sparing people's feelings because you don't want to be *mean*. You should tell the truth regardless.'

'But it may not be the truth,' Frankie says. 'That's my point.'

'Really, Frances, you're a hack, not a bloody vicar,' Kiera snaps. 'Stop trying to ruin your own story. I can't think why Charlie has been indulging this ridiculous attitude for so long. Anybody would think we were in a convent not a newsroom.'

There's silence in the small room. Frankie can see Caz hunching over her keyboard with embarrassment, clearly wishing she could disappear. Her own chest feels tight. She knows she ought to give in, but she can't. 'In that case, I don't think we should stop there. We need to include my question afterwards when I ask him if he had reason to dislike either of the girls.' Frankie feels uneasy thinking of his reaction, the intense way he looked at her. She won't admit it to Kiera, but she's staring to feel nervous of Brett Hollins.

'I don't think it adds anything, it was just some tedious to and fro between the pair of you about nothing.' Kiera stands up. 'I think I've hand held you enough for one day. Use those two clips. And don't fuck the rest of the report up.'

The door closes softly behind her, leaving them in the sound-proofed room. Caz lets out a sigh. 'Blimey. What a bully.'

'Yup,' says Frankie, trying not to feel too disappointed Caz didn't stick up for her while Kiera was still there. 'She certainly is.'

'Do you think he did it?' Caz asks, gesturing at the screen. 'Hell of an exclusive if he did.'

'I hope not,' says Frankie, with a lightness she doesn't feel. 'He knows where I work.'

Watching the report on TV with the rest of the team leaves her with an unpleasant aftertaste. The tissue of innuendo, the awkwardness of her attempt to diffuse Brett's victim blaming, and the nagging feeling he may have invented the creepy figure at the bar, all make Frankie uncomfortable. On the other hand, Kiera loves it. It's the most enthusiastic debrief the boss has given since she arrived, and when she smiles it almost looks genuine. Putting up with all that unpleasantness in the edit suite seems to have been worth it.

Frankie is sitting at her desk, staring at the blank computer trying to work up the will to get up and leave, when her phone bleeps.

Can't stop thinking about you. When are you free? I'd like to see you again . . . And not just on my TV. B xx

Her face flushes red, though there's nobody but her to see Brett's text illuminate the screen. She glances over at the newsdesk where Kiera is talking to Charlie, gesticulating about something. It's not only her boss's fault that she hasn't yet told Brett she has a boyfriend. Although she's ashamed to admit it, part of her has been flattered by the attention. He's ridiculously good-looking, after all. But even if she didn't love Jack, or have a general aversion to cheating, something about Brett doesn't feel right. The predatory way he looked at her, his cavalier attitude to Ava. It might be nothing more unsavoury than the bullshit of a player, but she doesn't trust him.

She swipes across the phone, opening her messages, finger hovering while she thinks of a reply.

Hi! Glad you liked the report. We might want to do a follow-up at some point so will be in touch. Frankie

She reads it again, trying to imagine his reaction. It's not the first time she's tried to avoid an awkward situation by pretending it didn't happen; she hopes Brett is smart enough to get the message. She presses send and stuffs the phone in her pocket, swings her bag onto her shoulder and walks out.

Jack is waiting for her in reception. He's chatting to Ernie at the front desk when she walks in. 'There she is.' Ernie nods at Frankie, proprietorial, as if she's a wayward daughter. 'Take care of her.'

'Thank God you're OK,' Jack says, squeezing her tight in a hug. They walk over to his car and Jack opens the door for her. 'That blog really freaked me out.'

'You're not the only one.'

'I hope you mentioned that creepy Brian guy to the police,' he says as she buckles herself in. 'Ernie just told me all about him, said he's a menace, wouldn't put anything past him.'

Frankie sighs. 'Zara thinks he's harmless, and it's her he's obsessed with, not me.'

'Yeah well, we can't be too careful, especially with the follow-up,' he says, turning the key in the ignition. 'I hope to God the police are going to take it more seriously. They sounded hopeless at that meeting you had earlier.'

'Follow-up?'

Jack looks at her, his face falling. 'I thought the police would have told you. I thought they'd be all over it.'

'All over what?' He doesn't say anything. They're not moving, still parked outside the newsroom with the engine running. 'All over what, Jack?' she says again. 'Is there another post?'

'Not a post, no, there's been a reply.'

'A reply?' She digs into her handbag and gets out her phone, clicking open the Internet. 'Saying what?'

'Don't look at that.' He snatches it off her. 'Let's wait until we get home.'

'Don't tell me what to do!' she shouts. Between Jack and Ernie treating her like a medieval maiden she's starting to feel claustrophobic as well as afraid.

'OK, sorry.' He turns off the ignition. 'But you don't want to be reading all the stupid comments,' he says. 'I really thought the police would have said something, I'm so sorry you're finding out from me.'

'Finding out what?'

'It might be a spoof,' he says, still clutching the phone as she tries to wrest it off him.

'Jesus, Jack!' she says. 'Just give me the bloody phone!' He hands it over and she loads the blog, scrolling down below the line. The words RAPE THE FAT CUNT leap out at her and she hands it back, feeling sick. 'Actually, you're right. Just point me at the comment you mean, I don't need to read all this.'

Jack flicks down through the posts, then puts his finger over one. 'There,' he says, and she leans over to look.

Many thanks to @Feminazi_Slayer2 for the tip-off. I currently have my hands full, but it's an interesting thought. I'm never one to ignore a plea to fight the Gynocracy. I will see what I can do.

@The_Norfolk_Strangler

'That's got to be a joke,' says Frankie. 'It can't be him. I mean look at the sign off!' Despite her bravado, the blood is buzzing in her ears.

'That's what I said. It could be a spoof,' says Jack, putting a hand on her knee. 'Though I guess if it's him, he has to sign off somehow, he can't use his real name.'

Frankie reads the message again, and this time she starts to feel truly afraid. It's not like the other comments surrounding it, full of violence, swearing and hyperbole. But the understatement seems more menacing. After all, why would a real killer need to vent his rage in words? 'Let's just get home,' she says.

Back at the flat Jack goes straight to the kitchen to make dinner, instructing Frankie to sit on the sofa and relax. Fat chance of that, she thinks. Calling DC Avery on the journey back has gone some way towards reassuring her, but not much. He told her they were almost expecting a troll might appear online claiming to be the killer in response to Feminazi Slayer's appeal. Part of her wonders if he said it to make her feel better. Even if it's true, she wishes he had warned her in advance. She picks up the post from the mat and flops down on the cushions with a glass of wine. There's a card from her mum, a water bill and another flier from the antiques shop. She turns it over. They must have money to burn sending out so many. She looks at the image again and does a double take. The crack in the vase has grown. She remembers the first one being just a hairline at the top, but this goes much further down, into the body of the alabaster. There's even a chip in the vase's lip.

'Jack,' she says, holding up the card. 'Do you know which place this is from?'

'That vase picture?' he says. 'No idea. There was one the other day too, but I chucked it. Bit annoying there's no address so we can't get taken off their mailing list.'

Frankie stares at the card. Her pulse racing. *It's nothing*, she tells herself, *the blog's just upset you*. 'Don't throw the next one away, OK?' she says, wishing her voice didn't sound so wobbly. 'There's something weird about them.'

Jack comes and sits beside her, taking the card from her. 'You don't think it's anything worrying?'

'I don't know,' she says, tears spilling over her cheeks. 'I don't know. Probably not. It's just been such a stressful day and I can't fucking *believe* that awful website's still up.'

Jack holds on to her while she cries and strokes her hair. 'It's all right, it's going to be all right,' he says. 'Listen, Frankie, I've been thinking. Would you like me to try and find out where this website is hosted?'

'Seriously.' She sits up. 'Could you do that?'

'I'm not sure. But I could try.' He looks a little shifty. 'And if I can't manage it, I know people who probably could.'

Frankie thinks about his chess games with nameless players in Russia and South America. She wonders what else he gets up to online. 'Would you get in trouble?'

'No,' he says, not very convincingly. 'I don't think so.'

'Then yes. Please try.' She hugs him tightly, feeling a surge of gratitude. 'I'm so lucky to have you.'

Ava

'Are you lonely, Ava?'

His voice, which has invaded my dreams too often, feels close. So close his breath is on my cheek. I startle awake. His face is just inches from mine, pale circles of skin around his eyes in the ski mask. I scream and lurch backwards. How did he sneak in here without my hearing him?

'Shhh, shhh,' he says, pressing a black-gloved hand against my shoulder, pinning me against the wall. 'There, there, no need to be jumpy. I just thought you might be lonely.' He sits back slightly. 'I get lonely.'

The fear that I've shoved to the back of my mind and tried to bury there crashes into my consciousness. It's like being hit over the head with a rock. He's going to rape me. 'Please no, please don't, you don't have to, there's no need, just please, please . . .'

'Please what?'

I hadn't realised that my gabbling was outside my own head. We stare at each other. I notice he's holding a torch in one hand and the overhead light is off. *Leave me the fuck alone!* I want to scream. But I can't say that, I need to placate him. 'I just don't know you very well.'

He shakes his head. 'Pathetic. Even covered in piss, stinking like a dustbin, you think a man might be interested. That's all you bitches have to offer, isn't it? But it's a sick delusion. The same age-old lie that you're all irresistible.' He flips the torch up and shines it in my eyes, making me blink and squirm. 'Women are unbelievable. All you have is a few years of being able to paper over the cracks, persuade guys you're not totally fucking disgusting, before your tits start to sag, and your faces fall to pieces, and yet you still think this little window gives you the right to rule the whole fucking world.' He rests his arms back on his knees, bouncing the torch against one ankle so that the light lurches crazily back and forth. 'It never enters your stupid skulls that men might have other things to think about, does it? That some of us might see through you? You're just silly little children.'

Still shocked from being dragged from sleep, I struggle to follow what he's saying. Other things to think about? Perhaps he's not going to rape me. Unless this is all an elaborate bluff. 'That's interesting,' I lie. 'In what way are women like children?'

He sighs. 'You wouldn't understand. That's the point.'

Keep him talking! 'I could try.'

'All right then.' He nods. 'How about this? Everything in life is run for *your* benefit. Men protect you, look after you and you're just ungrateful and whine for more. Like spoilt brats. And it's not good enough to be fawned over at home, you also want things all your own way *everywhere*. Demanding that you can have babies and still get fucking promoted. It's a sick joke, it really is.' He shines the torch in my face again. 'But woe betide any poor bastard who points this out. The Feminazis will make sure *his* life's ruined.'

I'm sitting with a man who locks women up for kicks and he's telling me *he* feels victimised. It would almost be funny if I weren't so frightened. 'Do you think it was better before? In the past,' I say. 'When men had more control over women.'

'Control over women?' He laughs. 'Well, that's a joke. Study your fucking history! Women have always been children, and men have always had to run around after them.' He shrugs. 'Though I guess in the past there was more *recognition* of this.'

'But you must have met *some* nice women,' I say, keeping the conversation going, as if this is a sensible exchange and he's not a psychopath. 'Some you thought were OK?'

He rolls his eyes. With the rest of his face blacked out by the mask, the gesture is especially hard to read. 'Is this the point where you ask me about *my mother*, Ava?'

'I don't know. I could do,' I say. 'But it might be a bit of a personal question.'

He stares at me. 'Full of surprises, aren't you? You're a hard nut to crack.'

'I'm just a person. Like you are.'

'Don't give me that.' He smacks the torch on the floor and the light lurches, plunging his face into shadow. 'I've got all the cards here. You're just a desperate little slag, scrabbling around hoping I don't kill you.'

It takes everything I have not to start crying. 'It's true you do hold all the cards,' I say, my voice quavering. 'But even so, we're probably more similar than you think. Everyone has things in common.'

'Really?' He flips the torch up and grins at me, his teeth shining white in the dark. 'You think we're similar? I don't think so. But you remind me a bit of someone else. Do you want to know who?'

I can tell from the way he asks the question that I'm not going to like the answer. 'Why don't you tell me?'

'Hanna. That's who you remind me of. The last one I had here. She was a tough nut to crack too. But she did in the end. You all do. You all end up begging and pleading to stay alive, as if that's going to make any fucking difference.'

Sitting here with him, talking about my own impending death, is so horrific it feels unreal. I'm so frightened that I'm starting to lose any sense of my fear, like freezing to death but slowly feeling less cold. 'It was just one moment out of her life,' I say, daring for once to contradict him. 'Just one moment when she begged, when anyone would beg. It doesn't prove anything.'

'Perhaps. But she's still dead, isn't she?'

He means to scare me, and he has. But I sense there's something behind his words besides the threat. It's the way he keeps mentioning her by name. 'You miss her, don't you? You liked

Hanna. You miss her.' His silence suggests that I'm right. 'What was she like? She sounds like a nice person.'

'She was nice,' he says. He darts a quick look at me. 'Nice for a *slag*, anyway. She'd had a shitty life. It was one of the reasons I picked her. I thought we might have something in common. Not a privileged bitch like you.'

'What had happened to her?'

'She grew up in foster care. Mum was a junkie. A couple of years ago she got assaulted by some lad in a club. I thought that was a lie. So many of you women lie about that shit. But after getting to know her, I think maybe Hanna wasn't lying about it after all. It's hard to say.'

Listening to him talk about Hanna, his voice gentle as if we're reminiscing about a friend rather than someone he murdered, I feel my chest tighten. What good is it going to do me, even if I get him to like me? Hanna must have tried the same thing and it didn't save her. Tears prick at my eyes. The thought of her trapped here, alive, hoping to escape, after whatever she had survived before, is unbearable. I wish I could reach her, hold her hand, make us both feel better. But she's dead. 'That sounds very sad,' I manage at last, my voice hoarse.

He shrugs. 'Well, we all have to die sometime.'

'I still think it's sad,' I reply, clenching my fists, not trusting myself to say more. Rage is stirring beneath my fear and I mustn't start shouting at him.

'Don't be sad for me.' He stretches out a hand to touch my arm. It takes all my willpower not to flinch. 'After all, I've got you now.'

When he says this his hand creeps downwards to rest on my thigh. I stay rigid, willing him to move it. He doesn't. 'Did you say Hanna's mum was an addict?' I say, to distract him. 'That must have been really tough.'

'Tough? How would you know, Ava, with your perfect posh family. Mummy's an *artiste*, isn't she? Or would that be *Maman*?'

I feel a chill. My mum is a French teacher at a secondary school. She's always painted, but only started getting her work into a gallery in Chichester in the last few years. Hardly a well-known artist. He must have stalked my family to know this. I think of Matt and my stomach drops. Is it possible he wasn't lying? Is he dead? He senses my distress, even if he doesn't understand the cause. 'Oh dear, was I being *mean*? Did I hurt your *fucking feelings*? Some people have everything. And they're not even grateful. The whole world is set up for the benefit of people like you.'

I want to scream, punch him again and again until he stops talking. 'I'm sorry you've had a difficult time,' I say.

'But you're not though, are you?' He grabs me by the shoulders. 'You're not *sorry*.'

His face is so close to mine, there's almost no space between us. It's a split second decision; not even a decision – it's instinct. I throw my head forward violently, smashing his skull with my own. It's painful but I'm expecting that. He staggers back in surprise. I fling myself on him, grabbing for his shoulders, trying to pound his head on the concrete floor. We wrestle silently. He's stronger than me, but I've got gravity on my side. For one soaring moment I think it's going to be like my fantasy, I'm going to crack his skull, knock him out and escape. Then he brings his knee up hard into my groin.

My body betrays me, reacting to the pain, even though I thought I had steeled myself against it. He flips upright like a scorpion and grabs me round the throat. I can't breathe.

'Thought you'd check out early, bitch? I can help with that.'

I scrabble against his face with my nails, tearing and gouging, but his skin is protected by the mask. It's agony, my lungs feel like they are going to burst. Then he releases his grip slightly, just enough to let me get some air. I don't even think of fighting back, I'm too desperate to catch my breath. I draw in the air in shuddering gasps, wheezing like an old woman.

'*I said* do you want to check out early?'

'No.' My voice is barely audible.

His grip tightens again, cutting off my air supply. 'Sadly, *you* don't get to make that decision.'

Terror is a scream in my head, a scream I can't release because I can't breathe. My legs look for his body but instead kick uselessly against the floor. This man is going to kill me. My body senses it, carries on fighting, even as my mind fractures and dissolves into darkness.

Frankie

'We're going to have to tread a fine line with this,' Charlie says. 'Ava's family are doing an appeal, but Frankie's also going back to speak to Lily's parents. We don't want to make it feel as if Ava is a lost cause.'

Kiera sighs. It's the morning meeting and by tradition, as the news editor, this is Charlie's domain, but she clearly isn't pleased by the arrangement. Frankie and the other reporters sit around in a circle, slumped on chairs or leaning against various desks. There's an odd atmosphere; nobody knows where the power lies. It reminds Frankie of dinner time with her mum and dad before their divorce, when she and her sister Natalie would turn from one parent to the other across the table, as if watching the world's most passive aggressive tennis match.

'Why are we going back to Lily's parents?' Kiera asks. 'I can see why we'd speak to them after the trial but why now?'

'They aren't happy with the media coverage,' Frankie says. 'They called me to say they feel the police and press are treating Sandra and Lily as second-class murder victims because they were sex workers.'

Kiera pulls a face. 'Interesting enough, I suppose, if they're not happy with the police. But it feels a bit small fry with a serial killer on the loose. Go along, see what they say, but we can't spare a camera.'

'But I thought that—' Frankie begins.

'That's enough, Frances. It's just one house in Lowestoft, you'll be fine.'

'I'd best be off now, then.' Frankie stands up. 'So I'm not late.' She walks out of the newsroom not looking back at Kiera or

Charlie. There's plenty of time to get to the interview, but she can't bear to spend any longer in the meeting.

The drive to Lowestoft takes Frankie across country, with little variety in the flat green landscape until she gets to the flash of silver crossing the River Waveney. It's not the sort of road where you pay huge attention to your surroundings, but about half an hour into the journey she becomes vaguely conscious of the white car behind her. It's some distance back, driving slowly, but while other cars turn off or overtake, this one remains steadily present.

She's just beginning to feel anxious when the white car turns off down a side road on the outskirts of Lowestoft. Frankie feels a wash of relief. She realises her hands are cramped from clutching the steering wheel and relaxes them.

The Sidcups live on Pakefield Street on the edge of the town. It's one of the prettiest parts, a row of small Victorian houses right on the coast. Lily's family home isn't on the side of the road with a direct view out to sea, but she would have grown up just minutes from the coastal path and the vast expanse of blue. Frankie parks up and unloads her camera kit before knocking on the front door. She notices the trellis in the shape of a heart is still on the wall, with pink autumn roses in bloom. Vicky Sidcup, Lily's mother, opens the door.

'Hello Frankie love,' she says. 'No Gavin today?'

Vicky seems to have aged since the last time Frankie was here. Her carefully made-up face is unable to hide the puffy red eyelids and dark circles beneath her eyes. 'Not today, I'm afraid,' she says. 'Just me.'

'Well, come in. You know the way. Ian's in the lounge.'

Frankie walks through to the back room, which looks out on the Sidcups' small garden. The garden where Lily is laughing in the photo her family released to the police. Ian Sidcup rises to shake her hand, but seeing she is laden down, takes the tripod instead. 'Here, let me have that. Bit heavy for you,' he says.

Frankie is conscious of pictures of Lily on every surface of the room. There are the annual official school photos of her as a chubby-faced child, hair tightly plaited, and others of her as a teenager on the beach with her younger brother, whose name Frankie can't remember. And in between the pictures, there are sympathy cards on the mantelpiece, poorly scanned supermarket poems that try to make sense of her parents' agony.

'Go on, sit down, make yourself comfortable,' says Vicky, coming in with a mug of tea.

'Thanks,' says Frankie, taking it. She perches on a wide leather footstool, which she hopes was not Lily's favourite spot. 'I'm really sorry you've been finding the coverage so hurtful. What sort of things did you want to talk about today?'

'We just want people to see Lily as a person, not . . . not . . .' Ian hesitates, struggling to find the words. 'Not what she was doing when she died. She had a lot of troubles, I'm not denying that, but she was our little girl, you know? And she had such a good heart. That's what did for her, really.'

'That *bastard*,' says Vicky. Frankie knows she means Lily's boyfriend, not the killer. The last time they met, Vicky told her he was to blame for Lily's drug addiction and the life she led to feed the habit.

Ian pats his wife's hand. 'We don't need to talk about him.'

'Did you say you weren't happy with the police too?'

'They've not been too bad,' Vicky says. 'Not really. It's more the papers.'

Frankie's heart sinks. If the Sidcups aren't going to criticise the police, she's worried Kiera might not run the story, meaning Lily's parents could be baring their souls for nothing. She puts her tea down on the carpet, starts setting up the tripod and camera. 'OK, well, we'll film this as a chat. Tell me whatever it is you want to say about Lily.'

Vicky and Ian talk to Frankie about their daughter for over half an hour. She hears all about Lily's love of animals as a child, how caring she was, what a good aunt to her brother Derryn's children, how she wanted children of her own some day. They tell her how upset they are by the media's relentless focus on the last two years of Lily's life. At one point Vicky has to break off to cry. The whole interview gives Frankie a pain in her chest, as if she's swallowed glass. Whatever she reports, it's never going to do justice to this family's grief, any more than the hackneyed rhymes on the mantelpiece about angels and stars can adequately describe their loss.

When she packs up, Frankie notices an old PC on a table in the corner. She thinks about the blog and feels relieved that the Sidcups don't seem to have read it. 'Before she went missing,' Frankie asks, 'when you saw Lily, did she mention any post or stuff online that had been bothering her?'

Vicky shakes her head. 'No, though Derryn has all her Facebook passwords and said she'd been getting some very odd messages.'

'I think they were sent after she died,' Ian says. 'They're odd but probably well-meaning.'

'Do you mind me asking what the messages said?'

'You can have a look if you like. Derryn's left her page up, so we can see whatever her friends post.' He moves over to switch on the PC. 'Lots of people loved her. Derryn's turned it into a tribute page.'

Frankie leans over to look. There are hundreds of messages. *Rest in peace Angel xxx Miss you beautiful girl.* She looks at Ian. 'It's lovely so many people care. Is it OK to see the weird posts you mentioned?'

'Sure.' He clicks down through the page. 'There you go. That's one. They're all the same. She got sent about five.'

He moves so Frankie can see the screen. Somebody has posted a gif. It's a crystal vase against a black velvet background. It wobbles slightly, then falls, smashing into fragments. Then the video restarts and the vase is whole. Then it smashes again, over and over on a loop. The footage looks grainy and flickers, like an old black-and-white movie. Frankie stares at the image, unable to look away.

'Odd, isn't it?' says Vicky who has come to stand by her shoulder.

'Very,' says Frankie, whose heart is pounding. She feels so frightened she can barely move. She thinks about the glass Hanna was sent in the post, the cards somebody has been sending to her house. The Sidcups are just behind her, but she doesn't feel safe; she's standing in a dead woman's home, with people who were powerless to protect their own daughter. 'Have you told the police about this?' she says at last.

'I don't think so, no,' says Ian. 'It was posted after she died. I think maybe somebody was trying to be kind, saying she was like a beautiful vase.'

Frankie watches the crystal smash again, the shards spreading outwards, jagged, towards the screen. She doesn't see any kindness in the image at all.

Ian insists on helping her out to the car, and hands her the tripod when she packs the kit into the boot. 'Thanks,' she says. 'I'll let you know when the interview's going out. It may not be today, but I'll keep you posted.'

Ian shakes her hand and she gets into the car. Frankie didn't film the vase on the computer screen, even though she knows that this is the one element that's likely to prick Kiera's interest. She tells herself it's because she's protecting the Sidcups from seeing their daughter's tribute page flooded by trolls, but the truth is more complicated. She doesn't want @Feminazi_Slayer2, or whoever has been sending her cards, to know what she suspects.

As she drives off, Ian and Vicky stand in the doorway by the climbing roses. She glances at them in the rear-view mirror, raising a hand in farewell. It's only as she turns to face the road that she sees the white car out of the corner of her eye, parked opposite the Sidcups' house. She whips round to look back. The car doesn't move. There's somebody sitting in it, though she's too far away now to see whether it's a man or a woman. She keeps driving, slowly, gripping the wheel, but the car doesn't follow her; instead it pulls out into the road and heads in the opposite direction.

Frankie continues along Pakefield Street until there's a space to pull over. She's shaking too much to drive. She turns the engine off and checks all the car doors are locked before getting her phone out of her bag. There's a message from Charlie saying he's sent Rachel to cover the Lindseys' press conference as Kiera was worried she wouldn't be back in time. She suspects it's a snub, but feels relieved. It means she's spared witnessing more desperate parents' anguish, and also that she has some time before she has to be back. Frankie takes Dan Avery's card out of her purse and calls his number.

They meet at Earlham Road police station. She explained on the phone it was a chat rather than a formal statement, and so Avery makes them both tea before leading her to a private room off the main office. She's interviewed a neighbourhood police team here before, and as she follows him, walking past desks with officers at work, it feels disconcerting. The prospect of being the subject of an interview feels very different to asking the questions.

'Thanks for seeing me, detective,' she says, hovering in the doorway.

'Please, it's Dan,' he says, gesturing her inside and closing the door behind them both. 'So tell me what's bothering you. Besides the obvious.'

Frankie sits down, and Dan takes a chair opposite. He's a slim man, probably in his mid or late twenties. She can't imagine him single-handedly grappling too many burly villains to the ground but he has a quiet authority that puts her a little more at ease. 'I hope this doesn't sound too crazy,' she says. 'I don't know if it's linked to the blog. I don't know if it means anything at all, but when I spoke to Hanna Chivers' flatmates they told me she had been sent glass in the post before she went missing and it really upset her. I thought that was creepy at the time. Then today I spoke to Lily Sidcup's parents and they showed me a weird message somebody posted on their daughter's Facebook page. It's a smashing vase.' Frankie swallows hard. 'Then, well, the next bit really is going to sound stupid.'

'Go on.' Dan doesn't look as if he finds her foolish. He's been writing everything she says in his notepad and now glances up, looking direct into her eyes. 'What else?'

'I've been getting pictures of a vase in the post,' she says, pulling the card out of her bag. She hands it over to him without looking at it. 'This is about the third or fourth we've got. My boyfriend and I aren't sure how many there've been, we threw some away.' Dan studies it, turning it over to look at the typed address on the back. 'They've all been like that, printed, no handwriting. But the main thing is, you see it's cracked? I think that crack is getting bigger. I can't be sure because we chucked the others, I thought it was a flier, but I'm almost certain in the first one the vase was virtually intact.'

'Do you mind if I keep hold of this?' Dan asks. 'And obviously let me have any others if you get them.'

'Of course,' she says. 'And the other thing. Well, this is almost certainly paranoia, but I thought I saw a white car follow me to Lily's house today. I lost it before I got there, but then when I left, I'm sure I saw the same car outside their house. There was someone sitting in it.'

'Did you get a good look at the person, or the reg plate?'

'No, I was too far away, and then they pulled out and drove off in the opposite direction. I was too flustered to clock the registration. I think the car was some sort of saloon. A Mondeo maybe, but I'm not very good with makes.'

Dan nods. 'Completely understandable,' he says. 'But if you see the car again, try and get the reg if you can, if you think it's safe. Is there anything else?'

The detective constable is looking at her with such sympathy that Frankie cracks. 'Yes,' she says. 'I just can't help feeling that the blogger on the website *is* connected to the killer, whatever your colleague says. I know you told me whoever is on there claiming to be the Norfolk Strangler is most likely a troll, but how can you be sure? And it doesn't reassure me at all that the blog's not a main line of enquiry. What if I'm the next target?'

Dan puts his notepad down. 'I know being targeted online like you've been is very upsetting. Do you want me to put you in touch with someone from victim support?'

'I don't need victim support,' Frankie says, exasperated. 'I want to be sure I'm not going to get kidnapped by some murdering nutcase!'

'I'm not part of the team investigating the murders,' he replies. 'But I promise you I'm going to tell them everything you've told me and I'm hoping someone from the investigation will call you in to speak with you, OK?' Frankie watches him closely, trying to judge if he is fobbing her off or not. 'I'm being serious,' he says, as if reading her mind. 'I'm concerned about everything you've told me and I want you to be extra vigilant. Try not to go places on your own, be very aware of your surroundings and always tell people where you are going.'

'You think I might be a target, don't you?'

'I don't want you feeling alarmed, these are just precautions,' Dan replies. He sounds calm but Frankie sees the flicker of hesitation before he speaks. She can tell he knows she's noticed. 'You can still call me anytime at all,' he says. 'But if you think somebody's following you again, please call 999.'

In the newsroom Frankie doesn't mention her visit to Dan Avery. As she walks in she's met by Rachel, who looks upset.

'Oh, you're back, are you?' she says. 'Kiera wants *you* to do the Lindsey family presser report, not me. I'm just good for fluffy stories about kids and garden fetes, apparently.' Rachel hands her the memory stick with the rushes on it. 'Then why send me? She's so bloody rude!' Frankie knows Rachel is angry with Kiera but feels some of her resentment has spilled over onto her. Kiera certainly knows how to foster a toxic working environment.

'I'm sorry Rach, that's bollocks,' she says. 'If it's any consolation that means she's dropped my interview with Lily's parents without even telling me.'

'Yeah, well.' Rachel sniffs. 'Never mind. Let's face it, none of it really matters, does it? Those poor parents, what they're going through. Puts it all in perspective.'

'It does.'

'There's one thing, before I forget,' Rachel says, tapping her arm. 'There are reporting restrictions about Ava's brother Matthew.'

'What restrictions?'

'He's not to be mentioned, apparently. Not sure why.'

'Bit weird,' Frankie says, then remembers Laura's remarks about him having depression. 'Maybe it's his health. I think some local rag blabbed his medical history.'

'Don't ask me, I'm the newsroom dullard.' Rachel shrugs. 'Just passing it on.'

Caz scrolls back through the footage with the cursor. Frankie sits beside her in the edit suite, sipping an instant coffee.

'You sure we've got time to listen to the whole thing?' asks Caz. As she scrolls back through the rushes, Ava Lindsey's parents flash and flicker on the screen. Frankie has already watched the family's press conference at an edit machine in the newsroom. After speaking to Lily's parents in the morning, witnessing the Lindseys' grief was especially gut-wrenching. Frankie wanted to scream at the killer, *just let their daughter go, you bastard!* But all she could imagine in response was the mockery in the posts of @Feminazi_Slayer2.

'They spoke for ten minutes max,' she says. 'I've already written a rough version of my voice-over, it's only about twenty seconds long.' She holds up a print-out of her short script as evidence. 'I'm leaving the other two minutes to the parents, better for the viewer to hear from them than me.'

'Right, let's have a listen, then.' Caz presses play. Frankie sits poised with her notepad. They watch the screen as DSI Nigel Gubberts leads Ava Lindsey's stricken parents into the room. There is a barrage of silver flashes, and frantic clicking, like a swarm of insects descending. Ava's mother is supported into her chair by a female police officer.

'The first bit was just Gubberts introducing them,' says Frankie. 'We can skip that.' Caz scrolls through until the camera zooms in on Ava's father. 'Yep, go from there.'

Eric Lindsey's eyes are red-rimmed and he's clutching a piece of paper, which he looks down at from time to time while he speaks. 'The last few days have been a nightmare—' He stops, swallowing. 'We keep hoping we will wake up, that none of it's real. But Ava's still not home.' He starts to shake, crying silently. After a pause, busy with more flashes, he starts speaking again. Every now and then, his voice dips and quavers. 'Ava is a lovely girl. Kind, compassionate. She wouldn't hurt anybody. We just want her home. Please, just let her come home.' His face crumples and his wife Celine takes his hand. Ava's mother is dry-eyed, her face immobilised by pain. Eric Lindsey starts speaking again. 'We would just like to appeal to anyone who thinks they might know where Ava is. Please think of your own child, or someone you love. Think how much you would want them home, safe. And then please, we're begging you, please call the police.'

'Ava darling, if you are watching this, we love you.' Celine Lindsey starts speaking. She has no notes and stares straight into the lens of the camera as if the intensity of her willpower will bring her daughter home. 'We are thinking of you, every minute of the day. Be strong, my angel. We are all waiting for you. We love you. *Ne quitte pas, chérie, reste forte.*'

'That's it,' says Frankie. 'They didn't take questions.'

'Jesus,' says Caz. 'How awful. Poor sods.' The Lindseys' grief has blasted into the edit suite, their anguish too vast to fit the small room let alone the confines of a two-minute TV report. But Frankie will have to try.

'Right,' she says, looking at her notes. 'We'll start on the natural sound of the press photographers, a couple of seconds of that.' Caz's fingers fly over the keyboard as she speaks, cutting the report as Frankie speaks. 'Then my script over the parents arriving: *It's been too long since the Lindseys spoke to their missing daughter, but they had a message for Ava today.* Then cut straight to the mother talking. In words *Ava darling* out words *every minute of the day*.'

'Don't you want all of the mother?' asks Caz. 'I thought that was the most moving bit. I don't think the accent was too strong, I know Charlie worried it might be. Though I didn't get her remark at the end. Was it French?'

'We'll use all of her clip, just split it in two. I was going to run the last section right at the end of the report.' She looks at Celine Lindsey, frozen on Caz's screen. There is a fierceness to her face she hopes her daughter has inherited. 'And yes, the last line was French. She said, *Don't give up, sweetheart, stay strong*.'

After the edit Frankie feels emotionally wrung out. The grief she's witnessed, tangled together with her own fears, feels like a physical knot being pulled ever tighter in her chest. She pays little attention to Kiera's debrief, which is as critical as ever, but when the boss has left, she heads over to Charlie to talk about the Sidcups. 'Are we running the report tomorrow, then?'

'I'm not sure,' he says. 'We can try.'

Frankie frowns. Charlie normally has absolute discretion about what goes into the programme. 'I can't drop them. They told me they feel like Lily is being dismissed by the media, as if she's not worth anything. If we don't run their interview, we'll just be reinforcing that feeling.'

'I know, I realise that.' Charlie sits back in his chair, running a hand over his eyes. He looks exhausted. 'But Kiera really isn't that keen.' He catches sight of Frankie's expression. 'Look, I promise at the absolute worst we'll run it this weekend, OK? We won't drop them.'

'OK.' Frankie's mobile, which she's holding, vibrates. It's an unknown number. 'Thanks, see you tomorrow.' Walking away from him, she answers the call. 'Hello?'

'Frances, it's Dan Avery. Hope I'm not disturbing you.'

'Not at all. Is everything OK?'

'Have you got access to a computer?'

Frankie heads over to her desk and moves the mouse, waking up the screen. 'Sure, what is it?'

'There's a post underneath that blog about you on *Killing Cuttlefish*. I'm sorry to ask you to look at it again, but I want you to scroll down to the bottom of the comments. There's a short video that's been posted by @Feminazi_Slayer2 and I want you to tell me if it's the same video as the one you saw on Lily's Facebook page.'

Frankie does as he asks, trying not to read the comments as she scrolls through them. She stops towards the end. @Feminazi_Slayer2 has posted a gif. It flickers black and white. The background looks like velvet drapery. A crystal vase falls and breaks, the shards smashing outwards, sharp and cruel. Then words appear, one after the other over the broken image, the red typeface getting bigger each time. Curiosity. Killed. The. **BITCH**.

'Have you seen it, Frances?'

'Yes,' she says, her voice hoarse. 'It's exactly the same as Lily's video. Except for the message. I think that's just for me.'

Frankie

At home she watches the TV, trying not to see the blog on Jack's laptop out of the corner of her eye. He has angled it away from her so she can't see the screen but she knows it's there. He wants to take over checking the site, as well as trying to crack it, so she doesn't have to look at the hateful thing. After @Feminazi_Slayer2 posted the gif of the vase smashing, he tells her, several others have uploaded the same image. This doesn't initially make her feel better, but Jack explains that means it might just be a meme, some weird MRA reference rather than a message from a killer. Other discoveries are less reassuring. It seems Feminazi Slayer is spawning copycat haters. The person who posted the YouTube video of Ava, @Anabolic100, has now written a blog about Frankie too, though Jack reassures her it's more a rant against female TV reporters in general. And whatever nastiness Frankie attracts, the greatest volume of bile is reserved for the murdered women. Like wasps swarming for a feed, the poisonous posts multiply, each more callous than the last. 'Listen to this one,' Jack says. 'It's by some weirdo called @CuckOff. Where *do* they get these names from? Anyway, Mr CuckOff thinks the women have been bumped off by feminists, just to generate hatred of men! Can you believe it? How crazy are these guys! He's probably lurking on another site somewhere, claiming 9/11 was pulled off by the CIA.'

In the end Frankie goes to bed to escape her boyfriend's commentary. She's grateful he is trying to take it off the Internet, but in the process, the website seems to be becoming an obsession. By the time he comes to bed, Frankie is asleep. She feels guilty the next morning, seeing the dark circles under his eyes. He can't really afford to spend all this time helping her out, the least she can do is appreciate it.

'I think it might be a VPN,' he says to her over breakfast. He looks at her blank face. 'A virtual privacy network. The site seems to be hosted abroad, somewhere that doesn't have a disclosure agreement with the UK. Otherwise the set-up of the site itself is quite straightforward – it's just a host, anyone can post their blogs on there, and they all go in the timeline. You can click through by section, most popular, most controversial, that kind of thing, but it's not curated very heavily. In theory you or I could post something on there if we joined up. Not that we'd want to,' he adds quickly, seeing her horrified face. 'But what's really annoying is the website protects all the bloggers from being identified too – once you join you're protected by the VPN.'

'Oh right,' she says. 'That sounds difficult to crack. Sorry it's causing you such stress.'

'I'm more worried about you,' he says, stirring sugar into his coffee. 'Do you have to go in to work today? Can't you call in sick or something?'

'I really can't,' she replies. 'What am I going to do, just disappear until the guy's caught? That could be weeks, or even months.' She doesn't add that the idea of being alone in the flat all day frightens her more than going to work and keeping busy.

Her phone rings on the counter, lit up with the newsdesk number. They both stare at it. 'I wish they wouldn't do that. Calling you at home so you can't even eat your sodding breakfast in peace,' Jack says. 'Can't they wait until you get in?'

Frankie sighs and takes the call. 'What is it?' she says.

'Frances, this is Kiera.'

Frankie hops off the stool, unconsciously standing to attention when she hears her boss's voice. Her bad-tempered greeting had been for Charlie. 'Oh, sorry, hi,' she says.

'There's some breaking news on the serial killer story,' Kiera says. 'I want you to go to the police presser, it's at nine thirty.'

'Oh God, they've found Ava, haven't they?' says Frankie, her face draining of colour. She's never met the psychology student but this almost feels like a personal bereavement. 'She's dead.'

The conference room is packed. Frankie has got there early and sits at the front, waiting for the police to arrive. She's avoided talking to people and is sitting right behind Gavin and his tripod. It's not only that she's depressed at the thought of Ava's death and it feels too sordid to speculate about where they found her body; after the blog post she feels oddly sensitive and exposed, as if a layer of skin is missing. She wonders if any of her fellow hacks have seen it. It's infuriating, but she can't help feeling ashamed and embarrassed, even though she knows it's not her fault. She keeps thinking of the horrible Photoshopped image, the harpy with the pendulous breasts.

'Mind if I sit here?' It's Luke Heffner. He's already moving Gavin's bag off the chair next to her before she has a chance to reply.

'Go ahead,' she says.

'Well, this is exciting,' he says. 'Must be the biggest story on your patch since Ipswich.'

She scowls at him. 'Hardly exciting, is it? A load of dead women,' she says, although part of her feels the pricking of guilt. All journalists have a morally queasy relationship to murder stories, and she understands Luke better than she'd like to admit.

'Oh come on,' he replies, his cut-glass voice drawling out the vowels. 'No need to play Mother Teresa with me. You've been all over the story. Must make a change from the pumpkin shortage for Halloween you lot normally cover at this time of year.'

'You're *such* a dickhead,' Frankie says, the words out before she can stop herself.

Luke laughs, not in the least offended. 'Takes one to know one. And well done with that blog exclusive by the way. Though I'm sorry about the aftermath. Now that guy really *is* a dickhead.'

Frankie couldn't feel more winded if he had just slapped her. 'How do you know about that?'

'Afraid it's one of the first things that come up when you google your name.'

'Well, that's fucking fabulous.'

'Don't worry, I can't see it making the news. Sad-sack blogger slags off local reporter for calling him out. Not exactly Hold the Front Page, is it?'

Luke's rudeness makes her feel oddly better. She quite likes him as a sparring partner, and at least he doesn't seem to have spotted the poster claiming to be the Norfolk Strangler. Before she can ask him what he was doing googling her, the investigation team walk in and the room of jabbering hacks falls silent. Then there's the familiar crescendo of clicks. Frankie flips off the lid of her pen, notebook poised.

Nigel Gubberts looks as if he has aged ten years since the last conference. The barrage of silver flashes illuminates every crease on his grey, sleep-deprived face.

'Thank you all for coming. As you may have gathered we've had a development in our ongoing investigation.' He pauses. 'I'm sorry to report that another woman from the Norwich area has gone missing.' There's muttering. It's not what his audience was expecting. The clicking and flashing accelerates. 'A young mother has not been seen for more than thirty-six hours and we understand her disappearance from her home is entirely out of character.' He looks behind him, as a colleague flashes a photograph up on the screen.

Frankie gasps. She knows that face.

'Amber Finn is a twenty-four-year-old mother of one from Costessey,' says DSI Gubberts. 'She works part-time at a supermarket and is also a sex worker . . .'

Frankie feels the warmth of Luke's breath as he moves close to her ear. 'Do you know her?'

'I interviewed her on Monday,' she whispers. Her ears are ringing. She can't quite believe this is happening.

'Christ,' he says, leaning back, his eyes lit up with anticipation of all the moving footage of the victim that's going to be at his fingertips. Top story on the ten. He'll be furious when he finds out Amber was shot anonymously.

Frankie can see Nigel Gubberts looking at them both and turns red. She wonders if he knows about the interview and blames her for Amber going missing. 'We understand Amber was very selective about her clients and about arranging childcare,' Gubberts continues. 'She saw clients in daylight hours and has never before failed to pick up her daughter from nursery. When she failed to turn up on Tuesday afternoon, nursery staff immediately reported her missing.'

In her mind Frankie goes frantically over the interview. She and Gavin were so careful. Surely the grey wall couldn't have identified Amber's house? And they didn't even film her in profile, she was just a shadowy blob. But the killer must have watched the report and recognised her. Anything else is too much of a coincidence. She thinks of the plastic toys in the corner of the room, of a little girl now missing a mother, and feels sick.

Waiting for the press conference to end is painful. She doesn't ask any questions; she doesn't have the stomach for it. There's no need in any case, as Gubberts gets such a comprehensive grilling from everyone else. She learns that Ava's body has not been found, which is a departure from the killer's previous MO. The police say they are working on the assumption she is still alive, and making every effort to find her, though none of the journalists sound convinced by that theory.

When the questions are finally over, Frankie darts out of her chair, trying to grab Gubberts' attention. A press officer blocks her way.

'No one-on-ones,' he says. 'You got the briefing.'

'I don't want to ask him anything,' Frankie says. 'I need to give him information. We interviewed the victim last week.'

The tall man scrutinises her for a moment. 'Wait here,' he says. He heads out of the door where Nigel Gubberts and his team have just left.

'Franks?' says Gavin. She can see from his expression he shares her anguish. 'We were so bloody careful. This can't be linked to the report, it can't be.' Luke Heffner is hovering expectantly by Gavin's elbow.

'What did the guy say?' he asks.

The press officer sticks his head round the door, gestures to Frankie and Gavin to come over, and she obeys, conscious of all the curious eyes on her back.

They step into a corridor, where Gubberts is waiting. 'Frances,' he says, holding out his hand. 'And Gavin. What can I do for you both?'

'We interviewed Amber last week,' says Frankie. 'It was anonymous, she wouldn't have been recognisable, but we thought you should know.' Gubberts is looking at her without much affection. On a personal level, their interviews have always been civil, but she knows there's no love lost between the East Anglian Constabulary and the press. 'You can obviously have the full tape and the report if you need it.'

'Thanks,' he says. 'I think we may have seen it. That the one where she said Donald Emneth was a dirty sod who tied women up?'

Frankie puts her hand to her mouth. 'Oh my God, how did you know it was Amber?'

'I didn't until now,' he replies. 'You're right, you couldn't possibly have known it was her from watching the report. Except you and your news editor overlooked the fact that one person would have known exactly who it was. And that's Donald Emneth.'

Ava

My head is pounding and my throat is agony. My mouth is so parched I can barely moisten it with my tongue. Everything hurts. For a few moments I think I have the flu, that I've been having the worst possible nightmares, that I've just woken up in my bed in halls, seriously ill but safe.

Then I try to move and realise my hands are tied behind my back and I'm not lying down but sitting, cramped against the concrete wall of the basement, propped there like a puppet. The despair that washes over me is so intense I think I'm going to pass out again.

I must be groaning aloud, as I can hear an unearthly moaning. Then with a sense of dislocation I realise it's not me making the sound. I think I'm going mad, that my senses are playing tricks on me, projecting my terror into delusions. I look round for The Stain, half expecting to see Hanna, dead and rotting, standing in its shadow.

That's when I see it.

In the corner of the room, there's a coffin-shaped box. Cardboard, not wood this time. For one crazy moment I think he's dug Hanna up, that she's in here with me. Then I realise it can't be a ghost. He's kidnapped someone else.

'Hello?' I call, or rather croak. My voice sounds scary and rasping to my own ears, God knows what it sounds like to whoever is in there. The moaning stops. I can imagine the fear of the person trapped inside. 'I'm not him. I'm not the kidnapper,' I say. 'I'm like you.'

There's no answer. I shuffle painstakingly across the cold concrete floor on my bottom, like a baby that can't crawl yet. It takes a long time. I almost give up when I'm in the middle of the floor, but then I see there is a pile of sandwiches and more cartons of water dumped by the box. Thirst, added to my overwhelming need for company, gives me the strength to continue. My limbs scream with pain from being pressed against the cold concrete and my jeans are wet and sore against my thighs where I must have wet myself again. I know I stink.

I draw up level with the box and hear a scuffling noise. It sounds like rats, clawing at the cardboard from the inside. Perhaps there *are* rats in there, and this is all part of his hideous experiment. I hesitate. But then I think about how frightened I was when I arrived, and somehow it makes me feel better, imagining I can offer some sort of comfort to somebody else. At least his won't be the first voice she hears.

'I think you've been kidnapped,' I say. 'That's what's happened to me. We're in a basement. I'm tied up, and you've been put in a cardboard box.' I hear the sound of gentle sobbing, and feel tears of sympathy spring to my eyes. I feel guilty at the relief it brings me not to be alone any more, because it means somebody else's life is over. 'I'm very sorry this has happened to you, I really am. But perhaps together we can work out a way to escape. My name's Ava Lindsey.'

'Ava?' says a voice from inside the box. 'Ava Lindsey? The missing girl? Oh my God, oh my God, no, no, no . . .' She dissolves into weeping again.

'I'm sorry,' I say.

'I want to get out of here,' she wails. 'Oh God, I can't stand it! I can't stand it!' She kicks at the cardboard in panic. It must be industrial strength, because although it buckles with the impact, the seams don't split.

'Wait,' I say. 'Which end is your head? Here, I'll tap on the box, let me know if it sounds like I'm tapping near your face or your toes.' I shuffle along to one end of the box, then turn round so my back is to the cardboard. I flex my fingers, flicking at the box with my knuckles. Not the loudest rapping, but enough for her to tell if it's right next to her head.

'I think that's by my feet,' she says. Her voice sounds a bit stronger. Perhaps concentrating her mind on a practical task is good for her nerves. 'Can you knock again?' I flick the cardboard. 'Yes, that's my feet.'

'OK,' I say. 'What I'm going to do now is sit right on the edge of the box here. If you can kick against the end, perhaps we can make the bottom collapse.' I manage to heave myself up. The cardboard bulges. She starts to kick frantically. 'My hands are tied so I'm sorry if I fall on you,' I say, trying to raise my voice. My throat is hurting from all this talking. She doesn't answer in any case; all her energy is focused on kicking. I lurch alarmingly as the box starts to crumple. Without my hands to save my fall, I hope I don't crash head first onto the concrete. The box collapses suddenly, and I land on her feet, the drop cushioned slightly by the buckling cardboard, but we both cry out in pain. I shuffle off her ankles as best I can.

'Is the cardboard broken enough for me to get out?' she asks.

'Yes, if you wriggle along, you should make it, you'll be able to push the flap out with your feet.'

I can hear her puff with exertion as a pair of black sensible shoes appear, with thick rubber soles. My first thought is that they look like a police officer's boots, but then my heart lurches as I see the blue trousers of medical scrubs. Painstakingly, my companion makes her way out.

She lies there a minute, red-faced, looking up at me, her cheeks wet with tears. Then she smiles. I think I will be grateful to her forever for the effort that smile must have cost her. 'Hi,' she says. 'My name's Daisy.'

Frankie

Gavin sits white-faced in his car, the engine dead, Frankie beside him. She feels on the verge of hysteria.

'Oh God, we killed her. We should never have run that report,' she says. 'Amber would still be alive if we'd been more careful. We *killed* her, Gavin.'

'Come on now,' he says. 'That's not true. She approached us! She wanted to talk about it. And maybe she's not dead. Maybe some daft punter has locked her up for a bit, like Donnie did.'

'Shit, Gav. I should never have used that clip about him tying her up.'

Gavin says nothing for a moment, well aware whose idea that was. 'You had to use it,' he says at last. 'It was one of the only things she really talked about in detail. And you used a clip of her saying he was a lovely man too, I remember it. Maybe Amber's disappearance has nothing to do with us.'

Frankie covers her eyes with her hands, wishing she could blot out reality as easily. 'God, I hope not,' she says.

Gavin looks at the clock on the dashboard, turns his key in the ignition. 'Look, we need to let the newsdesk know what's happened. And at the risk of sounding heartless, we need to drive straight to Emneth's house, the police are bound to arrest him.'

Far from expressing dismay at Amber's disappearance, Kiera is delighted by the idea that they might end up with exclusive footage of the Strangler being arrested. They drive to Donald Emneth's house in Costessey and sit in Gavin's battered Toyota, parked several doors down from his bungalow. The house is partly screened by lime trees, but they can see that all the curtains are drawn. Gavin's camera is out, ready on the back seat if the police turn up.

'Could be a longish wait,' he says, finishing off his homemade sandwich, and scrunching the cling film into a ball.

'Sorry,' says Frankie.

'That's not why I said it. Just worried about you. Been a hell of a week.'

'I've got you for company though, haven't I?'

Gavin laughs. 'Flatterer.'

'D'you reckon Amber really told Charlie she'd spoken to Donnie?' says Frankie. He had assured her of this several times on the phone and she's desperate for it to be true. It would go some way to assuage the guilt that's clamped, vice-like, round her heart.

'Never known him to be one for lying,' says Gavin. 'And it would make sense, wouldn't it? If she wanted to do the old guy a favour, surely she'd run it by him first.' He sits back in his seat and looks at her, his grey hair backlit from the sun shining behind him. 'Franks, this really isn't our fault. I don't want you driving yourself mad with guilt over whatever's happened. If anything, the police are to blame. If Captain Birdseye is a killer, they should never have let him go.'

'I guess so,' says Frankie. 'I guess Gubberts was keen to pass the buck when we spoke to him earlier, because he knows he'll be in for it if Emneth is guilty. But I still find it hard to see old Donnie as the Norfolk Strangler, don't you?'

'Why's that?'

'Well, I struggle to imagine him writing that blog, for a start.'

'But maybe the killer didn't write the blog?'

Frankie looks at Gavin, then away. She hasn't told him about the cards or the smashing vase online. Dan and Jack know, and that's enough. The fewer people she tells, the less real it feels. She stares out at the street. The house they are parked alongside has a floor-to-ceiling window. She can see a toddler sitting on the carpet watching telly, their mum or grandma ironing in the background.

'I know this whole blog thing's difficult for you, Franks,' Gavin says, reaching over to squeeze her shoulder when she doesn't reply. 'I realise it must be getting to you, it would me. But I mean, there's nothing to suggest the writer is the killer, is there? It's just some wanker who happened to gob off about Hanna Chivers. Just because . . .' Gavin trails off, his attention caught by the rear-view mirror. 'We're in business,' he says, swiftly stepping out of the car and grabbing his camera from the back seat. A police car passes them on the road. It pulls up outside Donald Emneth's house.

Gavin is already trotting towards the action, camera hoisted up on his shoulder, and she knows he will be in record. He stops, standing back from the house, a respectful distance to let the police do their job, but she's sure they will still be annoyed to see him there. She takes the keys out of the ignition, then locks up the car, walking along the pavement until she's standing next to him. Without a word, Gavin hands her the overhead microphone. It's on an extra long lead so she can angle it and try to pick up any sound from the arrest.

Either the police haven't seen them, or more likely they've decided to ignore them. An argument with the press isn't going to serve their purposes right now; it will only alert their suspect. Two officers walk up to Donald Emneth's front door and knock. Gavin and Frankie watch as it opens a crack. They catch a glimpse of a bearded face, then Donald Emneth tries to slam it shut, but the larger policeman already has his foot in the doorway. Together the officers wrestle with Mr Emneth, and get him in cuffs. He's shouting but they are too far away to hear what he says. They head towards his garden gate, Frankie holding out the microphone, to catch any sound. When he sees them, Donald Emneth aims a kick at Gavin, who steps neatly out of the way.

'Vultures!' he shouts. 'You've ruined my life! You've fucking *ruined* my life! I've lost everything because of you . . .'

'Mr Emneth, it's not advisable to be saying anything to the press at this stage,' says one of the officers, shooting a warning look at Frankie. 'If you two could stand back, out of the way. *Please.*'

They bundle Mr Emneth into the back of the panda car, then one of the policemen heads back to the house. Gavin continues filming, following the man with his lens, though the officer studiously ignores the camera as he walks past them. He's inside the house for about five minutes, and Gavin switches off record.

'D'you think that's our lot?' says Frankie.

'Let's just wait until he comes out,' says Gavin.

They hear the wail of a siren. Gavin switches his camera back on and an ambulance roars past them, blue lights on. It stops outside Donald Emneth's house and two paramedics rush in to the bungalow.

'Oh my God,' Frankie says.

A short while after the paramedics have gone in the policeman comes out of the house. He's talking urgently into his radio. He clocks them and stands in the doorway, finishing the call, then tucks it back into his jacket. He walks towards them.

'A word please,' he says to Frankie. He gestures at the camera. 'Not with that recording.'

'Of course,' she says.

Gavin switches the camera off but the policeman stands behind him, just to be sure. 'And you are?' he asks.

'I'm Frances Latch from the Eastern Film Company and this is Gavin Starling.'

'DS John Bellmont,' he replies, nodding to them both. 'I know we all have a job to do, but I'm going to ask you to be sensitive and refrain from filming when they come out.'

'Is she alive? Are there two of them?'

'We've found one victim and she's alive,' says DS Bellmont. 'But very distressed. She certainly doesn't need to be all over the evening news.'

'Is it Ava or Amber?'

'It's not for me to tell you that,' he replies. 'Not until the family have been informed.' While he's speaking, Gavin lowers his camera to the floor. The policeman turns round as behind him a woman is led out to the ambulance, supported on either side by paramedics and wrapped in a blanket. There's little they can see of her but Frankie notices her hair. It's not pink.

Ava

I smile back. It makes my face hurt. I put my hand up to my cheek and realise it must be badly bruised. It's hard to remember but I think he punched me. And there's dried vomit on my chin. I must look a sight.

'Are you a doctor?' I ask her, as she scrambles up into a sitting position.

'A midwife. At the Norfolk and Norwich,' she says, then notices my arms are behind my back. 'Here, let me get your hands free.' She scoots over and pulls at my wrists. I wince as she tugs and something cuts into my skin. 'Dammit,' she says. 'It's those plastic things, you know cable ties.' She lies back down on the floor, so her face is level with the restraints. I can feel her breath on my hands as she studies them. Then she pushes and pulls, even gnaws at them with her teeth. This seems to go on forever, and I have to bite my tongue not to cry out, it's so painful.

'I'm really sorry,' she says at last. 'I'm not sure I'm going to be able to get them off. He seems to have melted them closed as well. Your wrists look like they might be a bit burned.'

I try not to scream with frustration. 'Never mind,' I reply, my voice heavy with disappointment. 'Maybe we can try again later.'

'I'm really sorry,' Daisy says again. I notice she has blood on her bottom lip where the plastic must have cut her when she tried to bite through, and my anger evaporates. It's not her fault.

'There's water over there, if you'd like some.' I gesture with my head. 'I'd really love it if you could get some for me too.'

'Of course.' She scrambles up, grabs a bottle and sits cross-legged in front of me, unscrewing the top. 'I'm used to helping

187

women drink water,' she says. 'But normally under happier circumstances, when they're in labour.'

She has such an earnest face. Dark messy curls are all out of shape on the side of her head where she's been lying in the box, and as I drink she looks at me with wide grey eyes. Her kindness makes me feel better and worse at the same time. I start to cry.

She puts an arm round me, the way she must have put her arm round a hundred other crying women. 'There, there,' Daisy says. 'It's OK. It's going to be OK.'

Neither of us has any idea if that's true or not, in fact our odds must be pretty poor, but then I suppose medical professionals are trained to inspire calm, even in the dying.

'I guess you've seen a lot of death,' I say.

'Well, yes. Doesn't make me relish the thought though,' she says. 'And my job is mainly about life, fortunately.'

'He's mad,' I say, as she wipes tears and snot from my face with her sleeve. 'The guy who's keeping us here. He's completely insane. Got this massive grudge against women, he hates us. I've been trying to connect with him, to make him me see me as a person, but it doesn't seem to be working. And now I've gone and blown it anyway by attacking him, by trying to escape . . .' I trail off, thinking of his hands round my neck. 'He says he's running a fear experiment. I don't know why he's put both of us together but it must be for something awful.'

I see the flash of terror in her eyes. Then she swallows hard, makes an effort to stifle it. 'There's two of us and one of him. We must be able to out-think him. Overpower him even.'

'Not with my hands tied up,' I say, a little bitterly.

'They're so tight. I'm really sorry, Ava. Even if we made the decision to take chunks of skin off your wrists, the plastic's not going to fit over your hands. And I'm worried that the more we cut you, the bigger the risk of infection.'

She's a midwife, I suppose she must know about these things, though I can't help feeling she's given up a little easily. I look at her, suspicion pricking my heart, wondering if those pale eyes are as open as they seem, wondering if I can trust her. It's not her hands that are tied after all; perhaps it suits her to be the one free.

Then it hits me.

'That's why you're here. He's going try and set us against each other. Survival of the fittest.' We look at each other appalled. 'He might even have done it already. To some of the other women.' I start shaking, I can't stop myself, my whole body is shivering with fear.

'We don't know that,' says Daisy, putting a hand on my shoulder, trying to hold me still. 'We don't know what he's thinking.'

'I didn't even watch the news properly when I was free, I don't know anything about him. I don't know anything.' The reassurance I felt from Daisy's presence is starting to drain away. I wish she'd move her hand. Being tied up and trapped in the room is making me doubly claustrophobic, I want to pace about, and am moments from another panic attack.

Perhaps Daisy senses this. She grips my shoulder tighter. 'That's a really good idea,' she says, though I haven't suggested anything. 'We can go through what we know about him. I can remember quite a lot about the news reports, I'm a bit of a current affairs junkie.' She runs a hand gently over my forehead, smooths my hair, bringing me back to myself. 'Breathe in through your nose, out through your mouth. Deep breaths. Good girl.' I do as she says and start to feel better, though my throat and chest hurt when I breathe in. 'Right, according to the news he's killed three women. It's OK, stay calm. And he's kidnapped you. You must have been here quite a few days now, though I can't remember exactly when it was first reported. Your mum and dad have done an appeal, they seem really lovely—'

'What about my brother, was he on the appeal?' I interrupt.

'No, I don't think so. I think it's just been your parents.'

I let out a cry. 'Oh God, he told me he was dead, he told me he was dead! What if it's true, he must be dead, Oh God, oh God . . .'

'Hang on, who told you? The kidnapper told you your brother was dead?' I nod, my breathing ragged as I try not to give in to sobs. 'Well then, it's probably a lie. He has been in the news, your brother. It's in some of the reports about you. How you looked after him when he was ill last year. When he was in hospital. Maybe this guy just read the reports.'

Her words act as a brake, stop me from falling further. 'Really?' I ask, hardly daring to hope it's true. Daisy nods. 'Maybe he's OK, then,' I say. And I start crying again, this time from relief.

'There, there, sweetheart. I'm sure he's OK, he'll be OK. Don't cry. He'll be waiting for you. And I remember your mum gave you a message in French. That was the headline on one of the papers: Stay Strong, Sweetheart.'

'*Reste forte, chérie*,' I murmur. I think about my mum, waiting for me, believing I will come home. 'Thank you,' I say to Daisy. 'I'm sorry not to be much use. Just crying. Pathetic.'

'Don't be daft,' she says. 'You got me out of the box, didn't you?'

A clanking noise startles us both. I see my own fear reflected in her face. The door handle is turning. I realise we've been wasting time. We hadn't yet discussed a plan for what we should do if he came in and now it's too late. We stare at one another, frozen with terror.

He closes the door behind him. I hadn't warned Daisy about the padded ski mask and feel her stiffen as she takes in the round ball of his head, its strange shape distorting and dehumanising his features. 'Well this is touching,' he says, looking at us.

Daisy scrambles to her feet, standing in front of me, her legs wide and arms slightly out, as if shielding me. The combination of exhaustion, pain and having no hands free means I have no hope of standing on my own. 'What do you want?' she says.

'Didn't Ava tell you? I don't like questions.' He takes two steps towards her, and I see a blade glinting in one hand.

'Look out! He's got a knife!' I scream.

He laughs and waves it at us, cutting through the air as if it's a scythe. Daisy takes a step back, almost treading on me. 'The thing is, Daisy. I'm going to give you a choice. Either you let me tie you up, or I'm going to kill Ava.'

Daisy cowers backwards, still blocking him from reaching me, though whether from fear or design it's hard to say. He strides forward, thrusting the knife in her face, and instinctively she cringes away from its blade. He grabs me by the arm, dragging me roughly to my feet, making me yelp with pain. He presses the knife against my neck. 'Don't make me impatient,' he says to Daisy. 'Go stand in the corner, bitch, facing the wall, and put your hands behind your back.'

I think I'm going to pass out. I can feel the cold edge of the metal pressing against my skin, which is already raw from where he choked me. I will Daisy to obey him. She walks slowly to the corner and we shuffle after her. 'Lie face down on the floor,' he breathes in my ear. Wobbling, I obey. Immediately he rests his foot on my back, making it impossible for me to rise. I twist my head and watch as he hogties Daisy with one hand, the other pressing the knife at the nape of her neck. She winces as he pulls the cable tie tight. Once she's tied up, he gets a lighter out of his pocket and melts the ends of the cable tie together. Drops of hot plastic fall on the floor near my face, and Daisy whimpers. I admire her for not screaming.

'Right you,' he says bending down to me. 'Are you going to be good? Pull another stunt like last time and I swear this knife is going in your fucking eyeball. Understood?'

'Yes.'

He grunts and cuts the cable tie round my wrists. It hurts as he pulls, but once my hands are free, the relief is enormous. I bring my arms round so the palms are pressed on the cold floor. There's a sharp pain in my shoulders from the angle they had been pulled into, and I don't think I could get up yet, even if I tried.

'Right then, girls, a bit of swapsies for you. Let's see how you share the food now it's your turn without hands, Daisy.' He looks between us both, then claps his own in a parody of glee. 'Isn't this fun? You two must have lots to chat about, my little TV stars.

Though Daisy's got the edge on you, Ava, she's been swanning around on some Nazi Health Service documentary, spouting a load of nonsense. And I wouldn't get too fond of each other,' he adds, nodding at Daisy. 'Just like the NHS, I've got limited resources, not sure how long I can keep you both. But then, you must be used to those decisions all the time on the ward, bitch.' He moves to the door. My cheek is still resting on the concrete and I can hear Daisy crying softly. 'Only one of you can pass the experiment. That's just how it works.'

Frankie

In the newsroom Kiera is jubilant. Their network is the only broadcaster to have shots of the Strangler's arrest. They share the rushes with Luke and after the footage has appeared on Commercial Television's lunchtime bulletin, it gets played over and over on 24-hour news, their rivals having to run it with the company's EXCLUSIVE banner burned into the picture. One of the channels seems to be playing Donald Emneth aiming a kick at Gavin on a loop, Frankie has seen it so many times.

Her relief that Amber is alive dwarfs almost every other emotion. If she had been murdered, Frankie isn't sure she could have handled the guilt. She knows Gavin and Charlie also feel a sense of reprieve. The only one who appears unmoved is Kiera. 'Well at least we have an "in" with Amber when she decides to talk,' is all her boss says, as she leans against the newsdesk, one elbow skewering the newspaper Charlie had been reading. 'Given she's spoken to us before.'

Charlie raises an eyebrow at Frankie, but she doesn't respond. She's still annoyed he let her self-shoot the job in Lowestoft, even though he has no idea about the stress she went through as a result. 'Police have yet to charge Emneth,' he says, rolling his chair away slightly from Kiera. 'But it can only be a matter of time, given you saw Amber being taken out of his house.' He glances at one of the screens. They had abided by the police request and the only sign there had been a victim is a shot of the ambulance doors slamming and the vehicle pulling away.

'I guess they might only charge him with abduction,' Frankie says. 'Maybe he's not the Strangler.'

Kiera makes a face. 'Of course he is,' she says. 'The police say they've arrested him on suspicion of three counts of murder, why on earth wouldn't they charge him?'

'Well, even if he's only done for kidnap,' says Charlie. 'He's still looking at life. We'll run the footage and say there's been an arrest, but I think it's best we hold off on a report.'

'What about Ava Lindsey?' Frankie says. 'She's never been found. Shouldn't we ask the police what they're doing to track her down?'

'I imagine they're asking Emneth about her as we speak,' says Charlie. 'But yes, we should definitely press them on that. I suspect our friend Donnie has already left her remains somewhere, it seems to be how he operates. Luke and the national crew are staying up here, hoping that's the case. They're banking on the police finding another body.'

Frankie sits at her desk, in the rare position of having not much to do. The police, unsurprisingly, won't tell her anything about their search for Ava. She ought to feel delighted they've taken in Donald Emneth, not only for Amber, but for herself too, but there's a good reason she doesn't. Shortly after news of the arrest broke, Jack texted her to say there's been another comment from the poster calling themselves @The_Norfolk_Strangler.

Best not count your chickens too soon.

She tries to tell herself it's exactly what a hoaxer who had seen the arrest would say, but she still feels frightened. She's about to wander over to the kitchen to get a cup of tea, when the phone on her desk rings. The extension flashing isn't her personal line but the main newsroom number. She looks around to see if anyone else might be free, then picks it up.

'Eastern Film Company?'

'Grant Allen here, from Justice for Jailbirds. I'm after Frances Latch.'

Her heart sinks. Not him again. 'Speaking.'

'Miss Latch, I thought I recognised your voice. How about you keep your promise and have me on the show now Donnie's been arrested again?'

She stifles the urge to put the phone straight down again. 'Hello, Mr Allen,' she says, trying not to let her irritation show. 'Firstly, I didn't promise, and secondly I meant we might be able to interview you after the killer is *convicted*. The case is still active, there's not even been a trial yet.'

'Whether he's guilty or innocent, Donnie still has the right to be treated fairly by the press.'

'I couldn't agree more, which is why we can't interview you.'

There's a pause on the line. 'Slippery customer, aren't you?'

Frankie's patience is at an end. 'For somebody who wants to get on telly, Mr Allen, you have a funny way of going about it. Good day.' She puts the phone down with a clunk. 'Idiot,' she mutters. Her curiosity piqued, she types his organisation into the search engine on her computer. A link to *Justice4Jailbirds* appears. She opens it. The website looks like it was built a decade ago and never updated. There are no pictures and the font is tiny. She clicks on the *About Me* section.

Grant Allen is the director and founder of Justice4Jailbirds. He has helped countless men on their journey through the criminal justice system, from arrest all the way to support on the inside. Grant's passion for justice was born when his 17-year-old son Zach was sentenced to 12 years. He saw the way Zach was treated and vowed no other boy – or man – should go through the same. Click here if you'd like to get me on board your case!

None the wiser, Frankie googles Grant's name. Immediately dozens of results pop up, including several press clippings. She clicks on the most recent, an article from the *Norfolk Times*.

Time on the PlayStation, guv? The life of a con at HMP Halvergate

Prison campaigner Grant Allen has spoken out about the conditions newly convicted sex pest Jamie Cole can expect inside Norfolk's HMP Halvergate.

Cole, who is 22 and from King's Lynn, was convicted of raping one woman and indecently assaulting three more at Norwich Crown Court last month. He's been sentenced to 6 years in prison.

'It's a joke,' says Allen, 58, from Brandon. 'They don't have the staff there to look after people. When my son Zach was inside, they left him to rot away in his cell all day. Rehabilitation programmes? Don't make me laugh.'

Allen's son Zachary Allen was convicted of manslaughter in 2002 at the age of 17, after killing his girlfriend, 15-year-old Cathy Spencer, in a drug-fuelled row. He served 8 years. Aged just 16 at the time of the crime, Zachary Allen is now living under a new identity.

Inspired by his son's experiences, Grant Allen runs a support group for recently convicted prisoners, **Justice4Jailbirds**. He has attended the trials of several notorious villains, as self-described 'back-up support'.

Mr Allen says Jamie Cole can expect to spend lots of time on his PlayStation inside. 'At Halvergate they just leave you to your own devices, locked up in your cell for hours on end,' he says. 'I know people don't have any sympathy for prisoners, but it's an outrageous form of neglect. And you can forget about staff caring if you get beaten up – in fact they might join in.'

HMP Halvergate has strongly denied Mr Allen's claims, saying in a statement that it maintains 'the highest standards of care towards its inmates and takes seriously violence of any kind.'

Cathy Spencer's aunt, Amy Wrexham, has condemned Mr Allen for his remarks. 'The fact Grant Allen goes to the trials of men like Jamie Cole and offers them support just sickens me,' she told the *Norfolk Times*. 'What about support for the victims? Zachary Allen only did 8 years, and now he's out in the world somewhere, living his life with a new name and no real punishment for what he did. Cathy is dead and we are all living a life sentence without her. Where's the justice in that?'

Mr Allen, who is now estranged from his son, says Zachary

accepted responsibility for his actions many years ago. He maintains all criminals deserve to be treated with respect. 'Two wrongs don't make a right,' he told us.

Frankie reads the article again, frowning. Grant Allen attended Jamie Cole's trial and so must have heard Hanna give evidence. She wonders who else is involved in his *Justice4Jailbirds* organisation. Curious about his son, she types 'Zachary Allen + Cathy Spencer' into the search bar, looking for clippings on his trial. She opens the first to pop up.

Schoolboy pleads guilty to killing girlfriend.

17-year-old schoolboy Zachary Allen has pleaded guilty at Cambridge Crown Court to killing his girlfriend Cathy Spencer in an argument last year.

The court heard that Allen, who was 16 at the time of the offence, had been smoking super-strength cannabis – known as skunk – with 15-year-old Cathy Spencer at his family home in Brandon, on 12th August 2001.

Mr Edward Collins, acting on behalf of the defendant, told the judge that the pair had an argument on the landing, and in a moment of madness Zachary Allen hit Cathy Spencer over the head with a jug of flowers. She fell down the stairs and suffered serious head injuries, dying at Addenbrooke's Hospital two days later. In mitigation Mr Collins said that the 16-year-old boy was suffering from trauma following his mother's unexplained disappearance last year and that this, together with the effect of the drugs, had led him into being uncharacteristically violent. Mr Collins asked the judge to consider the defendant's age and early guilty plea when deciding the sentence.

Outside Court a solicitor read a statement on behalf of Cathy Spencer's family. 'We are pleased that Zachary Allen has finally admitted his guilt. However, nothing can bring Cathy back. She was a clever, funny girl with her whole life ahead of her. She loved Zachary Allen, who abused that trust in the most cruel way imaginable. We are all devastated by her loss, and have no idea how we are now to face life without her.'

The article includes a photograph of Cathy, a plump blonde teenager, laughing on a swing, but nothing of Zachary. Frankie supposes that as a minor, his image must have been protected.

She searches for anything about Zachary in her company's own archive, but there's nothing that adds to the press clippings: they don't have any images of him either. She stares at the picture of Cathy Spencer, trying to dispel the anxiety that's taking hold. The detail about how she died, hit over the head by a jug of flowers, makes her think of the gif of the smashing vase on Lily's Facebook page and the cards she's been getting in the post. She tells herself it's just coincidence but the fear lingers.

Eventually she stands up and wanders over to Zara's desk. She taps her friend on the shoulder. 'D'you fancy a proper coffee before you go into the studio? I'm heading into town to get some air, I might nip to that new place opposite the cathedral.'

'Oh lovely, thanks,' says Zara, rooting about in her bag for change. She's got her late-afternoon make-up on, ready to present the programme, and is wearing far too much eye-liner. As some-body who never normally 'does her face' Zara has yet to crack the art of applying cosmetics for the studio lights. Paul Carter's foundation is much more evenly spread.

'Don't be daft,' Frankie says, walking away. 'I can stand you a coffee.' As she heads out of the door, she tells herself she's almost abided by Dan's rule to say exactly where she's going.

Frankie walks into the city, head down, hurrying towards the cathedral close. The pavements seem particularly full, and she pushes past people in her agitation. Zachary Allen has made her very nervous. He must be just a little older than her, out for around seven years now, living under a new name. If anyone has a reason to hate women, surely it's him, the boy abandoned by his mother, whose life was wrecked by a row with a girl. She passes under the ancient stone archway into the green, away from the traffic, and takes a deep breath, feeling a little better to be out of the rush. The vast honey coloured spire rises in front of her, its edge hard against the clear blue sky. She sits down on one of the benches by the grass. There's a chill in the air and she pulls her coat higher up her neck.

Dan picks up almost straight away. 'Hi,' she says. 'It's Frances Latch here.'

'I was just about to call you,' he replies. She wonders if that's as false as when a journalist says it. Probably not, Dan seems an extremely earnest young man. 'Don't worry, I've seen there are more comments under the blog,' he continues.

'It wasn't all of them that worried me,' says Frankie. 'Or not enough to call. It's the one claiming to be . . .' She hesitates, looking round the cathedral green. An elderly couple are walking by on the path opposite, and not far behind them, a young mother with shopping hanging from her pram. 'The one claiming to be from the killer,' she says, her voice low.

'Yes, I know exactly which one you mean,' he says. 'Where are you, by the way? Somewhere safe to talk?'

'I'm at the cathedral green,' she replies. 'There's nobody nearby.'

'OK,' says Dan. 'Well, keep your wits about you. I also wanted to let you know that the major crime unit are taking apart Donald Emneth's computer right now, looking for any links to the website.'

'I thought they weren't pursuing it as a major line of enquiry?'

There's a pause. 'Well, it's obviously not the only reason they're looking at his online history,' he admits. 'But I've asked them to keep an eye out for links to the blog too.'

'Thanks,' she says. 'Also, have you ever come across Grant Allen?'

'The Justice for Jailbirds guy? Why, what about him?'

'I think you might want to check into his background, maybe look at his online history too. It seems he went to Jamie Cole's trial, which means he would have had all the details about Hanna, just like the blogger Feminazi Slayer did. He also keeps calling the newsroom asking to come on the show and hasn't been too pleased that I've said no. He rang just this morning, asking for me.'

'Was he threatening in any way?'

She thinks about the rasping voice on the phone. 'No,' she admits. 'Just rude.'

'Sounds about right. Grant's not known for his manners. But if he's not threatened you, that doesn't sound too out of the ordinary. Our Mr Allen's always trying to get in the papers. He's also very litigious, so mind how you go.'

'Is there no way you can question him?'

'Not really, no, not unless you've got something more to go on,' says Dan. 'We can't just go taking people's computers apart on a punt, there's got to be a good reason to suspect them. Sorry if that sounds harsh,' he adds, perhaps hearing the pompous tone in his own voice.

'And the fact he went to Jamie Cole's trial to provide the guy with back-up support doesn't give you enough to go on?' Frankie asks.

'It's interesting,' Dan says. 'And definitely worth bearing in mind. But no more than that right now. It's not as if Grant's made any secret of supporting Jamie Cole – it's not as if he makes a secret of anything, the man's a total loudmouth, as I'm sure you're aware having spoken to him.'

Frankie glances round the green. There's nobody within earshot. 'What about his son?'

'The lad that killed his girlfriend? Living somewhere under a new name, I believe.'

'Couldn't you find out who he is?' There's a long silence. 'Dan? Are you there? I just thought if anyone fits the bill for Feminazi Slayer, it's him. He killed his girlfriend by smashing a vase of flowers over her head, and a smashing vase is the image left online for Lily and now for me. And then I've been getting those weird cards, and Hanna got glass in the post . . .' She trails off, not wanting to say her idea out loud. The police have arrested Donald Emneth after all, and Dan's not going to want to hear her theory about an alternative killer.

'Zachary Allen's new identity is protected by court order, only a handful of people know who he is.' Dan sounds angry. 'And even if I found out, can you imagine what would happen if I leaked that to the press? I'm amazed you'd even ask.'

'For God's sake!' Frankie says. 'I didn't mean for you to tell *me*. I meant could *you* find out, as in you, the police, investigating the case!'

'Oh right,' says Dan. 'Sorry.'

'Never mind,' says Frankie. 'Probably just a "punt" as you'd call it.'

'Look, I'm really sorry not to be more helpful,' says Dan. 'Genuinely, I am. Keep me posted on Grant Allen, let me know if he contacts you again. But for now, let's see if Donald Emneth's computer throws anything up.'

Frankie says goodbye and stuffs the phone back in her coat pocket, disappointed. It's not that Dan's said anything unreasonable, but she was still hoping for more. After their last meeting, she had started to see him as an ally. She sits for a moment, looking out at the green without seeing it, lost in her thoughts. Then a movement catches her eye. There's a figure in a woolly hat and a dark duffle coat, standing near the cathedral doors. It's too far away to see clearly, but she gets the feeling whoever it is, is watching her. She stands up, and walks swiftly to the archway. With a sidelong glance, as if she's admiring the cathedral, she looks back. The figure in the duffle coat is heading towards her across the green.

Her heart beats faster and she quickens her steps. She can hear her heels ring out on the tarmac, echoing against the ancient stone as she walks under the shadow of the arch. On the other side she turns a sharp left and waits round the corner, watching to see if the figure in the duffle coat comes out. Two minutes pass. Three. There's nothing.

Frankie walks back into the cathedral green, trying to look casual. A couple of students are now sitting on her bench and she can see a woman walking a dog. But no sign of the figure in the coat. Whoever it was must have walked the other way.

'You're going loopy,' she says to herself, angry at being spooked. She crosses the road, heading back into town, resisting the temptation to turn round and check if she's being followed. In Tombland she darts into a sandwich bar to pick up the coffee she promised Zara. There's a short queue. She's watching the barista prepare another customer's order, thumping out the old grains into the waste, when a soft voice by her ear nearly startles her out of her skin.

'Fancy seeing you here.'

She turns round to see Brett Hollins behind her. He's wearing a shirt with the same carefully ironed collar she remembers from the bar, and a distressed leather bag hangs over one shoulder. He's also standing far too close. 'Where did you spring from?' she says, relieved to notice he's not wearing a duffle coat.

'Sorry, did I give you a fright?' He looks amused rather than apologetic. He places one hand on her upper arm, and gives it a squeeze. 'I didn't mean to scare you.'

There's no room to step backwards and Frankie's too embarrassed to ask him to remove his hand so she squirms slightly and he lets go, nudging against her breast with his palm as he moves away. She feels the blood rush to her face, not quite certain whether or not he did it on purpose.

'What'll you be having?' It's the waitress, but Frankie is still staring at Brett. He looks particularly smug, obviously mistaking the reason for her blush.

'I think it's your turn,' he says.

'Right, sorry, um, two lattes please,' she splutters, irritated that she's the one who's embarrassed. 'I don't think much of Schopenhauer,' she says to him, aware after she's said it that this is a ridiculous remark to make out of nowhere.

'Really? Why not?'

'He was a massive sexist, that's why.'

'He was a man of his time.' Brett looks sidelong at her. His brown eyes remind her of a fox, sly and inscrutable. An image from *Killing Cuttlefish*, her own face transposed onto a harpy, flashes into her mind. Could this man have set up the website? Or worse? She can feel her palms sweating. She's desperate to get away. 'And really,' he continues, 'it would be an anachronism to judge him. By today's standards *everyone* back then was sexist.'

'He was born after Mary Wollstonecraft, so that's no excuse.' Frankie takes the coffees off the waitress, one in each hand, and looks up at him, her chin jutting out with fear and anger. 'And you must know sexists today still look up to him as if he's some sort of hero? There's even an entire website named after that horrible essay he wrote on women, and the whole thing's stuffed with hateful misogynist posts.' She holds Brett's gaze, watching him as she speaks, trying to judge his reaction.

He smiles and reaches forward to push a strand of hair behind her ear, his fingers brushing her cheek. 'What an *extraordinary* woman you are.'

She flinches. 'Don't touch me!' she says, much louder than she intended. She's aware of the waitress and other customers staring. It's Brett's turn to turn red. She leaves him standing by the counter and rushes out of the café, spilling some of her drinks as she bangs the door open.

Ava

Daisy is the best thing to happen to me since I was kidnapped. I feel guilty even thinking that, but it's true. The relief of being with somebody kind and having somebody sane to talk to is overwhelming. I know she's as helpless as I am, more so now her hands are tied, but somehow I feel safer with her here.

We have tried our hardest to get her hands free, but she was right; even taking the skin off, the cable tie won't fit over her knuckles. I'm currently trying to work a metal hook free from Daisy's left shoe. If I can rub that against the plastic for any length of time, I might be able to snap it. We both need our hands free if we're to stand any chance of overpowering him.

Our plan is for me to stand behind the door when he comes in and try to grab him round the neck from behind, while she kicks him in the nuts. Not especially original, but we're short of options, and this is something we could attempt even with her hands tied. Part of me is reluctant even to try. If we fail, I don't think he will be as forgiving as last time.

'When you've tried to get to know him,' Daisy says, 'have you seen any glimmer of empathy, anything at all?'

'I think he liked Hanna. The girl here before us,' I reply.

'The *dead* one? Well, that's brilliant.' She pulls a face, and though it's not funny we both laugh. 'Oh God,' she says, flopping her head back against the wall. 'This can't be real, it can't be happening.' She sighs, closing her eyes. 'I should be on shift right now. There's a mum who had post-natal depression with her first baby and she's pregnant again. I'm meant to be seeing her today, or at least I think it's today, if today is today. Shit, you know what I mean.'

'I know,' I say. I've completely lost track of how long I've been here. 'I've probably missed the deadline for my coursework.'

She snorts. 'Think the university will let you off?'

I think of Professor Marks and go cold. 'He imitated my tutor. Fat Head, I mean.' That's our new name for him. Daisy thought of it. 'I don't think he is Peter Marks, not really, but sometimes I don't feel totally sure. It's hard to be sure of anything in here.'

'Jesus! What does this guy *want*,' she says, her mind, like mine, constantly revolving around the man who's keeping us here. 'Is it sex? I mean, has he . . .' She trails off, a mixture of fear and sympathy in her voice.

I shake my head to reassure her. 'No, not at all. I don't think he's interested.' I look down at my vomit-stained front and my filthy jeans. 'Not sure why. I look irresistible right now.' There's a touch of hysteria to the laugh that follows, but even so, laughing at him is making me feel better. 'Actually I think women disgust him. Not just sexually, in every other way too. He just hates us.'

'Do you think there's a pattern?' she says. 'Why he's picked us in particular?'

'Not the first women, I don't think. He just refers to them all as "the whores", they don't even get names. But Hanna he always refers to by name, and me.' I think of the way he says my name – *Ay-vah* – deliberately stressing the first syllable, as if saying it gives him extra control over me. 'And he claims he was stalking me for a while.'

'God, how creepy. I wonder if he's been hanging round the hospital, round any of my pregnant women. What a bastard.'

Her brow crinkles with concern and I love her even more, knowing that even here, in this awful place, she's thinking of her patients. 'He told me a lot about Hanna,' I say. 'I think I know why he targeted her. It's because she got a guy banged up for sexual assault. That and he felt they'd both had a hard upbringing.'

'That's weird. He kidnapped her because of something they had *in common*?'

'I think he went for me because he *didn't* want to sympathise. He's always going on about how privileged I am. And over-educated. Comparing me to Hanna.'

'So, we've got a woman who gets a man sent to prison, a smart university student and a midwife. All stuff, I guess, that he wouldn't like. Unless the whole thing is just opportunism.'

If he's been stalking me, I know there's something else he might hate. 'Also, I'm a lesbian,' I say, blushing slightly, though my face is probably too filthy to show it. I hope she doesn't look at me differently now she knows, that I haven't ruined things between us. But why should she? After all, I haven't added the part that might make her uncomfortable: *and I think you're beautiful.* 'Fat Head's not mentioned it.' I shrug, as if it's no big deal for me to have told her. 'But I know being gay doesn't tend to earn you many friends with misogynists.'

'We're never going to know, are we? I mean we could just go round and round and round and still have no clue why the fuck he's doing what he's doing.' She closes her eyes again and I think she's on the verge of tears.

'We're going to get out,' I say, my voice much firmer than I feel. 'We're going to get out and the police are going to catch him.' Still, Daisy doesn't say anything. 'Let's not talk about him any more,' I say. 'Tell me about you instead, tell me what it's like to deliver a baby. Talk me through the whole thing.'

'No two births are the same,' she says. 'And yet they're all the same. The wonder at the end of it. A whole new life.' She smiles and I feel that I'm seeing her as she really is, as her friends outside must see her. 'I've only been a midwife for five years, but however long I do this job, I can't see it ever getting old. I mean the shifts are bloody hard and exhausting, but it's the birth itself I'm talking about. The elation at the end, when you hold the baby, look at him or her and think, that's it, little one. You're in the world. It's *your* life to live now.' Daisy starts to cry, silently at first, then she's howling. I shuffle over, put my arm around her. I feel bad for upsetting her, though I know it's not my fault. 'I want my own baby, Ava. I want to hold my *own* baby. But that's never going to happen for me now, is it? He's going to kill us. That's it, I've had my life, it's all led up to this, and I don't get to have my baby.'

She's crying so hard and I don't know what to say to her. I can't offer her empty words, promising her that she's going to have a child one day, she'll be a mum, it will all be OK. Her words tear at my own heart, ripping it apart as I think of all the things I desperately want to do. All the places I want to travel to, the moments I want to share with my friends and family, all the love and adventure. Even just to feel the breeze on my face, to see the sky, to be free to walk out of the door. I start sobbing too. We sit there weeping, her head resting against my shoulder, filling the room with our grief and fear.

Frankie

Jack's breath comes slowly, his chest rising and falling. He's fast asleep. Frankie leans over to the side table, pressing a key on her phone so that the blue light illuminates their dark bedroom. 5.12 a.m. She's been awake for the past two hours.

She resists the temptation to speed the remaining hours until daylight by surfing the Internet. Her eyes are already burning. Above her the overhead light casts a slight shadow on the ceiling. It's strange, she thinks, how the blackness of night always contains further darkness, once your sight adjusts to the gloom. She tries to lull herself to sleep by keeping her breathing at the same steady pace as Jack's. There was another card waiting when she got home. A chunk of the vase is missing now, its mouth a jagged ring. It's sitting on the breakfast counter, face down, but the image is seared into her mind. Her breath speeds up and she wills herself not to panic. *I'm safe*, she tells herself, *I'm safe here*. Jack promised her he'd drop it off at the police station for Dan on his way to work.

She told him all about Brett last night, admitting that she and Zara had gone to see him at the bar on Saturday. He teased her, said he didn't mind, that he was sure Brett wasn't dangerous just keen, but she didn't like the way she caught him looking at her later when they were watching telly. She thinks he's disappointed. If they weren't both so stressed by the blog and the postcards, she suspects he would have let his anger show.

Brett has texted her twice. One a huffy message apologising *'if she got the wrong idea'* and the other telling her she intrigues him and asking her out for a drink. Frankie hasn't replied yet; Jack asked her to ignore him. She feels a bit embarrassed by her reaction in the café – perhaps Brett didn't deserve to be shouted at – but her nerves are frayed and his pushiness is not reassuring. She can't be sure Brett doesn't wish her harm, whatever Jack says.

The shadow on the ceiling lengthens as minutes then hours pass, and light starts to seep through the curtains.

In the newsroom Frankie feels barely awake. She sips her third coffee of the morning and tries to read the papers online, to see how they're covering Donald Emneth's arrest.

It's not a pleasant sight. The tabloids have pushed their reports to the far side of lurid. *Strangler Arrest* is the headline on one, above a screen grab of him aiming a kick at Gavin, mouth open and eyes crazed. She wonders if Emneth's chances of a fair trial really have been diminished, as Grant Allen claims. Although she hates to agree with the newsroom's most irritating caller, she thinks he may have a point.

'We've got someone on the line who wants to talk to you.' She looks up to see Emma from the planning desk hovering nearby. 'Have you got time to take it?'

'Not bloody Grant Allen *again*!'

'Who?' Emma looks puzzled. 'No, this guy's called Simon. He's calling about another missing woman. Sounds very upset.'

'Sorry, yes, of course I'll take it,' she says. Emma goes back to her desk and buzzes the call through. 'Frances Latch here. How can I help?'

'She's gone and they're not listening to me!'

The voice on the line is shrill with distress. This doesn't sound like a prank call. In spite of her exhaustion, Frankie's senses switch to high alert. She tries to focus all her attention. 'Simon?' she says. 'Is that your name? It's OK, I'm listening. First of all, who's gone missing and for how long?'

'My wife Daisy Meadwell. She's been gone over two days and they're not taking it seriously, they're not doing anything. I'm going mad here.'

'Who's not taking it seriously? Do you mean the police?'

'Yes, the police. We want to do a press conference and they're not having any of it.'

'Has your wife, has Daisy, ever gone missing before?'

'Yes but I explained to them that was different, that was before she was a midwife. I'm telling you, you don't get more reliable. She never misses a shift, never, not for anything, and she's always home when she says she'll be.'

The knot between Frankie's shoulder blades tightens. 'What exactly have the police said to you?'

'They've said I need to give her time to come home, that she's got form for taking a few days off. But that was *years* ago. She was practically a teenager then.'

'How many times has she been missing before?'

'You sound like the police,' he says. 'For fuck's sake, why does that matter?' There's a pause, which Frankie doesn't fill. 'Sorry, I didn't mean that. I'm under a lot of strain. Two or three times. But like I said, that was years ago.'

'Have the police said what action they're taking?'

'They've told me they'll issue a missing-person alert to other forces. But they should be doing more than that! They should be getting the message out on TV that she's missing, see if anybody's seen her. Why aren't they?'

'Mr Meadwell . . .'

'It's Simon.'

'. . . Simon, I'm really sorry your wife Daisy is missing. I honestly can't imagine what you're going through. And I can see how frustrating it must be that the police haven't done an appeal. But could it be for her own safety? Maybe they think it's less risky this way?'

'You're joking, aren't you? Isn't it *obvious* what's going on? They don't want the embarrassment of announcing she's missing while they question that Emneth bloke. But what if someone else has her? And how can *saying* that Daisy's missing be any worse than the fact she already *is* missing?'

Frankie hesitates. If Daisy *has* been kidnapped the police must think it's Donald Emneth, and Simon is right: putting out an appeal while they question him would be tantamount to admitting their interrogation isn't working. She can't see them holding their hands up to that in a hurry. Or maybe they genuinely don't think Mrs Meadwell is at risk. She wonders just how flaky Daisy's past might be. 'OK. How do you think we can help?' she says at last.

'I want you guys to put out an appeal on your TV show. If the police won't do it, you can.'

She doesn't need to speak to her boss to know Kiera would be delighted to break the news that there's another woman missing. Charlie is another matter. 'OK, Simon, I understand,' she says. 'But I'm going to need to speak to somebody more senior about this, to see if we can do it. Are you OK to give me your phone number? I promise we'll call you back within half an hour.'

Frankie takes Simon's details and hangs up. She heads over to the newsdesk and stands next to Charlie. As always he's on the phone, though since it's through the headset she can't tell until she's up close. He raises his eyebrows at her, and with one hand over the microphone mouths, *What's up?* 'It's urgent,' she says, quietly, so that whoever's on the other line doesn't hear.

'Ray, I'm going to have to go,' he says. 'I know it's a pain in the arse but just get whatever shots you can. And then have a fag break or something.' Charlie ends the call. 'Pissing off cameramen,' he says. 'It's what I do best.'

'We've had a tip-off.' Frankie sits on his desk. 'I've just spoken to a man who says his wife has been missing for over two days. She's a midwife, very reliable, though he admits she's gone missing before, several years ago. The police say it's too early for an appeal.' She looks at Charlie. 'He wants us to do it. But after Amber Finn, I don't know if we should. I don't want to put anyone else at risk.'

Charlie glances round. 'Let's head to the kitchen for a moment,' he says.

They walk across the newsroom, Charlie nearly tripping over a microphone cable. 'Watch it!' he says to the reporter, Marcus, whose desk the cable is trailing from, but the hunched figure doesn't respond, too busy editing at his laptop with the head-phones on.

In the kitchen, Charlie fills the battered kettle at the sink, then flicks its switch on. 'OK,' he says. 'You don't need to look so worried. We're just keeping this between the pair of us at the moment.' Frankie knows, even though he doesn't say it, that he is thinking of Kiera. 'What exactly have the police said to this guy?'

'As far as I can tell, they've told him that they will put an appeal out to other forces, but they want to give her time to come home on her own.' She watches the old kettle; the force of the bubbling as it boils is making it lurch about on its base. One of these days, she thinks, it's going to leap off the counter and splatter hot water everywhere.

'So they've not said doing an appeal would put her at risk.'

'Not according to Simon Meadwell, no.'

Charlie sighs. 'Well, we're obviously going to have to put a call in to the police to try and confirm all this. And I imagine we're not the only news outlet he's phoned.' A pop like a gunshot goes off as the kettle flips its switch. It sits there, still continuing to judder, as if recovering from an outburst of hysteria. 'How would you feel about going to his house and filming a short piece with him? On the understanding that we may not be able to use it if the police come down heavily against the idea?'

'In all honesty? I'd rather not. But I will if you really want me to.'

Charlie plops a couple of teaspoons of instant coffee from a vast plastic vat into two grubby-looking mugs, then pours the water out. 'I know the whole business with Amber Finn has hit you hard,' he says. 'But this man Simon Meadwell has a right to publicise his wife's disappearance. And unless there's a compelling reason why the police aren't doing that, there's no law against him airing his concerns on our programme.'

'Did she really say she'd told Donald Emneth about the interview?' Frankie blurts out. 'Amber, I mean. Did she *really* say that to you?'

'Frankie, Amber getting kidnapped was not your fault.'

'But did she say it?' She stares at Charlie, trying to read his face for clues, the way she would scrutinise an interviewee she suspected of lying.

'Yes,' he says. 'She did. So please stop tormenting yourself. And have you ever thought that perhaps Emneth was always going to kidnap Amber, and our interview is what led police to her? It might be the reason she's alive.'

Charlie doesn't blink as he looks at her, but she can see a nerve twitching in his left cheek. She can only try to believe him, for her own peace of mind. 'OK,' she says. 'It's just all really crap, isn't it? I wish they'd catch the bastard and have done.'

Charlie looks surprised. He hands her a mug, keeping one for himself. 'Don't you think they already have?'

'I guess so. I hope so,' she says. 'But there's still that bloody blog.' She realises as she says it that she's not mentioned the comments below the line. 'Actually, that's become even more of a shit show. There's now a guy on the comments section claiming to be the Norfolk Strangler. Saying he'll bump me off if things get less hectic for him. And that Emneth isn't the right guy.'

Charlie puts his mug down hard, nearly missing the edge of the counter. 'Oh God, Frankie. I'm sorry. I was really hoping you hadn't read all that.'

She stares at him. 'You *knew*?' He nods. 'Why didn't you say anything?'

Charlie rubs a hand over his face. He looks tired. 'A couple of the Tabs called the newsdesk the day the blog went up. They'd seen the post from the alleged Strangler underneath and wanted a comment. Obviously we couldn't let that happen. I called head office in London and the Society of Editors got dragged in to it. The company have asked them not to name you, explained it would put you at risk of more hate online, not to mention anything worse. So far they've stuck to the agreement.'

'And you didn't think I had a right to know all this?'

Charlie sighs. 'You've been under so much strain. I thought the last thing you needed was the added worry of it all ending up in the papers.' He draws a finger along the line of the countertop. 'And to top it off, Kiera wasn't delighted that I went straight to the bosses without consulting her and there was an almighty row. It felt like too much hassle to involve you in.'

She remembers the morning meeting when he had allowed Kiera to send her off on her own to Lowestoft. It made sense now. He had already stuck his neck out for her, much more than she could have imagined. 'Thanks,' she says at last. 'To be honest, I *have* been struggling with it all, so it was nice of you to try and spare me that extra worry. Although I'd rather you kept me informed next time.' She slumps against the kitchen counter, picturing Leonard Smythe from the *London Daily Times* with his prostitute theory. 'I hope the Tabs don't print anything. Fucking hell, that really would be the icing on the cake.'

'I don't think they will. That last Strangler post went up after Emneth was arrested, and they've all decided he's guilty if their front pages are anything to go by.' Charlie looks at his shoes, pained, and she wonders what's coming next. After five years of working together, she knows he hates anything that resembles emoting; he'd much rather trade good-tempered insults. 'I'm really sorry I didn't say anything, but when you didn't mention that post to me, I honestly thought it meant you hadn't seen it,' he says. 'And I'm sorry this is so hard for you. I wish there was some-body else we could send to film Simon Meadwell. If you really don't feel up to it . . .'

'It's OK,' she says, realising she would rather be busy than mope around the newsroom. 'I'll do it.' She raises an eyebrow. 'After all, no point pissing off Kiera any more than we have to. You've obvi-ously done a brilliant job of that already.'

Charlie snorts. 'Thanks,' he says, the familiar tone of sarcasm back in his voice. 'That makes me feel *much* better.'

Gavin is waiting for her in the Toyota, its engine running and fumes belching from the exhaust as she heads across the car park.

'Lunch in the fast lane again then, is it?' he says as she jumps in the passenger seat.

She smiles at the familiar joke, snapping the seat belt shut. 'I'm afraid so. Right.' She fishes out a scrap of paper from her pocket. Gavin's finger hovers over his satnav. 'It's on Trinity Street, just off the Unthank Road.'

The journey only takes a few minutes. The Meadwells live in Norwich's 'golden triangle', a short distance from the Eastern Film Company's offices in the city centre. When they arrive, they're forced to drive up and down the narrow Victorian terraced street, with its privet hedges and rose bushes, trying to find a parking space. Gavin eventually manages to squeeze the Toyota into a minuscule spot several doors away from the address they want.

There's nobody else about as they walk along the pavement. The houses on Trinity Street always make Frankie think of a child's impression of a home: two large windows at the front, each with a single cross for a frame, and a wooden door with a glass arch at the top. They reach the Meadwells' front path. Somebody has planted a row of white Japanese anemones in pots the same shade of deep blue as the front door. They're so unashamedly bright and cheerful, it seems at odds with the tragedy she knows is lurking within.

'Are you Frances Latch?' A tall man with dreadlocks looks down at her.

'Yes, and this is my cameraman Gavin.'

'You'll be wanting Simon.' He waves them into the hallway. 'Need a hand with that?' he asks as Gavin clatters past with the gear.

'No, I'm all right, mate, thanks.'

'Just through to the kitchen.'

They walk along the hallway, past the stairs to a small room at the back, where a man who must be Simon is sitting slumped over a wooden table. He looks up at them as they walk in, his eyes puffy.

'Thanks for coming,' he says, without getting up. He looks as if he hasn't slept in a long time. There are bags under his eyes, and his top is rumpled. Whatever fight Frankie heard in his voice earlier seems to have been extinguished by exhaustion.

'Here, take a seat, I'll put the kettle on,' says the first man, heading to the sink. Frankie and Gavin cram round the table.

'I just don't know what to do,' says Simon. 'I can't go into work, I can't concentrate, I can't do anything. I feel so helpless. I just want to find her, I just want her to be OK.' He looks over at his companion making the tea. 'My brother Nathan's been doing everything, I'd have gone to pieces otherwise.'

'Don't do yourself down,' says Nathan.

'I'm really sorry,' Frankie says. 'I can't imagine what it's like.' Her eyes wander over to a pink handbag and fluffy white scarf dumped at the end of the table.

'They're not Daisy's,' says Simon, seeing the direction of her gaze. 'That's Kelly's stuff. We live in a house share, she's a junior doctor, works with Daisy at the hospital. Actually, Nate.' He looks over to his brother. 'Are you OK to shut the door? We don't want to wake her, she's on nights at the minute.'

'I hope I explained properly on the phone,' says Frankie, lowering her voice, as Nathan closes them into the small room. 'We're not a hundred per cent sure yet that we can put out the appeal. My news editor is on to the police but they've been a bit slow getting back to us. The thing is, if they feel it would endanger Daisy – even if they're not right about that,' she adds, seeing Nathan's disgusted expression as he puts down her tea, ' – then we can't run it. I'm really sorry, I know that sounds frustrating, but we can't take that sort of risk. We have to be guided by what they say.'

Simon and Nathan exchange glances. 'What my brother and I don't get,' says Nathan, 'is why all these other women are considered worthy of an appeal but Daisy isn't? They've been off with us from the start.' He jerks a thumb at Simon. 'D'you know they even told him to calm down at one point?'

'Seriously?' says Gavin. 'What do they expect when your missus is gone?'

'That must have been very annoying,' Frankie agrees.

'It's more than *annoying*. It's racist,' Nathan replies. 'Daisy is God knows where and all they give a shit about is whether he raised his voice or not. I'll tell you why there's no appeal.' He thumps the table with the flat of his hand. 'It's because they don't think anyone wants to see an *angry black man* on the TV. They don't think people will have any sympathy, they clearly don't have any fucking sympathy themselves.'

'Nate,' says Simon. 'Please. It's not helping.'

'It sounds like the police haven't been great,' says Frankie. 'But even if that is the reason they're not doing an appeal, we're still stuck if they tell my editor it would endanger Daisy's life.'

Simon shakes his head, defeated. 'Whatever. Let's get on with the filming and hope you can use it. I have to do *something*.' His voice cracks. Nathan puts his arm round him, squeezing his shoulders. 'I just want her home. I just want her back.'

'Do you have any photos of Daisy?' says Gavin, sipping his tea. As always, Frankie thinks, she and Gavin are left navigating the shoals of other people's grief and despair with the cold practicalities of filming.

'Of course,' says Simon, standing up. 'I got some out for you.' He crosses to the pine welsh dresser, picking up a sheaf of photographs. He flicks through them. 'Some of us on holiday, that's a really nice one of her graduation, and that's our wedding.'

'That was a great day, wasn't it?' Nathan smiles, looking at the picture over Simon's shoulder.

'Can I see?' Frankie asks.

'Sure.'

Simon pushes the pictures to her across the table. The one on top is the graduation photo. Daisy's mortarboard is slightly askew on her mop of mousy brown curls. She looks shyly at the camera with wide grey eyes, standing slightly stiff and awkward in her robes. Frankie feels a catch in her throat as she flips through the other images. Daisy grinning in her wedding dress, holding Simon's arm as he gazes down at her, Daisy in a pub garden with Simon and friends. The last photo is slightly over-exposed, on a beach somewhere. She's holding a cocktail glass and has thrown her head back with laughter.

'She looks lovely,' Frankie says.

'She is,' says Simon, taking the photos back and stroking his fingers gently across the image of his wife's face.

'Have you got any home video of Daisy, on your phone maybe?' Gavin asks. 'That always helps too.'

'Probably,' Nathan replies. 'But you guys can get lots of video of her from Commercial TV. That's your channel, isn't it? She was in an NHS documentary recently, they filmed it at the Norfolk and Norwich. A day on the maternity ward.'

'Daisy's been on TV?' Frankie says, going pale, thinking of Hanna filmed in the hairdressing salon and her own newsroom's footage of Ava at the demo. All the most recent women have been on television.

'Why? Is that worrying?' Simon has picked up on her concern and looks anxiously between her and Gavin. 'Does it mean anything? Anything bad?'

'No, no, not at all,' Frankie says. After all, it might be nothing and it's not her job to alarm him. 'I'll call the channel and get them to send us some clips from the documentary.'

Gavin stands up. 'If it's OK I'll just get some shots of the three of you chatting and looking at the pictures.' Simon nods and Gavin gets to work, swiftly pulling up the legs of his tripod and clipping the camera onto its base.

She's filmed this sequence a hundred times before; it's one of the biggest clichés of the TV news report, going through photographs with relatives. But this feels different. It's not that long since she was sitting with the Sidcups, looking at pictures of their dead daughter, Lily. She hopes that Daisy has just taken off; perhaps the stress of working on an NHS maternity ward has got to her, and she needs some time out. But if not, she can't bear to think of what might be happening to her right now, even as her husband and brother-in-law reminisce about her happiest moments.

'Right. That's fine for the set-up shots,' says Gavin. 'Simon, are you OK to do the interview now? No need to move, I can frame you up where you are.'

'First, just your name for the tape please,' says Frankie.

'Simon Meadwell.'

'And Simon, why are you worried about Daisy, what's happened?'

'The thing you need to understand about Daisy,' he says, rubbing his hand nervously across his chin, his eyes flicking to the red light on the camera, 'is that she's the most considerate, responsible person. I know she did go missing a few times when she was young, but seriously, her family situation was a bit crazy and she's *nothing* like that now. She always texts if she's going to be late, like even from the supermarket if there's a big queue, she doesn't like me to worry. And she never misses a shift, you wouldn't *believe* how important her job is to her. Being a midwife, they work really long hours, and it's hard, you know? But she's only ever missed about three shifts her entire career, and that was only because she didn't want to give any of her pregnant ladies the flu.' He takes a deep breath. 'So that's how I know something's happened to her. When she didn't come home Tuesday, I knew straight away, something bad must have happened.'

'You don't think the stress of the job has maybe been too much for her.'

Simon shakes her head. 'She loves her job. And her patients. There's one or two I know she's looking out for right now. No way would she leave them in the lurch. No way would she leave me to worry like this.'

'And what appeal would you like to make?'

Simon leans forward across the table, his hands clenched. 'I'd say, let her go.' He turns from Frankie to stare straight into the camera. She had meant what appeal would he like to make to the public, not to a kidnapper, but seeing the intensity in his face she doesn't interrupt. 'Please,' he says softly, 'you've no idea how precious she is, how much she's loved. She's irreplaceable. I would do anything in the world to get her back safe, you can have anything, anything you want, you can have my life instead, please just let Daisy go. You don't need to hurt her.' Simon's voice wobbles, and his eyes are shining with tears. 'You don't need to prove anything. Daisy and me, we're not vengeful people, we will leave you alone. Just don't hurt her, *please* don't hurt her, *please* . . .' Simon breaks down. In all her time filming, Frankie doesn't think she's ever seen anyone lose it so completely. He is howling, all the anxiety and stress he's kept pent up, all the sleepless nights, all the agony, has suddenly and completely overwhelmed him. Nathan holds him as he sobs, and they rock back and forth. She realises tears are running down her own face. She touches Gavin's arm. 'Stop filming,' she says. 'That's enough.'

Ava

'And that's when I knew, I knew the baby was going to be OK, that we'd saved him,' Daisy says, her face lit up at the memory. 'After that, there was no question it's the job I wanted. And every baby since has been special too, but that little boy, he means something else to me. He must be three years old now, and whenever I'm down I think about him, imagine him running around, getting into mischief. Because I know he's only here because of me.'

We've been recounting our happiest times, things to make us feel better. Daisy's have made all of mine feel quite small. Her proudest moment is saving the life of a baby boy, after both mother's and baby's heart rates dropped through the floor. I'm not sure what my proudest moment is. We are sitting close together, blankets draped over us. It's so much warmer with Daisy next to me. Last night was the first one I didn't wake several times from the cold. I'd quite like to sleep soon even though I've no idea how late it is. The world outside the grille is dark, but it might just be early evening, not bedtime at all. Adrenalin is keeping Daisy awake, that and having her hands tied. I know having them wrenched behind her like that must be incredibly painful, but she's barely complained.

Love is important to Daisy. I've heard all about her wedding day to Simon. I've heard all about Simon too, from the dull (he works for Aviva, the insurance company) to the beautiful (whatever shift she's on he gets up extra early or stays up late, just so they can have a cup of tea together). It must be nice to be loved like that, I think. I've only had a couple of short, unsatisfactory relationships with guys, but my heart was never in it. And then there was Lina. I think about her, riding her bike next to mine, laughing. I think about kissing her, lying under the trees, the light and shadow on our faces, wanting to stay in that moment always. I haven't told Daisy about Lina. She looks a bit like her, for a start. And somehow I don't think a holiday romance would compete well with Simon, even though it meant everything to me.

I've told her about Matt though, and Laura, and my friends. And my mum and dad. It still feels small in comparison to what she has, and I realise that the six years Daisy has on me have given her so much more time at living. I've barely got started, though I'd never thought of it like that before. You don't really look at your life from the outside, you just live it. Until you realise somebody wants to take it from you.

I've had some dark thoughts, while she's been talking. About how, if one of us has to live, it ought to be *me*, because I'm younger, because I've had less time. But then that flips on its head and I think *she* ought to be the one who survives, because her life is so much richer than mine, because she helps so many women; she's literally out there, saving lives.

'I don't really want to talk about this,' I say, sorry to interrupt her, still lost in thought about the little boy she saved. 'But I think we should. That stuff he said about his experiment, about only one of us ...' I can't finish the sentence. I can't say the words, can't admit that one of us is going to die, even to myself. 'He's going to try and set us against each other, isn't he? I just want you to know, whatever he makes us do, whatever happens, I forgive you, OK?'

We're sitting next to each other. The Stain is behind our backs; she was understanding about the fact I didn't want to look at it, though it still bothers me, knowing it's there. She can't touch me because her hands are tied, but she moves one foot so it's resting against mine.

'I've been thinking about that too,' she says. 'The survival instinct is very strong, I've seen it in action, on the ward. People do anything to stay alive. So I don't know what either of us might do, if we're really pushed to it. But Ava, I think unless we manage to overpower him, or unless the police come, he *is* going to kill us both. It's a lie what he said about one of us surviving. So it's only a question of when, not if. And I don't want my last moments to be doing something terrible. That's not who I am.'

I don't say anything, just press my foot against hers. I can't say anything, because I don't know, I just don't know, if it comes down to it, if it's my life or hers, what I will do.

Frankie

The report is only just ready in time for Kiera's newly imposed broadcast deadline. Frankie double-checks it's been sent to playback, then sits back in her chair with a sigh of relief. She had known as soon as Kiera saw Simon's emotional interview that she would want to broadcast it. Frankie isn't sorry. Her earlier worries about airing his appeal were bulldozed by his desperation, and the police didn't give Charlie any convincing reasons why they shouldn't go public. But even though she's pleased to have reported Simon's story, she didn't share the general jubilation when the footage of Daisy from the NHS documentary arrived. She finds it creepy, as if the kidnapper wants to maximise news coverage by picking women who've been filmed. Unless that's the reason they were *targeted*. An idea she can hardly bear to contemplate, given the implications.

As always after a frantic self-edit at her desk, Frankie's shoulders have been wound up as if she's a marionette, and with all the other stress in her life, she has a howling dog of a headache, thumping and scratching against the sides of her skull. She takes the headphones off and turns over her phone. Two missed calls and a voicemail show up on her screen. She dials in to listen.

'Hi Frances, it's Dan Avery here. Just to let you know we're aware of the second blog and are on to it.'

Frankie sits forward again with a jerk. 'Shit,' she says.

'I'll call as soon as there are further developments,' the recording continues. *'In the meantime, please do take all the precautions we discussed.'* There's a pause, as if Dan is considering how much to

say. '*I pick up emails from my phone, so you can contact me that way if I'm not at my desk. But really, I meant it about calling 999 if you feel in danger. I think we should treat this as a credible threat, even if it's nothing to do with the murder enquiry. Take care.*'

For a moment she doesn't move, wondering whether it would be better not to look at the website, whether there's any point filling her head with more poisonous hate. But curiosity always wins. She types 'Killing Cuttlefish' into the search bar and the site loads onto her browser. @Feminazi_Slayer2's new blog is hidden part way down the forum. The title reads **Stalking Norfolk's Nancy Drew**. She clicks on the link.

Immediately a photo of her comes up in the crosshairs of a gun. It's a snapshot of her smiling in the studio, taken from a TV screen. There's a caption running alongside it: **Yoo-Hoo Nancy Drew!** Rather than an article underneath, she's confronted with a montage of pictures of herself. Many are screen grabs from reports or lives she's done, but all with a nasty digital addition. In several her face is blacked out, in others her head's been replaced with a pig's, and one has a red line of blood drawn round her neck. Some are shots of her on screen that have been zoomed in so far she's just a body part; a little more thigh than she had meant to show sitting down in an interview, or a tiny flash of cleavage.

The worst photos are the ones that aren't doctored. There's a shot of her leaving the flat, another of her getting into Gavin's car, and one from yesterday, sitting on the bench on the cathedral green. A single line of text sits beneath the montage.

Thanks to everyone who supplied photos! **We're watching you, BITCH.**

Frankie scrolls down to check the comments. She's hit by a barrage of obscenities and rape threats. She doesn't read complete messages, her eyes skip over them, but individual words and disjointed phrases jump out at her before she can un-see them. There's only one commenter she's looking for, and in the middle of all the '*fucking cunt*'s, '*throttle the bitch*'s and

'*LOL*'s, one post chills her more than all the rest: The fat bitch's days are numbered. Fancy giving her some love online before I visit? Beneath is a screen grab of her Twitter account. It's posted by @The_Norfolk_Strangler.

'Bloody hell, what *is* that?'

She turns round to see Zara standing by her shoulder, her face screwed up in a frown.

'It's that website,' she replies, her mouth dry. 'There's been another post about me.' She scrolls back up to the top, to the hideous montage. Her cheeks feel like they're burning and she doesn't feel able to stand up or move out of the way so her friend can see better as she leans over to read the screen. Instead she gets her phone out. 187 notifications on Twitter. With a feeling of dread, she clicks on the icon. A string of messages merge before her eyes into incoherent babble of abuse: **die in a fire feminazi bitch make sure you film it when you kill the cunt hope you get raped to death in your posh fucking flat die slowly fat waste of space . . .**

She gasps, sucking in the air as if she's been punched.

Zara spins round in alarm. 'What is it?' Frankie passes the phone over, her hand shaking. 'God, that's awful! Do the police know about all this?'

'About the blog. I don't know about the other stuff. God, it's so public.' She gestures at the phone. '*Anyone* can see this shit.'

'Is Jack home now?' Frankie notices Zara's eyes are fixed on the computer. She follows her line of vision. It's the photo of her leaving the flat.

She shakes her head. 'He's working late. I mean if I call him, I'm sure he'd come straight home, but I'd rather not when he has a deadline.' She doesn't like to add that she feels guilty about Brett and knows Jack has already been staying up all hours trying to crack the blog.

'In that case you're coming home with me. I mean it, no arguments,' Zara says when she opens her mouth to protest. 'There'll be more than enough dinner to go round. In fact, stay the night. It would do you good to be somewhere else for a change.'

Frankie feels like she might cry. 'Thanks. I'd love that,' she says.

In Zara's house on the Wellington Road, Frankie sits on her friend's familiar dog-haired sofa. The Hydes' black Labrador, Snoopy, has finished charging round the room barking with glee, and is now slumped against Frankie's knee, occasionally thrusting a wet nose at her for a sniff. Zara hands over a large glass of red wine and flops down beside her.

'Stew's on the hob,' she says. 'Mark's back in half an hour or so, and we can eat then.'

Frankie takes a gulp from her glass. 'I really appreciate this. It's all a bit stressful right now.'

'God, it must be. Fucking awful.'

Frankie smiles at her. She always appreciates Zara's bluntness, and right now it feels especially comforting. Snoopy yawns and leans more heavily against her leg. She sighs and takes another sip of wine. The living room is a jumble of Mark and Zara's different tastes; Victorian prints of birds cover the walls – Mark is a twitcher – but all the fabrics are from Zara's travels, most with the distinctive bright pink, earth shades and llamas of Peru. The furniture might politely be described as antique, but is really just old and scuffed. A wicker chair, which Frankie can't remember anyone but Snoopy ever sitting in, takes up too much room by the fireplace and various curiosities crowd the mantelpiece. There's a nineteenth-century jug, an Indian horse and a set of orange candlesticks. It ought to look a mess, but she always finds this room enormously homely and relaxing. Frankie realises with surprise that she feels more at ease here than in the new white flat she shares with Jack.

'I'm not sure what's going to happen with it,' she says. 'The police seem a bit useless.' They had called the station to report the Twitter abuse and received an underwhelming response. The officer answering the phone said Dan had left but advised her to take her account offline. That was it.

'You'd think they'd take it a bit more seriously since we've got a guy online calling himself the Norfolk Strangler, bloody hell,' Zara says, then sees Frankie's face. 'I mean I'm sure it's a hoax,' she adds quickly.

'Do you really think so?'

Zara nods. 'Obviously it's fucking scary, of course it is. But I do think it's somebody messing around, trying to upset you.' Frankie isn't sure how convincing she sounds. Zara leans over to scratch the top of Snoopy's head. The dog yawns and stretches. 'Do you want to talk about this though? Maybe you'd just like a night off from it all.'

'No, it's fine,' she says. 'It probably helps to talk about it, rather than it being locked away in my head.' She draws her legs up onto the sagging sofa, dislodging Snoopy, who whines and resettles on the floor, plonking his head down on Zara's feet. 'I ran my theory about Grant Allen past the police. Apparently he's a bit of a nightmare, very litigious. They don't want to disturb that particular hornet's nest unless they have enough evidence.'

'All the more reason to investigate, then,' says Zara. '*We* could always pay him a visit, if they won't.'

'You're joking, aren't you?' Frankie says. 'What, just rock up and ask him if he or his son have been blogging about me?'

'Don't be ridiculous.' Zara reaches for a laptop that is resting precariously on a pile of cushions, papers and rumpled jeans. 'People like that have massive egos, always think the press want to cover their every fart, why do you think he keeps calling?' She opens the PC and brings up the *Justice4Jailbirds* website. She scrolls down the page, squinting to read the tiny font crammed into the dated layout. 'God, what a shonky site,' she mutters, clicking on the *Contact Me* section. 'How about we ping him a message? Say we're doing a bit of background digging ahead of Donald Emneth's inevitable trial. I'll write it, say I've spoken to you, and that we don't want to miss out on his expertise. I'll ask if he'd like to meet to discuss coming into the studio as an expert to talk about it all.'

'You're awful!' says Frankie, leaning over to look more closely at the website. 'But actually it's not even that unlikely. He's exactly the sort of clickbaity idiot Kiera *would* have in the studio.'

'Right then. What shall I say?' Zara clicks on the button that reads 'send message' so a small box pops up on the screen. 'Shall I suggest we could pop round for a chat this weekend?'

Frankie hesitates. She had been caught up in the rush of Zara's mischief-making, but the reality of facing the man suddenly seems less appealing when she thinks about actually going through with it. 'What if he is Feminazi Slayer though? He was definitely at Jamie Cole's trial. Or maybe he knows who it is? Is it safe for us to turn up?' Particularly me, she wants to add, but feels too embarrassed to admit it. 'Dan Avery thinks the blogger might pose a threat even if he's not connected to the killer.'

'Is that what you've been thinking? That this Feminazi guy might be the Strangler?' Zara puts her wine down with a thump. 'Surely that's not likely? I know he's making your life a misery, but that doesn't mean he's bumped off a string of women.'

Seeing Zara's incredulous face, she feels both reassured and irritated to have her deepest fear dismissed. 'How can you be sure though? It's not just what's *in* the blog, and that's bad enough. He did target Hanna on there too, remember, not just me? And then there's this whole weird vase thing—' She stops, not sure she wants to share it all, but Zara is staring at her, waiting, and she knows she doesn't have a hope of deflecting her friend's nosiness now she's caught a whiff of something more. 'Hanna got sent broken glass in the post before she was kidnapped,' she explains, 'and now somebody's sending me postcards of chipped vases. There was a creepy smashing vase on Lily's memorial page and now there's the exact same image directed at me by Feminazi Slayer. And I think a car may have followed me to Lowestoft, though I can't be sure.' As she finishes, she realises that the whole thing sounds rather paranoid.

Zara is frowning. 'Have you told the police all this?'

'Yes, though I don't know how seriously they take it.'

'Could that be a good thing, do you think?' In reply Frankie makes a face. 'Sorry, I don't mean it's OK for the police to underplay your worries, but if they aren't too worried, hopefully that means you don't have to be either. Donald Emneth has been arrested now. Surely they must be pretty confident he's the killer?'

'I guess so,' Frankie says. 'But it's still bothering me. You know Zachary Allen, Grant's son, also killed his girlfriend with a vase?'

'OK, well, that is all a bit weird,' Zara says. 'Though it doesn't prove anything.' She sees Frankie's irritation and puts a hand on her shoulder. 'Look, I'm not discounting your murderer theory – if I'd been going through all that stuff you have I'd be absolutely crapping myself – I just don't think it should put us off visiting Grant Allen. He's been estranged from his son for years, hasn't he? We can let Mark know exactly where we're going, and tell Grant that our newsdesk knows where we are, just in case he has any funny ideas.' Zara runs a hand through her short hair. 'But I think the only way we're going to know if his organisation is linked to this Feminazi guy is by seeing how he acts around you. And then monitoring if there are any give-aways on the website itself.' Zara is looking at her, one hand hovering over the keyboard waiting to type.

'Oh, all right,' says Frankie, sitting back on the sofa. 'Let's see what he says.'

Full of beef stew and red wine, Frankie lies on the sofa bed in Mark and Zara's spare room as they get ready for bed. She takes a last look at her mobile, with its good-night message from Jack, and places it on the carpet beside her. There's the sound of the tap running in the bathroom on the other side of the wall, as Mark or Zara brushes their teeth. Thin curtains let the moonlight into her room, along with the orange glow of the lamppost on the opposite side of the street. This is the only space in the house that's plain white, and the only one that feels empty. Instead of physical objects it's full of longing for what it lacks: a baby.

Frankie tries not to think of that as she hears the click of the bathroom light next door. It's too painful imagining all the heartache that must be going on under her friend's cheery exterior. She knows the Hydes' second round of IVF starts in a month. At least Mark is a supportive partner; Zara told her once that he gave her all the injections because she found it too difficult to do it herself.

Zara had obviously filled him in on the blog before he arrived; he'd patted her arm with a murmured 'rotten luck' but hadn't asked her anything more. It was a relief not to have to explain it all. He hadn't looked too thrilled, though, when Zara mentioned their proposed visit to Grant Allen. With a pang of guilt, she wonders if the stress of tracking down the blogger is the best build-up to Zara's fertility treatment. Frankie turns over on the hard foam base of the sofa bed, fluffing up her pillow. On the other hand, knowing Zara, it's precisely the sort of distraction she would relish. A car passes the house, its headlights briefly illuminating the ceiling. She stares at the window, trying not to think of Feminazi Slayer's montage, or his message. *We're watching you.* Frankie closes her eyes. At least here, in her friends' house, she's safe.

In the morning she comes down to breakfast feeling crumpled in yesterday's work clothes. She and Zara had stopped off at the supermarket, just in case anyone was lurking near her flat, so she could get a toothbrush and spare pair of pants, but it means she didn't come with a change of clothes. She wanders through to the blue galley kitchen. The 1930s-style radio on the counter is playing Classic FM. Mark is there in a stripy knitted jumper, frying bacon. He raises a cafetière at her.

'Coffee?'

'Thanks. Can I help?'

He pours her a cup. 'All under control,' he replies.

'Morning!' Zara calls out. She's sitting at the dining table in the conservatory at the end of the kitchen with a coffee, her laptop open. 'Looks like we're in business.'

Mark shifts over so Frankie can get past. 'Not sure this is such a great idea,' he says, sticking some bread in the toaster. 'But you pair know best, I suppose.'

'No supposing,' says Zara with a grin. She puts her feet down off the chair next to her so Frankie can sit down. 'Mr Allen is keen to get his mug on TV, it seems. He can see us this afternoon.'

'That is keen,' says Frankie. 'What does he say?' Zara shoves the laptop over so she can see.

'*Dear Mrs Hyde,*' she reads. '*It's encouraging to hear that the Eastern Film Company aren't taking a narrow-minded view of Donald Emneth's arrest. I had my doubts from your colleague's rude reaction. Glad she's come round. Mr Emneth's already seen his name trashed by the mainstream media and it would be good if we could work together to rectify this. I'm at home in Brandon until 3 p.m. today and could spare half an hour for you both if you want to drop by. Regards, Grant.*'

'Anybody who uses the term "mainstream media" is bound to be a wanker,' she says. 'But aside from that, his complete lack of manners and the fact he's sympathetic to a guy who just kidnapped a single mum and possibly murdered a bunch of women, he sounds lovely.'

Mark steps down into the conservatory with two plates of bacon, eggs and toast. Zara jumps up from her chair to fetch the third portion from the kitchen. 'Still not sure this is a great idea,' he says as he puts Frankie's breakfast down in front of her.

'Don't be such a stick-in-the-mud,' says Zara, returning with her plate in one hand and a fistful of cutlery in the other. She spills it out on the table in a clanking heap. They help themselves to knives and forks.

'Thanks, this looks amazing,' Frankie says.

'You're welcome,' Mark replies. 'Seriously though, if he's the blogger aren't you just going to feed his obsession with Frankie?' He gives Zara a meaningful look. 'Not to mention give him some-body new to focus on.'

Frankie chews on her poached egg and toast, feeling uncomfortable. The last thing she wants is to be the cause of a row. 'Maybe we should give it a miss,' she says.

'Don't be so ridiculous, the pair of you!' Zara replies, sawing through her crispy bacon with force. 'I don't see how it can make things any worse for Frankie, the police don't seem to be doing much. Though you didn't tell them about Brett, did you? Do you think maybe you should?'

'Maybe. But there are so many creepy guys in my life. Hard to choose between them,' Frankie says, with a forced smile. She's beginning to wish they weren't going to visit Grant Allen; it would be much nicer to go for a long walk with Zara, Mark and Snoopy instead, perhaps all meet Jack in town for a pub lunch. Anything but keep thinking about the blog and all the abuse. 'If we are going,' she says, 'I'd better let Jack know.'

Zara rolls her eyes. 'You boys. No sense of adventure *at all*.'

Frankie can't get hold of Jack, which is odd, but she leaves him a message. They set off for Brandon in Zara's battered old Peugeot with Snoopy in the back seat. Until they get to the A11, Zara lets him sit with his head lolling out of the window, barking at passing cyclists. The sky is clear blue and the air crisp. It makes Frankie feel even more depressed about spending her Saturday on the county's most monotonous A-road rather than out in the countryside.

'We'll say he's yours,' Zara says, pushing her dark glasses on top of her head as they approach Brandon. 'If Grant's the blogger he'll know you don't have a dog and his reaction might tell us something.'

'He can't be, surely,' she replies. 'I mean he wouldn't agree to see us if he were.'

'One thing this job should have told you a long time ago is people are bonkers,' Zara says. 'They never do what you expect.'

They drive down the high street, then on to the town's outskirts. Grant Allen lives in a bungalow on one of Brandon's small meandering residential roads, all of which seem to have been named for Catholic saints, near the border with Thetford Forest Park. It looks like an unremarkable place, with neatly trimmed lawns and carefully raked plots of gravel. Frankie wonders if any of the neighbours know about Mr Allen's work at *Justice4Jailbirds*. Or the years his son spent in prison.

'Is this it?' she asks, as they pull up outside a house with a mock Tudor diamond pattern on the windows.

'Yup,' says Zara. 'Nice gnomes,' she adds, nodding at two little figurines on the freshly mown lawn. They appear to be fishing in the world's smallest ornamental pond. 'Snoopy will drink from anything. If we're not careful he'll end up knocking one in.'

'Sounds like a great way to ingratiate ourselves.'

The front door opens as they get out of the car and a barrel-chested man with silver hair walks over. He looks like the type of hale pensioner who might star on the cover of *Saga* magazine. 'Grant Allen,' he says, holding out his hand. 'You the ladies from the Eastern Film Company?'

'That's right,' says Zara, shaking hands. 'I'm Zara Hyde, this is my colleague Frances Latch, who you've spoken to before.'

Frankie extricates herself from a bone-cruncher handshake. Grant Allen is wearing glasses with thick blue frames, the same colour as his cable-knit sweater. He's so close, she can smell the cigarette smoke on him. 'How are you with dogs?' she asks, as Snoopy's bark booms from inside the Peugeot and he scrabbles against the glass. 'Can I bring mine in or would you rather we left him out here?'

'Rather he stayed where he was, if it's all the same to you,' says Grant, eyeing the drooling Labrador with distaste.

'Of course,' says Frankie. 'I'll just wind the window down a bit.'

'Thanks for seeing us at such short notice,' Zara says.

'I couldn't refuse the woman who brought down HMP Halvergate, could I?' he replies, with a grin. 'Made my year, watching you expose those bastards on the telly. Of course, *I'd* been saying the place was bent for years, but nobody gives a toss what the father of a lad who's actually been inside has to say.' His face darkens. 'Not like I have *direct experience* or anything.' Grant seems to have slipped from friendly to aggrieved in a matter of moments. Humouring him could make for a heavy-going afternoon, Frankie thinks.

'Well, *we're* interested in what you have to say,' Zara says, with a shamelessly oily smile. 'That's why we're here.'

He waves them over towards the bungalow. 'I'll do what I can,' he says as they follow him over the driveway's crazy paving. 'Poor Donnie's already taken a pasting. Going to be hard for the old boy to get any justice.'

'D'you know him, then?' Frankie asks.

'No, why?' Grant stops abruptly. He looks at her sharply, perhaps still harbouring a grudge over their phone calls.

'It's just you used his nickname.'

'Common enough for Donald,' he says. 'Lucky guess.'

They step inside. The front room looks more like a gym than a home, every inch of floor space is covered in fitness equipment. He gestures for them to take a seat. Frankie and Zara have to inch past a massive exercise bike to reach the grey sofa. The place reeks of stale tobacco. Grant Allen may have iron biceps but his lungs must be full of soot.

'I'll get us all a brew,' he says, pushing aside a punch-bag that hangs in the archway between the living room and the kitchen. It swings in the empty space after he's passed through.

'Blimey,' mutters Zara.

Frankie looks at the floor. There's a pile of *Justice4Jailbirds* flyers stacked at the foot of the sofa. She picks one up. The text is riddled with exclamation marks. She thinks about the vicious but controlled tone of Feminazi Slayer's blogs. If it *was* Grant who wrote those posts, he did so in a different voice to the excitable one he uses for his campaign website. She turns the leaflet over. On the back are mugshots of some of the prisoners Grant is helping. Jamie Cole is there, along with three others. With a start she realises all four men pictured have been imprisoned for violent offences against women.

'It'll be Donnie's face on the next one. If he accepts my help,' Grant says, standing in the archway, watching them. He pushes past the punch-bag, gripping three mugs of tea. 'There you go.' They take a mug each and Grant perches on a bench press opposite. 'So, ladies, what do you want from me? Fire away.'

'At this stage,' Zara says, 'this is more of a punt. As Frankie explained to you, we couldn't do anything until after Donald Emneth's trial – if he ends up being charged – but we'd be interested in talking to you as part of our coverage when the verdict's in.'

'Are we talking a ten-second clip or time in the studio?' he asks. There's an unmistakable gleam of hunger in his eye. Everyone wants to be on TV, thinks Frankie.

'That all depends on our editor,' Zara hedges, well aware that even Kiera might not want Grant Allen spouting his controversial views on the studio sofa, racking up complaints to Ofcom as well as longed-for clicks to the website.

'I'm really interested in your motivation,' says Frankie. 'It's unusual that you're not concerned about the men's guilt or innocence.'

'No, it's not,' he says. 'Zach was guilty. Just because you've committed a crime society thinks is beyond the pale, doesn't mean your human rights go up in a puff of smoke.'

'Does Zach help you with your campaigning at all?' Zara asks, pretending she doesn't know about their estrangement. 'He must appreciate what you're doing.'

'We're not in touch,' he says, looking away. It seems to Frankie that Grant's pugnacious stance wavers slightly; there's an almost imperceptible sag in his shoulders. For the first time she feels a flicker of sympathy. 'I don't get any help. Justice for Jailbirds is a one man band.'

'Sorry to hear about Zach,' she says. 'That must be hard.'

'I can understand why,' he replies. 'I try not to take it personal. The lad wanted a whole new life, forget about the past, all the shit that happened. And I'm not exactly a fade-into-the-background kind of guy, am I? Be bound to shoot my mouth off at some point and spoil things for him.' He looks round the room, which Frankie has already noticed is devoid of any photographs. 'The campaigning is like a secret signal between us. As long as I'm out there, talking about it all, he knows I'm thinking about him.'

Frankie isn't sure that constant reminders of the time he spent in prison would be the most welcome connection for Zach but she nods sympathetically.

'It must be hard for you though,' says Zara.

'Harder for him,' Grant shifts over on the bench press to get a wallet out of his back pocket. 'I can't really have any photos out,' he says. 'Might give the boy away. But I always keep this with me.' He hands over a tiny crumpled picture to Zara, who leans over to take it. She holds it out so Frankie can see. A younger, beaming Grant is holding a baby in the crook of one arm. With the other he's holding a woman's hand; you can just see the edge of a floral skirt, but the rest of her has been sliced off the photo. It must be Zach's mother, the one who left, Frankie thinks. She hands the tiny relic back. 'He's a bright lad,' says Grant, returning the photo to his wallet. 'I'm sure he's doing all right for himself somewhere. Took his A-levels in prison, did really well. I was dead proud.'

'Was he bitter about everything that happened?' she asks. 'I guess he must have been.'

'No more than most.' Grant looks between her and Zara, a slight frown on his face. 'Look, I could talk about my boy all day,' he says. 'But it's not going to bring him back into my life. It's Donnie you're here for, isn't it?'

'Of course,' Zara agrees. 'It's just interesting for us to know the background to your work. And very sad to think of all Zach went through at such a young age.' She pauses, waiting to see if he takes the bait and talks more about his son, but Grant is now watching them both with a wary expression.

'You were saying a crime doesn't cancel out someone's human rights,' Frankie says. 'Is that where your interest in Donald Emneth lies?'

'Exactly. And it's not like anyone else is interested. I daresay you ladies don't do it on *purpose*, but it comes across like the whole media are kicking the poor bastard like a dog when it's down.'

'How do you think cases like this should be treated?' Zara asks.

'With a sense of proportion,' he replies.

Frankie wonders, but doesn't ask, what proportion looks like when applied to murder. 'Do you mean the context of the crime?' she says, carefully.

'That. And the aftermath. As I say, just because you did something wrong doesn't mean you should be treated like dirt.' He leans over and adjusts one of the weights on the press. 'That's just hypocritical, isn't it? That's the justice system acting as bad as the criminal.'

'Quite.' Zara nods vigorously. 'I see you've got Jamie Cole on your leaflet. Did you know one of the women Donald Emneth may have killed gave evidence against him?'

'Hanna Chivers? Yeah, I remember her from the trial.'

'What did you make of her?'

He shrugs. 'Look, I'm not here to defend what Jamie did. It was out of order, he's banged up, end of. And I'm not one to speak ill of the dead either. But she was a bit of a piece, was Hanna. So far as I could see.' He looks at Frankie, gives a wink. 'And I saw you say your bit on the news, slagging off some blogger who said the same, but doesn't mean it's not true, just because you don't like a guy's turn of phrase.'

At the mention of the blog, Frankie feels her face flush red. She feels suddenly naked and hemmed in, conscious of all the equipment surrounding her, the images of her Grant might have in his head. 'Have you read the blog?' she says, her voice coming out sharper than she intended.

A smile flickers at the edge of his mouth. 'Might have done. Hard to say. I read a lot online.'

She's seized by the urge to stride over and shake him, demanding if it's him, or if he knows who's behind it, but before she can follow up with another question, Zara butts in. 'It's called *Killing*

Cuttlefish,' she says. 'Pretty vile site. I'm sure you'd remember it, if you came across it. Very unusual name.'

Frankie glances at her in surprise. She hadn't expected Zara to slap their cards on the table quite so openly. Grant's smile fades. 'Really? I'd have thought you ladies were all in favour of free speech. Regardless of how "*vile*" it is,' he says, making quote marks round the word. 'After all, some of the stuff printed about Donnie in the MSM was more than "*vile*", it's probably stuffed up his chance of a fair trial.'

'But it's like you said earlier, no point being hypocritical,' says Zara. 'If it's vile to slander Donald Emneth, it's vile to do it to Hanna Chivers, don't you think?'

Grant's knee is jigging up and down on the bench press. 'No, it's not the same. You have to look at where the power is. Hanna had all the might of the courts and the police behind her. Donnie's just out there on his own. Hung out to dry. Hated. It's not the same at all.'

Frankie isn't quite sure what courtrooms Grant has been in, where victims hold all the cards, but it's not reminiscent of any trial she's sat through. The longer they spend chatting to him, the more his world view seems similarly skewed to that of Feminazi Slayer, and yet she feels that it can't be him. His voice just doesn't feel similar to the one that's been going round and round in her head. 'If we did have you on the programme,' she says, 'how would you feel about the fact the victims' families would be talking too? That's presuming Donald Emneth is convicted.'

'It's a free country.'

'It wouldn't change what you had to say?' Frankie says. 'I mean, wouldn't it make you uncomfortable knowing they were watching?'

'I've got a thick skin,' he says. 'Cathy Spencer's family are always slagging me off. Never stopped me telling the truth before.'

This isn't what Frankie meant at all. There's a moment when nobody seems to know what to say, then she and Zara look at each other. 'Well, it's been very helpful meeting you . . .' Zara begins, as they both rise from the sofa.

'Is that it then?' Grant says, staying where he is. 'All this way for that? Aren't you going to give me some sort of guarantee you'll have me on the programme?'

'It doesn't quite work that way,' Zara says, inching past the exercise bike, before tripping on a dumbbell. She steadies herself, but yelps as Frankie bowls into her ankles.

Grant shakes his head at them, then stands up with a sigh. 'Well, I hope you pair are who you say you are,' he follows as they clamber past all the equipment to reach the door. 'That this wasn't some bogus visit. If you print anything defamatory about me, my lawyers will have you, I can promise you that.' He winks, so Frankie guesses it's meant to be a joke, though he doesn't sound very jolly.

'Mr Allen, you only have to turn your TV on at half past six to see me sitting in the studio of the Eastern Film Company,' Zara replies. 'There's no question of us being imposters.'

'And thank you again for your time,' Frankie adds. 'We do appreciate it.' She's already got one hand on the door, but Grant Allen barges in front of her before she can open it.

'I'll have *that*, thank you,' he says, snatching the flier from her fingers. She stares at him in astonishment. 'Cost me money to have them printed.'

Allen is grinning, his face inches from hers. She knows he must be trying to be funny but it's such a sudden invasion of her personal space, she has the urge to shove him out of the way. 'Let me past please,' she says. Grant Allen steps back so she can open the door.

'No need to be so touchy,' he says. 'Though I thought you were a slippery customer over the phone.' He closes the door before either of them has a chance to reply.

There's the sound of a key locking them out as soon as they step onto the crazy paving.

'Good Lord,' says Zara. 'Absolutely *barking*.'

They make their way to the car and Zara starts up the engine. 'Not now, Snoopy,' she says crossly, as the Labrador yaps and leaps about the back seat with excitement. Frankie turns back to look at the house as the Peugeot drives off. 'Is he watching us?' Zara asks.

'No.'

'Probably knocking seven bells out of that punch-bag,' she jokes. But neither of them laugh.

Ava

We hear his footsteps on the stairs, and look at each other in terror. Without saying anything, I yank Daisy onto her feet and we walk to the door. She stands in front, I'm just to the side, so I can grab him when it opens. I can see she's shaking. I am too.

He stops outside the door. His breathing is heavy. 'Nice plan, girls,' he says. 'But I have a gun.' There's silence. We look at each other, and I see my own confusion on her face. 'You're so fucking stupid. I've been *listening* to you. The room is bugged, bitches. I've got a nice little spy cam in there too, so I can watch you from home.' Daisy's mouth is half hanging open. 'Did you honestly think I'd leave you both alone to plot? Especially after your little stunt, Ava.' He laughs. 'So, here's how it's going to go. As soon as I open this door, I'm firing the gun. If you girls want to survive I'd stand well back and away, or somebody's head's going to get blown off. Of course, I might hit one of you anyway, but you'll have more of a chance if you move it. So on the count of five, four, three . . .'

Daisy and I run to the far side of the room, at an angle from the door. There's an explosion as it swings open and a bullet ricochets off the wall. I don't know where it ends up. We're both unharmed and so, unfortunately, is he.

Fat Head slams the door shut with his foot. He's wearing the familiar ski mask, the black gloves, and he's holding a huge gun. It looks like an old hunting rifle, the sort I remember my grandfather keeping on his farm. There's no sign of a bag of provisions.

'Very touching, all your little stories,' he says. 'What lies you tell.' He turns to Daisy. 'You're the worst. White guys not good enough for you? Dirty little slut. And I had no idea you were a fucking *dyke*, Ava, thanks for that extra information. Must have been Christmas for you here, a little girlfriend all tied up.'

I don't reply. The thought of him listening, hearing all about Simon, Daisy's wedding, my childhood with Matt, makes me feel hollowed out inside. And it's obviously done nothing to activate the bastard's non-existent empathy.

'But there's one thing Saint Daisy hasn't told you, Ava. A nasty little secret. I'd be pretty worried if *I* were sharing a cell with *her*.' Daisy looks at him in bewilderment. He stares back, clearly expecting her to understand, and becomes agitated when she says nothing. 'Enough of this!' he shouts. 'Don't just stand there like a couple of gormless cows.' He points at Daisy. 'You come here, lie face up on the floor.' He gestures at his feet. She hesitates. 'I said *move!*'

She leaves me and does as he asks. He rests one foot on her neck, holding her head still with the toe of the other. 'You.' He points at me. 'Come over here. Turn your back to me. One false move and I stamp out your girlfriend's windpipe.'

I walk over and he ties up my hands, then slips something over my neck, I think it's a piece of string. I shake my head violently, but it's stuck there, loose and dangling from my throat. I hear a thump and a cry as he kicks Daisy. 'Up you get, bitch.'

It's a struggle for her to stand up with her hands tied, but she manages. We're facing each other and I see her eyes widen when she sees whatever it is round my neck. 'No!' she gasps.

'What is it?' I say.

She doesn't say anything, all I can see is the look of horror on her face.

'Go on, tell Ava what it is.' Still she says nothing and he points the gun at her head. 'Tell her!'

Daisy looks at me, holds my eyes with hers. They're shining with tears. I think she's trying to tell me something, silently, but I don't know what it is. 'It's a garrotte,' she says.

I scream and try to shake it off my head, backwards and forwards, but it won't budge. He laughs. 'Shall we tell Ava your little secret now?' he says. 'Stop shaking your head like a crazy bitch!' he snaps at me, swinging the gun round. With difficulty, I force myself to stand still. Terror has built a loud ringing in my ears and my chest is soaked with sweat. 'Well, you're obviously not going to tell her, so I will.' He leans closer to me. 'Daisy's a *murderess*.'

There's a pause while we both stare at him. I turn to Daisy. At first I see only confusion on her face, then a flash of fear. 'You're insane,' she says.

'Daisy doesn't just bring lovely little babies into the world. She *kills* them.'

'That's a lie!'

'When that black bastard brings you a cup of tea in the morning, what does he say to you? Good luck killing babies today, darling!'

'You're a liar!' she shouts.

'Just because they're small, doesn't mean they're not alive, that you're not killing them.'

'Abortion isn't murder,' I say, finally understanding.

'No it couldn't be, could it?' He turns to me, spitting the consonants, venom in every word. 'Because it's something *women* do. Only men can be murderers. Women can kill as many babies as they fucking like and nobody bats an eye! That's what you do on your ward, isn't it? Getting the final say on who lives and who dies, like a coven of fucking *witches*.'

'You've no idea what you're talking about,' Daisy says. I can't tell if her voice is so low from fear or anger.

'It's not murder,' I say. For a moment I imagine running through the arguments, telling him that it's a pregnancy, not a baby, before being hit by the utter futility of trying to convince this man of anything. I look at his hated puffball face. 'It's *not*,' is all I say.

'So, you're really confident Daisy's not a killer,' he replies, circling us both. My legs start shaking. 'We'll see about that.' He stops next to Daisy, raises the gun so that its muzzle is pointing at the back of her head. He holds it with one hand, reaching into his pocket with the other, bringing out a knife. 'Ava can tell you my finger's on the trigger,' he says, leaning closer to her. 'And both you bitches know it works and it's loaded. So don't try anything.' He cuts the cable ties round her wrist with the knife. 'Walk towards Ava. Go on,' he says, shoving the gun against her. 'Don't make me say it twice.'

I walk backwards as they head towards me, I can't help it. I hit the wall with a thump, my hands scraping the concrete. I know without checking that I'm standing against The Stain. He's forced her to stand really close to me, so close I can't move. Daisy is not looking at me; her eyes are fixed at the side of my shoulders, on the wall. I can see she's crying even though she's not making a sound. Behind her, he is clutching the gun, grinning.

'Daisy,' I say.

She raises her eyes to mine. We're staring at each other, and I realise I have nothing I can say to her. I can't plead for my life. It would mean her blood on my face as he blows off her head. Her grey eyes, which I thought were so beautiful, will be the last thing I see.

'So, you're not a killer, Daisy Meadwell,' he says. 'That's what *you* say, but *I* know you better. Now. I want you to tighten the garrotte around Ava's neck.' I try to move to the side, but he pushes her towards me with the gun. 'Don't be stupid,' he snaps. 'From this distance I can kill you both at once. Take hold of the cord.'

Up until the point her hand moves to take the string, some part of me had been unable to believe this was really happening, but now it's all moving too quickly, and I have to make it stop. 'You don't have to do this,' I gabble, trying to look him in the eye, desperate to make him feel something. 'Please. We can talk, can't we? There's so much more to say to each other. You don't want to do this, you don't. You *can't* want to do this.' I'm crying so much I can hardly get the words out. 'Think about Hanna, think how you miss Hanna.'

'I miss Hanna, you stupid bitch, because *I miss killing her*. I miss snuffing her miserable little life out.'

Daisy has tightened the garrotte, not enough so that it hurts, but enough that I'm terrified she's actually going to do it. I thrash about, and instantly she lets go. 'I can't do this,' she wails. 'I can't, I can't!'

'Yes, you can,' he says, soothingly. 'Go on. Think of Simon. This is the only way you're ever going to see him again.'

She looks at me. I see resolve stiffen her face and I start to scream. But then, instead of taking hold of me again, she flings herself backwards. The gun goes off, but she's knocked it wide and the bullet hits the wall. She's grappling with him, both hands round his wrist, trying to make him drop it. With his free hand, he's grabbed the back of her head. It happens so fast, shock freezes me to the spot.

'That's not who I am!' she's screaming. 'That's not who I am!'

With a single violent twist, he turns her head. I hear a snap. Daisy falls to the floor, crumpling at an unnatural angle. She's lying at his feet. His chest is rising and falling with exertion, but she's lying there completely still.

He turns to face me, raising the gun to point at my face. 'Guess it's just you and me,' he says.

I want to scream but I can't make a sound. My eyes meet the two black holes of his gun, and I'm mesmerised by its malignant stare. I can't even drag my eyes down towards where Daisy is lying on the floor. I'm afraid if I blink he will shoot me.

'I'm kind of glad, even if it's not what I planned. You were definitely my favourite.' I'm aware of him nudging Daisy with his foot but I can't look down at her. 'Not going to say anything, then?'

Words try to force themselves into my mouth, heaved there by a bubble of air from my lungs, but the only sound that comes out is a gagging noise. I start to whine, a barely human sound. I can't speak even though my life depends on it.

'That's better!' he says. 'That's what I like to see! It's what my experiment's all about.' He strides towards me, still pointing the gun at my head, and I collapse onto the floor like a rag doll. I feel like I've been cut off at the knees. He bends over me, the gun tucked under his arm, and drags me back onto my feet, holding me at arm's length. I know if he lets go I will fall. 'You're covered in cracks, Ava,' he says. He sounds excited, his breath is fast and shallow and his lips, close to my face, are moist. 'Absolutely covered in cracks. Just a few more blows with the chisel and you're going to shatter all over my hands.' He lets go suddenly and I collapse again, scraping my shin on the concrete. 'That's right!' he says. 'Smash!' He walks over to where Daisy is lying and kicks her. 'Smash! Just like the other one. Like all the other ones. You're just like all the others, Ava.' He tilts his round head, staring at me where I'm lying on the floor. 'In fact I don't think I'm going to call you Ava any more. You can be Hanna. You're more like Hanna than Ava now anyway.' He bends down, carefully placing the gun down behind him on the concrete. 'I'm breaking you in, Hanna. You're not going to fight me any more, are you? So you won't need these.' He takes the knife out of his pocket and cuts the cable ties around my wrists. Released from their restraints, my hands fall limp to the ground. He picks up the gun and stands up, then walks to the door.

'Night, night, Hanna,' he says, turning to look at me again. 'Have fun with Daisy. Don't stay up too late talking together, will you?'

There's a scrape and a clang as he shuts the door behind him. Then the sound of the bolt and his receding footsteps.

The silence in the basement is absolute. Daisy's body is a crumpled shape at the edge of my vision. I still can't look at her. I struggle with the garrotte around my neck, trying not to think that her hands only just touched it, or the price she paid for letting go. Only when it's off do I allow myself to look at her and truly understand what I see. She's not moving.

'Daisy?' I say softly. 'He's gone. You can get up now.' I know in my heart she can't hear me, I know she's dead, but I'm so desperate for her to be alive that I go through with the make-believe, trying to fool myself for another few minutes. I shuffle over to her on my knees. Her face is turned away from me, her head at a strange angle. I push aside thick curls, feeling for a pulse at her neck. I can't bring myself to smooth the hair from her face, or look at her eyes.

There's nothing, but I hold my finger there a long time. 'Maybe I can feel it better in your wrist,' I say, my voice wobbling. I pick up her hand. It's heavy and slack in mine, the skin already going cold. I press my finger against the soft hollow by the bone, willing a faint pulse into existence, but I can't feel anything. I sit back on my haunches and gently pull her head and shoulders across my lap. Her neck feels loose as I move her. When I'm holding her gathered against me, I finally dare to smooth the hair from her face. Her eyes stare upwards at nothing.

I grip her more tightly. 'I'm sorry, I'm really sorry,' I say, my voice breaking. Guilt and grief rack me. '*It should have been me, it should have been me.*' I rock back and forth, clasping her in my arms, unable to let her go. I try to comfort her, even though she can't feel it, stroking her face gently and calling her name. I think about the little baby boy she saved, of all the knowledge stored in her mind and the skill in her hands. It seems impossible to think all that has gone, obliterated, along with her memories of Simon and the future that was so close to her she was almost holding it.

I don't know how long I rock back and forth grieving for Daisy, but when I'm still I can feel she has grown cold, as icy as the touch of the concrete floor beneath me. Daisy is not going to be Daisy for much longer. She will start to decay. She's becoming a corpse. I look at The Stain behind us and dread washes up in my stomach. Perhaps it has already sucked her life into its horrible dark shape; it's growing larger, lines running down from it like a pregnant spider.

I start to shake. 'It's just a mark on the wall,' I say to myself. 'There's nothing there.' I try to hold on to the pieces of my mind, which feel like scraps of paper caught in the wind. I think of my grandfather, laid out in his bedroom in the old farm-house, my father sitting beside him reading a book, waiting for the undertakers to take him away. *The dead are nothing to be afraid of.*

I calm myself by performing the last rituals of respect. It's all I can do for her. I close her eyelids gently with my fingertips so that she looks peaceful, then allow myself to hold her for one last time. She's a dead weight in my arms. 'Goodbye, Daisy,' I say, stroking her hair. 'I promise I'll try to find Simon, and tell him how brave you were. I'm so sorry.' The tears drip over my cracked lips as I speak. 'Forgive me. I have to let you go now.'

I lean over and kiss her on her freezing forehead, then gently roll her off my lap onto the floor. Before I can change my mind, I drag her by the ankles to a corner of the room, just below the window where it's coldest. I arrange her so that she is lying on her back with her arms by her sides.

She's so pale now. She looks less like Daisy and more like a waxwork copy. It will be easier if I can think of her that way. I stare at her, willing myself to disconnect. I notice that the corner of her mouth is slightly open and move to close it, then stop, my hand hovering above her. My shoulder blades prickle as I wonder where he has installed the spy cam, if it's streaming video of me right now, but I don't turn round. It's possible that he won't be home yet, so isn't watching me, but I don't know.

An idea has come to me and I don't know whether to be appalled by it or relieved that somehow I still have the will left to survive.

With a silent apology to Daisy for the pretence, I start wailing, pulling at my hair. A clump comes out in my fingers. I keep it tight in my clenched fist, then fall forwards across my dead friend. I hope her face is screened from view by my head and shoulders, as I push the hair into her mouth and down her throat with my fingers, then hold her jaw shut. At some point I slip from pretend-ing to real weeping. I lie there sobbing, my wet cheek resting on her cold one. It would be so easy just to lie down next to Daisy and wait to die.

I force myself to sit back on my haunches. I look at her. *I'm not going to die here.* I say to her in my mind. *I'm going to live for both of us. We will make him pay.*

Daisy says nothing, but I hope the forensic officers who examine her will understand she can still speak. When her murderer dumps her body, she will give the outside world a message that I'm still alive.

Frankie

Waking up in her own bed, Frankie doesn't get the sense of happiness and anticipation a Sunday morning would usually bring. Instead she finds herself wishing she could have slept a little longer, blotting out her anxiety. She stares at the bedroom blinds. Could one of the website's followers be hanging round her flat, even now, waiting to snap a shot of her on his phone when she goes to the window in her pyjamas?

It doesn't help that she and Jack had a terrible row last night. He was furious she and Zara had been to see Grant Allen; there's a dent in the living room's new white sideboard where he kicked it. It's a small enough mark that she hopes the landlord won't notice, but the fact Jack lashed out physically, even at an object, leaves her with a feeling of disappointment that squeezes at her chest and won't let go. She tries to tell herself he only reacted that way because he cares about her, because he's worried about the blog, but the look of fury on his face was unlike anything she's seen from him before.

Beside her, Jack's chest rises and falls with a slow, steady rhythm and she hopes it might lull her back into a doze. But the sight of him is less comforting than it should be, and her mind is whirring, already on high alert. With a sigh she sits up and slips out of bed, picking up her phone off the bedside table. She walks into the living room. The curtains are closed. She doesn't open them. The river view has lost its appeal, the sight of joggers on the path opposite makes her nervous. Frankie wanders over to the kitchen, flicks on the kettle.

She checks her messages as it boils. Nothing from Simon Meadwell. She had asked him to text if there was any news. But perhaps Daisy has come home and he's too embarrassed to get in touch after making such a fuss, or too happy to remember to text her. She hopes so. A hot cup of tea in her hands, she wanders across to sit down on the sofa where she left her laptop last night, pulling it onto her knee.

For a moment she stares at the blank search engine. Then she types in the address for the hated website. If she can't avoid thinking about it, she might as well tackle her fear head on. Zara remains convinced the blogger could be Grant; that his knowledge of Jamie Cole's trial and misogynist world view make him a prime suspect. Frankie isn't sure. Though she can't get the idea of Grant's son Zach out of her head. Last night when Jack was shouting, a terrible thought had flashed past, so insane she feels guilty for entertaining it, even for a moment. It was just the sound of the names, she tells herself; Jack and Zach. And the fact they both have dead mothers and estranged fathers. She blushes. Just because the connection popped into her head doesn't mean she actually suspects her own boyfriend, she's not *that* crazy.

She brings up @Feminazi_Slayer2's previous posts, ignoring the last couple about her, and those about the murders. There's a long list. She glances back at the door, wondering if Jack will be cross at her for looking at the blog again. But she can't let it rest. She clicks on one from a year ago, titled **Big Game**. The first thing she sees is the photograph. A woman in a bikini has been Photoshopped so that she appears to be lying amongst a pride of lions. The crosshairs of a gun are superimposed over her chest. Frankie feels a pain in her own. The image is reminiscent of the one used against her. She forces herself to read the article beneath it.

So you want to use your game on the biggest game of all? You've come to the right place. This post will teach you how to hunt and destroy the 10. By the time you've finished with her, she'll be hovering at 3. Anyone will be able to smash her.

But I'm going to say this now: This post is not for snivelling Betas, desperate to turn the 8s, 9s, and 10s out there in the wild into the Loyal Girlfriend. If that's your game, my friend, then look elsewhere for tips. And maybe grow some balls while you're at it.

This post is for THE SLAYER, the man who wants to smash his ten . . . And leave it broken.

The first thing to understand is that before you can fuck the Wild 10, you need to fuck with her head. Big Time. Everything you do should aim to lower her social value, challenge her sense of herself and invalidate who she thinks she is. You need to condition her so she's reliant on you for validation; reward behaviour you like, punish behaviour you don't. And later, when you leave, you're going to do so with maximum impact.

I'm assuming if you've read this far, you've got your standard game off pat. You know how to open a girl on the street, in a club, wherever. You can engage her interest and reel her in. But if not: Don't even think of trying these techniques until your game is at an advanced level.

TIP 1 TOUCH TOUCH TOUCH

Touch her like you own her. Right from the start. Don't ask permission, just get hold of her. If she puts up resistance, carry on. She needs to get used to it. We're not talking rape here, you don't want to get arrested, but **BE ASSERTIVE.**

TIP 2 PUSH PULL

Yes, you all think you know about this one. But we're talking about upping the ante to the max, until her head's spinning. So you're calling her goodnight three days in a row then radio silence for a couple of days. All over her one date, then don't so much as hold her hand on another. Hang off her every word, completely ignore her . . . You get the picture.

TIP 3 NEGGING

Again you think you know this one. But we're not just talking a few well-placed negs here, just to make her more receptive, we're talking about lowering her sense of herself . . . **PERMANENTLY**. But be subtle, you need to ramp it up slowly. Remember the frog that didn't notice it was being boiled alive because the water started off tepid? That's your model.

So let's say you want to give her a complex about personal hygiene. Start by offering her tic tacs before you kiss. When she asks why, smile, act sheepish and tell her that her breath smells. Progress to getting her to shower before sex, because she 'smells sweaty'. Buy her expensive perfume and ask her to use it liberally. Trust me, by the time you've progressed to telling her she's disgusting, you've primed her to believe it.

Frankie stops reading, unable to listen to the hateful voice any longer. She feels physically repulsed. The over-confident tone makes her think not about Grant Allen, but Brett Hollins. She remembers the feel of his hand on her arm in the café. Her eye travels to the blog post, picking out the words TOUCH TOUCH TOUCH. Brett's obviously not used to being turned down. Would he want to share his pick-up expertise online? Although what she's read goes beyond pick-up tips; it reads more like a recipe for domestic abuse.

Frankie scrolls absently through the article. If only she had mentioned Brett to Jack ages ago, when it wouldn't have been a big deal. She's sure one of the reasons he got so angry last night is because he thinks she's been hiding so many things from him.

'Up already?'

She swings round, pushing the laptop off her knee. Jack is standing behind the sofa. She didn't hear him walk out of the bedroom. 'I've got a lot on my mind.'

Gently, he strokes a strand of hair behind one ear. 'I know, it's stressful. And I'm really sorry about losing it last night. Shall I make us both a coffee?' She sees him frown as he catches sight of the screen, abandoned on the seat beside her. 'What's that you're reading? *Dating* tips?'

She hurries to close it, embarrassed to be caught out. 'No, it's that website. I've been looking at Feminazi Slayer's previous blogs.'

Jack moves away, walking off to the kitchen. He flicks the kettle on. It boils in moments, still hot from Frankie's tea. 'I wish you wouldn't do that. I thought you were going to let me deal with it.'

She jumps off the sofa and follows him, leaning against the kitchen counter as he spoons ground coffee into the cafetière, pours in the water. 'I know, but it's been useful just having a quick look. I think it rules' – she stops, not wanting to mention Grant Allen by name – 'it rules certain people out.'

Jack groans. 'Not him again. What were you and Zara thinking, knocking on the doors of random madmen?' He gets the milk from the fridge, his back to her. 'You're not the police. You don't need to go off eliminating suspects, for God's sake.'

'I know,' she says. 'But it's driving me crazy just sitting around like some sort of target.'

Jack presses down the plunger and pours out the coffee. 'So rather than sit around, you go out seeking danger and make yourself even *more* of a target?'

Frankie takes the cup he's holding out to her. She feels weary from constantly having to explain herself. 'Let's not do this. Again.'

He leans against the counter beside her, touching her shoulder with his. 'It's not about giving you a hard time. I'm sorry if it comes across that way. And I've already said sorry a million times for the kicking the cabinet thing. I really *am* sorry about that,' he says. 'It was a stupid thing to do. But I live here too. And it's not nice for me either, knowing the pervert paparazzi are lurking around.'

'Pervert Paparazzi? Good name for it,' Frankie says, thinking of the montage.

'Can we just forget about them for today and go out for breakfast somewhere nice? Please?'

She clutches her mug. It's too hot but she doesn't put it down. He's looking at her hopefully, like a puppy, his hair still mussed from where he slept on it. She wants to tell him that she'd rather stay in together with the curtains closed, preferably back in bed, snuggled under the duvet, blotting it all out with a book. But that seems hypocritical given what she just said about sitting targets. The mug starts to burn her fingers. She puts it down. 'Of course,' she says. 'Great idea.'

*   *   *

Frank's Bar always feels like home, but today she can't relax. She keeps looking at customers wondering if any might be stalkers, surreptitiously taking pictures. Jack tucks into his cooked breakfast, seemingly unaware of her heightened anxiety. One man in particular, who is sitting alone at a table across from the bar, seems to keep catching her eye over his Sunday papers. She glares at him and he quickly looks away.

'Are you listening? Did you hear a word I just said?' Jack asks.

'What? No, sorry,' she replies.

He rolls his eyes. 'I was saying the project at the lab should be done by next month, so why don't we both try and book some leave off? It'll be November, off season, we might get a last minute deal somewhere nice.'

'That's a great idea,' she says, only realising after he's suggested it how desperately she wants to get away, have a break from all the horrors that are building in her head. 'Where d'you fancy?'

'I can't afford much, not right before Christmas, but I was thinking we might find a deal in Southern Europe. Italy is probably too expensive, but you never know.'

'That would be amazing,' Frankie says. She can already picture them both walking the streets of a medieval hill town in wintry sunshine, winding their way to the top and leaning over the ramparts to look out at the olive groves spread out below. Jack breaks her reverie, taking her hand across the small table. She smiles, then notices a movement from the man behind him.

'What?' says Jack. 'What's wrong?'

'That guy behind you over there – no don't look – I think he's watching us.' She can feel Jack grip her fingers.

'He'd better bloody not be.' Jack has gone pale. The man behind them is hidden by his newspaper again. 'What's he doing?'

'He's stopped now,' she says. She tilts her head, trying to see the coat hanging behind his chair. Could it be a duffle?

Jack lets go of her hand. Neither of them has finished their cooked breakfast. He stares down at his half-eaten egg, pushing at it with his fork. 'Are you sure he was looking this way? I mean maybe it's just because he recognises you from the news or something.' Frankie hears the question he didn't ask in his tone of voice.

'I'm not imagining it,' she says, flushing. 'He's definitely been acting oddly.'

'Right, well no point us hanging out here, then.' Jack sticks his hand in the air to call for the bill.

'What are you doing?' She glances round, looking for the waiter to give the opposite instructions. 'We've not finished.'

'I've lost my appetite,' he snaps. With a sense of shock, Frankie realises he's annoyed with her.

'It's not *my* fault this is happening,' she says. Jack looks at her, saying nothing. 'What? You think I brought this on myself?'

'I think you're reckless,' he says. 'What were you *doing* yesterday? Gadding off to see some sodding madman. Poking about in a hornet's nest, asking him about his killer son.'

They are arguing in hissed whispers, but the tables at Frank's are tightly packed and a couple of curious students are clearly earwigging.

'How do you know he had a son in jail?' Frankie has been careful to keep information about Grant Allen to a minimum. 'Have you been scouting him out?'

'Your bill,' says the waiter, breaking across their argument and leaning in from behind her to place the tab on the table.

'Thanks,' says Jack, putting down his card. There's an awkward pause while they suspend hostilities long enough for the waiter to take the credit card reading.

'I can't believe you've been checking up on me,' Frankie says when the waiter has moved out of earshot. 'As if it's not bad enough being stalked by a bunch of website weirdos, my own boyfriend is spying on me!'

'How can you compare me to that?' Jack pushes his chair back, furious. 'I've been looking out for you,' he says, no longer bothering to keep his voice down. 'Not bloody stalking you! Who wouldn't check out some nutter their girlfriend's been visiting? And to sit there accusing me of snooping when you know I've been spending *hours* of my time trying to help. I don't know why I bother.'

They walk past the curious diners. Frankie's face is burning hot with embarrassment. As they pass the man with the newspaper, Jack flicks the pages with a finger. 'And you can stop goggling,' he says.

Frankie looks back to see the man watching them in open-mouthed astonishment. With a stab of mortification, she recognises him, and finally understands why he tried to catch her eye. It's the press officer from a lobby group for local manufacturers that she interviewed last year. She turns round, hurries out of Frank's with her head down. Somehow she doesn't think he will be emailing her more story pitches any time soon.

Frankie and Jack continue arguing on the walk back to the flat until the hopelessness of trying to make things up smothers them into silence. She steals a glance at him as they clump along King Street, hoping to see a glimmer of sadness, anything that might give her the space to reach out a hand, take his arm, ask if they can't just forget it, put it down to stress. But he's staring straight ahead, lips pressed, his chin jutting out. This isn't working, she realises with a jolt. The thought beats a tattoo with their footsteps: this isn't working, this isn't working.

They reach the apartment building and both instinctively scan the car park for loiterers; Frankie with a small nervous flick of the head, Jack spinning round, scowling. They go in, head up the beige communal stairs, but when she opens the door to their apartment, Jack stands back.

'I'm going to the lab,' he says. 'Do a bit of work. I think we both need some space.' He's about to leave, then hesitates. 'Don't forget to lock the door. And call me if you're worried. I can come straight back.'

She nods, then locks herself in, leaning for a moment against the newly painted wood. She turns to face the white room. The curtains are still drawn. The Scandi layout, which so impressed her when they first came here, feels bland. It's a room without personality. They haven't even had time to put any pictures up. And without the river view to draw the eye, the open-plan room shrinks. It feels like the opposite of space.

A wave of claustrophobia hits her. She takes a step backwards, meaning to walk back into town again, but fear stops her. What if the blogger and his army of watchers are out there, waiting for her?

She heads to the sofa, picks up the remote and turns on the TV. It's a Sunday afternoon film, a Roger Moore James Bond. She can't remember which one it is, but the sight of him raising an eyebrow, improbably disarming baddies half his age, is oddly comforting. It reminds her of rainy afternoons in childhood, watching whatever Bond film was on with her sister Natalie while their mum made spaghetti in the other room. She sits back on the cushions with a sigh. She thinks about giving her younger sister a ring, but it's getting a bit late with the time difference. Natalie is in Australia now, spending a year at the Sydney office of the wine company she works for. Her loyal boyfriend Alex is waiting for her in London.

She thinks of Jack and her heart drops. They've only been living together six weeks and already the relationship is unravelling. On the perspex coffee table is the one personal object on display from their life together; a blue glazed bowl from the pottery shop at Clay. It's empty, as neither of them could think of what to put in it.

On the screen, Roger Moore fires missiles from a magical speeding car. She met Jack during an afternoon's filming at the John Innes. Everyone imagines journalists getting dates that way, being asked out by the people they interview, but it was the first time it had ever happened to her. She can still remember the excitement of their first dinner, not much more than a year ago. Jack had looked ridiculously attractive in his glasses, constantly topping up her wine, so eager to impress. And then the texts every night, the minibreak to Scotland three months later. Zara had nicknamed him Clark Kent, a tribute to his geeky charm.

She had thought a year was plenty of time to get to know some-body, that they were more than ready to move in. But his bad temper this weekend has taken her aback. With a wince, she thinks of him flicking the press officer's paper as they left the bar, their half-eaten food still on the table. She makes an attempt in her own mind to excuse him, thinking of all the stress he's been under.

Her phone vibrates. She reaches for it, hope fluttering in her chest that it might be an apology. It's a text from Charlie.

Emneth has been charged. First appearance at court tomor-row. You OK to cover that? Kiera would like you to go.

Frankie sags with relief. The police must feel secure they have their man. Whoever is posting their bile online, the Norfolk Strangler is off the streets.

Sure, no problem

she texts back.

The closed curtains catch her eye as she leans over to put the phone down on the table. She rises and walks over to the window, opening them with a single firm movement. She looks out. There's nobody on the path across the river. The sun's reflection shines on the surface of the water in rippling spots of silver.

Frankie sighs, leaning her forehead on the cool glass. Without a killer on the loose, the blog has lost some of its power to disturb. But at the back of her relief is still the persistent drip of anxiety, like a tap she can't quite turn off. She thinks of Amber Finn and her little girl, remembers sitting in the front room with its pile of plastic toys, listening to her defend Donnie. God knows what horrors he put her through. Amber had known Donald Emneth for years, yet as it turned out, she hadn't known him at all.

Ava

I knew Daisy for only two days, but she was more than a friend. She was hope.

Now she's nothing but a heap in the corner, dead, and I can't escape her. I have to do everything in her presence. Eat one of the sandwiches we should have shared. Pee in the awful, stinking, plastic bucket. Sleep.

I leave the light on in the night and the bulb blows. I think it's because she's angry with me. I want to crawl over to her, say sorry again, but I don't dare.

The garrotte lies in the bottom of the waste bucket. There are times I wish I had the strength to use it. At least then I would cheat him of my murder. There are so few choices left to me and if I have to die, I would rather die alone than with him watching. I glance at the ceiling. Unless he *is* watching.

I keep hearing her scream *That's not who I am!* The horror of the images, of him twisting her neck, plays over and over in my mind. I try to think of her living instead. I remember her sitting back on her heels, as we talked together. 'We ought to have a name for him,' she said. 'To make him smaller. He's pathetic really, hiding behind that puffed-up mask.' I see her again, the way she frowned, lost in thought. 'Fat Head!' she said. 'That's what we should call him.' I think of her laughing. I can't keep the image of her smile in my mind for long; the replay of her murder starts to drown it out. But this time when I hear her scream, I notice something else. I actually listen to her words, and understand: she didn't beg. I remember him saying that we all beg and plead to stay alive. But Daisy never did.

I turn to look at her but I can't see anything more than a vague shape in the dark. It's no longer safe to speak aloud in here, even to myself, but I talk to her in my head. I imagine her answering, telling me not to kill myself, that it's a false choice, that my life has value and I must never forget that. All night I promise Daisy that I will try to be like her: to be strong, to be brave, whatever happens.

He comes to take her in the morning, and all my resolve to be strong deserts me.

'Are you going to be trouble?' he asks, pointing the gun at me. The sight of it liquefies my insides; even after all I've suffered I still can't get used to staring death in the face. But although I'm afraid, it strikes me how the gun diminishes him as well as frightens me. Here I am, weak, half-starved, with a dead woman. And he's still scared of us. Daisy's right. He *is* pathetic. He gestures for me to move away from her, then bends down and swiftly slings her over his shoulder.

'Sandwiches are by the door,' he says. 'And I've treated you to some chocolate. Though I wouldn't eat it all, I've got another visitor planned, and she's a real fatty. Shouldn't think she'll thank you for scoffing the lot. Though the nosy slag could do with going on a diet.'

Of all the threats he could have made, this is the worst. The thought of another woman, brought here, tortured, while he amuses himself is unbearable. 'Why are you doing this?' I say, my voice rising. 'What's *wrong* with you?'

'Oh it's like that, is it?' he shouts. 'I bring you fucking chocolate and you can't even say thank you?'

I'm not playing this game any more. I know being nice isn't going to save me. I stare at him, looking at Daisy hanging over his shoulder. 'That's not who I am,' I reply.

The breath whistles through his teeth. 'We'll see about that, bitch. Don't play tough with me. Once the fat slag's here, you'll be *begging* for mercy.'

He slams the door shut and I'm alone.

Frankie

The magistrates' court is packed for Donald Emneth's first appearance and Frankie is wedged so close to Luke Heffner she's almost sitting on his knee. Still, she knows she's lucky to have a seat; a number of furious hacks are trapped outside after the clerk told them they'd have to rely on Malcolm from the Press Association for copy. Not that there will be much to report at this stage; the hearing is really just a formality so Emneth's case can be referred to the Crown Court.

'Well, this is fun,' says Luke, his plummy tones lowered into a gossipy whisper. 'The Bad Guy getting his comeuppance. And you must be feeling smug after that Daisy Meadwell interview. What a cracking piece of TV. Have you heard anything more?'

Frankie knows it's a rare compliment from a competitive hack but Luke's praise makes her feel guilty rather than pleased. 'I texted Simon this morning. She's not home yet.'

'Hmmmm. The midwife went missing before they nabbed Donnie Emneth, didn't she? Not going to look too good for the police if she's dead. They've had all this time to question him. Though I'm sure the defence team *here* will be chuffed if they can argue it was someone else.' He nods at the barristers sitting a few feet away. 'He's going down for Amber either way, I suppose. And we're going to be *laughing* after sentencing with that interview you did to play with. Though it's a shame,' he adds, looking at her reproachfully, 'that you didn't get *any* shots of Amber when she wasn't disguised. Let's just hope she agrees to another interview.'

'Yes, sorry about that,' Frankie says. 'I should have made a contingency plan for if she got kidnapped or bumped off.'

Luke either ignores or misses her sarcasm. 'Always good to plan ahead with a serial killer story,' he says. 'Just in case.'

Frankie wants to jab him in the ribs, but part of her is increasingly wondering if she deserves to feel morally superior. Is he so very different from her and Ray, congratulating themselves on filming Donald Emneth in case he's guilty? And at least Luke doesn't have any reason to feel even partially responsible for Amber's ordeal. They're all wallowing in the same gutter after all; she just happens to have got her hands dirtier than the rest.

'Cheer up,' says Luke, patting her arm. 'It's not your fault.' Frankie looks at him in surprise, taken aback that he's sensitive enough to pick up on her sense of guilt. 'After all,' he goes on, looking down at his notebook. 'Ten to one she'll talk again and if not there will always be shots of her arriving at court.'

Frankie can't help snorting with laughter, but before he can ask her what's so funny they rise for the entrance of the judge.

The district judge, Ralph Meyer, greets the court and everyone sits down. As always, when the hearing starts, the dryness of the proceedings helps keep the drama of the crime contained. Even murder feels neutered by the to-ing and fro-ing of the lawyers' meticulous discussions. In any case, there are severe limits on what Frankie can report. All legal arguments are off limits, and strictly speaking she shouldn't even include details about the defendant's appearance, though the press push the boundaries all the time. But even though she can't mention many of the details, it's useful background to know ahead of the trial.

Along with the rest of the hacks she keeps stealing glances at Donald Emneth where he sits, slumped and despondent, behind the glass of the dock. He's a different man from the eccentric who gesticulated wildly at her in his garden, or leered at her chest. His face is haggard and he's shaved badly, with red-blotted patches of tissue paper stuck to his chin. Can she mention that in the piece to camera, maybe? His response to the judge confirming his name and address is barely audible. He stares at the floor while his defence brief argues that his client is prepared to plead guilty to the false imprisonment of Amber Finn, but denies any involvement in the murder of Lily Sidcup, Sandra Blakely and Hanna Chivers. There's no mention of Daisy Meadwell or Ava Lindsey. At the thought of either of them lying dead somewhere, like Hanna on the wasteland, she feels sick.

The hearing takes less than ten minutes and then Donald Emneth is told his case will be referred to the Crown Court and led out of the dock again. There's a collective rustle and scraping of chairs as the journalists all get up to file.

'Well,' says Luke, raising his eyebrows at her as they shuffle along in the queue to leave the court. 'This could get very interesting. Maybe the police don't have their man after all.'

'What makes you say that?'

'He's obviously not one of those psychos who pleads not guilty to everything, regardless of the evidence. He's prepared to hold his hands up to the first charge, isn't he? That means they don't have overwhelming proof he's implicated in the murders. Looks to me like he kidnapped Amber because he was peeved at your interview,' Luke says, with crushing insensitivity. 'And then PC Plod nobbled him for the killings because those women were abducted too and he's creepy.'

'Not *just* because he's creepy,' Frankie snaps, her stomach sinking as the weight of Luke's argument hits her. 'Keeping a woman prisoner is a tad incriminating, don't you think? And they must have other evidence, surely? He probably only admitted that one because it's the least serious charge.'

Luke shrugs. 'Perhaps.' He gets out his mobile from his pocket, despite the court clerk's furious stare, and starts to type out a message. 'But where's the pink-haired student? Or your midwife? I'm going to warn the newsdesk this killing spree might not be over. Just in case.'

Outside the court Luke wanders off to his sat truck without saying goodbye. She watches him cross the road, already combing his hair, getting ready for his lunchtime live. Luke's nothing to her, but it's still galling the way he drops her at the end of their conversation as if she were an empty Coke can. She starts trudging up the road to the office. It's a grey day and the wind quickly freezes her legs through too-thin tights. She dismisses Luke from her mind. She still feels exhausted after the stress of last night. Jack got home after she had gone to bed and they had lain next to each other under the duvet with the lights out, both obviously tense and awake, but neither breaking the silence. She passes the cathedral close, trying not to think of whoever it was in the duffle coat and whether they took her photo.

On the road opposite she can see the sandwich shop where she last bumped into Brett. She thinks about Feminazi Slayer's pickup blog. Its tips do seem a bit crude for Brett; he has much more charm than that. But that doesn't mean he's not involved with *Killing Cuttlefish*. She visualises the website's homepage, the slick graphics, the James Bond-style opening montage. Perhaps she needs to be braver. Frankie gets out her phone, checks the time, then calls Brett's number.

He is waiting for her outside The Blue Bicycle, no cigarette this time; instead he is scanning the street and smiles when he spots her walking towards him. He leans in to kiss her on both cheeks. She stands stiffly.

'I was hoping you might call—' Brett begins.

'What's your Schopenhauer dissertation on?' she interrupts. He parts his lips in surprise. 'I can check with the UEA if you won't tell me.'

'It's not a secret,' he says, perplexed. 'It's about Schopenhauer's influence on the early animal rights movement, if you must know. Why the urgency?'

His answer is not what she expected. For a moment she hesitates, worried she might be about to make a fool of herself, then ploughs on. 'Have you ever seen this website before?' She hands him her phone, the homepage of *Killing Cuttlefish*. He takes it from her with a frown, then hands it back.

'No,' he says. 'What's this all about? I was hoping you were here to—'

'That site I just showed you takes its name from Schopenhauer's essay *On Women*. I believe I mentioned it before,' Frankie says, interrupting him again. 'The site's very sophisticated, the police can't find out where it's hosted. It's also full of hateful posts about women, including Ava Lindsey, saying she deserved what she got.'

Two red spots appear beneath Brett's perfect cheekbones. 'And what exactly does this have to do with *me*?'

'You told me Ava and her friends were drunk, that you're not surprised somebody "with an agenda" might try and pick them off. Just the sort of victim-blaming crap that's spouted on that site. And what did you mean by an *agenda*?' she says, gaining in confidence as she allows anger to take hold. 'That sounds like the sort of word one of the bloggers on *Killing Cuttlefish* might use for their warped world view. So I'm asking. *Are you hosting that website?*'

'OK, I've had enough of this,' Brett says. His face is taut with fury. 'I like a challenge in a woman but not a fucking fruit loop. You're not even *that* hot.' He steps back towards the door of the bar, looking her up and down. 'And don't even think of calling me again or I'll make a formal complaint.'

Frankie isn't sure if her face is flaming from embarrassment or the cold by the time she swipes herself into reception. Mortification doesn't even begin to cover her feelings about the confrontation with Brett. To make matters worse, she's not even sure it achieved anything, as nagging doubts about his involvement remain. Of course he would be angry if he's innocent, but wouldn't he also deny it even if he were involved? And it's not like he didn't say all those things about Ava drinking. She doesn't know what to think.

'Cold out there?' Ernie the security guard greets her as she heads past his desk, breaking her reverie. He's always friendly, but since the blog post, all the guys on the security desk have gone out of their way to be extra supportive.

'Just a bit. Why, my nose the same colour as my jacket?' she asks. She's wearing her bright red winter coat, easy to spot when doing lives in the dusk. Almost every female reporter she knows owns one, except for Zara who won't be parted from her ancient Barbour.

'Not just your nose,' he laughs. 'You look like you've been in a wind tunnel.'

She rolls her eyes at him and heads into the newsroom. From the newsdesk, Priya beckons her over. She's wearing a blue fluffy jumper so thick she wouldn't look out of place on a reindeer sleigh.

'How was our Strangler, then?' she asks, rolling her chair backwards to give Frankie room to perch on the desk.

For a moment, Frankie struggles to focus on Donald Emneth, her thoughts still on Brett. 'He looked like he's had better days,' she says at last, pushing aside an empty mug and sitting down. 'Guilty plea for Amber, not guilty for the rest. And nothing more on Ava Lindsey. Which just feels odd.' Frankie thinks of Ava's family, so desperate for her return, and Simon Meadwell still waiting for news.

'Guess the police must know something we don't,' says Priya.

'I guess,' Frankie says without conviction. 'Are you really sure we can squeeze a report out of this?'

Priya grimaces. 'Between you and me? No. But Kiera wants something. I've suggested a studio live. Just rehash the basics, that he spoke to confirm his name and address, when his appearance at the Crown Court will be. The usual.'

'Nice easy day for me in that case,' Frankie says. 'Though there was one other thing. You know that smug guy from national, Luke Heffner?' Priya nods. 'He thinks the police may have fucked up. That Emneth's not a serial killer.'

'God, he's so vain, he *would* think he knows better than a squad of sodding murder detectives.'

'I know, he's not my favourite person either. But I think he might have a point.'

'Really? Well, *only time will tell*,' says Priya, over-enunciating the journalist's cliché. 'But that's a story for another day if these charges don't stick. We can't very well float that theory now.' She doesn't seem too bothered about whether or not the right man's behind bars, Frankie thinks. Though why should she be? Nobody claiming to be the killer has been talking about Priya. To her and all the rest of the team, it's just another court case.

It takes Frankie about ten minutes to write her studio live, then she sits slumped over her desk, clearing her email. At lunchtime she heads to Tesco and is picking up a sandwich when her phone rings with the boss's extension.

'Where are you?' It's Kiera. She sounds breathless and cross.

'I'm just at the supermarket, I'll be—'

'Come back now! We've had a tip-off.' Frankie wrestles with her purse, counting the pennies into her palm as her boss barks out of the mobile wedged between her shoulder and ear. 'A farmer just rang the newsdesk. He's found a body at the edge of his land. I want you to get over there. Now.'

'Oh God, the police were right, then. Emneth must have killed Ava. Her poor family.' She notices the cashier looking curiously at her, hands over the change and hurries away from the till.

'Right, my arse,' says Kiera. 'Our guy swears the body wasn't there this morning. She's only just been dumped. That's why he called us.'

'Shit,' says Frankie, breaking into a run. 'I'm on my way.'

Gavin is already filming when she arrives. The farm is on a small road, about ten miles from Methwold, deep in West Norfolk. A satellite truck covered with a rival broadcaster's branding is parked up near the familiar Toyota. Further along the verge, Luke Heffner is filming a piece to camera while forensic officers in their distinctive white boilersuits troop back and forth through the gate behind him. The farmer obviously called a few newsrooms, she thinks. Frankie walks up to Gavin, waits quietly until he's finished his shot.

'All right, Franks?' he says. 'Got lots of action shots. Securing the scene, all the usual. Don't think we were first on Farmer Giles's list. That lot' – he gestures at the truck – 'were already here when I arrived.'

'Any sense of who it is?'

Gavin shakes his head. 'Nah. But I overheard one of them say Gubberts is heading over, which got your friend over there excited.'

She glances over at where her 'friend' Luke is standing. He's finished filming his piece to camera and is talking animatedly into his mobile. She can hear his voice, but only catches the odd phrase; 'exciting development' and 'top fucking story' being a couple that stand out.

She glances at Gavin and sees her own discomfort written on his face. 'Doesn't feel right, does it?' he asks, wrinkling his nose. 'I thought they'd caught the bastard.'

'Maybe they have, maybe the farmer's wrong about the body only just being dumped.'

'Don't think so,' Gavin replies. 'They've put the tent up right by a public footpath. No way you could have had a body lying there for days and nobody see it.'

Luke makes his way towards them, keeping off the long grass and striding confidently over the rutted tarmac. 'What did I tell you this morning?' he says to Frankie, tapping his nose. His cheeks are pink, either from the chill or adrenalin. 'Instincts of a bloodhound. The police will be crapping themselves. What a fuck up!' He looks delighted. Gavin turns back to his camera.

'Did you get a clue who it is?' she says.

'Yes. It's Gubberts. He's coming over.'

'No, I mean, do you know who's died?'

Luke flicks through his notepad, scanning scribbles of shorthand. 'The farmer came out to the fence before you guys arrived. Police warned him away but we had a brief chat off the record. No pink hair he said. So I don't think it can be the student.'

'But who else could it be?' says Gavin.

'Wasn't there that chap you interviewed? With the missing wife?'

'Oh God, I hope not. Poor Simon.' Any relief Frankie felt at hearing the victim didn't have pink hair evaporates. She thinks about Simon in his kitchen on Trinity Street, imagines him getting the news, making the final journey to identify the body, still hoping it isn't Daisy. Then the crushing realisation.

'Any chance you could give him a bell now, see if he'll talk to us?'

'Not today, Luke, seriously,' she says. 'Give the poor bastard a break. This'll be the worst day of his life. You could at least *pretend* to have a heart.'

Luke flushes. Behind him she sees Gavin shake his head. For once it seems she's hit home, though whether it's the insult or the prospect of a major interview evaporating that's annoyed Luke, she can't say. 'No, you be serious,' he retorts, jabbing a finger in the air before her. 'Simon Meadwell has been royally shafted by the police. They obviously left his wife exposed to the real killer, while they pissed about with the wrong guy. Don't you think he might want to talk? That he has a right to? They denied him a press conference and now look what's happened!'

'So that's why you want to interview him? For his own good?'

'Don't come across all holier than thou with me,' Luke says. 'You're no better than the rest of us, you just want to feel superior. Well, too bad. If you don't want to make difficult phone calls, don't be a fucking hack.'

'All right, that's enough!' says Gavin. 'It's not a good look, you know,' he says to Luke. 'Bickering like you're in the playground rather than standing yards away from a dead woman. Have some respect.' Luke is about to reply, but Gavin raises his hand to cut him off. 'And Franks, I'm sorry, but he has a point. Maybe just text Simon, say you're around if he wants to talk.'

'But we don't even know if it's his wife in that field!'

'Doesn't matter. You need to make contact, give him the option.' She knows he's right but can't bear to admit it in front of Luke. Gavin lays his hand on her arm. 'You'll find the words.'

She nods and walks a little away from them both to text. She can see Gavin leaning in to Luke, hears him say '*remember the blog, she's under a lot of pressure*' but turns away again when Luke looks towards her. She gets out the phone, unlocks it and stares at the blank screen. Self-loathing sits in her stomach like curdled milk, bobbing against her insides. Maybe Luke's right, maybe she is in the wrong job. She starts to type.

Hi Simon, I'm so sorry to bother you at such an incredibly difficult time. Please know I'm always here to talk if there's any message you want to give. Thinking of you, Frankie.

She presses send before she can think better of it, then walks back to her colleagues. Gavin nods at her.

'Look,' says Luke, inclining his head and staring down his nose like an especially patronising teacher. 'Maybe I was a bit . . .'

'Don't mention it,' she says. 'I'll let you know if he gets back. And obviously share any interview.'

'Thanks. Well, I'll just . . .' He waves in the direction of his own cameraman, who is still filming, and sets off. They watch him go.

'Don't mind him,' says Gavin.

'I don't,' she replies.

It's a long day standing by the roadside. The cars pile up as more and more journalists get a whiff of what's going on. Once the 24-hour news channels start broadcasting their first lives, police have to close off the road, making them all park further away. It means nobody has the chance to shout their questions at DSI Gubberts when he arrives. Instead he drives past the pack and gets out of his car several metres behind the police cordon. But even though he's safe from their shouts, his grim expression, zoomed in and caught by Gavin's camera, tells its own story.

The chat amongst the reporters is that this is the Norfolk Strangler's latest victim, either Ava Lindsey or Daisy Meadwell, and although the police press office won't confirm this, they don't deny it either. Frankie keeps checking her phone but Simon never answers her text message.

Sky News is the first to throw their hat into the ring. 'This discovery,' Frankie hears their presenter say, 'throws open the awful possibility that Norfolk's serial killer is still at large. So far police are refusing to comment . . .' After that everybody piles in on the speculation. The farmer's tip-off that there had been no body in the field first thing that morning, the likelihood the police have let a killer slip through their fingers with 'devastating consequences'; all of it is aired, picked apart and mulled over.

Through it all Frankie finds herself distracted, thinking about the posts below Feminazi Slayer's blog. Claims to be the Norfolk Strangler ring less hollow now. She doesn't even know if anything has been found on Donald Emneth's computer that might give her reason to relax. Dan's landline rings out when she calls him, but she leaves a voicemail. She thinks about the gif of the smashing vase, the message to her appearing across it in red letters, and feels afraid. If Emneth isn't the killer, it's a bigger news story, but one she doesn't want to become part of herself.

When it's time for her own live on the evening news, Frankie puts her professional face on and stands solemnly in front of the illuminated blue and white police tape in her bright red coat, listening to Paul Carter intone his ponderous throw into her earpiece, '. . . this grim discovery raises many questions. Questions that the police are so far refusing to answer. Our reporter Frances Latch is live at the scene. Frances.' And then she's off. Relaying the smattering of facts, gesturing into the blackness behind her, the crime scene now obliterated by the winter dark. She finishes speaking and stands, her expression serious, waiting for the clear. 'Thanks, Frankie,' the director says in her ear. 'That's all we need from you. You can head home.'

Her face relaxes, showing the exhaustion she's feeling, and she yanks out the earpiece. 'That's it, Gav,' she says. 'We're good to go.'

They walk back to their cars. 'Long old day,' Gavin says as he swings himself into the battered Toyota. 'Hope you've got Jack waiting at home for you with a hot dinner.'

Frankie gives a tight smile. 'Yeah, hopefully.' She slams the car door shut behind her and starts up the engine. Gavin waves as he drives past, the opposite way to where she needs to go. Several other journalists seem to be leaving the scene too. She pulls into the road and starts down the dark lane. She turns the radio on but it's yet more chat about the Norfolk Strangler so she switches to a Motown CD.

At first she doesn't think anything of the headlights behind her. There are a number of cars on the road. But after a while, when she's taken several different turnings, losing cars at each rural twist and turn, she realises there's now only one vehicle behind her. She's always been a cautious driver and doesn't like to hold other people up, so slows down, giving them room to pass, but instead of overtaking, the car behind also slows down. Frankie feels the sweat leak through her palms onto the steering wheel. In the dark it's hard to see the car's colour.

'Come on, get a grip,' she tells herself. She puts her foot to the accelerator and speeds along the black fenland road. The two white dots behind recede into the distance. She breathes out in relief. She mustn't let this story get to her. Keeping up a steady pace, she fiddles with the volume on the controls and Marvin Gaye's singing grows louder. As she looks up, she sees the two lights in her rear-view mirror growing bigger and brighter. The car behind is gaining on her. She speeds up, but so does her companion. The car is white, the same saloon she saw in Lowestoft.

Her eyes still on the road, Frankie scrabbles with one hand for her phone, reaching into her bag on the passenger seat. She's driving at speed and it's hard not to veer about. Eventually, she manages to dig it out and clutches it against the steering wheel. No signal.

'Shit!' Frankie glances at the satnav. She has no real idea where she is, a B-road somewhere in rural Norfolk in the dark. She wants to fiddle with the settings, find out where the nearest service station is, but as she reaches for it, the car behind gives an angry burst of speed and taps her back bumper. Frankie screams. Her car lurches onto the wrong side of the road and for a moment she thinks she's going to end up in the ditch. Her tormentor speeds up still further, so they're driving directly abreast, and she can't get back into her lane. In the dark it's impossible to see who's driving the other car, but their head seems unnaturally large.

For a moment they're side by side, then Frankie comes to her senses and slows down. The car ahead speeds off, honking. She just has time to register that the number plate in front has been blacked out by gaffer tape before it disappears.

She wants to pull over, have a minute to collect herself, but she doesn't dare stop in case the other car comes back. Instead she keeps speeding along the road, taking in breaths in frightened gulps. There's still no signal, but even if she called 999 now, the car seems to have gone and she doesn't know what she could say. Frankie tries to calm herself down. Maybe it wasn't the same white car. Maybe it was just some idiot, out to give whoever they met on the road a scare. Nothing more. She tells this to herself, over and over, but her heart is thumping and her head hurts, every sense on high alert. Back in the correct lane, her hands shaking, she turns off the CD. She needs all her concentration. Frankie drives back to Norwich, the only soundtrack accompanying her is the blood pounding in her ears.

Frankie

At Jack's insistence she reports the road rage incident to the police. She's so shaken up by the time she gets home, it's impossible to hide what's happened, and the shock draws the pair of them into a tentative truce.

She sits on the sofa in a big cardigan, her feet tucked under her, while a saucepan of spaghetti boils on the hob. Jack hands her a cup of sugary tea. 'Franks,' he says, sitting down beside her and resting his hand on her knee. 'Please don't take this the wrong way. But I really don't want you working on the Strangler story any more.'

She doesn't reply, just strokes a finger up and down the side of the hot china, back and forth, back and forth. Deep down she knows he's right but she can't see a way out. Not with Kiera so keen for her to cover it. Her boss has the look of a woman who can smell a media award on the horizon. Frankie knows Kiera would not be forgiving of anyone who jeopardised the biggest story to hit their patch in years.

She doesn't dare tell Jack about her confrontation that day with Brett. She tells herself it must just be a horrible coincidence that she's the victim of road rage straight after making him angry. 'I don't think the driver really *was* the killer,' she says, not very convincingly. 'Honestly, it was probably just some random knobhead.'

Jack looks horrified. 'Jesus! I meant the stress isn't good for you, not that your life's at risk. I thought the driver might be one of those creeps that've been uploading photos on the blog. Isn't that bad enough? If you think it might have been the killer in that car, why would you even consider carrying on?' He grips her knee. 'That's it. You've got to stop.'

'Even if it was him,' she replies, her voice wobbling. 'What makes you think I'm any safer sitting around on my own at home? When that blogger's posted our address online? And we've been getting all those weird cards? At least at work I've got a bunch of people looking out for me.'

Jack rubs his hands over his eyes, pushing his glasses upwards. Then he flops back on the sofa. 'Fuck it. Let's get away. Take that holiday early. Just disappear for a couple of weeks.'

For a moment she's tempted, imagines them packing their bags, heading to Norwich airport in the morning. The predictable anonymity and security of the departure lounge. Then reality kicks in. 'Oh come on,' she says, forcing a laugh. 'Do you really think I'd be given leave at this short notice? That Kiera would say, yeah sure, just disappear in the middle of a massive story?' She shakes her head. 'Thanks for suggesting it, Jack. I really appreciate it. But it's fine, honestly. I'm sure the police will catch him soon and then it's all over until the court case. I've just got to plough through a few more days.'

'Are you sure the police are taking it all seriously enough? I would have thought they'd have done more by now.'

'I'm sure Dan's doing everything he can,' she says. 'He's been fairly supportive so far.' She sips her tea, wishing she felt as convinced as she sounds. She likes Dan, but he was only lukewarm about pursuing Grant Allen. And after all, the police were wrong about Donald Emneth. What other mistakes might they make?

The phone call that rips through her sleep the next morning makes her gasp. Frankie thinks it's the alarm ringing and goes to switch it onto snooze, her heart hammering with the shock of being jolted awake. Then she realises someone is calling. It's an unknown number.

'Hello?'

'Frances, it's Luke Heffner here.'

'Luke?' she says, sitting up, astonished. Jack groans and turns over. She gets out of bed, heading to the living room. She thinks about their row. Surely he's not calling to apologise? 'What do you want? What time is it?'

'Yeah, sorry to disturb you early and all that, but I wanted to speak to you before the presser today,' he replies. 'I've just had an old friend from the *Mirror* get hold of me, wanting to talk to you. He says Leonard Smythe has run a piece about an anonymous reporter, who my mate says is you, getting threats from someone claiming to be the killer. I checked out the blog and he's right. You didn't tell me you'd been getting personal messages from the Strangler, what's that all about?'

For a moment she is too shocked to reply. Frankie suddenly has a sense of piranhas circling, of what it would be like to be the centre of a media storm. She has to steer him off course. 'Oh that,' she says, with an air of unconcern. 'The police say it's a hoax. Just some saddo. Not linked to the murder investigation at all.'

'Really?' Luke sounds disappointed. 'Not even considering it?'

In the privacy of her dark flat, Frankie lifts two fingers up at an imaginary Luke's head. 'Nope. But thanks for your concern.'

'Oh well, had to ask.'

'Course,' she replies. 'And Luke? Don't pass my number on please. After all, if it did turn out to be something, I'd obviously give *you* the exclusive.'

Luke laughs. 'You're so full of shit. But of course I won't pass your number on. I'm not that much of a twat.'

'Sure you're not,' she says, suddenly unwilling to be sucked into their usual banter so soon after all he said yesterday. 'Bye.'

Frankie looks down at her phone. 6.55. Luke really is shameless. She checks her email. There are messages from the *Mirror*, the *London Daily Times* and the *Express*. She forwards them all to Charlie.

Some of our fellow hacks have been sniffing round about the blog again in spite of your efforts. There's even a report in the LDT

though I'm not named. Sent you the emails. Can you tell them all
police think it's just a hoax and get them to piss off, please?

Frankie stands a moment, lost about what to do. The curtains
are all closed, yesterday's dishes, undone, on the countertop. She
knows she should go have a shower, start getting ready for the day,
but all she wants to do is hide.

Frankie frustrates any of her colleagues who might have been
undeterred by Charlie's email by turning up late to the press
conference. She slinks into the back and shuffles into the only
empty seat, part way along a row. It's not just her fellow journalists
she wants to avoid: she's also nervous about who might be watching later. If the killer is following the wall-to-wall television
coverage of his exploits, she's no desire to take centre stage on
shots of the presser. Instead she slumps down in her seat, hoping
she's out of the reverse camera's line of vision.

The conference is operatic in its savagery. Ten minutes in, and
her companions are still on the attack. Much has been made of the
police blunder over Donald Emneth, and how such a mistake
could have been made, as well as outrage expressed over the
additional anguish inflicted on the Lindsey and Meadwell families. Like a thunderstorm on the horizon, the sense of a looming
IPCC investigation is heavy in the air.

'You've confirmed the dead woman is Daisy Meadwell,' she
hears Malcolm from the Press Association say. 'What message do
you have for her grieving husband who begged you to investigate
her disappearance?'

Frankie frowns. Kiera will be cursing as she watches the live
feed. That ought to have been *her* question. Simon is their contact
after all. He's still not replied to her text, but she knows if Kiera
has her way she will inevitably end up on his doorstep at some
point this afternoon.

'We *did* investigate her disappearance,' says DSI Gubberts. He
runs a hand over his face. He's sweating so much it looks as if he's

just stepped out of the shower. 'And we are in contact with Mrs Meadwell's family, who have our sincerest condolences. Next question please.'

'Flora Hitchinson, BBC. Will you be dropping all charges against Donald Emneth?'

'I'm afraid I can't comment. That's a decision for the CPS.' Gubberts points a finger at the front row. Frankie sees the familiar bouffant hair. 'Yes?'

'Luke Heffner, Commercial Television News. As my colleagues have pointed out, your investigation so far has been a series of preposterous blunders with unimaginable consequences. Do you feel personally responsible for the death of Daisy Meadwell?'

Nigel Gubberts's cheeks grow pink. There's a hush in the room. 'Nobody is responsible for the death of Daisy Meadwell apart from the person who decided in cold blood to kidnap and murder her,' he replies. 'And that's the case, Mr Heffner, with all murders.'

Frankie feels a pang of sympathy. Gubberts *must* feel responsible for Daisy, whatever he says. And however much the police may have screwed up, ultimately she agrees: he's not the real villain here. There's a pause. Gubberts is scanning the room. All hands are down. Luke's unsubtle thrust of the spear seems to have brought the bloodletting to an end. 'Any more questions?'

She shifts on her seat. Nobody has asked the one thing she's genuinely curious to know. It's now or never. With a sigh, she sticks her arm in the air.

'Yes, Frances?'

'You said earlier that you now believe Ava Lindsey is alive. What new evidence have you discovered to suggest this? Was something found at the crime scene?'

Gubberts blinks at her. He appears surprised not to be fending off another attack. 'I'm afraid I can't tell you the answer to that,' he replies. 'Not without compromising the investigation.'

★　　★　　★

'Frances!'

She turns around, feeling hunted, standing with her hand on the door of her car, trying to see where the shout is coming from. She had slipped out of the presser early to avoid the other journalists.

'Frances!' Dan Avery is jogging towards her across the tarmac. 'I thought I might catch you here today. Have you got a sec?'

She thinks of Kiera pacing up and down the newsroom, furious at her failure to capitalise on the Meadwell lead, no doubt already planning to send her off to intrude on Simon's grief. 'Sure,' she says.

They head back across the car park to the station. Dan swipes them out of reception and through a corridor, then ushers her into a small room. It's empty apart from a couple of chairs and a table covered in boxes. 'Excuse the mess,' he says, pointing her towards one of the chairs. 'I haven't booked out a room and I knew this was free.' He sits down opposite. 'I wanted to tell you we've had Martin Hungate in for questioning.'

'Oh my God! Really? About the serial killings?'

Dan shakes his head. 'About the blog. We decided that email he sent about you gave us enough to take him in for questioning, particularly as he's got previous. He wasn't too pleased to see us, as you can imagine, though he handed over his computer readily enough.'

'I take it you didn't find anything?'

'On the contrary,' Dan replies.

'Oh my God! It's him? He's the blogger?'

'Not quite,' says Dan. 'But we found clear evidence that those comments from the user claiming to be the Norfolk Strangler were made from his computer. The only thing is, he said it must have been his girlfriend Debbie. I know, I know,' he says, as she rolls her eyes. 'We thought that was rubbish too. But it turns out he's telling the truth. We've looked at the time the comments were posted and he was at work then, we can corroborate that. Whereas the comments were definitely all made from the computer at their home in Wells.'

'Really? You're sure it was her?' Frankie asks, reluctant to believe the person who has caused her so much stress is a woman, and an abused woman at that. 'I seem to remember her mentioning she had a son.'

Dan shakes his head. 'She's admitted it. Says she felt you were unfair in your coverage of her and her partner and she wanted to give you a fright. She seemed very shocked to learn making threats like that was such a serious offence. It'll be an open and shut case at the mags.'

'And what about Martin Hungate's alibi for the killings?'

'Why would he need one?' Dan says. 'He's not a suspect if he didn't post the comments.'

'Of course.' Frankie sits back heavily in her chair. 'Sorry, I didn't think. I'm just wound up after a load of my beloved fellow journos piled on wanting to know all about it. At least this will shut them up. And then there was my scare with the white car last night.' She sees Dan's puzzled expression. 'I guess the team at 111 didn't pass the message on to you, I did ask them to. Last night, heading back from the crime scene, I got chased then shunted by what looked like the same saloon that trailed me to Lowestoft. There was gaffer tape over the number plate.'

Dan looks horrified. 'Are you OK? Why didn't you call 999? I've *told* you to do that if you ever think you're in danger.'

'I couldn't, I didn't have a signal on my phone, and by the time I did, the car was long gone. And yes, I'm OK, physically I mean. But otherwise? No, I'm not.' Frankie pulls her jacket downwards, straightening it, trying to collect herself. When she looks up at Dan, there's an anxious frown on his face, which doesn't make her feel any better. 'I don't think I've ever been more afraid. I don't trust anyone, I don't know what to think. This whole saga with Daisy and Donald Emneth makes me feel like the police don't have a clue what they're doing. And I don't see why the blog isn't being taken more seriously as part of the murder investigation. You said the murder team would have me in for questioning, why hasn't that happened?'

Dan gets up and goes to the door, makes sure it's closed. He sits down heavily. 'If I talk to you about this, do I have your word you are not going to use this in a story?'

For a moment Frankie imagines Kiera's reaction if she brought her a scoop on the Strangler. The inside story from the police. Just as quickly she squashes the thought. Her life is more important. She makes an effort to look Dan in the eyes. 'You have my word.'

'The investigating team don't believe there's a credible threat to your life,' he says, speaking slowly. 'But I do. I think you're right. To me it seems quite possible there's a link between the blogger, the cards you've been getting and messages women in this case have received.'

Frankie lets out a cry and covers her mouth. 'Jesus Christ!'

Dan holds his hands out, palms down, as if trying to steady a spooked horse. 'Please, try not to get too alarmed. I said it's *possible*. Not definite. Really, I'm not certain. I just think we shouldn't dismiss the idea, that's all. And I want you to take every possible precaution.'

'They didn't find any link to the blog on Donald Emneth's computer, did they?'

Dan shakes his head. 'There was nothing.'

'Oh my God,' says Frankie, gripping her knees. 'If he's killed Daisy and Ava, he'll want another, won't he?'

'We don't think he's killed Ava.'

'How can you possibly *know* that?'

Dan glances at the door again, then turns back to her. 'This is more than my job's worth, if you repeat it. Promise me it goes no further.' Frankie nods and with a sigh, Dan continues. 'They found Ava's hair hidden on Daisy's body. For various reasons we don't think the killer put it there. We think Ava is trying to tell us she's alive.'

For a moment Frankie takes this in. Imagines the circumstances Ava might have found herself in that led to such horror. Her mind baulks at the images that crowd in, but one sticks stubbornly, flicking back over and over, like the pages of a book left out in the wind. Hanna's body with the hair over her face. Dan presses a hand on her shoulder. 'I'm sorry. I shouldn't have said anything. But I just want you to be careful.'

Frankie doesn't say anything for a while. She knows Dan is her best shot at finding whoever is targeting her. 'I went to see Grant Allen this weekend,' she says at last.

Dan releases her shoulder. 'That's exactly the sort of thing I'm talking about.'

'I didn't go on my own,' Frankie replies. 'I went with a colleague. And a dog. And anyway,' she says, 'you said there wasn't enough to take him in for questioning, so what else could I do? I really think there might be something going on with him and his son. Are you sure you can't track Zach down, make sure he's not still living in the area?'

Dan shakes his head. 'If I did look into it, would you *promise* not to pursue that lead yourself?'

'Of course,' Frankie says. Though this time she doesn't mean it.

Kiera is even angrier than she imagined. Her boss shouts at her in front of the rest of the newsroom, demanding to know why she let Malcolm from PA steal their thunder on the Meadwells. Nobody steps in to defend her, though Priya looks embarrassed when she catches her eye. She wonders if Kiera has deliberately waited until Charlie's out of the room to have a go, but then again, maybe he wouldn't have said anything in her defence either. The character of her old familiar workplace is changing, slowly being poisoned by fear, even though there's only one bully.

She's halfway to the Meadwells' house with Ray when her phone vibrates. It's a text from a number she doesn't recognise.

Hi. We're too upset to talk. Also Si wants to wait so we don't hurt the Lindseys. Only good thing that can happen now is they find Ava. But I can tell you we're not letting this rest. We're going to make sure the police pay for this. Nathan.

Frankie sags back in her chair and starts to cry. From the driver's seat, Ray glances over at her in alarm. 'What's happened? Franks? What's wrong?'

'I'm sorry,' she says, putting the heels of both palms up to her eyes to stop the tears. 'Nothing. Nothing's happened. Shit, I'm being ridiculous. Sorry. You can head back. They don't want to talk.'

'It's that Kiera, isn't it?' Ray says, pulling over. 'I knew I should have said something. I won't let her have a go when we get back. If she starts being a bitch again, I'll tell her where to go.'

'No, it's not Kiera,' Frankie says, wiping her face. 'Or only a little bit. I'm just really relieved we don't have to bother them, I wasn't looking forward to it. And to be honest, I'm finding this whole story a bit much. You heard about the blog?' He nods, embarrassed. 'Yeah, of course, everyone has. Well, there'd been some hoaxer on there, claiming to be the killer. Said they were looking out for me. Turns out it's all bullshit, but it's still been a strain. The rest of the press pack jumped on it.' She doesn't tell him about her conversation with Dan, everything she's learned about Daisy and Ava; she can't.

'God, I'm not surprised you're rattled,' Ray says. 'Can't Charlie move you onto another story?'

'It's not up to Charlie,' she says, turning and looking out of the window at the pavement where they've parked. 'Not any more.'

Somehow, Frankie makes it through the edit. Nathan's text gives her an exclusive line, not much, but just enough to mollify Kiera for her feeble question at the press conference. It's Zara's day off and she's not sure if it's her imagination, but a couple of her colleagues seem strained with her. She wonders if Ray might have mentioned her outburst in the car, and they're worried she'll cry all over them, or maybe they think Kiera's anger might be catching.

The shift over, she heads to her car and is about to open the door when she hears a scuffle above her. On the grassy slope lined with trees that overlooks the car park, she sees Ernie grappling with someone. It's Brian. 'Take your hands off my fucking phone!' Brian's shouting, trying to wrestle free from Ernie, who's much too strong for him. Frankie recognises his coat. Not the usual red parka, but a duffle.

She scrambles up the bank. 'What's going on?'

'Call the police!' Ernie says, out of breath from trying to contain the struggling Brian. 'The little creep's been taking pictures of you!'

Frankie stares at Brian, incredulous. 'You!'

'You've got no right to stop me!' Brian is red in the face and furious. 'No different from what you do, is it? You film people without permission! Fucking hypocrites!'

'The police, Frances. Now!' Ernie says.

Frankie calls Dan's number. 'Hi Dan, it's Frankie. Can you get a team over to the newsroom? Our security guard has just got hold of a guy taking photos of me in the car park . . .'

Brian aims a kick and catches her in the groin, not hard, but it's a shock. She drops the phone. Ernie leans towards her, anxious she's been hurt, and Brian twists free. 'The bastard!' he exclaims as Brian speeds off down the road. Without stopping to think, powered by rage, Frankie sets off after him. 'Frances!'

'Call 999!' she shouts, not turning round to see if he's heard. She charges over the busy road, just as the lights turn green. Ernie is left stranded on the other side, gesticulating as the honking traffic revs past him. Frankie runs into the old town, thumping hard into startled shoppers. 'Sorry!'

Brian is surprisingly fast. He makes it into the cathedral close and tears down towards the houses on the green, disturbing the peaceful silence with his thumping footsteps. Frankie hurtles after him. He speeds into Hook's Walk and Frankie follows, her lungs feeling as if they are about to burst. She slows down slightly, her breath coming in gasps. She knows Hook's Walk ends in a dead end unless Brian cuts across the field. Instinctively she feels for her phone in her pocket, then remembers she dropped it at the car park. Ernie must be close behind, she tells herself, and it would be easy enough for the police to track their route. She carries on, puffing her way to the edge of the path across the field. There's no sign of Brian. She hears a sound and spins round. He must have been hiding in one of the doorways at the end of the alley and is trying to sneak past, back up Hook's Walk. Frankie hurls herself at him, knocking him to the floor. His phone spins wide across the cobbles and she grabs it. They both get unsteadily to their feet, chests heaving.

'Give it back!' Brian says.

'Why were you taking photos of me?' Frankie asks. 'It's that website, isn't it?'

'None of your business!' Brian shouts, snatching for his mobile. Frankie darts out of the way.

'You're pathetic, you know that? I even felt sorry for you! Why would you do that to me?' She looks down at the phone in her hand. The screensaver is a young woman sprawled out on scrubby grass in a pink top. It looks like she's asleep, but Frankie knows somehow that she's not. She stares. It takes her a second to register that she's seen her before, another to realise it's Hanna Chivers. She doesn't see Brian's punch coming.

Sprawled on the floor, Frankie just has time to roll out of the way of the kick Brian aims at her head. His next catches her in the ribs. 'Nosy bitch!' he spits, spraying saliva. He stands over her, aiming kicks, while holding out his phone to take a picture of her lying on the ground. She's winded but knows she has to get off the floor. She manages to sit up, protecting her head with her arms, but she's squashed against the wall and can't move further out of the way. Brian is so busy trying to hit her, he doesn't see Ernie, running towards them down Hook's Walk. 'Got you, you bastard!' he roars, throwing him face first to the ground. He sits on Brian, twisting his arms behind his back. 'One move before the police arrive and I'll bloody kill you!'

Frankie's head is banging but she's desperate to get to Brian's phone. She picks it up from where he dropped it near her feet, swiping across the screen. The first photos she sees are her lying on the cobbles, her face twisted in terror. She works backwards. Dozens of photos of her. There she is getting into her car, sitting with Gavin, walking with Jack. There are some of Zara, Rachel and Priya too, even Kiera. Several of the photos have been edited; the crosshairs of a gun sit superimposed on her face. She recognises one. It's the image of her used on the blog.

'*You're* Feminazi Slayer?' Brian doesn't answer. 'I knew you were the same person, I bloody knew it! Was it you following me in the car? Sending all those cards?'

'Put it down, Frankie,' Ernie warns. 'The police will need that phone, it's evidence.'

Frankie keeps on swiping. Photos of her fly past. Then she gasps. This is something different. It's a poor-resolution shot of a woman in a dark concrete space, taken from high above. The woman is thin, sitting on the ground, holding her knees in her arms, looking upwards but not seeing the camera, her face anguished. Ava Lindsey.

'Oh my God.' Frankie's hand flies to her mouth. 'What have you done to her?' Brian's face is squashed into the ground but his eyes swivel to look at her, full of hate. '*Where is she?*' she screams.

'Stay back, let the police deal with it,' Ernie warns but Frankie doesn't register him.

'What have you done with her, you bastard!' she shouts. 'Where is she?'

Brian closes his eyes, shutting her out. He says nothing.

Ava

He's not been back since he took Daisy away. I must have got through to him last time he was here, made him see his own pettiness, but if so, it was a hollow victory. I think he means to starve me into submission. Or maybe he's sitting at home, watching me die slowly, without feeling the need to come back.

Everything hurts so much and I'm so tired. I can't think any more, everything in my head is falling apart. I don't want to do anything but sleep. I wish I could dissolve, be nothing more than a stain on the wall, escape from whatever he's planning, for me or anyone else. Sometimes I imagine the police will find the message I left with Daisy, and then I feel a prickle of hope again, but it's hard to keep believing things will be OK. I don't have the strength to lie to myself any more.

I try to be brave. I try to think of defying him the way Daisy did, but it's not helping. I think I'm going to die in here.

Frankie

When Dan Avery drops her off back at the flat, Jack is home. He had wanted to come to the station, to be there when she gave her statement, but she insisted that he finish work. There was nothing he could do while she was in the interview room, she told him. It's true, but their recent rows also mean she doesn't feel as close to him as she should; the only person she really wanted nearby was Dan.

Jack's been cooking his fail-safe chilli con carne, to have dinner waiting for her when she arrives. The worktop is strewn with spice jars, onion skins and empty kidney-bean cans, and steam rises from the pan, turning his face red.

'Thank God they found him!' He goes over to Frankie, enveloping her in a massive hug.

'Careful!' She winces, still sore from where Brian kicked her in the ribs.

'Sorry.' He lets go and stands back. 'I can't believe it was some creep who you all knew about at work! Talk about under your noses.'

'Yeah, well,' Frankie says, feeling sick at the thought that the man who has killed so many women was also obsessed with her news programme. Obsessed with her.

'At least we know you're safe now, that's all that counts.'

'Well, it's not really, is it?' she says, pulling up a stool at the counter and inching herself onto it. 'What about Ava?'

'I'm sure the police will persuade him to tell them where she is. Can't they offer a plea bargain?'

'He's going down for life. Nothing he does about Ava changes that. What can they possibly offer him that's more than the sick power he's enjoying by letting her starve to death?' Frankie feels close to tears. She keeps thinking of Ava's face staring at the ceiling, waiting to be rescued, time running out. It makes her want to scream with frustration.

'They'll find her,' Jack says. 'They will.'

'Dinner looks good, anyway,' says Frankie, changing the subject. She stares at the chilli. She ought to be starving but has no appetite.

'Shit, that reminds me,' Jack says. 'I bought some jalapeno cheese at the deli, it's still in my bag.' He gestures at the pan. 'Don't let it burn.'

She slides off the stool as Jack hurries to the bedroom. The meat is sizzling and she gives it an idle nudge with the wooden spoon. There's a bleep. Jack's phone is lying beside the hob. She glances at it, half notices an alert that's come up on the black screen, then does a double take.

@Cuttlefish_Eater someone has liked your post!

Frankie picks up the phone, staring at the message. She taps to read it and types in his code. The phone takes her straight to the post, a picture of her walking along the street at Wells two weeks ago, with the caption I spy Nancy Drew! Jack comes back in, waving the cheese. He stops when he sees her expression.

'What's this?' she asks.

'What's what?'

She looks back at the screen, enunciating slowly. 'Who's Cuttlefish Eater?'

'Have you been going through my phone?' He strides across, snatching it from her, hurting her fingers as he grabs it. The gesture is so like Brian earlier that she takes a step back, staring at him, almost too shocked to speak.

'Have you been posting photos of me on that website?'

'You've no right to go through my stuff!'

She moves away from him, away from the burning hot pan. 'I'll take that as a yes then.'

'You shouldn't be snooping through my phone. You know I'm trying to crack that site, what do you bloody well expect?' He takes the chilli off the hob, slamming it down on the breadboard where it hisses on contact with the wood.

'Have you been posting stuff about me?'

'Look at that!' He points at the pan, jabbing his finger. 'You've gone and ruined the chilli!'

'Who gives a fuck about the chilli!' she screams, hysteria building. Her whole body is shaking as adrenalin hits her. 'Have you been posting about me?'

'I had to post something to get them to trust me. You told me to do what I needed to do, what did you expect?' His face softens, and he reaches a hand out to her. 'After all, you went and saw Grant Allen, didn't you? And Brett. You didn't ask me what I thought about that.'

The pan's no longer hissing, but the noise seems to be continuing in Frankie's ears. She stares at Jack and feels like she's looking at a stranger. He takes a step towards her. 'Stay away!' she shouts, holding a hand out to stop him.

'Come on, Franks, don't be ridiculous. It's me!'

She grabs her bag, heading backwards for the door, not taking her eyes off him. 'I'm going to stay with Zara.'

'What? Frankie, no! Don't be stupid. I'm sorry I shouted but you shouldn't have snooped through my phone like that.' She turns and opens the door, steps into the corridor, slamming it behind her. 'Frankie!' she hears him yell, as she runs down the stairs. But he doesn't open the door and follow her.

'Well, I think we can safely say Jack's a first-class pillock,' Zara says, handing her an enormous glass of red wine. 'And you may be looking for a new boyfriend pretty soon. But surely you don't think he's anything worse than that?'

'I don't know, I don't know what to think about anything at the moment,' Frankie replies, running a hand through her hair. She's bundled up underneath one of her friend's Peruvian blankets, with

Snoopy the dog snoring by their feet. Mark has been dispatched to the kitchen so they can talk, and is now sitting at the table with his headphones in, watching *Breaking Bad* on the laptop. He's consoling himself for his banishment with a giant slab of chocolate cake.

'I know you've not met his mum and dad, and Jack's been a bit cagey in the past. But Grant Allen's son? Come off it, he doesn't look anything like him for a start.'

'Maybe it's a bit far-fetched,' Frankie admits.

'Just a *bit*.' Zara smiles.

'But don't you think it's really weird that his mum's dead and I've not met *any* of his other family? Wouldn't you want to keep your dad extra close after a loss like that?'

'It depends,' says Zara. 'Grief can tear people apart as well as bring them closer together. It's not unusual for families to fall out after a loss. Maybe he blames his father in some way.'

'That's what I'm worrying about!'

'I *meant*, maybe Jack blames his dad for still being alive, when his mum's dead. Or maybe he doesn't like his dad's new partner and the whole thing's just too painful. Franks, you've got to let this Grant Allen thing go, it's absolute madness. Swearing at your girlfriend and behaving like a bit of a twat doesn't mean you murdered your ex. Besides,' she says, picking up her smartphone. 'We've looked at that wretched website and it seems he's being truthful. Cuttlefish Eater is blatantly fishing for information. Not exactly the behaviour of somebody skilled at leading a double life, is it?'

Frankie snorts. She can always rely on Zara to make her feel better. 'No, you're right. I was being hysterical.' She sighs, tears smarting at her eyes. 'I'm still probably going to have to dump him though. I really thought he was the one, but I can't see a way back after this. I was so happy that day when we went to Wells. I can't believe he posted a picture of our lovely day together on that horrible site.'

'That's a worry for another day,' Zara says, taking a swig of her own wine. 'Don't make any decisions now. You've been under so much strain lately, it's enough to send anyone loopy.'

'Thanks.'

'You know what I mean. Seriously, you need to take a break. Take tomorrow off, call in sick, *stuff* Kiera.' Zara waves the wine glass at her, sloshing some of it over the side. 'Jesus, it's not even a sickie, you just fought off a serial killer, you *ought* to be nursing your bruises, lying in bed. I'm not taking no for an answer. You can stay here, take the old slobberer for a walk if you feel like it. Just have some breathing space.'

Frankie is about to protest but realises she doesn't want to. 'OK,' she replies. 'You win.'

Zara leans over and hugs her. 'God, I'm relieved he didn't hurt you, old girl,' she says. 'And I can't believe I didn't let Ernie report Brian to the police. I thought the bastard was harmless, just some lonely saddo. If only I had been tougher, so much might have been different. Dear God. All those women . . .'

'It's not your fault,' Frankie says, holding her close. 'It's nobody's fault but Brian's. Don't even say it.'

It feels strange watching Zara and Mark leave in the morning. She stands in the doorway with Snoopy, who barks as Zara clambers into her battered Peugeot. Her friend gives a wave as she drives past the house, then the car turns the corner and Frankie's alone.

'Come on, boy,' she says to the dog at her feet. 'Let's go inside.'

Snoopy pads after her into the house and flops across the rug in the centre of the living room. In the kitchen she turns the radio onto a station playing jazz, before sticking a jug of milk in the microwave and making herself an enormous cafetière of coffee. Propping her feet up on a mound of furry dog, she sits back on Zara and Mark's sofa with a homemade latte. She stares at the ceiling, trying not to think about Ava, hoping the police are on their way to wherever Brian has hidden her. Her phone rings. It's Jack.

'I'm sorry,' he says when she picks up. 'I know that's probably never going to be enough, but I am. I'm really sorry.' She doesn't say anything, a lump forming in her throat. 'Franks, can you hear me?'

'We were so happy that day. How could you do that?'

'I know, it was unforgivable. I don't know what to say. It's just that site has been driving me nuts and I was desperate to find out who was behind it.' He sighs. 'And I didn't even need to.' His laugh sounds close to tears. 'I know this is too late, they've caught the killer anyway, but I think I've cracked it. Last night, after you left, I managed to find an address in the UK linked to the site. I think it belongs to whoever is hosting the thing.'

'Oh my God, how did you do that?' she asks.

'Not legally,' Jack replies. 'If you decide to tell the police, I'll get done for it.' His voice breaks. 'But I don't know how else to tell you how sorry I am, or what you mean to me. I'll text you the address, then it's your choice what you do with it.'

He ends the call and a moment later her phone bleeps. It's a Norfolk address, on Hock Drove, near Feltwell. Frankie stares at the screen for a long time, her coffee going cold. She could be looking at the address of the person who knowingly hosted the posts of a serial killer. If they were sympathetic to Brian, might they even have some idea where he's keeping Ava? She's desperate to give the information to Dan, but knows that unless she has compelling evidence, he's not going to investigate. And giving him that evidence would mean giving Jack up.

Frankie chucks the phone on the sofa. 'Shit,' she says. It startles Snoopy, who looks up at her with his sad Labrador eyes. 'Come on, Snoops,' she says to the dog. 'We're going for a drive.'

She locks up Mark and Zara's house and heads to her car, getting the camera gear out of the boot. She unravels the radio mic, and attaches it to the inside of her shirt, underneath her jumper. Snoopy watches her patiently as she tucks it out of sight. She makes sure it's remotely connected to the matching radio mic on the camera then switches them off to save battery. Best to set it up now. If she's going to get a secret audio record-ing of her confrontation with whoever has been hosting the website, she doesn't need them cottoning on to what she's planning while she faffs around on the doorstep trailing wires under her bra.

'In you get,' she says, letting the black Labrador into the passenger seat. She feels reassured that Snoopy will be keeping her company. She looks over at him, sprawled on the seat beside her, as she releases the handbrake. 'Let's nail the bastard.'

Adrenalin and Radio 1 at full volume keep Frankie going along the A11, but when they get to Thetford Forest, she starts to feel more anxious. It's a flat, relentless landscape, and hard to calculate distance. The trees flash past her on either side, tall and thin, on and on, while the grey sky hangs low overhead. Feltwell isn't a million miles from Methwold, and the memory of her late-night car chase lingers. It's small-scale terror compared to all the other things Brian has been doing, but it still makes her angry.

She tries to build up a cover story, wonders whether direct confrontation is best or if she should pose as an admirer of the website. Her car continues to eat up the miles and the closer she gets, the less she feels like carrying on. She can't imagine what she's going to say to whoever opens the door.

'Come on!' she says, louder than she intended. Snoopy looks over, blinking, as if she's talking to him. She nods at him, encouragingly. 'We've dragged ourselves all this way, it would be pointless to give up now, wouldn't it?' The dog just yawns, showing off a great curl of pink wet tongue, then settles back down, resting his head on his paws.

By the time Frankie reaches the narrow turning of Black Drove, and the first farmhouse is behind her, her isolation is total. The road is more of a track, with no space to turn round, though the probability of meeting an oncoming car seems remote. She feels flattened by the vast horizon, the sky a large hand pressing on the car. In the distance it's hard to tell if a line of scrubby trees is broken by the dark smudge of a barn; instead all she can see are grey shapes like bristles, jutting up out of the flat miles of green. Either side of the tarmac, she knows, the ditches run deep.

'Not the place for a get-away drive eh, Snoopy?' The dog doesn't open his eyes. He seems to have fallen asleep. She carries on along the track for fifteen minutes or so, until the satnav tells her an even narrower turning is Hock Drove. For a minute she sits at the junction, her indicator ticking. She cranes round in the car. The view behind is identical to the one in front; the empty flatness feels uncanny it's so absolute.

'Sod it,' she murmurs, turning back and swinging the car onto the lane. 'We'll just have a quick scout,' she says to the still-sleeping dog. 'See if there's anyone there, and leave.' She puts her foot down slightly, speeding up over the rough surface.

Frankie sees Hockwell Farm long before she reaches it. A small flint house, it's dwarfed by the squat, dark shape in front of it. A corrugated barn. It looms up as she gets closer and drives into the wide muddy yard. There's the noise of the handbrake as she yanks it up, then nothing but the sigh of the wind around the car.

'Come on, then,' she says to Snoopy, who's woken up, startled by the abruptness of their stop. 'Let's be quick. Get it over with.'

Reaching in her pocket, she flicks on the radio mic. She gets out and opens the passenger door. Snoopy jumps out and she clips his lead on, then leads him round to the boot, opening it and reaching for her camera. She switches on the sister radio microphone and presses record. She glances at the house. The distance should be near enough for the mic she's wearing to pick up any conversation.

She slams the boot shut and walks towards the door. 'Here goes nothing,' she says, rapping smartly on the wood. There's no reply. She knocks a second time, louder, waits again. Still no answer.

'Well, this was a waste of time,' she says to Snoopy, who sits patiently beside her on the doorstep. She looks in through the window, which, she now realises, is coated in grime. There's a massive pile of unopened post on the kitchen table, and resting on the sink, a jug, half-covered in mould and flies. Nobody can be living there, yet somebody must have moved all those letters.

Frankie is suddenly uneasy. 'Come on, Snoopy, let's be going,' she says, almost falling over her own feet in her haste to get back to the car. She's jerked to a stop by the dog, straining against his lead. Snoopy is sniffing the ground, where Frankie now sees there's a line of boot prints in the mud. They lead to the mouldering structure of the barn. Frankie's breath hisses through her teeth. She tugs hard and Snoopy lets out a deep growling bark, so loud and unlike any noise she's heard from him before that she drops the lead in surprise. Instantly, he's off, careering across the yard, kicking up the mud. He disappears at the side of the barn.

'Fucking hell! Snoopy! Snoopy, come back!' Frankie looks after him, torn between her growing sense of anxiety and the realisation she can't charge off in the car and leave Zara's beloved pet alone in the middle of nowhere. She reminds herself that the killer has been caught, there's no need to panic. She dithers a moment, torn, then gets her phone out of her pocket. The bars waver between one and two. There's just enough signal to make a call.

'Hello?'

'Dan, it's me, it's Frankie. Listen, I want to give you the address where I am right now. It's on Hock Drove near Feltwell. I think it might belong to the person hosting the website where Brian's been blogging.'

'What?' Dan's voice goes up a notch with incredulity. 'What the hell are you doing there? Leave now, you hear me!'

'It's fine, Dan, I do door knocks all the time. It's not like Brian's here, is it?'

'Leave now! I mean it! Get in the bloody car!'

His tone has her rattled. She looks through the window at the post on the table, her unease icing over into fear. 'I just have to get Zara's dog then I'll go. But I wanted to let you know where I am, it's a bit weird here.'

'Frankie! Listen to me. You have to leave. We don't think Brian took the pictures of Ava. Do you understand? The team have been through his computer and photos of Ava and the other victims were *shared* with him. He didn't take them himself. *He got them through the website.*' Frankie stares at the boot prints in the mud and feels cold. 'Are you listening? You can't be anywhere near whoever hosted that site, get in your car and leave now.'

'I can't. I need to get Zara's dog.'

'Sod the bloody dog!' Dan shouts.

'I can't,' says Frankie, thinking of the empty nursery at Mark and Zara's, of all Snoopy means to them. 'I'll call you in fifteen minutes. Probably less than that. OK? In the meantime this is the address. No, listen, take the postcode.' She recites it to him and ends the call before she can change her mind.

Without looking back at the house, she runs over to the barn. Her heart is beating so quickly it makes her feel shaky. She walks swiftly alongside the corrugated wall, which bulges outwards, khaki paint peeling from the ridges. Round the corner, the wide doors are open. She stands looking at the empty space. It smells of must and creosote. The dirty concrete floor rolls out in front, and some rotting hay bales have been dumped at the back. She can see muddy paw prints leading towards them across the dry floor. There are older boot prints too, where the mud has dried.

'Snoopy!' she hisses. 'Come back!' No Snoopy appears. Feeling sick to her stomach, she clatters across the empty space, her footsteps echoing in the rafters above.

There's no sign of the black Labrador behind the bales; instead there's the dark opening of a stairway into a basement. Dread squeezes her heart. She doesn't want to go down there.

'Get back here! Snoopy!' she shouts. He barks in answer but doesn't return. 'Fucking hell, you fucking stupid dog!' Frankie says. She heads down the concrete stairs, breathing in the cold stale air. At the bottom, Snoopy is wagging his tail, tongue lolling, delighted to see her. She grabs his lead and yanks it. 'We're going! Now!'

That's when she hears it. A muffled banging. Frankie turns and looks back. Snoopy is barking at a wooden door. It's locked by a massive rusty bolt and a Yale latch. There's another thump.

She jumps. All her instincts are screaming at her to leave, but instead, as if she's watching herself in a film, Frankie walks forward and places her head against the cold, heavy wood. She thinks about the photo of the concrete cell on Brian's phone. 'Hello!' she shouts. 'Anyone in there?'

In answer Snoopy barks wildly, leaping at the bolt, drowning out any reply. 'OK, OK,' Frankie says. 'We'll check it.' She winds his lead around her wrist, to stop him charging off into whatever's behind it, and draws the bolt back with a scrape, then presses down the latch with a click. Immediately the door pushes open, and something or someone falls into her arms, almost knocking her over. She screams in shock and scrambles back, brushing the person off.

And there on the floor in a heap, covered in filth, is a woman. She raises her head to look at Frankie, who gasps. 'Ava!' she says.

Ava

There's a blonde woman staring down at me, her eyes wide, her mouth opening and closing as if she'd like to say something but can't.

I'm flooded with relief. For a moment we stare stupidly at each other. I can't believe it. I can't believe I'm out. Then the terror surges back.

'We have to get out of here! We have to leave! He'll come back, he's got a camera in there.' My voice is a hoarse croak, it's so long since I've spoken aloud. But I see the fear cross her face. She's understood me.

She reaches down and drags me to my feet. The dog is barking, snuffling at my legs with its wet nose, making it hard for me to stand up. I feel so shaky and weak.

'Lean on me,' she says. 'Here, put your arm round my waist.' I do as she says and she drags me towards a concrete staircase. 'One step at a time, there we go.' She's going too quick for me, and I almost fall. 'Sorry, it's OK. Catch your breath.' It's agony to wait, knowing he might come back. I'd rather she dragged me bodily across the concrete.

'It's fine, I'm fine,' I lie, and somehow we manage to hobble up the rest of the stairs. We're in a huge dark cavern, but even this is too bright for me after the place where I've been kept.

'Right, my car's just outside and I've already called the police,' she says as we shuffle as fast as we can. The barn seems to stretch on forever in front of us. 'I'm Frankie, by the way, and I know you're Ava Lindsey. I'm a journalist.'

I don't have the breath to reply, but squeeze her hand where she's holding me. I don't think I've ever felt anything so reassuring as the warmth of her flank against mine. At last we reach the entrance, and step out into the bright grey light of an autumn day. I'm so overwhelmed I'm afraid I might faint. In front of us, nothing but wide flat green. I was right about my location. There's nothing for miles.

'Nearly at the car,' the woman says, hustling me along the corrugated side of the barn. I can hear her panting and I don't think it's just the exertion of helping me along. I can see she's terrified. Beside us the dog trots happily, nose in the air, tail wagging.

We round the corner and she stops with a gasp. The dog starts barking again. I can see two cars. A silver one parked across the entrance of the yard. And another in the middle of the tarmac. Leaning against it is a familiar, wiry figure. I let out a whimper. 'Oh my God, oh my God, it's him, it's him.' Frankie grips me so tightly it hurts. He's not wearing the puffball mask and the wind blows tousled grey hair from his scalp. He's older than I expected.

Neither of us moves. With a slow casual movement, he stands up from the car. That's when I see the rifle resting by his leg. He raises it so it's pointing at us, and walks across the yard. 'Nice to see you ladies,' he says.

'Grant Allen?' Frankie's voice is incredulous.

He grins at her. 'Nosy little bitch, aren't you?' He takes a step closer, pointing the gun at me. 'You've saved me the trouble of fetching you. But you can let that one go. She's mine.'

'Let's be sensible about this.' Frankie puts her arm in front of me. 'You need to put that gun down.'

'Or what? You'll set your ferocious dog on me?' We all look down at the black Labrador, which gazes stupidly back, its tail thumping the floor in celebration at all the attention. He laughs and turns to Frankie. 'I don't think so.'

'The police are on their way,' she says, her voice wavering. 'But it doesn't have to be like this. Really, it doesn't. We can say you let Ava out yourself, that you were feeling remorseful, that you were going to turn yourself in. It would count, you know, at sentencing, I'm sure it would count.'

I see his eyes narrow, sense his change of mood. I want to warn her to stop talking but she ploughs on, oblivious. 'Look, Grant,' she says, somehow flashing him a smile that doesn't look entirely insincere. 'I mean it. If we get our stories straight, I'm sure we can make you look more sympathetic . . .'

'Frankie,' I whisper, clutching at her arm. I can see she's used to taking charge, getting people to do what she wants, but that's not how he works. His face is expressionless, but I sense the rage coming off him in waves.

'It's OK, Ava will back you up,' she continues. 'Won't you, Ava? She'll say you let her out. That you were really sorry about what you'd done, that you—'

He points the gun and fires. She collapses. I sway on my feet as she falls but somehow I'm still standing. On the ground her face is turned from me, but I see the blood already spreading across the tarmac.

'She was getting on my nerves.' He's not even looking at her; instead his eyes hold mine. 'That's better, isn't it? Just the two of us again.'

Neither of us notices the dog before it springs. He's knocked backwards, the gun flying from his grasp as the dog claws, growling, at his throat. Its jaws snap in his face and he seizes its muzzle, giving the furry head a sharp twist. Immediately, it goes limp. He pushes the lifeless animal away from him, then puts his hand out, feeling for the gun. It's not where he dropped it. He looks up to where I'm standing, shaking so hard he must be able to see the gun trembling, as I point it at his head.

'Give the gun to me, girl,' he says, making an impatient gesture. I'm so used to obeying him, my hand twitches to do as he asks. But I stay where I am. With a sigh, he leans his weight onto the ground to stand up.

'Stay where you are.'

'Don't be a silly girl. We both know you're not going to shoot.'

He shifts himself upwards again and this time I yell at him. 'Don't you fucking move!'

'Or you'll do what, Ava? Shoot me?' he says. 'You don't even know how to use it. And besides you don't want to. I've been watching you, you're a good girl. You listen, not like the others. You're even better than Hanna. You know you belong to me, there's no way out, that bitch was lying about the police . . .'

I can't bear him talking, I can't bear his voice, I have to make him stop. The scream that's been trapped in my chest ever since he took me prisoner bursts out of my lungs and I run towards him, firing the gun. I don't stop running until I'm standing over him.

'*I said don't move!*' He's writhing on the ground, clutching his leg. There's a red stain spreading out along his trousers from where I hit him. I gesture at him with the rifle. 'Or I'll shoot you in the other leg.' He stares up at me, this man I've feared and hated for so long, his unknown face twisted with pain. Without the puffball head he looks pathetic. 'Didn't you hear me? I told you not to move. At all. Do you understand?'

He nods. I turn, desperate to get back to Frankie, to try to save her, but then I see him shift himself out of the corner of my eye and think better of it. I swing round and shoot him in the other leg. 'I don't trust you,' I say.

I leave him then, howling in pain, and stumble back to where the blonde woman, Frankie, is lying on the tarmac. I flop down, placing the gun beside me, and feel for a pulse in her neck. It's there but very faint. 'It's OK, Frankie,' I say, pushing the hair from her face. I've no idea if this is true or if she can hear me. She murmurs and her eyelids flutter. 'You're going to be OK, I'm with you, you're safe. The police are on their way.' I'm terrified of moving her but know I have to try to put some pressure on the wound. Red has already seeped out from underneath her body onto the earth. I roll her gently. She's been shot in the ribs on her right. Her coat is already soaked from the inside. I have nothing to try to staunch the bleeding but my own filthy top. I take it off and press down hard. I'm worried it isn't hard enough. My hands are shaking, it's freezing in just my bra, and I'm so weak. I hope to God she was telling the truth about the police. Pressing down with all my body weight onto my left hand, trying not to think about the wetness between my fingers or what organs I might be squashing, I rifle through her pockets with my right hand, and bring out a mobile phone.

I swipe across the screen to call 999. 'I need an ambulance!'

'Go ahead, caller, where's the emergency?'

'Oh God,' I falter. 'Oh God, I don't know where I am. I don't know! Can you track me from the phone? Please, please come quickly, please, I need an ambulance, she's been shot. And police. We need the police.'

'We'll find you, don't worry. You say someone's been shot. Are you in a safe place to make this call?'

I hear a groan and look over to where he's curled up on the ground. 'Safe enough. Please, please just come quickly. You can't let her die, not again, not again, he can't kill her again. Oh God . . .' My hand is shaking so much, I can hardly keep a grip on the phone. If I start crying now, I'm going to be swallowed up by hysteria. The operator seems to sense my distress, pulls me back from the brink with his calm voice.

'It's OK. Take a deep breath, you're doing really well. Help's on the way. What's your name?'

'Ava.'

'Ava, I'm Tony. Now, can you tell me the casualty's name and where they've been shot?'

'Frankie. And she's been shot in the right side. There's a lot of blood. But it's in the side of the ribs, not the centre. I don't think . . . I don't think he hit her heart.'

'She's been shot in the side?'

'Yes.'

'Have you checked her pulse?'

'Yes, and she's breathing. Or she was just before I called, I'm not sure now.' I peer down at her ribs. It's hard to tell if they are rising or falling. 'I think she is.'

'You did just the right thing. Now without moving her, can you apply pressure to the wound. If there's any material like some clothing handy, fold it and press it down on the place where she's been shot, to try and stop the blood flow as much as you can.'

'I am, that's what I'm doing, but oh God I moved her already, I moved her! I had to, she fell on the wound, and I knew I had to put pressure on it.'

'That's OK, Ava, you did the right thing. You're doing really well, I know this must be very difficult. Help will be with you soon. Just keep applying the pressure to Frankie's wound. Are there any more casualties at the scene?'

Any more casualties. I look over to where he's lying, not moving now. I suppose he is a casualty, as well as a killer. Thanks to me. 'There's the man who shot her. He's injured. I had to shoot him in the leg. Both legs.' It hits me that the bastard's going to take precious medical resources away from Ava when the ambulance arrives and I almost regret that second shot. 'I had to shoot him. He killed Daisy.' My voice starts to break; talking about her, I'm back in that room, trapped, and I can't stop the tears. 'He killed her, he just killed her *like she was nothing*, and then he left us alone. Oh God, I thought I was going to die, I thought I was going to die. He killed Daisy.' I take a gasp of air. I'm drowning, I'm going to pass out. Perhaps sensing the change in pressure, Frankie shifts very slightly. I grip the phone. I have to stay in the present, I can't abandon her, not again. 'My name's Ava Lindsey,' I say. 'I've been held prisoner. I don't know how long for. And when Frankie found me, he shot her.'

There's the slightest pause on the phone. 'Ava Lindsey? I've heard about you on the news. You must have been through so much. I'm really sorry. But you're going to be OK now, Ava, help's on its way. We've found you, you're near Feltwell in Norfolk. A caller had already sent the police to your address. They're going to be with you really soon. Are you injured?'

'I don't know,' I say. 'I've not been shot, but I don't know, it's hard to remember everything that's happened since he took me. Please, when are the police going to be here? Please don't let her die.'

'It's OK, you're being really brave, the police are right round the corner, and there's an ambulance with them. They're already on Black Drove, that's the road near where you are. You should be able to hear them soon. Can you hear them?'

I pause, straining to listen. At first I think the sirens must be my imagination, but then the sound gets louder and louder. 'I can hear them, I can hear them! But he's parked his car across the gateway!'

'The police will get rid of it, don't worry.' As the operator speaks, I can see two panda cars and an ambulance over the hedgerow.

'Over here! *Over here!*' I scream. The tops of heads bob up and down as they run alongside the hedge, then I see two uniformed officers scramble over the bonnet of the silver car, followed by paramedics. 'They're here, they're here,' I say.

I drop the phone as I reach out my arm to the paramedic running towards me.

One of them, a man in his thirties, kneels beside me. 'We've got it from here, don't worry. We've got her.'

I feel warmth – perhaps a coat – around my shoulders and somebody is lifting me to my feet. 'It's OK, Ava, you're safe now. My name's PC Anne Ratcliffe.' There's an arm round my waist and a gentle tug, but I don't move. I don't want to walk away from Frankie, leave her lying there. 'Don't worry. They're going to look after her, we need to get you warm.'

I stumble towards the gate without looking back. I can't bear to see anyone offering the bastard first aid. The police are already moving the silver car; I guess he must have given them the keys.

Fat Head has a name, Frankie said his name, I should tell the police what he's called, but I can't remember what she said. Anne Ratcliffe is opening the back door of a panda car, we must have walked to the other side of the hedgerow without me realising. She's holding the door open, saying something, but I can't hear her over the buzzing in my ears. The inside of the car yawns dark and cramped, like a cage. I don't want to get in there. I start struggling against her.

'No, no, no!'

'It's OK,' she says. 'I'll get in with you, you won't be on your own. I'm sorry, but we have to get you to hospital. And on the way, we can try and get your family on the phone.'

Another police officer comes round from the front of the car while she's trying to get me into the back. 'We don't know if the family's been told yet,' he says.

'Well radio now and get them to call!'

I don't get into the car, but I stop resisting. 'Is my brother OK? Can I speak to him? Is he OK?'

Anne looks uncomfortable. 'I don't know your family, love, sorry. But there's no reason your brother wouldn't be OK, is there?'

'He said Matt was dead.' I gesture at the silver car. 'When I was . . . when I was locked away, he said Matt was dead. But he must have been lying, he was lying, wasn't he? He was lying!'

'I'm sure he must have been. We will try to get hold of your family as soon as we can. But you're freezing. Please, Ava, you can trust me, you have to get in the car. We need to get you to hospital. And the sooner we get there the sooner you can see your family.'

I clutch hold of her hand as she helps me into the car, and then she follows me in, sitting beside me. I look down at my hand gripping hers and am shocked by how filthy it is. My skin looks grey. 'I'm sorry,' I say.

'You're OK, Ava,' she says. 'You're being really brave.'

The officer in front has started up the engine. I crane my head to look round. I can't see Frankie. I don't know if they've already loaded her into the ambulance. 'She'll be OK, won't she? I'd be dead if it weren't for her.' Flat fields, the waving heads of reeds, all are a blur as we drive along, the ambulance getting smaller behind us. The road must be very rough; we're jouncing around and I can feel my bruises as we thump along the tarmac. I hate to think of Frankie racing along this road with her injury. 'They won't let her die, will they? Can't they send a helicopter?'

'She's in the best hands,' says Anne. 'Colin, any news on the family please?'

'They're calling them now. Then they'll ring through on your phone.'

'Can't I call? Can't I call my mum?' I can't believe this didn't occur to me before, I'm not thinking straight, and make a grab for Anne's phone as she gets it out of her pocket, but she keeps hold of it. 'Please! I want to speak to her, she'll be so worried.'

'I promise you it's better this way, sweetheart. After something like this, even good news can be a shock. It's best they tell her and then put you straight on the phone afterwards.' I'm about to argue, but the phone rings, and the sound of it feels like a punch in the stomach. I sit frozen. I can't believe this is happening, that I'm going to hear my mum's voice, that I'm alive, that I'm going to see her again. Anne has answered the call. 'She's sitting right here, I'll put her on.' She hands me the phone but I'm so overwhelmed, I can't find the words.

'Ava? *Mon ange! C'est toi? Vraiment c'est toi?*'

'Mum, it's me.' She's crying, asking me over and over if I'm OK, if it's really me. 'I promise I'm OK, I promise, but what about Matt?' I finally manage to say. 'Is he all right? Can I speak to him? Is he there?'

'*Oui, oui, il est ici!*'

'Sis?'

It's Matt's voice. It's really him. 'You're OK! Oh Matt thank God, you're OK! I've been so worried.'

'You were worried about me? You were fucking kidnapped and you were worried about *me*? You mentalist!' He's laughing and crying at the same time. But I'm sobbing so hard I can't answer him, I can't speak at all.

One Year Later

'Take your time, Ava, remember what we talked about. Just centre yourself, breathe in deeply and count to seven as you let the breath go.'

Air exhales from my nose, slowly, slowly. I'm in Dr Scott's office, or Rosie as I call her. I like this space. Clean lines and bright. Always feels sunny, even on an overcast day. I don't like the dark.

She wants me to talk about how I feel now the trial's over, now that he's doing life. What *do* I feel? I think there are many types of prison. That's what I'm discovering. I can't tell her that.

Does that sound ungrateful? I hope not. It's hard for me to admit that some days can be difficult. How can anything be hard after what I went through? Survivor's guilt is what Rosie calls it, that and a large helping of post-traumatic stress.

Of course, I'm glad Grant Allen is in an actual prison. That he's never coming out. I call him that now, rather than Fat Head, though it was hard at first to acknowledge he even had a name, that he could be a real person and have done what he did. After I escaped, he still wasn't done with me. He tried to file an attempted murder charge. When that wouldn't fly, he went for GBH, his lawyer arguing that the force I'd used wasn't 'proportionate'. That's not uncommon, the police told me. It's a way of continuing to victimise somebody, a refusal to let go. They didn't press charges.

Rosie is looking at me, waiting for me to say something. She has a kind face, dark curly hair and bright red glasses. I've never told her, but her hair reminds me of Daisy sometimes. But then so much makes me think of Daisy, it's not like looking at Rosie is harder than anything else; she's never out of my head. 'I feel relieved, I do feel relieved that part of it's over, that they found him guilty. And I'm glad he didn't get parole. It means a lot I'm never going to have to worry about him getting out, and go through all that. But it still doesn't feel finished, not the way I expected it to.'

The trial was everywhere, on the news every evening, then again in my nightmares. Giving evidence brought it all back. I wasn't in court for the verdict; it made my skin crawl to be in the same room with him. I imagined myself being brave, staring him down in the dock, but when I took the stand I found I didn't want to look at him. And then all the families; I could feel their eyes on me as I spoke, wishing it was their daughter who had lived to give evidence rather than me. Rosie told me it wouldn't have been like that, that they would have felt pleased I escaped, that I helped get them justice, but I'm not so sure. Either way, I didn't want to be there. The liaison officer told me any details I asked to know.

We weren't the only ones, me, Daisy, Hanna, Lily and Sandra. The police found three more bodies at the farm. Two other sex workers, a woman called Mary Fenny and another they've yet to identify. The police say she might have been an illegal immigrant, here for a better life, but she met Grant Allen instead. And then there was Carol Denham, his former sister-in-law, buried in her own fields. She was retired, a widow with no children, and a recluse. Almost a year she'd been dead, and nobody reported her missing.

The prosecution argued that in some ways Grant Allen *wanted* to be found. The way he kept going for higher-profile victims, no longer leaving them buried in the mud on Hock Drove, but dumping them where the police were sure to discover them. All those deaths raised questions about the disappearance of his wife, Lydia Allen, the mother of his son Zach. Police dug up every address he's ever lived at, but there was no body, and if she really had fled abroad, as he claimed, all those years ago, she's proved impossible to trace.

Zach. I cannot believe Grant Allen was a father, that he watched his own baby grow up, cared about him even. There was talk that Zach might not have killed his girlfriend at all, that he took the rap for his dad, and that's why Grant started the *Justice4Jailbirds* campaign: guilt. Rosie says it might make sense, that perhaps all that rage he inflicted on others was displaced anger he felt towards himself. But who knows. They were never able to bring that up at trial. Zachary Allen, whoever he is now, didn't take the chance to claim his innocence. I'm not sure I even care why Grant Allen did it; there's no explanation that would make me feel better about what happened.

I've been staring at Rosie's pale grey carpet so long, it takes me a while to realise it's started to blur, that my eyes have filled with tears. That happens a lot. 'Sorry,' I say, though she's told me a million times I've nothing to say sorry for. 'It's just . . . Whatever he gets, it doesn't bring back the lives he took.'

The lives he took. How inadequate. But I find it painful to name them aloud, even Hanna who I never met.

'No,' says Rosie. 'You're right.'

'So in that sense justice isn't *fair*, is it? Just an exercise in damage limitation, after all the damage has been done.'

'But it's good that you helped ensure he can't hurt anyone else, isn't it?'

'Yes, but only after it was too late.'

'Ava, we've talked about this. You can't blame yourself. If it were reversed, what would you want Daisy to feel about you?'

'I'd want her to live her life, to be happy.'

'Exactly. And by doing that, by allowing yourself to be happy, it's a form of honouring her memory.'

I know she's right. Partly. But I also know there were times when Daisy and I were together that I didn't feel that way. That part of me wanted to be the one who lived, and I can't help feeling, if she exists somewhere, she must feel cheated, maybe even angry that I'm living my life while hers was stolen. There's an empty space in the world I can never fill; not only Daisy, but the child she wanted but never carried.

I look at the clock. I can't believe an hour has gone by already. 'I'm making you late,' I say.

Rosie shakes her head. 'There's no rush. And it's a big day today. How are you feeling about the meeting now it's finally here?'

'Nervous. But in a good way, I think.'

She smiles at me. 'It's all going to go well. And I'm here, if you need to speak to me before next week.'

I wait downstairs in the hospital canteen. I'm early, and every time somebody walks in, my heart beats a bit quicker, then I relax again. This isn't the best place perhaps; it's the same hospital Frankie was brought after Grant shot her, where her family were rushed when she lay unconscious and critical.

Frankie. She and Daisy are entwined in my memories, the women who took my place. She was Grant's next target, that's what the prosecution argued. That blog had alerted the police, made her more challenging prey, but Grant had still wanted to kill her, he would have gone for her anyway. The car chase proves it. Or that's what I tell myself.

I've seen her a million times in my imagination. The way she stood in that doorway, the light behind her, so I couldn't see her face. I've watched her old reports online too. It was painful to see her covering my case, to look at her standing just feet away from where Daisy's body had been dumped. I couldn't escape those reports of hers this last week. They were used endlessly in the television coverage of the verdict; the reporter at the scene who rescued the girl but paid the price.

The door opens and it's a brunette. I'm about to turn back to my coffee, then I freeze, because I recognise that face, even without the blonde hair. She's walking over to my table, stooped slightly to one side: the consequence of her meeting with Grant.

But instead of the guilt I expected, I feel the same flood of relief as when I first saw her. Yes, she's marked because she found me, will always bear the scars, but she's alive. And that's partly thanks to me too.

'Ava,' she says, standing over my table. She's smiling, her eyes shining with tears. 'It's good to see you again.'

Frankie hugs Ava close to her. It's a relief to see her looking so much stronger than she remembered. The thin, filthy creature who clung to her at the farm on Hock Drove is gone, and in her place is a tall young woman with a dark crew cut. It doesn't look as pretty as the pink bob, but it suits her better.

'God, it's good to see you,' she says, finally letting go. 'Thank you so much. The hospital told me what you did. After all you'd been through I can't believe you had the presence of mind. It's thanks to you I didn't bleed to death.'

Ava turns red. 'Oh, it's all anybody would have done. *You* were the one who saved *me*.'

'Well, we're quits then, as my friend Zara would say. Fancy another coffee? And maybe a cake or something?'

'Great, thank you.' Ava reaches for her purse, but Frankie waves her away.

'Don't be daft.'

From the queue she glances back at Ava. It makes her ridiculously happy to see her sitting there, like a normal student, like any twenty-one-year-old. On the outside at least. Frankie knows Ava quit her course at the UEA, that the pair of them have spent the past year in a state of stasis. Although she suspects that the business of recovery has been harder work for Ava than it has for her. Frankie has just had to learn how to live with one lung. God knows what memories Ava is still laying to rest.

She returns to the table with the coffees and two huge brownies. 'I know for a fact these are good. I lived on them during rehab, much to the doctors' disapproval.'

Ava takes a sip of coffee. 'You look great.'

'Thanks. You too,' Frankie says. There's a pause as she works up the courage to broach the unmentionable. 'I'm so glad you shot him.' Ava looks startled and Frankie wonders if she's said the wrong thing. But there's not much room for small talk after what they've been through. She ploughs on. 'Don't get me wrong, I know you had to shoot him. But I'm also really glad. Is it OK to talk about this?'

'Yeah, it is. I don't normally, I try to give him as little space in my life as possible, but this feels sort of different.'

'How you didn't blow his head off, I've no idea.'

'I don't know either,' says Ava. 'I've thought about it. It's almost like I knew he wasn't worth it. Though sometimes I'm sorry I didn't, to be honest.'

'Don't be. Prison's no fun for control freaks like that. This way the bastard gets to suffer for longer.' Frankie's will to vengeance is cheerily expressed and rounded off with a bite of brownie.

'Can I ask *you* something?' Ava says. 'Why were you there that day?'

'Nosiness really.' Frankie makes a face. 'Or rather it was mainly because some dickhead, a guy called Brian Clifton, was writing a nasty blog about me.'

'That's the guy who had the photos, isn't it?'

'Um, yeah,' says Frankie, aware that this must be yet another trauma for Ava, knowing that pictures of her being tortured are still out there somewhere on the Internet. The police will never be sure they've traced them all, neither the photos of her nor of the other women Grant Allen abused. 'That's the one,' she says. 'He had incriminating stuff on his phone, and I really thought he was the killer. He was arrested for it and everything. At the same time my boyfriend had been playing about on the deep web, trying to track down the website that was hosting Brian's blog posts. He connected with some pretty unsavoury types, did some snooping through personal data and came up with an address. It was the farm. I went there hoping to catch the person who hosted it, force them to admit what they'd done. I thought they might even be able to put pressure on Brian to say where you were.' She pauses, not wanting to make herself out to be more of a hero than is honest. 'And it wasn't entirely selfless, I was also beyond furious about the blogging. It made my life utter hell.' Frankie blushes, suddenly aware that her stress over Feminazi Slayer was nothing compared to what Ava went through.

'Sounds like your boyfriend's pretty smart,' Ava says. 'I ought to thank him too.'

'Ex-boyfriend.' It still makes her sad, thinking about Jack. 'In order to get in with the website he shared some photos of me, both on the blog and privately. Nothing sexual,' she adds, seeing Ava's face. 'But it was still too much of a betrayal. I know he didn't do it to hurt me, he was just trying to help, but I couldn't get past it, I couldn't trust him any more.'

'No, I can see that.' Ava looks down at her hot drink. 'It's weird, you know, talking to somebody else that Grant Allen hurt. He did so much damage, but he was such a nothing, wasn't he? Just a small pathetic person, who made up all these grand-sounding reasons for wanting to inflict pain.'

'Yes.'

Ava looks up and holds her gaze. They sit a moment in silence. The connection between them, through their shared experience of horror that day, feels too intense for words. 'What are you up to, now it's all over,' Frankie says at last.

'I'm starting at a new university in a few months. In Bristol this time. UEA transferred my degree.'

'Really? That's brilliant.'

'But before that I'm going on holiday with my brother. A long weekend in Amsterdam.'

'Amsterdam's lovely, you'll have a great time.'

'What about you?'

'I've spent a lot of the past few months on nappy-changing duties. My friend Zara has had a little boy. He makes a lot of noise for something so tiny.'

Ava twiddles with her coffee cup, without drinking. 'I was sorry you've not been back reporting.'

'Well, I might do eventually. Haven't decided yet. Think I've had enough of telly though, I've been wondering about trying print or more likely radio.' Frankie sighs. 'And I'm not too keen on the boss at the Eastern Film Company, so I don't really want to go back to the old place, much as I miss it.'

'I guess you're sitting on an exclusive if you wanted to use it.'

Frankie wonders if Ava is trying to sound her out, whether she would mind either way. 'I wasn't planning any interviews about what happened,' she replies, thinking of Luke Heffner turning up one weekend on her doorstep. It makes her smile to remember. The cheeky bastard had even brought a bottle of champagne. She had happily invited him in, even given him a glass, but he still left without what he came for. Kiera's disappointment at being turned down was less gracious. 'I haven't spoken to anyone,' she says. 'Not just because I knew I'd have to give evidence, but also it didn't feel like my story to tell.'

'That's the thing, isn't it? It doesn't even feel like *my* story.' Ava takes a deep breath, willing herself to say their names. 'Because it's also Hanna's story, and Lily's and Sandra's. Those three women who died before, Mary, Carol and the nameless one.' She closes her eyes. 'And Daisy.'

Frankie takes her hand. Behind them, a small child is wailing. The hospital café is not a private backdrop for Ava's grief. It's full of people dealing with the stress of illness, waiting to visit relatives, or in for treatment themselves, as she once was; there's a man in a hospital gown in a wheelchair and an elderly woman with a mobile drip in her arm. 'I met Simon, Daisy's husband,' Frankie says. 'After she died, he didn't want to do an interview. Because of you. Because the only thing he wanted after that was for you to be found alive.'

'Don't,' Ava says. 'Don't be kind.' She withdraws her hand. 'I'm sorry, it's the one thing I can't talk about. I can't bear to think about her, it's too much.'

'Of course. I'm sorry.'

'Don't be. It's not your fault.' Ava is picking at the skin around her nails, an unconscious gesture, but Frankie notices it must be a frequent one, as her fingers are red. Ava sees her looking and stops. She meshes her hands together. 'How would you feel about telling the story if I spoke to you too?'

For a moment Frankie can only stare at her. 'Are you serious?'

'There's no other journalist I'd speak to.'

Frankie feels the old familiar tightening of her stomach, the tingle of anticipation at an exclusive. Once a hack, always a hack. 'That would be . . . Well, that would be amazing. Are you sure though?'

'There'd be some conditions. You'd have to report it, obviously. No obsessing about Grant Allen and his motivations. And we'd have to get Simon to agree. I can't talk about Daisy for him, that would have to be his decision.' Ava sits back in her chair. 'Also I'd want to be editorially involved. It would be us telling our story, not me being the subject.'

In spite of herself, Frankie visualises a prime-time TV documentary taking shape before her eyes, imagines filming with Gavin again, the look on Luke Heffner's face when she asks him to give the perspective of 'the press'. 'Sounds reasonable,' she says. 'But are you really sure you want to do this? There'd be a lot of publicity. Other media would want to talk to you too.'

'They already do,' she says. 'I think they always will, it's another thing I can't escape. I'd rather own the story than just be it.'

'I can understand that.'

'So what do you think?' Ava is watching her, the grey eyes direct and challenging, just as she remembers in the missing-person photo at the police press conference all that time ago. But to Frankie she no longer looks like a victim. Instead she sees a young woman who has been through hell and is starting to grow stronger in spite of it.

Frankie smiles. 'I think you just persuaded me to go back to work.'

Acknowledgements

I wrote the first couple of chapters of this book a few weeks before my son was born and the rest on maternity leave. Babies don't take a starring role in its pages, but for me this novel will always be associated with the seismic shift that is new motherhood. The author Stephen King suggests writers work on their first draft with the study door closed, but in this case it was while the baby slept – or my mother took him to the park.

It was a truly wonderful year, if an exhausting one. A huge thank you to everyone who helped me through it. My family – in particular my husband Jason Farrington and my mother Suzy Kendall – all the new parents and babies in my NCT and pregnancy yoga group (who put up with endless cancellations), also Jo Jacobson, Andrea Binfor, Rosie Andrious and everyone who came to visit while I stuck to the house like a limpet. Most of all, thank you to Jonathon: just like in your favourite story, 'the world is much more lovely since the day you came along.'

I'm indebted to many people for giving me feedback on earlier drafts. Thank you to Joyce Eliason, Geoffrey Case, Linda Agran, Jason Farrington, Eugenie Harper, Ruth Grey Harper, Tom Harper, Alexander Harper and Suzy Kendall. Thank you to David Old from Bedfordshire Police who has helped me out many times as a journalist, and did so again for this book. A big thanks to Maca, aka DS Graham McMillan of Beds, Cambs and Herts Major Crime Unit, for giving up his time to answer endless questions about policing. Thanks also to DCI Christopher Beresford and Garry Dix of Bedfordshire Police for pointers on cyber crime. Any liberties I've taken with procedure are entirely my own.

I owe a huge debt to my second family – my colleagues at ITV News Anglia who have been unendingly supportive both personally and professionally. I am so lucky to work with you. By rights everyone should be listed here, but I have to single out news editor Andy Thomson, who has spent years checking my TV scripts for errors and then advised on the final draft of this book. He also supplied the gun. Metaphorically speaking, of course.

Thank you to Nathalie Hallam at Caskie Mushens, all the writers at #TeamMushens and to everyone at Hodder – to Cicely Aspinall, Rachel Khoo in marketing, Helen Parham for the copyedit, and Tom Duxbury for the cover art. To Rosie Stephen for the hours you spent on publicity and supporting me at events – not to mention all the conversations about feminism! To Ruth Tross for making this book the best version of itself, for always making the editing process rewarding and for being so thoughtful in every way; it is such a huge pleasure working with you.

And of course thank you to Juliet Mushens. Ever since I waddled into your office as the fattest pregnant writer ever to sign with an agent, you have been there for me. Your agenting style combines Elle Woods and Dorothy Parker – with a dash of The Terminator – and as a friend, you are the kindest and the best.